BOOKS BY TIM JEAL

A Marriage of Convenience
Until the Colors Fade

A Marriage
of Convenience

Tim Jeal

Simon and Schuster · New York

Published by Simon and Schuster
A Division of Gulf & Western Corporation
Simon & Schuster Building
Rockefeller Center
1230 Avenue of the Americas
New York, New York 10020
Designed by Dianne Pinkowitz
Manufactured in the United States of America
Printed by The Murray Printing Company
Bound by The Book Press, Inc.
1 2 3 4 5 6 7 8 9 10

Library of Congress Cataloging in Publication Data

Jeal, Tim.
   A marriage of convenience.

   I. Title.
PZ4.J428Mar 1979   [PR6060.E2]   823'.9'14   79-840

ISBN 0-671-22872-2

PART ONE

CHAPTER ONE

Shortly after three in the morning, Clinton was wakened by the trumpet call to stables, and at once his heart was beating fast. From the squadron lines, across the dark parade ground, came the clash of hoofs on cobbles and the confused neighing of horses being led to water at an unfamiliar hour. The barracks, so still a few minutes before, now resounded to shouts of command and the rumble of boots on the iron troop-room stairs.

By the time his servant came to call him, Clinton had already pulled on cavalry overalls and a heavily frogged patrol jacket. After lighting more candles, the man eased his master into his riding boots and, when Clinton had checked his revolver, helped him with his sword belt and scabbard slings. Having put on his hussar busby, Clinton chose a cutting whip and then took the cape held out to him. He did not leave the room at once after the trooper's departure, but stood awhile by the window, breathing deeply to rid himself of the slight queasiness at the pit of his stomach. He wished profoundly that the next three or four hours were over.

As adjutant of the 15th Hussars, Clinton Danvers had found little to enjoy during the first six months of his regiment's tour of duty in Ireland. July 1866, and ahead of him almost a year till the end of the posting. Although the monotony of rural garrison life made many of his brother officers impatient for any form of military offensive, Clinton was more relieved than depressed to have escaped involvement for so long. No lover of the Irish, he had nonetheless never looked forward to receiving orders for direct action against the Fenians. Now that these orders had finally arrived from Dublin, his feelings, in spite of the recent murder of two troopers, remained largely unchanged. Blaming Irish poverty more on the people's incompetence as farmers than on the rapacity of their English landlords, he felt scant sympathy for the rebels, but the idea of using regular cavalry against a half-armed rabble still pained him—his distaste owing more to pride in his profession than to any tender feelings for the republican Irish. Just as a prize-fighter would feel ashamed to hit a hamstrung man, Clinton considered that horsemen skillful enough to split pegs in the ground with their swords at a full gallop deserved better of their opponents than to be made to feel common butchers.

When Clinton entered the stables, troopers with lanterns were hard at work grooming and saddling horses, their efforts rising to fever pitch as they saw the adjutant arrive. Since the second-in-command was due to retire and the colonel drank heavily, Clinton virtually ran the regiment, and in a way which many officers resented. Compulsory riding school for all ranks twice a week, except in the hunting season, and the prohibition on maneuvers of private carts containing officers' luxuries were measures which had been fiercely opposed. But with these, as with his insistence that every subaltern learn to shoe a horse, Clinton had got his way in the end. He almost always did. Not that he either was or seemed to be a martinet. There was too much ease in his manner for that. It was an airy light manner but far removed from swaggering; at his most offhand, he still somehow conveyed a latent energy that might suddenly burst forth. His pleasure in himself was not vanity, as his detractors claimed, but something in his being: a possession like health or luck which radiated from him. His lips were finely curved, and, even in repose, a faint smile seemed to play around the corners; his eyes too were mobile and expressive, made memorable by flecks of gold in the brown irises. The first impression left by his face was of youthfulness; a closer look revealed a slight hollowness beneath the cheekbones and lines beside his mouth that made him seem a little older than his twenty-seven years.

Those envious of Clinton for his outstanding horsemanship, and the daunting reputation for courage he had brought back from the Third China War, took some comfort from persistent rumors about the magnitude of his debts. In public, though, he gave little indication of concern or depression about his position; and in truth, this resilience did not surprise many of his colleagues. On his father's death, a decade earlier, Clinton Danvers had become the Fifth Viscount Ardmore; and, however much in debt he might be, a handsome cavalry officer with a title could usually count on exchanging these assets for an heiress's fortune. If Lord Ardmore's long struggle to avoid this course had been known about in the mess, few of his brother officers would have understood his scruples.

As Clinton walked between the rows of stalls, listening to the rattle of chain collars and the shouts of troop sergeants rising above the splashing of water and the scrape of shovels, he started to feel more relaxed. As always, the smell of damp straw and the unique ammoniac tang of the stables pleased him. When his stallion was led out into the yard, he patted his warm flank. Under the horse's soft satin coat, he could feel the firm sinewy muscles. Clinton loved the animal's alert pricked ears and the exact and delicate way he raised his hoofs to paw the ground, movements remarkably light for such a powerful horse. While waiting for him to be saddled, Clinton wandered into the saddle room. In the shadowy lamplight, polished leather glowed like old mahogany, and bits and stirrup irons glinted dull blue against the walls.

Watching the stream of troopers coming and going with saddles and bridles, Clinton did not notice a tall athletic-looking man enter from the other end of the room. The clink of spurs on the stone flags behind him made him turn. An officer, roughly Clinton's age, stood saluting him. Clinton returned the salute and smiled.

"My troop will be ready to mount in five minutes, sir," said the newcomer.

Clinton nodded. "My lot shouldn't be far behind."

Dick Lambert had served with Clinton in China, and they had been imprisoned together shortly before the fall of Peking. The experience had been so harrowing that, four years later, they still rarely spoke of it. Lambert was Clinton's closest friend in the regiment, and was expected to be the next adjutant when Lord Ardmore bought his majority. Though the light of the oil lamps was poor, Clinton could tell that Dick was annoyed. Beneath his black mustache his lips were tight and unsmiling.

"I've just seen some gunners limbering up a nine-pounder."

"That's right," replied Clinton breezily.

"You didn't say a word about artillery at the conference yesterday."

"I didn't want to argue about one miserable little field gun." Clinton smiled apologetically. "Actually it should be rather useful."

Lambert said nothing for several seconds, but stood slapping his whip against one of his boots. At last he looked up, anger thinly disguised as incredulity. "I'm surprised you think the two best troops in the regiment need help from the horse gunners to deal with fifty Irishmen."

Clinton picked up a duster and with apparent unconcern ran it over the crupper of a saddle. "Could be more than fifty," he said soothingly. "If they're the ones who attacked the constabulary barracks at Dromina, some of them are going to have new Enfields. Farm buildings aren't hard to defend."

"So we storm the place while they're asleep. Attack on both sides . . . Your plan, my lord."

"I've changed it."

Lambert unexpectedly grinned. "You can't intend to blow them to bits with artillery."

"Hardly."

"Right, so we're back to storming it. Unless you're planning a siege." Lambert's ironic expression faded. "For God's sake, Clinton, don't pay scum like that the compliment of taking fieldpieces. You'll make us the laughingstock of the army."

"Too bad. I'm not going to lose any men. Imagine hand-to-hand fighting in a warren of small rooms. We'd have troopers shooting each other in the chaos. That's a job for infantry, not cavalry."

"My troop won't mind that. Don't we owe them the chance to get even?"

Clinton was well aware of what his friend meant. One of the two soldiers murdered by the Fenians in May had been in Lambert's troop—a young recruit, shot from behind a hedge while exercising horses. He sighed and shook his head.

"Sorry, Dick. Kill them and they'll be martyrs. Let them kill some of us and they'll be heroes. But take them all alive and they'll look fools." From the square came the trumpet call "Prepare to mount."

Lambert looked hard at Clinton as he adjusted the chinstrap of his busby. "They'll just carry on till we give them some real discouragement."

Clinton clapped Lambert on the back. "If my way doesn't work, we'll try yours next time."

Dick remained silent, but from his expression Clinton sensed that he had now worked out what tactics would be employed.

"Try again, will we?" he asked with elevated brows. "Lose the kind of gamble you're taking, and who'll be fool enough to give either of us a second chance?"

Clinton laughed quietly as he walked to the door. "A gamble? Lose? My dear Dick, you know I only bet on certainties."

"I find that most comforting, sir," replied Lambert gravely.

Their eyes met for a moment, but this time without pretense of ironic detachment. A curious glance passed between them, as fleeting as light on water, but as distinct: a wordless affirmation of complicity, proof of an alliance safe in all essentials from surface differences of opinion on military matters. In any case, as both men knew, decisive execution, even of a poor stratagem, could usually be relied upon to outweigh its defects. Only hesitance and lack of confidence in command were fatal failings, and Clinton had never given Dick cause to reproach him with either.

As they walked out into the yard, Clinton touched Lambert's arm. "A bet with you, Captain Lambert? A hundred guineas to a shilling that we'll take them all alive."

Lambert's impassivity suddenly gave way to an affectionate

smile, which he quickly suppressed. "Course we will, my lord," he returned with marvelously feigned incredulity that Clinton could even contemplate any other result. "Unlike you, sir," he added, "I never bet on a certainty—even with odds like that."

A moment later, Clinton was watching him striding into the gloom to where his troop were dressing on their markers.

When the cavalcade of horsemen left the town of Carrick-feeney and clattered over the stone bridge spanning the river, the sky was only partly overcast and the countryside lay tranquil under the soft and kindly light of the stars. In the water meadows, cows loomed through the grayness like peaceful ghosts under the dim silver of the willow trees. But soon the clouds thickened, and, passing through woods, even with eyes accustomed to the dark, the horses often stumbled on ruts and fissures in the road. The air became oppressive and very still, heavily laden with scents of damp earth and long woodland grass. Coming out of the trees, they rode on through country more prosaically Irish: a patchwork of small irregular fields enclosed by crude earth and stone banks. Here and there, scarcely distinguishable in the darkness, ricks of hay and long piles of peat dotted the approaches to small thatched cabins.

An hour after leaving barracks, the stillness was broken by a rumble of thunder, and after it, a light wind rustled through the ears of the uncut corn. The rain was not slow in coming, and when it did, the downpour was relentless. Only as the first faint smudges of dawn made wan blurs in the thick sky did the circling storms finally move away, leaving the land sloppy and overflowing. The ditches, choked with summer vegetation, made little impact on waterlogged tracks. Drenched and steaming, the horses all looked black, whether chestnut or bay, and their flattened wet manes made their necks seem strangely thin. Every movement sent little streams of water trickling down from the fur of Clinton's hussar busby into the gap between the chain fastening of his cape and his skin. The reins in his hands were sodden and greasy, and his whole body felt clammy and cold. From every overhanging tree, large drops of water still fell, and the hoofs of the horses in front splattered him with mud. Near the center of the column, the team of horses pulling the field gun were having a hard time. Often the gun crew had to dismount and heave the wheels out of the mud.

Clinton's original intention had been to rest and feed both men and horses before the attack, but the delays caused by the state of the roads had now ruled this out. The growing light was not his only reason for anxiety. As so often with similar expeditions against the Fenians, his column was acting on information sold to a resident magistrate and relayed back to the regiment from general headquarters in Dublin. Without these mercenary betrayals, the army would have had few successes against the groups of rebels operating in the countryside. Although Clinton had memorized the informer's directions, and had added further details culled from army maps, he was still constantly worried in case they took a wrong turning. The information might of course be false or, worse still, a trap. For this reason every trooper rode with a loaded carbine held at the support ready for instant use.

When they passed a disused limestone quarry, listed in the directions, and shortly afterwards entered a thin belt of trees, correctly described as mainly oaks and rowans, Clinton felt more confident. Five minutes later, his doubts were finally allayed. Ahead of them, at the bottom of a shallow depression, stood an isolated group of farm buildings, dominated by a large barn with a slate roof. No detail was wrong. Beside the barn was the farmhouse, with a lean-to shed against the side wall and one bricked-in window at ground level. The place looked derelict and would have seemed deserted were it not for a faint smear of turf smoke issuing from a chimney. As the informer had claimed, the buildings were surrounded by meadow grass and overgrown root fields. In spite of this lack of close cover, Clinton was momentarily tempted to get it over and do what Lambert would have done in his place, namely order an immediate gallop across the fields and then the storming of the buildings. But he mastered the impulse. It was possible that lookouts posted in the woods had seen their approach and crept back unseen to the farm to alert the rest of the Fenians.

Keeping the horse gunners and his own troop with him,

Clinton hastily conferred with Lambert before ordering him to have his men dismount and take up positions in subsections at the edge of the woods six hundred yards behind the buildings; from there, a few well-directed volleys would thwart any attempted escape in that direction. Less than a mile to the right, across a rough tract of gorse and bracken, was a swollen river. In this area Clinton felt he could afford to be less vigilant. If driven down to the banks by mounted troops, the Irish would surely surrender there, rather than face the near certainty of being shot dead or wounded while swimming across. Having heard Clinton's plan during their ride, Dick now conceded that the lie of the ground would be excellent for it if the vital first stage succeeded.

Before riding off, he turned in the saddle. "Don't forget, sir, my lot go in first if your bluff's called."

"It won't be."

Lambert raised his hand in salute and rode off at speed. As soon as he had gone, Clinton sent his sergeant major and two troopers crawling into the root field to get within hailing distance of the farmhouse. The light was better now, and the men made what use they could of the slanting line of a low wall for cover. The nine-pounder was already being unlimbered at a spot just in front of a spinney of straggling elders and blackthorn. From there, still partially hidden, it could be brought to bear on the large barn without endangering the farmhouse.

While the gun was got ready, Clinton ordered his troop to form two lines and to draw sabers. Then he explained what he wanted of his subalterns. If the men inside the house did not surrender at once, but made a run for it towards the river, the front line, led by him, would ride through them and break any attempted stand; the second line were to take prisoners, only striking to kill those who fired on them. Since even disciplined infantry rarely turned to face cavalry at anything under company strength, he did not anticipate more than a few stray shots. Kneeing his horse round, Clinton watched the loaders ramming home the charge and inserting the shell. To the instructions of their lieutenant, the gunners turned the elevating screw and then inched the muzzle to the left.

After a long stare down the line of sight, the young officer came over to Clinton and saluted. "Ready, sir," he said briskly, looking up at him with a badly disguised smirk. "Should wake them up a treat, sir."

"You won't miss?" asked Clinton with a touch of the familiar irony which marked the relations of cavalry officers with their counterparts in the Royal Horse Artillery.

"Not unless it moves, sir."

Clinton smiled. "Give the order then."

A moment after the shouted command, the kneeling bombardier pulled the lanyard and the gun recoiled sharply. The shock waves from the report made Clinton's horse curvet and whinny, but he quickly controlled him. As the smoke cleared, Clinton saw a gaping hole in the roof of the barn and a jagged rent in the upper part of the wall.

He heard the lieutenant shout, "Stop the vent and sponge."

In the silence that followed, Clinton raised his field glass to see if he could catch any movement in the windows of the house, but there was none.

Several seconds passed, and then, to the letter of his orders, the sergeant major yelled from his advanced position in the root field, "You're surrounded. Come out and surrender, or we'll blast you out."

Clinton waited tensely. To his right the gunners were reloading; behind him he heard an occasional horse snort and the creak of saddlery; but no sound or sign came from the farmhouse. If the sight of what a single shell had done to the barn was insufficiently impressive, he was prepared to drop a couple more into the yard directly in front of the house before issuing a final ultimatum. If this intimidation failed, and the men stayed where they were, Clinton had no intention of carrying out his threat of massacre. Instead he would be obliged to storm the place; and with every vestige of surprise thrown away, he knew the process would be bloody on both sides.

The danger had always been that the Fenians would be so well aware of the government's long-standing reluctance to increase support for the rebels by making martyrs that they would recognize the shots as a ruse to get them into the open. But Clinton had never given this sort of logical thought any chance against the instinctive terror struck in the hearts of recently awakened men by shells bursting within yards of their hiding place. His worse fear was that they had received advance warning; even a few minutes would have given them time to steel their nerves for holding out. He was agonizingly conscious that unless they had already panicked, every passing moment increased their chances of thinking rationally.

Without waiting any longer, Clinton gave the order for the next round to be fired. The shell exploded ten feet from the house and blew in the door and every visible window frame. The brickwork was pitted and scarred in a wide arc. Clinton watched with a sinking heart as the dust slowly settled and still nothing happened. With a great effort of control, he called cheerfully to the artillery officer, "Perhaps they went out for a walk."

"Just the weather for it, sir."

Ten more seconds—an eternity to Clinton—and then a sight that brought a derisive cheer for the gun crew: a white sheet was thrust out of a window by an unseen hand. Then very hesitantly some half-dozen men came out into the yard holding up their hands. Before Clinton had time to enjoy his relief, a rapid stutter of small-arms firing from Dick's men on the fringes of the wood told him that the majority of the Fenians had preferred to try their luck at the back. Now that the threat of having to storm the farm had been lifted from him, he felt only mildly disappointed not to have achieved a tidy surrender.

Detailing a corporal and three troopers to take charge of the men in the yard, Clinton turned to his trumpeter. "Advance in line."

The man sounded the call; and as the front line moved forward, calls to trot and then to canter followed. With swords held at the carry, their sodden capes opening to reveal frogged braid and gleaming buttons, the line thundered down across the fields towards the rough ground between the farm and the river. Behind him, the even thudding of hoofs and the rapid but fresh breathing of the following horses exhilarated Clinton with a feeling not unlike that of leading the field in a hunt. Glancing over his shoulder briefly, he allowed himself the pleasure of admiring the line, his eye caught by the swaying plumes and red busby bags. With none of the tension of a charge against a waiting enemy or moving cavalry, Clinton gave himself up to the beautifully smooth action of his stallion, feeling entirely at one with the animal, not holding him back as he quickened his pace before leaping a wall, nor urging him on over a wide ditch. The horse took these obstacles as if they did not exist, and Clinton merely gave him the rein, anticipating his movements with instinctive ease.

A hundred yards ahead, he saw the fleeing men stumbling through the tall bracken, throwing away their weapons, blundering into gorse bushes, tripping, falling. A small group led the rest and seemed likely to reach the thick sedge and reeds beyond a line of willows at the water's edge.

"Right shoulders," he shouted to the trumpeter, wheeling to cut them off. Checking his horse a little as the ground grew rougher, he came up with the stragglers and tightened his grip on the hilt of his saber. One man stopped, another flung himself out of the way.

"Stand where you are," roared Clinton, catching glimpses of terrified faces as he flashed by. Between him and the willows was a bank of blackberry bushes; with a slight touch of his heels, he urged his horse over it. The stallion landed badly on a steep little slope. Almost before Clinton had righted himself in the saddle, he saw the blurred shape of a man crouching low in his path, a black thing held up apparently to the shoulder. Clinton crouched in the saddle and cut cleanly with his sword, carrying the full weight of the horse into the blow. The man spun away, falling with outstretched arms. In the fleeting glimpse Clinton caught of him, he saw a young lifeless face, and the blackthorn stick he had mistaken for a gun lying harmless in the grass. With a nauseous sensation in his stomach, he rode on, all his earlier elation spent.

He swore aloud as he saw that four Fenians had already reached the reeds well ahead of him and the dozen hussars close on his heels. His success had already gone sour; more deaths would ruin it completely. These men were not soldiers, and his pride as well as his humanity revolted against being obliged to treat them as if they were. Around him, troopers were dismounting and snatching their carbines from the straps behind the saddle cantles. Clinton shouted to the Irish to stop and save their lives, but now hussars were plunging into the reeds, forcing their quarry on. Two gave themselves up when they saw the speed of the current; two others, regardless of the repeated shouts to halt, launched themselves into the swirling tea-colored water. A sergeant, acting on Clinton's previous orders, told his men to fire, and one of the Fenians was hit in the first burst of shots. His companion by then had reached the far bank, and could have escaped into the thick overhanging undergrowth, but looking back, he hesitated and then dived in again, in a suicidal attempt to rescue his compatriot.

"Get them out. Don't shoot," bellowed Clinton, scrambling from his horse and running to the bank. By the time three hussars had waded into the water, the Irishmen had been swept down to a bend where the river was waist-deep. Seconds later, a floundering struggle ended with the sharp crack of a carbine fired from the shore. The rescuing Fenian staggered, seemed to freeze, and then fell face downward into the brown water. Before anyone moved to prevent it, he was washed downstream with the current.

Shocked, and shaking with anger, Clinton strode towards the point from which the shot had come. He saw a uniformed figure enter the river lower down and strike out to reach the man who had just been hit. Clinton told a trooper to go and find out who this soldier was; then, slightly mollified by this disinterested act, he went on to try to discover why the shot had been fired. The corporal responsible told him that the man had pulled out a knife and had tried to stab the soldiers or-dered to arrest him. When this weapon was fished out of the muddy water, Clinton sighed and asked no further questions. The body of the Irishman who had been shot first had been dragged up onto the grass; Clinton had seen enough corpses to recognize the unmistakable attitude of death. The now certain fact that the other Fenian's bravery had been futile from the beginning added to Clinton's desolation.

Returning to his horse, he was overtaken by the trooper he had sent to bring back the name of the soldier who had gone to the aid of the hapless Irishman.

"Trooper Harris, sir."

"Did he get the man ashore?"

"Yes, sir. Done for, he was—the Irish lad. Between the eyes, sir."

The man had said this with pleasure and seemed surprised that Lord Ardmore did not commend the accuracy of the corporal's shot. Clinton stood a moment, as if thinking of something else, and then turned on his heel. Above the farm the low clouds were breaking up, and the sun began to come through, shimmering on the wet grass. Somewhere in the bracken the croak of a pheasant seemed to answer the faint cries of a wounded man.

An hour later, when the two troops were once more winding their way along the cut-up woodland track, with four dead Fenians roped to the gun limber, and twice that number of wounded, moaning with every sliding tilt of the farm cart carrying them, Clinton looked ahead over his horse's ears at the silent phalanx of prisoners trudging between the double line of their mounted escort. Behind him, his men riding in columns of threes were laughing and joking with each other. Not one had been hurt and no horses lost.

"Your trouble," murmured Dick, who was trotting next to Clinton, "is you're too damned pigheaded to be satisfied with anything short of the impossible."

"It's called optimism," replied Clinton, smiling in spite of himself.

"Try a bit of the other. Expect the worst, and anything else is a pleasant surprise."

"You're no more a fatalist than I am."

Dick shook his head as if in sorrow. "Expecting too much again. Just because I haven't the sense to follow it myself, you brush aside my perfectly good advice." He paused as they reached the top of a rise. Ahead of them, beyond the trees, the valley opened out into a wide blaze of dandelions and purpling heather. "I'll tell you something," Lambert went on confidingly, "You're one of the only two men I've ever met who doesn't hold a quite different theory of life from the one he's patently acting on."

"I wonder if I can guess who the other is."

Lambert shrugged modestly. "Myself?"

"For a cynic, you're a good friend, Dick."

Glancing in front, Clinton saw that the body of the man he had killed had slipped slightly on the limber, so that the gashed head hung down and lolled, knocking against the metal with each jolt of the wheels. A thin trickle of blood ran down from the forehead across the youth's open eyes. Following the direction of Clinton's gaze, Lambert touched his horse and rode up to the cornet immediately behind the gun carriage. Clinton saw him point his whip at the corpses and heard him tell the cornet to cover them.

On their return to barracks, Clinton warmly congratulated all ranks on the efficiency with which they had carried out their duty.

That evening most of the officers of the 15th Hussars were uproariously drunk by the time they poured out of the mess dining room into the anteroom in their many-buttoned blue and gold mess jackets. Only the duty field officer and the orderly officer for the day were unable to celebrate their returning adjutant's success. A cornet had just purchased his lieutenantship, so tradition obliged him to pay for yet more champagne. Another subaltern had parted company with his horse on parade the day before, so he too was "fined" in the customary manner, and the mess servants were sent scurrying out for more bottles. Later, the junior officers would probably set about tent pegging on each others' backs, and the smallest among them would end up in the horse troughs. Listening to their loud laughter and arrogant self-assertive voices, Clinton wished he had drunk enough to feel utterly detached. Had he ever been so puerile and absurd as these young men? Very likely he had, and only five years earlier. It would be a long time before he reached the age of sentimental recollection of youthful idiocy; at present his memories made him feel mildly uncomfortable. All that scorn and mockery and blind ignorance of human limitation.

The war in China, and two months spent in daily terror of summary execution, had given Clinton's illusions of invulnerable self-sufficiency a lethal mauling. On his return to England, this experience had been followed by another of equal educational force. For the first time he had been worsted in love—by an older married woman, who had cast him adrift after a year of promises to elope with him. An unbroken sequence of earlier successes had left him ill-prepared for suffering at the hands of a woman. Afterwards he very rarely spoke of love with cynical superiority, although in the two years since, he had remained entirely immune.

Since dinner had left the assembled company too addled to play cards, bets were placed on whether the pips in a particular orange would come to more or less than a certain number. The fruit was solemnly cut open with a saber and its contents examined. A similar wager was made on the number of serrated leaves on top of a pineapple; then it was the number of horses depicted in the battle prints on either side of the cabinet containing the regiment's presentation silver, the contestants having to guess without looking. Clinton did not stay long in the anteroom before leaving for his quarters.

As he walked along the side of the parade ground, the slow ache of anxiety, which had oppressed him intermittently for the past month, returned insidiously. In a week he would be back in England for a fortnight's leave, and then everything would have to be settled. His financial difficulties had almost all been inherited from his father, but with current outgoings on mortgage interest and debt repayment exceeding his income by nearly three thousand pounds a year, the origins of his predicament did nothing to make it any more palatable. Recent correspondence with his bank had made it inescapably clear that his credit was exhausted, and that unless he were ready to leave the army at once, and so save the additional thousand he spent annually on regimental bills and subscriptions, he would have to sell the house and estate which his family had owned for two centuries. The choice was not one which Clinton was prepared to make.

Two other options remained. The negotiation of a substantial loan from his brother, or marriage to an heiress who had already given him good reason to suppose he would be accepted. Believing the odds to be heavily against the loan, marriage seemed the likeliest outcome. He had always lived by the belief that a man's destiny could be controlled by what was within him, regardless of external facts; and indeed until recently his moods and emotions had seemed strong enough to change his perspective of the world from within. Now, more and more, everything seemed forced upon him from without. Until recently he had only recognized one kind of freedom: the freedom to do the things he wanted; now he knew he lacked another variety, just as desirable: the freedom not to have to do what he did not want. Though he had foreseen his present problems years before, he had always secretly believed in a miraculous escape. His uncle might die or some less predictable piece of good fortune could arise. Meanwhile, he had assured himself, all he could do was live for the present, and in the end take the cards fate dealt him without complaint. While the crisis had been in the future, this course had served him well enough. Yet marriage for money to a woman he did not love—when she herself loved him sincerely—no longer remained the largely unobjectionable solution it had seemed before becoming an imminent and all but certain event. If the girl in question wanted him for his title, Clinton would have seen marriage to her as a fair enough exchange of assets. But since Sophie Lucas had already turned down two suitors with titles and fortunes, this conscience-saving consideration did not in any sense apply.

One of Dick Lambert's sayings was that to love before marriage was to squander an inheritance before getting it, and Clinton himself was not bad at justifications when he applied his mind. Love might be a reasonable basis for an affair, but a lifetime needed more rational criteria. How often do people fall in love disastrously with partners almost the opposite of what they would have chosen if logic rather than random attraction had been the means of selection? And in any case, wasn't love usually more to do with pride and sensual possessiveness than with gentler emotions? Far better trust money than love; money tended to last better. Although Clinton could laugh about the subject when talking to Dick, it did not alter his instinctive feelings.

In his last days before leaving for England, Clinton pinned his hopes on persuading his brother to help him. The chances seemed remote, but Clinton was not entirely without hope. He believed he had a carrot which an avaricious man would find hard to resist. In the meantime, when his thoughts returned to Sophie, he tried to allay his misgivings by reminding himself that the motives for a deed usually changed before it had been performed. One way or other, the next few weeks would determine his future.

CHAPTER TWO

"To be illegitimate is a misfortune. To be illegitimate *and* the elder son of a dead peer is something worse, because nobody's going to have to be a genius to work out why you're plain Mr. Danvers and not my Lord Ardmore like your father before you."

This much at least Esmond Danvers would sometimes volunteer to friends about his origins. Occasionally he might also remark, in the same ruefully ironic tone, that he was only born out of wedlock because his mother's divorce proceedings went on longer than expected and delayed her marriage to his father by a small matter of two months. Anybody hearing him, who also happened to know that his younger brother, now serving in the cavalry, had inherited the Ardmore title and everything else in the family worth inheriting, would inevitably have been impressed by the apparent lack of resentment in his voice. But that was only to be expected in a man whose two decades in the City might have served as a useful text for a sermon on self-help.

From solicitor's articled clerk, Esmond had progressed in five years to a partnership in a practice dealing mainly in company law. An invitation to join the board of a small private bank had followed; and because a number of the largest borrowers were bill brokers, he had learned a lot about the discount market.

Attracted by the large sums to be made discounting bills of exchange in a rapidly expanding market, he had ventured everything on winning a substantial slice of this lucrative field. Nine years later, at forty, he found himself sole proprietor of one of the three most successful discount houses in the city.

Among men of business, who measured strength of character by a man's capacity for hard work, Esmond's ruthless exclusion of most human pleasures in pursuit of his financial aims had made him seem a man of iron. And though some were perfectly aware that the men who strove hardest to seem invulnerable were often those with the worst weaknesses to hide, very few of Esmond's associates would have thought this in any way applicable to him. Esmond himself knew very well that boyhood rejection by his father had played an important part in his early determination to prove himself; but this, he considered, had long since ceased to have any relevance, especially after his father's death a decade ago.

Every now and then he wondered whether something more obscure than the logic he believed he lived by had been responsible for his avoidance of close relationships until he was forty—until his success and wealth had become incontestable. Had he really denied himself so much for so long, just because it had been logical to establish an unassailable position in the City before allowing competition from other distracting influences? Perhaps—and this thought had crossed his mind once or twice, only to be swiftly dismissed—perhaps he had needed to succeed before he could believe himself worth loving, had needed to feel invincible before he could once more risk dependence and possible rebuff. Far better to claim love as the just reward of success rather than sue for it humbly from a position of weakness. He wasted little time on such thoughts, preferring facts to theories; and the facts of his life seemed straightforward: at forty, he had swept every obstacle aside and made a fortune; the time had come to fall in love, marry, and have children. Time had inevitably become more important than it had been. When Esmond finally made up his mind that he had found the perfect woman, he very soon convinced himself that ultimate failure with her would destroy him. Success had become more than a habit to him.

A year before, if told that he would fall in love with an actress, and worse still a widow with a young daughter, he would have thought the prediction laughably improbable. Indeed to start with he had tried to persuade himself that his liaison with Theresa Simmonds was just another of the clandestine affairs that had supplied his wants in the past; but when she had refused to let him set her up in a house, the intensity of his fears that she might be seeing other men had shattered any pretense of limited involvement. Without any claims on her and unable to see her except when she chose, he was wretched enough to consider proposing marriage, but his caution would not allow that until he knew more about her. Instead he had asked her to live with him in his own home. She had refused on the grounds that it would ruin his social existence and harm his business, but he sensed that the sacrifice he had been prepared to make had won him a new respect. In fact, mixed in with genuine nobility of motive, there had been an element of calculation on his side. Believing that his love was greater than hers, he had concluded that the surest way to cement their relationship was to make the comfortable life his money made possible indispensable to her. This could only happen if she lived with him. Certain that his true strength lay not in passionate avowals but in maturer virtues—understanding, dependability, and loyalty—Esmond made himself her rock to cling to. At times this role made him feel like an athlete in a straight jacket, but calm persistence finally overcame her scruples about living with him.

Two months after this first victory, Esmond felt sure enough of himself to propose marriage. She had avoided a decision by promising an answer in three months' time if his feelings were still the same. Knowing Theresa too well to suppose he could force her hand, Esmond had accepted this. Though disappointed, he knew that if he showed no signs of reproach but continued to behave with undemanding devotion she would find it very hard to refuse him. By making him wait, she would realize that she had given him cause to hope.

On a warm August evening, with almost the whole three months still to run before he could expect her final answer,

"When I'll be at the theater."

"Yes." Esmond's surprise was masterly. "You can't want to sit listening to him moaning on about his debts?"

"If I had an only brother, wouldn't you be rather surprised if I tried to stop your meeting him?" As so often when she asked her most loaded questions, Theresa's tone was soft and caressing.

"I'd be delighted for you to meet Clinton."

"So you'll ask him to come earlier on Friday?"

"Dearest, you know I can't leave Lombard Street till six."

"Then change the day."

"He leaves for the country on Saturday."

"And after that he goes back to Ireland? How difficult it all is for you. I think we'd better forget about it, don't you?" Her serious face and meekly apologetic manner were too much for Esmond.

"Dear God, I'm the devious one." He laughed. "All right, I didn't want you to meet him just yet. Not till he's made a few decisions."

This time Theresa laughed. "Might I have influenced him in the wrong way?"

"Of course not." Esmond sighed, knowing that he was now going to have to tell her at least part of the truth. Not wanting to meet her smiling eyes, he gazed past her at the veneered surfaces of the bureau by the window. "He's going to ask me for a loan. Nothing new in that; but this time, if I don't oblige him, he's going to claim I'm forcing him into a mercenary marriage. In fact he's brought it on himself by refusing to consider getting out of one of the most expensive regiments in the army."

"It can't be easy to give up a career," she suggested with a personal emphasis that made Esmond even sorrier that Clinton had ever called on him.

"He doesn't have to give it up," he replied with asperity. "He could exchange into a less exclusive regiment, or sell his estate." He did his best to master the rising bitterness in his voice. "When the rest of us are in debt, we have to cut our costs or face the consequences. But nobody's going to get Clinton to recognize anything so tiresomely obvious. Life owes him what he wants."

Esmond was less optimistic than usual. Theresa had been late back from the theater, and this always made him uneasy. The fact that other men desired her both deepened his pride in possession and disturbed him—just as he was disturbed and inflamed by her physical closeness to the leading man on stage. The differences between her stage self and her real self fascinated him. He loved the contrast between her feminine gentleness and the toughness it concealed. Because she had often lived from hand to mouth, and knew what it was like to plunge from luxury into want, she lived intensely for the moment—an irresistible trait to a man who for years had mortgaged the present to the future.

When Theresa entered the room where he was sitting, Esmond wanted to ask what had delayed her, but as usual he suppressed the urge. Having frequently expressed his absolute trust in her, he did not intend to spoil this by seeming suspicious. In fact, the pleasure of seeing her immediately banished the irritation he had felt while waiting. As she crossed the room, the lamplight kindled copper glints in her hair and lent her face a misty softness.

"How was it?" he murmured.

She kicked off her shoes and sank down on a low sofa. "Another audience like that and I'll run screaming through the auditorium."

The exaggerated pathos of her expression made him smile. "You mustn't let me miss that."

"You mean it might make you come near the place?" She laughed in the slightly husky low tone he loved and then looked at him intently. "Why don't you come any more? You know I like talking to you between the acts."

"I feel out of place backstage."

"You could sit in front and only come behind in the intervals." She took the combs from her hair and let it fall loosely to her shoulders. Esmond turned away and glimpsed himself in the mirror above the console table near the door. A dignified, rather solemn man with graying hair and impeccably tailored clothes stared back at him. In general Esmond did his best to avoid conversations about Theresa's career. Before she accepted him, he thought it would be most unwise to admit that he would expect her to give up the stage after marriage. He met her inquiring green eyes for a moment; she was waiting for him to answer.

"It's not so much where I sit," he began slowly. "I suppose I don't like to see you in that part." A discussion of the play and her performance seemed safer than a dissection of his attitudes to the theater.

"Peg isn't virtuous enough?" she asked with a faint hint of ridicule.

"You're not her, that's all."

"I do try, you know."

"I meant it as a compliment. I didn't mean that you don't play the part well. . . . It's just that for me, knowing you—" He broke off, seeing how unconvinced she looked. She motioned him to sit next to her. As Esmond obeyed, he tried to divert his attention from the soft rise of her breasts under the lace chemisette in the yoke of her dress. Close to, she looked pale and rather tired. She might joke about the strains of her profession, but they were real enough. Saturated with tenderness, he longed to say aloud what he so often thought: Why work and tire yourself when you can depend on me for everything? But that was what she refused to do; she would let him buy neither her clothes nor any of her daughter's necessities.

"Why not be honest?" she said coaxingly. "It's nothing to do with the play. You don't like the theater or the people."

"Nothing of the sort. I'm an intruder there. Anyway that's how I feel; and when I'm on edge, I can't help giving a false impression. I know they think I'm superior—even contemptuous." He paused, aware of the close scrutiny of her long-lashed eyes, and wishing that she were not so skilled at hiding her thoughts. "Too rich and too fastidious. In their position I'd probably feel the same."

She smiled sweetly and seriously. "Actors only envy more successful actors. Other kinds of success don't count."

"I didn't mean they envied me."

She was sitting with her knees drawn up and her hands clasped round them, rocking very slowly back and forth. She said gently, "You can't help not liking them; I don't myself, half the time." She released her knees and sat up straight. "You are funny, Esmond. I know you think most of them are vain and rather vulgar. You're a dear to blame yourself, in case you hurt my feelings, but I'm not fooled."

He forced a laugh. "So I *am* superior and fastidious."

"Of course not." She leaned forward so close that he could not resist kissing her satiny cheek and then her finely curved lips.

"What am I?" he whispered.

She tilted her head and studied him. "Reserved. More discriminating than some. I like that." She smiled. "After all, it's why you like me. You're not conceited like most self-made men." She flicked a strand of hair from her forehead and frowned. "You're far too good at avoiding subjects you don't like. Quite devious, although you seem to be so straightforward."

"When have I been devious?"

"That's what I mean." She laughed. "You sound so virtuous; it's that seriousness of yours. I'm so glad you're not brash and debonair."

"When?" he insisted with firm good humor.

"Sunday," she replied after a silence which he had interpreted as an admission of defeat.

Now he wished that he had not pressed the point. On Sunday evening when he had been dining with Theresa, Clinton had called without any warning. Esmond had sent down a footman to say that he was not at home; he had explained this unbrotherly act to Theresa by saying that Clinton only ever came to talk about money and could never be bothered to say when he was coming. Esmond had also told her that he felt under no obligation to hear about his brother's financial difficulties on the one evening of the week that he was able to spend with her. But really, as it now seemed that she had guessed, Esmond had had other reasons for not wanting to see Clinton when she was in the house.

"You mean when I wouldn't see Clinton?" he said ingenuously. "I sent him a note. He's going to come back on Friday evening."

He paused awkwardly, noticing that she looked puzzled. He still had not explained why he had wanted to delay a meeting with Clinton. Damn the man, he thought; damn him. "Too hot in here," he said, getting up and drawing back the heavy swagged curtains. A light breeze made the candles on the mantelpiece flicker, casting moving shadows on the silk-hung walls. Esmond stared out at the lighted windows on the far side of the square. "You see," he announced, turning, "if he meets you now, he'll do his level best to get you to persuade me to help him. He can be very plausible—oh yes, and charming. And of course he'd misrepresent everything and make me out the worst miser in the world. I don't mean you'd believe him, but there'd still be plenty of scope for unpleasantness."

Theresa sat smoothing the folds in her dress, her face betraying no hint of what she was thinking. She asked without apparent interest, "Could you help him if you wanted to?"

Esmond grimaced and thrust his hands into the pockets of his frock coat. "He'd want at least ten thousand. Not the sort of sum anyone lends at the drop of a hat on indifferent security. Frankly there's no reason why I should try to raise it."

"I suppose," she began diffidently, "if you were fond of him, and trusted him to repay you . . ." She raised her hands. "I'm being very stupid. He got everything that should have been yours."

"That wasn't his fault." He managed to smile. "I don't hate him, if that's what you're driving at. I'm not sure how I feel. He was only seven when I left home. . . . In some ways we're more like acquaintances than brothers."

"And that's all you'll tell me?" she asked, coming up and laying her head against his shoulder. She saw his frown. "Not about him, Esmond. About you, and what mattered to you."

He looked down at her upturned face and smiled, the whole of his personality conveyed by the self-deprecating sadness of his hooded eyes and the folds of irony at their corners.

"You really want me to bare my wounds?" He kissed her forehead gently. "Ah, you want to share the pain. It's all gone, you know. Only a reminiscent twinge every now and then." He moved away, shaking the bunch of seals on his watch chain.

"The odd thing is how on earth such little scratches troubled me for as long as they did." He sat down on the sofa which Theresa had just left. "Your husband died, leaving you with a daughter of three and no means of support. Nothing I've ever known has made me suffer like that. My parents were unhappy —like thousands of others. They eloped; father was cut off by his family; he was robbed by moneylenders. A bad start for a marriage, but nothing exceptional. Granted, I made it somewhat worse by arriving before the wedding day. A little bastard isn't the best addition to a bride's trousseau. But I won't flatter myself—the recriminations and quarrels would have come along nicely without me. Anyway I was about four when my father started to stay away. As children often tend to, I blamed myself. If I'd done this or that better, shown a greater liking for horses, he would never have left me. It sounds pathetic, but that sort of guilt can be quite a comfort; it's much better to feel one's had some kind of say in events, even if a disastrous one. Also I worshiped the man and didn't want to blame him. I was a fool of course, but not without a few excuses, I like to think. He was as tall as a mountain with a voice like God's, a hero in the Opium War, famous sportsman, excellent raconteur—though his mistresses would be better judges of that. Come to think of it, he was just about everything I was never going to be. Clinton's a lot more like him." He looked at Theresa. "How am I doing?"

"I'll tell you when you've finished," she murmured, sitting beside him again. As she took his hand, the wry smile that had seemed engraved on his face faded.

"When I was ten, he left us for the best part of a year. I took it worse than Mother. The other women had finished it for her. After a time, I think he revolted her. That didn't worry him though. One day he came home, quite out of the blue, and announced he was back for good. If I'd been older, I don't suppose it would have surprised me much. After all, what does every nobleman want sooner or later? Years later, Mother told me he didn't beat about the bush. Either she agreed to try to give him the legitimate heir he wanted, or he'd divorce her. I'm sure he would have done it if she hadn't given in. I didn't know what was going on, but I'd have been blind and deaf if I'd not realized how miserable she was.

"I pleaded with father not to upset her any more. The first couple of times he kept his temper. After that he hit me whenever I said a word about her. There's an aphorism about its being harder for a man to forgive the person he wrongs than the person who wrongs him. At any rate, I forgave, but he didn't. Now I suppose I can see the humor in it. In effect I was begging him not to give her the child who would disinherit me. My innocence must have made his guilt worse.

"After Clinton's birth, I didn't really exist in his eyes, even though I did get better at shooting and managed to ride passably. I knew there wasn't going to be enough money for both of us to go into the army or get equal shares of anything, but the gap in our ages softened the disappointment. I got over it after a while; but—and this is the strangest bit—I went on thinking that one day I'd win back his good opinion. I used to sit imagining his saying that he knew how sad he'd made me and wanted to make it up. I went on making excuses for him, trying to please.

"Then they separated. Mother and I were sent to Ireland—father had a small estate there—and Clinton stayed on at Markenfield. Father kept him most of the time. He spent a few months a year with us in Ireland. That went on a year or two, then I came to London. Father died in a shooting accident when Clinton was eighteen. The coroner said it was an accident. It looked like suicide to me from what I heard. Who knows? I hadn't seen him for five years. Clinton got all the land and property; we share a family trust, which is just about the only reason we still see each other. News filters through from time to time. A while ago he bit some high-class whore's leg and was taken to court by her. He covered himself with glory in China and was lucky to get out alive. He nearly caused a scandal with a cabinet minister's wife a year ago. An active sort of life." He shrugged and stared at the floor.

"How strange," said Theresa, "and now you're the one with the whip hand. I wonder how you'll use it."

Esmond rose and held out a hand. "I'm tired and it's late."

She seemed on the point of asking another question, but instead she nodded and took his hand.

The following day, Esmond did not go to the City, but took Theresa and her daughter Louise to Greenwich Fair. He had kept the outing a surprise till the last moment; but, as with most of his surprises, the careful planning was soon evident. The picnic, bottles of chilled wine, and all the other requirements for the day had all been stowed away in the landau before he made his announcement.

Louise was precocious for eleven, but the experience of driving through the streets in an open carriage with a liveried coachman on the box was still enough of a novelty to delight her. Often she tried to seem unimpressed by the trappings of her new life, and the result was a juvenile sophistication that made Theresa cringe. Later, alone with Theresa, Esmond would say that he found the child's gaucheness touching or innocent. Her positive views, many of which had first been uttered by her grandfather, usually made Esmond laugh. Unaccustomed to children, he had no preconceptions about what she already knew, or what she might want to talk about; and this meant that he rarely spoke to her mechanically or with condescension. At first Theresa had half suspected that he might be trying to win over Louise as a matter of policy, but later she had revised this opinion. He seemed quite simply to enjoy giving the child pleasure.

In his immaculate frock coat and silk top hat, Esmond always looked out of place in places of popular entertainment, as if he had lost his way and ended up mysteriously in a circus tent or fairground without knowing quite how. This was the impression Theresa got that afternoon at Greenwich, watching with him the trapeze artists and the caged lions and tigers from Wombwell's Menagerie. Apart from a definite disinclination to have his fortune told, and an equal aversion to visiting the booths which housed the freaks and prodigies, he seemed to enjoy himself. The main event of the afternoon was the ascent of a richly painted hot-air balloon high above the gingerbread tents and hucksters' stalls.

At home again afterwards, drinking hock and seltzer in the principal drawing room, while Louise chattered to Esmond about the fair, Theresa was troubled by the undermining guilt that had rarely been entirely absent ever since she had refused to give Esmond a positive answer about marriage. He had assured her many times that he cared nothing for the social position he had thrown away by having her live with him. Yet this had not made her feel better. Considerate to a fault, it would be typical of him to conceal his regrets. Just as he would inevitably conceal any losses in the City that he suffered as a result of scandalous rumors. She was fond of Esmond, admired him. Louise was captivated; Theresa's father had frequently told her that she would be the greatest fool in the country if she lost her chance of marrying Esmond. And yet she could not steel herself to decide.

At twenty she had married because she could not endure days, or even hours, away from the man she loved. Her husband had been poor, and arrogant as only the young and ambitious can be. From the start he had made it plain that neither love nor marriage would ever be permitted to hinder him in his pursuit of fame as one of the great actor-managers of the day. Illusion or not, just a glance or a touch had made her heart race and her breath come fast. She had accepted him without thought for what had gone before and what would very likely follow. Long before consumption had killed her husband, Theresa had recognized that the real life of romantic love, after its first bright soaring, could be a poor twilight thing, doomed by the false images and expectations that had once sustained it.

Now, in her early thirties, she told herself she had finally left that delightful and delusory world where love is always true, and always going to last. Never again, if she had any sense, would she grant handsome youthful men all desirable qualities simply because she delighted to look on them. And Esmond, after all, was a striking man, and not yet old. He was not frivolous or vacillating; he had principles; he was loyal. Though distinguished, he never sought, as many actors did, to use conversation as an opportunity to impose his personality and trumpet his achievements. She had come to like his long angular face and heavy-lidded eyes, which perfectly reflected his sardonic humor. His low quiet voice, which had at first seemed a little monotonous, now appealed to her, just as his formality and shyness had come to do. Often she was sure she loved him. So why subject him to suspense which his kindness made cruelly undeserved?

At times she very nearly relented, but never reached the point of no return. Before she did, from out of her restless searching past came ghosts of faces—not more than three or four, and none of them extraordinary at first sight, though undeniably attractive in their ways—each one of which, for a brief month or two, had once been magically transformed and made beautiful beyond expectation. And choice, resistance, reason, had all been swept away like gossamer. When she thought of this, Theresa could not escape the difference between such devastating changes and her slowly altering perception of Esmond's qualities. In truth, he had acquired rights of possession almost without her realizing it, by patience and the kind of imperceptible encroachment which, given time, can establish rights of way to the most unyielding hearts.

Perhaps in three months she would know whether such things mattered, whether a love built so consciously could justify the sacrifice of an independence not easily won. Her other fears were harder to define. Sometimes she wondered whether his refusal to be demanding or possessive was quite as reassuring as she had once thought it. His ability to maintain such close control of himself, when deeply committed and involved, often struck her as uncanny. A man who trusted a woman, and praised her as a paragon of every virtue, was imprisoning as well as flattering her; for how could she ever disillusion a person who thought so well of her? There were times when she felt obliged to resemble his exalted picture: not making a scathing remark, not saying what she thought, but acting out involuntarily the gentle role his kindness had cast her in.

Theresa and Esmond dined early that evening, as they always did before she left for the theater. As dinner drew to a close, Theresa reminded him of the weeks before she had agreed to live in his house. With an exhausting provincial tour just finished, and another looming close, she had been tired and

Esmond was less optimistic than usual. Theresa had been late back from the theater, and this always made him uneasy. The fact that other men desired her both deepened his pride in possession and disturbed him—just as he was disturbed and inflamed by her physical closeness to the leading man on stage. The differences between her stage self and her real self fascinated him. He loved the contrast between her feminine gentleness and the toughness it concealed. Because she had often lived from hand to mouth, and knew what it was like to plunge from luxury into want, she lived intensely for the moment—an irresistible trait to a man who for years had mortgaged the present to the future.

When Theresa entered the room where he was sitting, Esmond wanted to ask what had delayed her, but as usual he suppressed the urge. Having frequently expressed his absolute trust in her, he did not intend to spoil this by seeming suspicious. In fact, the pleasure of seeing her immediately banished the irritation he had felt while waiting. As she crossed the room, the lamplight kindled copper glints in her hair and lent her face a misty softness.

"How was it?" he murmured.

She kicked off her shoes and sank down on a low sofa. "Another audience like that and I'll run screaming through the auditorium."

The exaggerated pathos of her expression made him smile. "You mustn't let me miss that."

"You mean it might make you come near the place?" She laughed in the slightly husky low tone he loved and then looked at him intently. "Why don't you come any more? You know I like talking to you between the acts."

"I feel out of place backstage."

"You could sit in front and only come behind in the intervals." She took the combs from her hair and let it fall loosely to her shoulders. Esmond turned away and glimpsed himself in the mirror above the console table near the door. A dignified, rather solemn man with graying hair and impeccably tailored clothes stared back at him. In general Esmond did his best to avoid conversations about Theresa's career. Before she accepted him, he thought it would be most unwise to admit that he would expect her to give up the stage after marriage. He met her inquiring green eyes for a moment; she was waiting for him to answer.

"It's not so much where I sit," he began slowly. "I suppose I don't like to see you in that part." A discussion of the play and her performance seemed safer than a dissection of his attitudes to the theater.

"Peg isn't virtuous enough?" she asked with a faint hint of ridicule.

"You're not her, that's all."

"I do try, you know."

"I meant it as a compliment. I didn't mean that you don't play the part well. . . . It's just that for me, knowing you—" He broke off, seeing how unconvinced she looked. She motioned him to sit next to her. As Esmond obeyed, he tried to divert his attention from the soft rise of her breasts under the lace chemisette in the yoke of her dress. Close to, she looked pale and rather tired. She might joke about the strains of her profession, but they were real enough. Saturated with tenderness, he longed to say aloud what he so often thought: Why work and tire yourself when you can depend on me for everything? But that was what she refused to do; she would let him buy neither her clothes nor any of her daughter's necessities.

"Why not be honest?" she said coaxingly. "It's nothing to do with the play. You don't like the theater or the people."

"Nothing of the sort. I'm an intruder there. Anyway that's how I feel; and when I'm on edge, I can't help giving a false impression. I know they think I'm superior—even contemptuous." He paused, aware of the close scrutiny of her long-lashed eyes, and wishing that she were not so skilled at hiding her thoughts. "Too rich and too fastidious. In their position I'd probably feel the same."

She smiled sweetly and seriously. "Actors only envy more successful actors. Other kinds of success don't count."

"I didn't mean they envied me."

She was sitting with her knees drawn up and her hands clasped round them, rocking very slowly back and forth. She said gently, "You can't help not liking them; I don't myself, half the time." She released her knees and sat up straight. "You are funny, Esmond. I know you think most of them are vain and rather vulgar. You're a dear to blame yourself, in case you hurt my feelings, but I'm not fooled."

He forced a laugh. "So I *am* superior and fastidious."

"Of course not." She leaned forward so close that he could not resist kissing her satiny cheek and then her finely curved lips.

"What am I?" he whispered.

She tilted her head and studied him. "Reserved. More discriminating than some. I like that." She smiled. "After all, it's why you like me. You're not conceited like most self-made men." She flicked a strand of hair from her forehead and frowned. "You're far too good at avoiding subjects you don't like. Quite devious, although you seem to be so straightforward."

"When have I been devious?"

"That's what I mean." She laughed. "You sound so virtuous; it's that seriousness of yours. I'm so glad you're not brash and debonair."

"When?" he insisted with firm good humor.

"Sunday," she replied after a silence which he had interpreted as an admission of defeat.

Now he wished that he had not pressed the point. On Sunday evening when he had been dining with Theresa, Clinton had called without any warning. Esmond had sent down a footman to say that he was not at home; he had explained this unbrotherly act to Theresa by saying that Clinton only ever came to talk about money and could never be bothered to say when he was coming. Esmond had also told her that he felt under no obligation to hear about his brother's financial difficulties on the one evening of the week that he was able to spend with her. But really, as it now seemed that she had guessed, Esmond had had other reasons for not wanting to see Clinton when she was in the house.

"You mean when I wouldn't see Clinton?" he said ingenuously. "I sent him a note. He's going to come back on Friday evening."

"When I'll be at the theater."

"Yes." Esmond's surprise was masterly. "You can't want to sit listening to him moaning on about his debts?"

"If I had an only brother, wouldn't you be rather surprised if I tried to stop your meeting him?" As so often when she asked her most loaded questions, Theresa's tone was soft and caressing.

"I'd be delighted for you to meet Clinton."

"So you'll ask him to come earlier on Friday?"

"Dearest, you know I can't leave Lombard Street till six."

"Then change the day."

"He leaves for the country on Saturday."

"And after that he goes back to Ireland? How difficult it all is for you. I think we'd better forget about it, don't you?" Her serious face and meekly apologetic manner were too much for Esmond.

"Dear God, I'm the devious one." He laughed. "All right, I didn't want you to meet him just yet. Not till he's made a few decisions."

This time Theresa laughed. "Might I have influenced him in the wrong way?"

"Of course not." Esmond sighed, knowing that he was now going to have to tell her at least part of the truth. Not wanting to meet her smiling eyes, he gazed past her at the veneered surfaces of the bureau by the window. "He's going to ask me for a loan. Nothing new in that; but this time, if I don't oblige him, he's going to claim I'm forcing him into a mercenary marriage. In fact he's brought it on himself by refusing to consider getting out of one of the most expensive regiments in the army."

"It can't be easy to give up a career," she suggested with a personal emphasis that made Esmond even sorrier that Clinton had ever called on him.

"He doesn't have to give it up," he replied with asperity. "He could exchange into a less exclusive regiment, or sell his estate." He did his best to master the rising bitterness in his voice. "When the rest of us are in debt, we have to cut our costs or face the consequences. But nobody's going to get Clinton to recognize anything so tiresomely obvious. Life owes him what he wants."

He paused awkwardly, noticing that she looked puzzled. He still had not explained why he had wanted to delay a meeting with Clinton. Damn the man, he thought; damn him. "Too hot in here," he said, getting up and drawing back the heavy swagged curtains. A light breeze made the candles on the mantelpiece flicker, casting moving shadows on the silk-hung walls. Esmond stared out at the lighted windows on the far side of the square. "You see," he announced, turning, "if he meets you now, he'll do his level best to get you to persuade me to help him. He can be very plausible—oh yes, and charming. And of course he'd misrepresent everything and make me out the worst miser in the world. I don't mean you'd believe him, but there'd still be plenty of scope for unpleasantness."

Theresa sat smoothing the folds in her dress, her face betraying no hint of what she was thinking. She asked without apparent interest, "Could you help him if you wanted to?"

Esmond grimaced and thrust his hands into the pockets of his frock coat. "He'd want at least ten thousand. Not the sort of sum anyone lends at the drop of a hat on indifferent security. Frankly there's no reason why I should try to raise it."

"I suppose," she began diffidently, "if you were fond of him, and trusted him to repay you . . ." She raised her hands. "I'm being very stupid. He got everything that should have been yours."

"That wasn't his fault." He managed to smile. "I don't hate him, if that's what you're driving at. I'm not sure how I feel. He was only seven when I left home. . . . In some ways we're more like acquaintances than brothers."

"And that's all you'll tell me?" she asked, coming up and laying her head against his shoulder. She saw his frown. "Not about him, Esmond. About you, and what mattered to you."

He looked down at her upturned face and smiled, the whole of his personality conveyed by the self-deprecating sadness of his hooded eyes and the folds of irony at their corners.

"You really want me to bare my wounds?" He kissed her forehead gently. "Ah, you want to share the pain. It's all gone, you know. Only a reminiscent twinge every now and then." He moved away, shaking the bunch of seals on his watch chain.

"The odd thing is how on earth such little scratches troubled me for as long as they did." He sat down on the sofa which Theresa had just left. "Your husband died, leaving you with a daughter of three and no means of support. Nothing I've ever known has made me suffer like that. My parents were unhappy —like thousands of others. They eloped; father was cut off by his family; he was robbed by moneylenders. A bad start for a marriage, but nothing exceptional. Granted, I made it somewhat worse by arriving before the wedding day. A little bastard isn't the best addition to a bride's trousseau. But I won't flatter myself—the recriminations and quarrels would have come along nicely without me. Anyway I was about four when my father started to stay away. As children often tend to, I blamed myself. If I'd done this or that better, shown a greater liking for horses, he would never have left me. It sounds pathetic, but that sort of guilt can be quite a comfort; it's much better to feel one's had some kind of say in events, even if a disastrous one. Also I worshiped the man and didn't want to blame him. I was a fool of course, but not without a few excuses, I like to think. He was as tall as a mountain with a voice like God's, a hero in the Opium War, famous sportsman, excellent raconteur—though his mistresses would be better judges of that. Come to think of it, he was just about everything I was never going to be. Clinton's a lot more like him." He looked at Theresa. "How am I doing?"

"I'll tell you when you've finished," she murmured, sitting beside him again. As she took his hand, the wry smile that had seemed engraved on his face faded.

"When I was ten, he left us for the best part of a year. I took it worse than Mother. The other women had finished it for her. After a time, I think he revolted her. That didn't worry him though. One day he came home, quite out of the blue, and announced he was back for good. If I'd been older, I don't suppose it would have surprised me much. After all, what does every nobleman want sooner or later? Years later, Mother told me he didn't beat about the bush. Either she agreed to try to give him the legitimate heir he wanted, or he'd divorce her. I'm sure he would have done it if she hadn't given in. I didn't know what was going on, but I'd have been blind and deaf if I'd not realized how miserable she was.

"I pleaded with father not to upset her any more. The first couple of times he kept his temper. After that he hit me whenever I said a word about her. There's an aphorism about its being harder for a man to forgive the person he wrongs than the person who wrongs him. At any rate, I forgave, but he didn't. Now I suppose I can see the humor in it. In effect I was begging him not to give her the child who would disinherit me. My innocence must have made his guilt worse.

"After Clinton's birth, I didn't really exist in his eyes, even though I did get better at shooting and managed to ride passably. I knew there wasn't going to be enough money for both of us to go into the army or get equal shares of anything, but the gap in our ages softened the disappointment. I got over it after a while; but—and this is the strangest bit—I went on thinking that one day I'd win back his good opinion. I used to sit imagining his saying that he knew how sad he'd made me and wanted to make it up. I went on making excuses for him, trying to please.

"Then they separated. Mother and I were sent to Ireland—father had a small estate there—and Clinton stayed on at Markenfield. Father kept him most of the time. He spent a few months a year with us in Ireland. That went on a year or two, then I came to London. Father died in a shooting accident when Clinton was eighteen. The coroner said it was an accident. It looked like suicide to me from what I heard. Who knows? I hadn't seen him for five years. Clinton got all the land and property; we share a family trust, which is just about the only reason we still see each other. News filters through from time to time. A while ago he bit some high-class whore's leg and was taken to court by her. He covered himself with glory in China and was lucky to get out alive. He nearly caused a scandal with a cabinet minister's wife a year ago. An active sort of life." He shrugged and stared at the floor.

"How strange," said Theresa, "and now you're the one with the whip hand. I wonder how you'll use it."

Esmond rose and held out a hand. "I'm tired and it's late."

She seemed on the point of asking another question, but instead she nodded and took his hand.

The following day, Esmond did not go to the City, but took Theresa and her daughter Louise to Greenwich Fair. He had kept the outing a surprise till the last moment; but, as with most of his surprises, the careful planning was soon evident. The picnic, bottles of chilled wine, and all the other requirements for the day had all been stowed away in the landau before he made his announcement.

Louise was precocious for eleven, but the experience of driving through the streets in an open carriage with a liveried coachman on the box was still enough of a novelty to delight her. Often she tried to seem unimpressed by the trappings of her new life, and the result was a juvenile sophistication that made Theresa cringe. Later, alone with Theresa, Esmond would say that he found the child's gaucheness touching or innocent. Her positive views, many of which had first been uttered by her grandfather, usually made Esmond laugh. Unaccustomed to children, he had no preconceptions about what she already knew, or what she might want to talk about; and this meant that he rarely spoke to her mechanically or with condescension. At first Theresa had half suspected that he might be trying to win over Louise as a matter of policy, but later she had revised this opinion. He seemed quite simply to enjoy giving the child pleasure.

In his immaculate frock coat and silk top hat, Esmond always looked out of place in places of popular entertainment, as if he had lost his way and ended up mysteriously in a circus tent or fairground without knowing quite how. This was the impression Theresa got that afternoon at Greenwich, watching with him the trapeze artists and the caged lions and tigers from Wombwell's Menagerie. Apart from a definite disinclination to have his fortune told, and an equal aversion to visiting the booths which housed the freaks and prodigies, he seemed to enjoy himself. The main event of the afternoon was the ascent of a richly painted hot-air balloon high above the gingerbread tents and hucksters' stalls.

At home again afterwards, drinking hock and seltzer in the principal drawing room, while Louise chattered to Esmond about the fair, Theresa was troubled by the undermining guilt that had rarely been entirely absent ever since she had refused to give Esmond a positive answer about marriage. He had assured her many times that he cared nothing for the social position he had thrown away by having her live with him. Yet this had not made her feel better. Considerate to a fault, it would be typical of him to conceal his regrets. Just as he would inevitably conceal any losses in the City that he suffered as a result of scandalous rumors. She was fond of Esmond, admired him. Louise was captivated; Theresa's father had frequently told her that she would be the greatest fool in the country if she lost her chance of marrying Esmond. And yet she could not steel herself to decide.

At twenty she had married because she could not endure days, or even hours, away from the man she loved. Her husband had been poor, and arrogant as only the young and ambitious can be. From the start he had made it plain that neither love nor marriage would ever be permitted to hinder him in his pursuit of fame as one of the great actor-managers of the day. Illusion or not, just a glance or a touch had made her heart race and her breath come fast. She had accepted him without thought for what had gone before and what would very likely follow. Long before consumption had killed her husband, Theresa had recognized that the real life of romantic love, after its first bright soaring, could be a poor twilight thing, doomed by the false images and expectations that had once sustained it.

Now, in her early thirties, she told herself she had finally left that delightful and delusory world where love is always true, and always going to last. Never again, if she had any sense, would she grant handsome youthful men all desirable qualities simply because she delighted to look on them. And Esmond, after all, was a striking man, and not yet old. He was not frivolous or vacillating; he had principles; he was loyal. Though distinguished, he never sought, as many actors did, to use conversation as an opportunity to impose his personality and trumpet his achievements. She had come to like his long angular face and heavy-lidded eyes, which perfectly reflected his sardonic humor. His low quiet voice, which had at first seemed a little monotonous, now appealed to her, just as his formality and shyness had come to do. Often she was sure she loved him. So why subject him to suspense which his kindness made cruelly undeserved?

At times she very nearly relented, but never reached the point of no return. Before she did, from out of her restless searching past came ghosts of faces—not more than three or four, and none of them extraordinary at first sight, though undeniably attractive in their ways—each one of which, for a brief month or two, had once been magically transformed and made beautiful beyond expectation. And choice, resistance, reason, had all been swept away like gossamer. When she thought of this, Theresa could not escape the difference between such devastating changes and her slowly altering perception of Esmond's qualities. In truth, he had acquired rights of possession almost without her realizing it, by patience and the kind of imperceptible encroachment which, given time, can establish rights of way to the most unyielding hearts.

Perhaps in three months she would know whether such things mattered, whether a love built so consciously could justify the sacrifice of an independence not easily won. Her other fears were harder to define. Sometimes she wondered whether his refusal to be demanding or possessive was quite as reassuring as she had once thought it. His ability to maintain such close control of himself, when deeply committed and involved, often struck her as uncanny. A man who trusted a woman, and praised her as a paragon of every virtue, was imprisoning as well as flattering her; for how could she ever disillusion a person who thought so well of her? There were times when she felt obliged to resemble his exalted picture: not making a scathing remark, not saying what she thought, but acting out involuntarily the gentle role his kindness had cast her in.

Theresa and Esmond dined early that evening, as they always did before she left for the theater. As dinner drew to a close, Theresa reminded him of the weeks before she had agreed to live in his house. With an exhausting provincial tour just finished, and another looming close, she had been tired and

your argument, how should I understand what you're doing now? Aren't you waiting? Making me wait? Taking the risks you couldn't bear?" He pushed back his chair and smiled. "I'm afraid, my dear, in matters of confidence you've always had the advantage." The clock on the mantelpiece struck the quarter. "Perhaps you ought to go?"

Theresa nodded dumbly. This was not the first time an attempt to ease her conscience had left her feeling worse than before. Nor could she in any way blame him for what she had brought upon herself.

When Esmond was at work in the City and Louise doing her lessons with her governess, Theresa often felt bored and listless in the museumlike tranquility of her lover's Italianate mansion. Idleness gave her time to read and think, and yet she often wished she was not left so much alone in the day. But, ostracized by Esmond's City friends, and knowing he would dislike it if she were to invite theater people to the house, there seemed no help for it. She might have minded less if she had been expected to do more for herself. But with everything she could possibly need already in the house, and a dozen servants in readiness to bring whatever she might require, there was scarcely any reason for her to go out. Apart from occasional excursions in Esmond's landau, her career survived as her only link with what she thought of as the ordinary world.

At four o'clock, Louise finished with her governess, and Theresa usually spent the rest of the afternoon, until Esmond's homecoming, with her daughter. After sitting for hours in the formal elegance of the main reception rooms, Theresa liked coming to Louise's small room with its wallpaper of red flamingoes on dark green and its tables and shelves cluttered with pottery animals and pert-faced china dolls. Less pleasing was a brightly painted plaster statue of the Virgin surrounded by unlit candles; for though Theresa had herself been brought up a Catholic, her daughter's religiosity sometimes struck her as excessive.

When Theresa entered, Louise was sitting cross-legged on the bed reading a book. Theresa sat down next to her and asked what she would like to do. Ignoring the question, Louise looked at her intently. "Do soldiers go to hell for killing people?"

"I don't think everything your nuns told you should be—"

"Never mind," the child went on impatiently. "They must be cruel to kill people; you can't deny that."

Theresa looked at her in bewilderment. Used to extremes of gaiety or moroseness, she still could not always judge which to expect. "Why are you so interested?" she asked.

Louise swung her legs round and jumped off the bed. She laughed and began to pirouette about the room, her short white dress and petticoats whirling out around her and her red hair flying. "When you don't tell me things, I feel ill. Will you feel ill if I don't tell you?" Louise's eyes looked even larger than usual in her pointed elfish face.

"I doubt it," Theresa replied with a smile.

Louise tiptoed closer and whispered melodramatically, "He's coming. That's why I'm interested."

"Who's coming?"

The child executed another derisive pirouette. "*Him* of course. The lord . . . the viscount, silly." Theresa remained silent. "Didn't you know?"

"Of course."

"When, when?"

"Tomorrow evening. How did you hear?"

"With these," said Louise pointing to her ears. "The servants tell me everything—except whether we're going to see him."

"I'm afraid you'll be in bed."

"I'll watch from the window."

"I don't think Esmond would be very pleased if—"

"Esmond's never cross with me. You said he'd refuse to let me ride in the brougham with Miss Lane when it's not being used, but he didn't." Louise ran over to the window. "I'll hear his carriage and I'll look out." She lifted the net curtain and pressed her face to the glass for a moment before turning quickly. "Will he wear his uniform?"

Theresa squeezed her hand affectionately. "Yes, and his sword will be dripping with blood."

"Nonsense, it'll be in a scabbard." Louise looked thoughtful. "I wonder how many people he's killed."

"Darling, he'll be dressed just like anybody else."

"How could he be? Lords have special tailors."

"Better than Esmond's?"

The child looked suddenly depressed. "How will I know who he is? And from high up too."

"Perhaps he'll wear his coronet."

Louise made a face and turned her back. Even when treating a subject humorously, she disliked being made fun of. The way she mixed insight with naïveté made it difficult to joke with her.

"Will you see him, Mama?" she asked after a silence.

"Esmond wants both of us to wait. He's coming to talk business."

Louise considered this and frowned. "Farraway says his squadron cleared the road to Peking for the whole army."

"Perhaps he exaggerated a little," Theresa suggested quietly. She wished that Louise did not take everything she heard from the servants so seriously.

"Farraway says that he was captured trying to save the journalists and the diplomats—the ones they hung up by their arms and feet. They hung him up too and nearly cut off his head." She looked at her mother wide-eyed with horror, and made a swooshing noise with her lips as she brought down her hand. Like sin, pain and death were subjects she enjoyed being shocked by. She stuck out her chin. "It's all true. Ask Farraway."

Theresa said nothing. If the incident was the one she thought—and it sounded extremely like it—she was nonplussed that Esmond had not told her that his brother had been involved. The treatment of the civilian hostages, and the soldiers who had tried to free them, had become as notorious in the China War as the Black Hole of Calcutta had been in the Indian Mutiny.

"You're sure Farraway said he was tortured?"

"Of course I am. He must be brave as well as cruel. Probably he's more cruel though."

"Why?"

"Otherwise we'd be allowed to meet him. If he was nice, Esmond would ask him to luncheon."

"Esmond's very good to you, you know."

"Because I'm always nice to him and never bad-tempered."

Theresa caught a glimmer of reproach in Louise's eyes but pretended not to notice. "It'd be very odd if you weren't nice, darling."

Louise bit her lip, her expression suddenly tragic. "You must always be nice to him, Mama." She flung her arms round Theresa's neck and hugged her fiercely. "Say you will . . . please say it."

Theresa kissed her on the cheek before disentangling herself. "You don't think I'm nasty to him, do you?"

"If you are, he could turn us out," stammered Louise, close to tears.

"Of course he wouldn't. Anyway, if we ever go away, we'll always be together."

Louise pulled away. "In some wretched place. I'd be sent away to school again." A rebellious light shone in her eyes. "I wouldn't stand it; I'd get expelled, I swear I would. I'd say dreadful things."

"What things?" murmured Theresa.

"About you." Louise sobbed. "Grandpa told me you could marry him, but don't want to."

"That wasn't right of him, my love."

"You'll burn in hell if you don't marry," moaned Louise.

"Didn't the nuns ever tell you that lots of saints led lives that shocked people? Of course I'm no saint, but God always forgives people who ask him to. Dearest, you must trust me to do what's best." Theresa stroked the child's hair until she was calmer. After a while, she said as cheerfully as she could, "This is what I'm going to do. I'll ask Miss Lane to let you stay up later than usual. You can watch out for Lord Ardmore from the schoolroom; you'll get a better view from there. And I want you to tell me what he looks like. Will you?"

Louise nodded solemnly, but in the end could not help smiling. Later Theresa played cards with her, and though Louise betrayed none of her earlier misery, the memory of it haunted her mother for days afterwards.

CHAPTER THREE

 A few minutes after eight o'clock, Louise, who had spent the best part of an hour staring down from the schoolroom, was shocked to see an ordinary hansom draw up. She had expected a barouche or phaeton. The man who got out was wearing a felt hat, which maddeningly hid his face; and, just as bad, his clothes looked quite unremarkable: a beige morning coat edged with dark braid, and matching trousers. Determined to get a closer view, Louise left the room, making out to her governess that she was going to bed. No sooner out of sight, she darted down a flight of stairs and hid herself behind the banisters on the half-landing. Esmond would be sure to see his brother in one of the rooms on the first floor.

Clinton paid his driver and ran up the steps under the pillared portico. He was soon admitted by a footman in a blue livery coat and silk stockings. Clinton disliked calling on his brother at any time, and had not been pleased to be sent away and summoned like an errand boy. However, since Esmond not only advised the family trustees on all financial matters, but also represented his last chance of escaping a forced marriage, Clinton had pocketed his pride.

Though largely indifferent to everything about his brother's house, the massive statue of Ceres in the hall always irritated him, so typical was it of Esmond's dry humor to make the Roman goddess of plenty every visitor's introduction to his stack of treasures. Clinton had long considered Esmond's love of ancient bronzes and statuary a fine example of the self-conscious way in which rich men cultivated rare tastes, partly to impress and partly for something to do with their money. Refusing to give the footman his hat or cane, Clinton followed the servant up the stairs.

From her hiding place, Louise caught her breath as halfway up the first flight Lord Ardmore unexpectedly turned. A second later she was struggling not to laugh. Without any sort of amusement on his face, the viscount took careful aim and tossed his hat over the banisters. It caught momentarily on the statue's only undamaged ear and then slipped to the ground. The first footman, who Louise had always thought pompous, stood rigidly staring at his feet. When Lord Ardmore said, "Fetch it for me," Louise almost choked. After the hat had been retrieved, Clinton once again measured the distance with his eye, and this time successfully landed the missile on the deity's head. The absolute solemnity of both peer and servant during this episode finally proved too much for Louise, and a strangled laugh broke from her lips.

Clinton looked up and was amazed to see a girl's face staring at him through the banisters on the next landing. He reacted slowly, but when he did, he wasted no time; pushing the servant aside, he dashed up the next flight four steps at a time. The girl had already placed another floor between them, but Clinton rapidly cut back this lead. On the fourth landing, he caught a glimpse of her flying skirts disappearing down a corridor, and slipping and sliding on the polished floor, he sprinted after her. She fled round a sharp corner, and when Clinton turned it, a baize-covered door blocked his path. On the other side he found himself in an empty corridor with some dozen doors leading off it: servants' bedrooms. But the girl had looked far too young to be in service, and in any case no servant would have run away. A servant's child perhaps? If so, Clinton could not believe that she would have dared sit watching people on the main stairs. The thought of Esmond's having an illegitimate daughter and then leaving the evidence to wander about his house was too preposterous to entertain.

Intrigued, and convinced that his quarry had only momentarily gone to earth, he decided to wait. He retraced his steps along the corridor, as though leaving, and then tiptoed back again. Less than two minutes later he was rewarded by a gingerly opened door and the child's face peering round it. This time Clinton made no mistake as he pounced; but, though he caught her sleeve, the next second she had torn herself free with a strength and determination which her thinness and delicate appearance made surprising. They were now facing each other from opposite sides of a small typically furnished servant's bedroom containing nothing more than an iron-framed bed, a chest of drawers, a rush chair, and a washstand. The girl had lost no time in running to the other side of the bed, where she now stood trembling with very real terror.

Clinton smiled and backed away a couple of steps to reassure her. "You run fast, little lady," he said with a laugh. Her only answer was a stifled sob. "Do you live here?" She shook her head and started to cry in earnest. "I never meant to frighten you. Why didn't you stay where you were?"

Still weeping, Louise shrank into the corner by the washstand. As Clinton moved round the end of the bed, intending to comfort her, she sprang forward onto the bed, jumped down and fled to the door.

Abandoning any idea of further pursuit and more puzzled than before, Clinton shook his head. As he reached the door, he saw on the floor a small scrap of lace, part of the child's cuff that had come away when she had pulled free. He picked it up and hurried down to the reception room he had been about to enter several minutes earlier. He was glad to arrive there before his brother, who, he supposed, had been delayed by his outraged servant. Whether the events of the past few minutes would be of any use in his coming interview Clinton had no idea, but the girl's desperate flight made it at least seem likely that Esmond would rather have kept her existence to himself.

As Clinton waited, every object his eye fell upon spoke of Esmond's prosperity and exacting taste. Around him, pale walls and stark contrasts of black and gold, dark equestrian bronzes and gilt Empire chairs, above an ebony cabinet a mirror framed by gold acanthus leaves, and statues everywhere—on wall brackets, tables, marble pillars flanking the mantelpiece. Figures in porphyry, alabaster, and basalt: a whole classical mythology. Believing that the next twenty minutes would determine whether he would escape the marriage he had struggled so long to avoid, Clinton was understandably nervous.

Most of his present difficulties stemmed from his father's determination that his heir should never, as he himself had done, either marry a poor woman or run up debts in early manhood. To prevent this, Ardmore had devised a will which had locked up every free shilling of capital in a family trust. Neither Clinton nor Esmond could legally touch his respective share of this money until Clinton's thirtieth birthday—still three years distant—unless, before that, Clinton should marry a woman bringing a dowry in excess of £20,000. Outrageously unjust to Esmond, the will had not helped Clinton either, since it had obliged him to let Markenfield, the family's principal estate, for a purely nominal rent, to compensate the tenant for carrying out essential repairs which he himself had been unable to afford. In the meantime, Clinton's outgoings, both on regimental charges and mortgage interest, had regularly outstripped his income by three thousand a year. The will, far from preventing his living beyond his means, had actually guaranteed that he did so; nor had the powerful incentive to marry an heiress proved effective while he could still negotiate new mortgages on his property. Now at last his borrowings had reached the limit of the security he could offer. Clinton's aim was to secure a loan from Esmond large enough to see him through till his trust capital came due. Otherwise marriage would be all but inevitable.

As it grew darker, a maid in a black silk dress entered unobtrusively and lit two lamps whose white Parian shades diffused a cool even light throughout the room. Drops of rain were beating against the windows when Esmond came in wearing his usual frock coat, his silk cravat held in place by a pearl pin.

"Still the same old sense of humor," murmured Esmond, taking Clinton's hand. "I can't believe you really get much fun out of distressing servants." He clicked his tongue as if reproving a child. "Sending the poor fellow racing up and downstairs like a retriever."

"I'll think of something more amusing for him next time."

"I'm sure he'll appreciate that." Esmond sat down and gestured to Clinton to do the same. "I was going to offer my congratulations, but perhaps that ought to wait till you've been accepted." Esmond eyed Clinton with nicely feigned anxiety. "You've not come here because you anticipate difficulties with the young lady?"

"Same old sense of humor," Clinton said wryly. "Last time I saw her, she wept buckets when I left."

"Most affecting. Women really are the oddest creatures. The way you've treated her, it's quite beyond me why she lets you anywhere near her. You honestly don't deserve her, Clinton."

"That's true."

"You don't know when you're lucky, never have done. The girl's a wonder—pretty, sweet-natured . . ." He paused, as if searching for a word.

"Rich?" suggested Clinton sharply. "As a matter of fact I'm perfecting a special form of words. I, mortgaged acres and distant expectations, take thee, immediate prospects and money in the funds, to be my wedded wife, to have and to hold for dinners, balls, and soirées, to bore and to tolerate till death us do part."

Esmond frowned and said quietly, "Do you suggest that the lady's fortune is a disadvantage?"

"I suggest," said Clinton, getting up, "that you should help me avoid this marriage you find so entertaining."

"Entertaining?" Esmond looked thoughtful. "I don't think that's quite right. I've never been very entertained by your problems." Though his tone was inoffensive, even mild, Clinton was chilled by it. Esmond brought his hands together in a silent clap. "Well, little brother, how do I help you?"

Forcing himself to be calm, Clinton gazed out into the street, where a brougham was waiting, the poor horse's ears back in the downpour. He turned. "You make loans, Esmond."

"Indeed I do—by the purchase of bills of exchange."

"There are other forms of security. I have certain expectations."

"You mean Uncle Richard? That dreadful old man."

"I don't like him myself; but I'm still his heir, and his fortune brings in fifteen thousand a year."

The tight stretched smile on Esmond's face seemed suddenly to snap. "It's out of the question."

"You don't even know what I'm proposing," objected Clinton.

"Don't I?" said Esmond with a harsh laugh. "You're asking me for so many thousands now, and in return you'll sign over Uncle Richard's fortune." He let his hands fall heavily on the gilded arms of his chair. "For a start, bill brokers don't keep large reserves like a bank, and frankly, even if I did, I'd still say no."

"Because I might die first?" asked Clinton, doing his best to make light of his brother's reaction. "For God's sake, he's in his seventies. Why not insure my life if you're worried?"

"I'm afraid insurance companies don't give cover for every kind of risk."

"You mean he may change his will?"

"Of course he could. No moneylender would even consider the idea. So you came to me with it. I'm flattered you think me so philanthropic."

"You know the man. That's why I'm asking you. He'd only change it if he married. Is it likely? You know it isn't. He's a worse misogynist than you."

"Appearances can be deceptive," said Esmond, flushing deeply.

"He's dead on his feet. That money's as good as in your hands, but rather than oblige me you'd see me in hell first."

Esmond listened politely, as if unaware of Clinton's anger. Then he looked at him sadly. "I don't know why you have to think the worst of me. Listen, what would you say to me if I accepted your proposition, and a week later he died? Wouldn't you accuse me of taking advantage of your present difficulties to rob you? That's the real reason I won't consider it."

Clinton leaned against the window frame and watched the rain.

He heard Esmond say almost sympathetically, "Even if I did finance you till you get the trust money, what would happen then? All the capital would go in repaying the debt. You'd be back where you started."

"That's not true. There's enough in the trust to pay you back and redeem the main mortgage on Markenfield. The lease ends about the same time. The next tenant would have to pay a proper rent."

"All right," replied Esmond soothingly. "Your debts mount by two thousand a year instead of three. You buy five years more and beggar yourself in the process. That's what it amounts to."

"With Markenfield unencumbered, I could raise enough for seven years."

"And what if your uncle didn't die by then? You'd be bankrupt." Esmond let out his breath slowly. "You wouldn't find an heiress then, and dear old Richard would change his will. Hard times, Clinton."

"There's no chance he'll last seven years. We both know that."

Esmond nodded. "The odds are in your favor. I'd say five to two. But that's not good enough when losing means destitution. You must marry her, and that's an end of it. Either that or sell Markenfield."

"What would you think of any nobleman who sold what he held in trust for future generations of his family? I can't throw away two hundred years."

"I understand that; it's not something Father would ever have done—one of the few things that can be said in his favor." Esmond shrugged. "I'm sorry, Clinton, he was a good father to you. I doubt if we remember the same man. A pity really."

Looking at his brother's sad, unforgiving eyes, Clinton wondered how he had ever allowed himself to believe that he might help him. Of course Esmond had turned him down; there had never been any other possibility. Between them the past still flowed like an impassable river, treacherous and deep. His anger and disappointment were fading now, rather as though an icy wind had swept the inside of his skull, leaving nothing behind. He supposed that he had been humiliated, but it did not trouble him; instead, to his surprise, Clinton felt a confused sense of freedom; there was nothing else to be done, no more hopes to be destroyed. With a detachment far less solemn than resignation, he imagined himself in a country garden, mouthing conventional endearments to a girl who meant little to him. The scene, though vivid, was as if glimpsed from a great height—the human figures mere specks in the landscape.

Only when he had left the room did the staircase remind Clinton of the girl. He brought the scrap of lace from his pocket and went in again. "A young lady gave me this," he said, dropping the child's cuff on Esmond's knee.

"That wasn't quite what I heard," Esmond replied mildly. "Her name's Louise—my mistress's child."

"You a father?" Clinton laughed, genuinely astonished.

"Her mother was married. She's a widow."

"You lucky dog." Clinton sighed, pleased by the lines of irritation on Esmond's brow. "I like older women too."

"If I shared that taste, my mistresses would be old enough to be grandmothers. Men of my age find women of thirty delightfully youthful."

Clinton smiled. "Calculation and sensuality—that's what I like about women that age. They enjoy the present but always keep something back for the future. Young girls offer the whole dish at once. Lechery's fed better in careful spoonfuls."

"I'll take your word for it." Esmond twisted his lips disdainfully. "You never had much time for love, did you, Clinton?"

Clinton leaned nonchalantly against the mantelpiece. "Maybe once or twice a century." he picked up a head of Pallas Athene and kissed her marble lips. "In the meantime vanity must have its little conquests and boredom its diet of excitement."

"I wonder if you're really as cynical as you pretend."

Clinton's hand shook slightly as he replaced the head on the mantelpiece. "I'm afraid one has to have one's capital intact for romantic passions. Wouldn't you say mine's dribbled away in the small change of flirtation?" He took a step towards Esmond. "Men who marry for money can't be expected to babble on about sentimental attachments."

52

"I meant no offense."

"I'm sure you didn't." Clinton looked at him quizzically. "I suppose you're going to make her an honest woman . . . being a man of principle."

"I intend to marry her if that's what you mean."

Clinton smiled ingenuously. "It's a most remarkable thing. I've known about a dozen men who intended to marry their mistresses; but somehow, God knows why, they never seemed to find the right moment."

Esmond looked at him steadily. "I'm not a liar or a hypocrite, Clinton. I've already asked her. I'm waiting for her answer."

"Sounds a clever woman. If she grabbed you straightaway, you'd think she was after your money and nothing else."

"You think I should kick her out so she comes crawling back?"

"Might be an idea."

"Then let me tell you this: She's turned down richer men than I am, and she's not a banker's widow either, in case you're thinking of making any more funny remarks. She's an actress. Does that amuse you?"

"Not in the least. I'm quite partial to them myself from time to time. What sort of parts does she play?"

"I've said all I mean to. I wouldn't have told you anything unless I'd thought you'd find out anyway sooner or later." Esmond moved across to the fireplace and rang the bell. "Will you dine with me?"

"Perhaps another evening. If I'm accepted by the girl, I'll have to come back to talk about the marriage settlement. Any contribution I make is going to have to come from the trust."

Esmond smiled when they had shaken hands. "I sometimes wonder if we'll ever see each other again when the trust's wound up."

"You'll have me in tears," said Clinton, picking up his cane and crossing to the door. About to open it, he looked back. "You had a long wait before seeing me bow to the majesty of financial facts. Was it as enjoyable as you expected?"

Esmond stood stiffly with folded arms, a slight tightening of his lips the only sign of his annoyance. "There's an old saying,

Clinton: In important matters, it's very rare for a man to be cheated by anyone but himself."

"They believe *that* in the City?" Clinton laughed, pushing open the door. He paused a moment on the landing, and then, rapping the buttocks of a marble Aphrodite with his cane, started lightly down the stairs. Not caring to wait while a servant fetched a hansom, he set out on foot.

The rain had stopped, and evening sunlight was gleaming on wet pavements and on the stuccoed façades of the houses as he left the scene of his defeat. With every step, he felt his anger returning and keen regret for the many things he had left unsaid. His efforts to seem lighthearted and insouciant now struck him as worthless affectation. The only result of them had been to let Esmond off lightly.

Esmond stood to get his trust money at once if the marriage with Sophie went ahead. Otherwise he would have to wait a further three years. Clinton could not understand or forgive his own failure to make pointed use of the financial advantage Esmond had secured for himself by refusing any sort of help. Clinton's conviction that Esmond had no real need of the money made him regret his silence still more. But at the time, his principal concern had been to hide the full extent of his anger and depression.

For years, Clinton's most vivid boyhood memories of Esmond had centered on his sardonic disparagement of the pursuits he liked best: hunting, steeplechasing, and the other interests he had shared with his father. Later, Esmond had become more subtle, praising the army whenever they met and belittling his own commercial activities, simply to give added force to apparently casual remarks about the China War being fought solely to protect the interests of British merchants. Esmond's claim to have been envious of cavalry officers had been his standard way of ridiculing a society which despised trade and yet derived from it much of the wealth which made such snobberies possible. Until recent years, the difference in their ages had inevitably placed Clinton at a disadvantage in these exchanges; nor had the undoubted fact that Esmond had been wronged made matters easier.

In the past, Esmond had seemed especially fond of representing Clinton as a charming and carefree idealist, while he bemoaned the loss of his own joys and illusions in the wicked City. It was this recollection which now made Clinton angriest. Esmond would have found it deliciously ironic that he, the world-weary broker, should intend to marry for love, when the young idealist was on the verge of a cynically profitable union. The ingenuity Esmond had shown in reversing these old roles, while talking about his virtuous actress, grated harshly on Clinton's nerves. And what he had heard about the woman herself annoyed him almost as much as Esmond's attitude.

Here was an actress—possibly unsuccessful—in her thirties, with a daughter to support from what she could earn in the most precarious of all professions. When offered riches and security by a devoted cultivated man, had she gone down on her knees and thanked God? Not she. It stung Clinton personally, as Esmond had probably known it would, that this unknown woman, with reasons for marrying quite as persuasive as those which had crushed his own resistance, had stood firm. By what right had she valued herself so highly? Or did he actually believe a word of it?

At the ornamental gates which separated the square from the public highway, Clinton stopped abruptly, and then started back purposefully in the direction of the mews which ran behind Esmond's house. A few shillings would be enough to elicit from a groom or stableboy the name of Esmond's actress and the theater where she worked. Clinton did not intend to damage his brother's chances with her, but what better medicine could there be for his bitterness than to find the woman a calculating bitch instead of an angel? And really there was nothing unlikely about an actress making a fool of Esmond while casting around for an even bigger fish.

With several days to kill before leaving for the country on his marital mission, Clinton would in any case have been curious to see the woman capable of melting Esmond's self-contained heart; now he had additional incentive. When the time came to propose to Sophie Lucas, it would be particularly consoling to reflect that if Esmond's marriage ever happened, it would be, on the girl's part, no more a mutual love match than his own.

CHAPTER FOUR

 Early the following evening, Clinton sat drinking brandy and water in the smoking room of the Cavalry Club, idly listening to snatches of conversation about the relative merits of cutting and pointing swords.

"Experts be damned," an elderly general was saying. "Give a big strong fellow a saber as sharp as you like—but can he make any impression at all on a leg of mutton covered in sacking and leather straps? That's my point."

"You mean your edge, sir," said a younger officer.

"In the Mutiny," said another, "the Ninth Lancers had a short spike set in the hilts of their swords; in melees it was better than any kind of blade. A blow in the face with the hilt and that was that."

From there, the conversation passed on to whether the lance was an outmoded weapon. Looking around the room, from face to face, Clinton supposed that few if any of these officers would consider it reprehensible to marry for money. Most would undoubtedly label objections to such a time-honored practice as sour grapes or humbug. As a rule, Clinton himself was largely immune to serious doubts about the accepted code of behavior his class lived by—his faith in part due to social habit, in part to a cast-iron assurance of his position in society.

If this certainty made him arrogant, it also left him almost entirely free of the ambitions and jealousies which drove the majority to try to outstrip each other.

Esmond of course described this aristocratic virtue as complacency. Not for the first time since their meeting, Clinton cursed his brother. Nobody else on earth was better at forcing him up against his own inconsistencies and the questionable moral assumptions he shared with most of his friends.

Rarely had he known the strange detachment he felt now, sitting in a room where he had previously been so much at home. What did he really feel about these men he had seen on scores of occasions over dinner and cards?

Lord Hampden, one of a group of men playing whist by the window, was known to have debauched his bride in the guard's van on the way back to his ancestral home after his London wedding. The story had much amused Clinton, not least because the girl had been the exceptionally virtuous daughter of an earl. Now, two years later, Hampden kept two mistresses, and even so found time to visit Kate Hamilton's assignation house. In the present company, Clinton doubted whether there was a single married man who was faithful to his wife. Yet all of them would cry shame on the husband who paid his wife's dressmaker's bill himself, instead of giving her a large enough allowance to cover it. Captain Malcolm, another of the card players, had deliberately compromised an heiress, so that she had been forced to marry him, and had not been shunned for it. But Malcolm now expected her to be faithful and would furiously demand an apology for any slur on her reputation. Sir Richard Benham, asleep in an armchair by the door, had a wife who had carried on a series of intrigues after she had given her husband three sons, and because she was discreet and Benham feigned complete ignorance, life went on as before. But were any man to cross the room and say to his face that Lady Benham was an adulteress, he would leave no stone unturned in the law courts to clear his wife's name. Should he fail, in spite of his own affairs, he would undoubtedly cast her out without compunction.

Ridiculous though Clinton thought this, he could no more stop himself finding a sexually abstemious man a prig than he could help feeling sympathy for unfaithful wives whose husbands bored them. It seemed obvious to him that disappointed women would gravitate to men of greater energy and confidence. If he himself were ever to bring about the social ostracism of a married woman, Clinton knew that the same code that would compel the husband to disown her would also oblige him to take her up and support her for as long as she needed his protection. He would expect to be forced out of his regiment and would think it perfectly natural that none of his married friends should ever again receive him in their homes. But where in this strange pattern of honor and deceit would his own marriage find its place? Would he behave just as Hampden and Benham had done? In company, he often smiled over axioms which he found privately distasteful; probably every man he knew did the same. To display tenderness of conscience was to be an ass.

A man had duties, undoubtedly, especially if he was an officer; but when women spoke of their duties or moral scruples, these things were trifles—just so many fortified positions which they loved to have stormed by determined men. "Treat them like fools and they'll worship you" had been an important part of Clinton's father's advice to him. It would have been remarkable if Clinton had learned to respect women as well as love them.

He had dined early in order to be in time for the theater, and he was leaving the club when he met Richard Hawtrey on the stairs. Hawtrey, a handsome cynical man with white regular teeth and a small carefully trimmed mustache, had been a subaltern with Clinton in the 15th Hussars before exchanging into the Royal Scots Greys. Clinton knew the man disliked him.

"Met Dicky Folliat at Tattersalls yesterday," drawled Hawtrey. "He's out for your blood and no mistake."

"Can't imagine why," replied Clinton curtly.

"Cutting him out with that Lucas girl. Keep an apple dangling and it attracts more than a single wasp."

"Who told him I had any interest?"

Hawtrey grinned and jingled his watch seals. "Told him herself. Good as said it was my Lord Ardmore or nobody." He lolled against the banister with one hand thrust into a pocket of his peg-top trousers. "Just as well these heiresses are vain enough to think up more reasons than money for their attraction."

Clinton stepped forward menacingly. "Are you speaking of Miss Lucas?"

"I spoke generally, my lord," replied Hawtrey with mocking deference.

"That's fortunate, Mr. Hawtrey. In future anything said touching her will be my personal concern. You may tell Captain Folliat that." With a slight nod to Hawtrey, Clinton turned on his heel.

What point pretending after that? he asked himself as the hall porter opened the door for him. He was no freer than any of the others, and he might as well accept it. The code allowed no exceptions even to the proudest, since pride itself was its cornerstone.

From a box in the second tier, Clinton looked down at the assembling audience. Not a regular visitor to the respectable theater, he was surprised to see that the old pit benches had been pushed back under the balcony to make way for expensive orchestra stalls. As he preferred popular melodramas, burlesques, and extravanganzas to polite sentimental comedy, the composition of the audience at the Princess's Theatre did not please him. Many of the men were in dress coats and the women wearing tulle, velvet, and silk evening dresses—clothes which Clinton considered appropriate for the opera but not in an ordinary playhouse. Used to the mixture of classes at the Surrey and the Standard, where the pit and gallery were always filled to bursting by a boisterously enthusiastic orange-sucking crowd of mechanics, dock laborers, and costermongers in greasy fustian and corduroy, Clinton found the refined impassivity of predominantly middle-class audiences as lifeless as the plays they watched—purged of sexual suggestion, politics, and low comedy. The plays of Congreve and Vanbrugh, which he had often enjoyed with his father, were now rarely performed except in bowdlerized versions.

But with his special reason for being there, Clinton was perfectly content to admire the decorative improvements made during Charles Kean's long management: the gold leaf framing the boxes, the sparkling chandeliers, and the blue empyrean above, where painted gods floated in clouds. Helped on by a bottle of Clos Vougeot and a cigar, he was soon caught up in the pleasantly expectant mood which filled the house with the first squawky dissonant chords of the orchestra tuning up. Within minutes the heavy curtain rollers began to turn with a faint creaking, and the richly swagged draperies lifted to reveal a romantic painted drop with a blue lake, bosky trees, and a distant eighteenth-century house. Clinton was now impatient for the orchestra to finish their brief introductory piece, after which their role would be limited to musical backing at moments of high emotional crisis.

The play, *Masks and Faces,* by the spectacularly successful team of Tom Taylor and Charles Reade, had been frequently revived since its first performance more than a dozen years earlier. And though it was an artificial sentimentalization of theatrical life in the previous century, it had a strange effect on Clinton almost from the beginning. Very loosely based on the life of Peg Woffington, who had started life as a Dublin watercress seller to find later fame acting with Garrick at Covent Garden, the action was inevitably more concerned with Peg's goodness of heart than her violent temper and numerous affairs. The theme of a woman with a doubtful reputation and a heart of gold was anything but new, and yet for other reasons Clinton became quickly involved.

Theresa Simmonds, in real life an actress living with a rich man, was playing the part of an actress facing the dilemma of whether to do just that. After several scenes of indecision, Peg high-mindedly rejects wealthy Sir Charles Pomander, instead falling for a simple country gentleman, who later turns out to be married to a sweet young wife. Angry and wounded though she is, Peg heroically sacrifices her own feelings and, after some gentle ridicule of her deceitful swain, brings about a reunion between him and his wife. All of which had about as much to do with the real Peg Woffington as milk has to do with brandy. But the play had plenty of witty lines, and once or twice a sense of pathos coming close to genuine tragedy.

Theresa's first entrance had disappointed Clinton. Some actresses mysteriously seemed to fill the stage and command it. But though she lacked this elusive quality, Theresa undeniably had others: a mocking laugh which could quickly turn to gravity, well-timed ironic turns of the head, alertness of eye, and grace of movement. She could also convey invisible struggles with conflicting emotions. But her vivacity, clear voice, and the delicious sting she gave to her wittiest lines seemed wrong for a woman evidently intended by the authors to be the epitome of mellow sensuousness and warmth. Theresa's demure pose, concealing subdued mischief expressed by arched eyebrows and watchful eyes, would have made her ideal for numerous roles in Restoration comedy. She could seduce with her eyes and lips, but in attempting Peg's more blatant coquetry, the effect was false. But the audience that night was a bad one—a particular disaster in comedy of any kind, when response is everything.

All the time Clinton wished that her face were not masked by a layer of white makeup in the eighteenth-century manner, and further disguised by period dabs of color on her cheeks and a prominent beauty spot. Her powdered wig made it still harder for him to judge what she would look like off the stage. At least her figure was not concealed by the tight fit of her low-cut scarlet bodice, which plumped up her breasts pleasingly.

Clinton was not impressed by her until comparatively late in the play, and he had till then been principally held by the theme of marriage, money, and fidelity. But her reaction to the revelation that her country gentleman was married showed what she might be capable of if better cast: a subtle blend of anger, dignity, and self-mockery, shot through with a sorrow that was neither maudlin nor pathetic.

"You forget, sir, that I am an actress. A plaything for every profligate who can find the open sesame of the stage door. Fool to think that there was an honest man in the world and that he had shone on me. What have we to do with homes and hearths and firesides? Have we not the theatre, its triumphs and full-handed thunders of applause? Who looks for hearts beneath the masks we wear? These men applaud us, swear to us, cajole us, and yet forsooth we would have them respect us too. Stage masks may cover honest faces and hearts beat true beneath a tinselled robe."

The passion in her voice both pleased and puzzled Clinton, the sentiment of the speech being so much at variance with her prevaricating behavior to Esmond. He frowned, and thought for a little; then he smiled to himself and summoned the box attendant and asked for pen and paper. It took him very little time to dash off a note and hand it to the waiting attendant for delivery.

Dear Miss Simmonds,

I beg a few words with you, not as a devoted follower of Thespis, but as a sincere friend and colleague of Mr. Danvers, to talk of what must concern you, namely his unhappy disregard for the high repute which he lately enjoyed. I shall present myself at the stage door after the final curtain.

Trusting to your kind consideration, I am honored to be, dear madam, yours very truly,

Frederick Higgs

It had rained during the performance, and the gas globes over the stage door were reflected, elongated and iridescent, in the black mirror of the pavement. Clinton pushed his way through a group of waiting men, his eye caught by fur-collared coats, gray whiskers, and glinting monocles. Across the road a streetwalker was hovering, and several urchins watched the men warily, doubtless waiting for the best opportunity to attempt to pick their pockets. Clinton announced his fictional name to the doorman and, to the fury of those who had been denied entrance, was immediately admitted.

Backstage the air was stuffy and overheated, savoring of ammonia and the glue used in the scenery; up a flight of badly lit stairs, Clinton heard the noise of washbasins and people laughing and calling to each other. Here in the dressing-room corridors, the musky scent of makeup mingled with the pungency of hair warmed by curling tongs and the odor of damp powder.

An old crone of a dresser with thin yellowy hair opened Theresa's dressing-room door and reluctantly let Clinton in. In front of a dressing table covered by a grease-stained cloth and dotted with bottles and jars, the actress sat sponging her face while the dresser unpinned her wig. Without moving, Theresa scrutinized Clinton in the mirror. She had made no preparations for the arrival of a strange man, and was wearing a dirty waist-length cotton chemise to protect the dress she had worn in the play.

"Well sit down, Mr. Higgs," she said, waving a bare arm impatiently in the direction of a sagging armchair next to a cracked cheval glass. As the dresser lifted off the wig, Theresa shook out her own rich copper-colored hair, which fell to her shoulders, at once softening and transforming her face. Without the stiff black mascara around her eyes and the white layer of makeup, Clinton was suddenly aware of the beauty of her eyes and skin. Disconcertingly, she had not wiped the carmine from her lips.

"Don't you think it rather presumptuous, Mr. Higgs, to involve yourself in a man's affairs without his consent or knowledge?"

"Concern for his well-being compelled me, madam."

"I'm a fiend, isn't that so, Mary?" she asked the dresser, who was now waiting to unhook the back of her dress. "Demanding this spot for my entrances, that one for my exits, bullying everyone in sight . . . ruining my lovers."

The old woman shook with silent mirth and then broke into wheezy laughter. "You demand anything, Miss Simmonds? Bully people. . . ? Oh dear me . . . oh . . ." Her laughter caught her breath and changed to a violent fit of coughing.

Theresa turned and faced Clinton. "Being a humanitarian, I'm sure you won't want to delay Mary's getting home." She stood up and picked a towel from the floor, which she handed to the dresser. "Put that over Mr. Higgs and we can get on."

Mary advanced on Clinton and looked at him sternly. "No peeping, mind," she croaked, dropping the towel over his head.

While Clinton was shrouded, Theresa's bodice was carefully unhooked and her skirt unlaced at the back. As Theresa stepped out of the dress, wearing only a petticoat, Mary, herself bent and withered, cast a solicitous eye over her mistress's full upward-tilting breasts. There was nothing that younger girls could improve on there. She hastily fetched Theresa's long cambric dressing gown and, with a covert eye still on Clinton, helped her into it.

"You can go, Mary; and you may come out now, Mr. Higgs, if you haven't suffocated."

How in his own character he would have responded to having a damp towel placed over his head Clinton did not know, but in the role of Mr. Higgs, he thought it best to accept any indignities gracefully. The stilted awkwardness of his note had predetermined his behavior, however ill it accorded with his appearance.

When the dresser had gone, Theresa sat down on her dressing stool and smiled kindly at Clinton, as though trying to help a gauche, embarrassed boy. "You look like someone well accustomed to coming backstage, Mr. Higgs. A man much in society, I'd imagine."

Clinton studied the peeling flower-patterned wallpaper with dignity. "Society and I, madam, only have a nodding acquaintance. Insignificance has that advantage." He leaned forward and said as solemnly as he could, "Mr. Danvers is not a happy man, Miss Simmonds. It's not right, you know, to tantalize a man of his character."

"You sound like a physician, Mr. Higgs."

"It needs no special knowledge to diagnose his disease and prescribe the cure."

"Which is?" asked Theresa, her face completely composed but her eyes glinting.

"Marriage, madam."

"I'm sorry?"

"Marriage is the cure. Why do you live as his wife in fact, and yet refuse him the honorable satisfaction of making you that in law?"

Theresa lowered her eyes. "The life of an actress makes me unfit for that honor."

"You mock me, Miss Simmonds."

"On the contrary; rank is not an illusion but a cruel hard fact."

64

Knowing very well that she was being insincere, Clinton had no idea how to make her honest without abandoning the restraints imposed upon him by being Mr. Higgs. "Should an artificial social distinction," he asked, "part two people in other ways ideally suited?"

Theresa bowed her head. "Mr. Danvers is no ordinary broker. He is a nobleman's son. His brother is a viscount."

"Actresses have married dukes."

"I cannot marry into his family, Mr. Higgs." She clasped her hands as though violently agitated. "His brother would prevent it."

"His brother?" echoed Clinton, bemused but also suspicious. Yet when he looked directly into her eyes, Theresa gazed back at him without the least trace of mockery; in fact, tears were beginning to brim over.

"If you knew a fraction of the things I know about that man, you wouldn't doubt me."

"Tell me some." He sighed, wondering where his mistake had been.

"He once bit an actress's leg; he likes chasing young children." She rose and leaned against the wall for a moment before coming close to Clinton; her manner was conspiratorial. "I hardly know how to say this, Mr. Higgs." She lowered her voice to a whisper. "He's about to contract a scandalous marriage to a woman old enough to be his grandmother." She looked into Clinton's eyes, her own opened wide with horror. Clinton fought to stop himself smiling, but in the end could not help himself. She shrugged her shoulders and turned away. "You're a poor actor, Lord Ardmore," she said quietly.

"You knew all along?" he asked, annoyed to have done so badly, but amused too by the absurdity of his situation.

"From the moment you walked in. My poor daughter described you down to that little scar over your eye."

Clinton did his best to laugh. "What can I say?"

"What about what you intended to?"

"That's no longer possible. I'm afraid my brother might find it in rather doubtful taste."

"And how would you describe what you have done?"

"Provided an intelligent woman with an excellent opportunity for making a fool of me." Her regal scorn was so superbly convincing that he laughed out loud. "You really should try that expression on the stage; poor old Sir Charles would take to his heels before his exit. How can I help what Esmond's told you about me? That old story about biting an actress. The lady in question asked me to bring her a necklace in my mouth on my hands and knees."

"So you bit her like a dog. How witty, my lord."

"I thought so at the time." Clinton got up. Her disdain no longer seemed so funny. He said mildly, "Aristocratic villains are more common in plays than in life."

"How fortunate," she murmured, removing the carmine from her lips.

"One day someone will write a melodrama with a bestial heroine and a virtous aristocrat instead of the other way round."

"As a burlesque it might be successful."

Her ability to deal out sarcasm in a quiet, almost gentle voice left him speechless. Looking at her silky hair and her milk-white skin, lightly etched with the first faint traces of age at the corners of her eyes, he was filled with admiration for this woman, so unlike the pampered daughters of luxury.

A widow of thirty-two or -three could not be ruined by slander like a girl hoping for marriage; more experienced and therefore less prone to the emotional upheavals of younger women, she could afford to be herself serenely. With little time to waste, she would choose with greater caution and, with less histrionics, feel more. He wanted to explain that he knew he had been mistaken in coming to see her in the way he had, but his mind felt dulled by the wine he had drunk during the play.

In the brief silence which followed her last words, the doorman knocked and told her that her coachman was waiting. She held out a formal hand, which Clinton took with equal formality. She smiled wistfully. "Goodbye, Lord Ardmore." As he was going out, she called him back and said with a hesitance that astonished him, "If you'd chosen any other subject, I wouldn't have—"

"Whipped me so hard?"

"It was a good practical joke—your letter. I mean that."

"You're kind to take that view."

"Perhaps I can hope to meet you properly at your brother's house?"

"So we can all laugh about it?" Clinton smiled and shook his head. "I think not, Miss Simmonds."

The stage door had been locked, so he was shown out through the dimly lit auditorium. Trying to remember exactly what he had hoped to achieve, he found himself laughing aloud. Nothing could have made any difference to his predicament. Tomorrow Theresa would be equally passionate about the hearths and firesides, which probably meant nothing to her; tomorrow he would leave London to propose to Sophie, with about the same degree of sincerity. Dooming some to deceit, others to nobility—life going on.

CHAPTER FIVE

A hot windless day in late July, and the country lying tranquil under a soft haze. The meadows after the cutting of the hay looked brown and scorched, and the leaves on trees and hedges were tarnished and dull. Clinton had been met at the station by one of the Lucases' coachmen, and had asked the man to drive him to Ammering Court by the longer way, which took them through Dinsley Woods and up onto Aylsham Ridge. Already the hindquarters of the horses were flecked with streaks of sweat, and their legs were hidden, except for the occasional flash of a metal shoe, in clouds of driving dust which billowed out from under the blurred wheels of the black and yellow phaeton.

Up on the ridge, Clinton told the coachman to stop, and jumped down without waiting for the step to be lowered. He clambered over the nearest gate into a field where the air was heavy with the scent of hedgerow honeysuckle and freshly mown hay. From the nettles in the ditch behind him came the constant chirping of grasshoppers. Ahead lay a wide panorama of fields and woods: white checkering of barley stubble, golden squares of wheat, greeny brown patches of pasture, all sloping away to the darker tints of a thickly wooded valley. On the far side was a farmstead with ricks and barns, and to the right a rolling park skirting a small village. Near the gray spark of the church spire stood a long line of elms, an avenue, and at its end a massive Elizabethan house in dark red brick. Clinton had not seen Markenfield for five years.

He thought of the dark paneled rooms and the bright thick panes of diamond-shaped glass, the armorial windows in the hall staining the floor with reds and blues, and the gray leaded roof where he had loved to sit in summer. More vivid than any sights were remembered smells: beeswax on mellowed timber, linseed oil in the gun room, the mossy pithy smell of the logs in their baskets, waiting to be burned.

Closing his eyes, he could see the pictorial story of John Gilpin on the nursery wallpaper and the holes in the skirting where he had placed traps for the mice whose dried skins had provided winter clothing for his lead soldiers. Again he was in the village church tracing the grain of the wood in the family pew with his fingernail, confusing Biblical names with real people, watching his father's bored face during the sermon. He tried to recall the pictures in the long gallery, but there were tiresome gaps; what had been between Romney's portrait of his grandfather and Marco Ricci's painting of people walking in the Mall? With furniture and china too his memory was poor, and yet he could remember every door and corner under the pantiles in the yard behind the servants' hall. The leather fire buckets filled with sand outside the butler's pantry, the dangling bell rope in the kitchen passage used for summoning the outdoor servants, and the rows of polished jelly molds and gleaming meat covers on the long shelves of the kitchen dressers—all these had remained far clearer in his mind than the wealth of detail in the famous Soho tapestries.

Sophie had often come over to Markenfield from Ammering Court with her parents. On the first occasion Clinton could remember, he had been twelve and she seven, and she had said that unless he played trains with her along the narrow paved paths in the topiary gardens, she would scream and say he had punched her. From the age of fifteen she had regularly told him that one day they would marry. Until three years ago, Clinton had treated the idea with tolerant amusement.

With his hands thrust deep into his pockets, he stood for

several minutes with half-closed eyes before walking slowly back across the field to the carriage.

When the clock in the cupola over the stables struck three, Sophie was close to tears and her maid was little more composed. Sophie had tried on and rejected not only her pannier dress with looped side flounces, but also her redingote princess dress, her Balmoral bodice, and her favorite white silk walking dress with Greek key pattern frills on the skirt. In the end, still dissatisfied, she had selected a scarlet Garibaldi shirt and a Zouave jacket, which she had not worn for two years. While the maid was pinning up her chignon, she moved, and the girl accidentally pricked her neck, making her scream with pain and anger. As soon as the chignon had been secured in a net of black chenille, she told the servant to leave and sat down on the bed, her arms clasping her knees. Her forehead was burning and her head throbbed with going over and over the same thoughts. How, after her last letter to him, could Clinton be coming unless he intended to propose? Yet when she had seen him in London three months earlier, just before his departure for Ireland, she had been equally convinced that he would ask her.

Her mother was enraged with her, and her father could not bring himself to speak about Clinton. She was making a fool of herself, they said, refusing to go to town for the Season and behaving with impossible rudeness to every other eligible man her mother had asked to dine with them during the two brief weeks which she had grudgingly consented to spend in London that spring. Didn't she realize that he was playing with her in an insulting and humiliating manner? According to Sophie's mother, her daughter's heroic fidelity to Lord Ardmore was due to diseased pride—a twisted determination to go on loving him whatever he said or did, thus proving herself in some inexplicable way victorious. Often her mother accused her of loving her pain and resentment more than the actual man.

Sophie's passion for Clinton had begun in earnest shortly after his return from China three years earlier, when the change in his appearance had both shocked and thrilled her. A

thinner, paler face with the eyes and cheekbones more prominent and distinct lines scored at the corners of his mouth. He
had spoken and smiled far less, and had often worn a haunted
remote expression that had puzzled and fascinated her. She
had had no idea what he had been thinking about, and this,
combined with the uneasy alertness common to men who had
spent many months in danger, had made her love him more.
When she had heard that he was having an affair with Lady
Cawthrey, she had been ill with grief and anger, yet because
she had admired the woman's poise and inaccessible beauty,
her rage towards Clinton had been tempered by an equally
powerful feeling of jealous desire. Lady Cawthrey's love for
Clinton had increased his value still further in Sophie's eyes.

Sophie was too much a realist to feel that she understood
him, but his mystery was what she loved best; even the idea of
vices and bad women attracted as well as revolted her. When
she had been sixteen, he had patiently helped her improve her
riding and had sometimes ridden beside her when hunting to
make sure that she kept up with the field. Her memories from
these days were still like precious stones to be taken out, polished, and admired, regardless of whether Clinton himself had
any memory of them. For almost a year after his father's suicide, Clinton had remained at Markenfield with a handful of
servants, living the life of a recluse. Then he had let the house,
bought a cornetcy in the cavalry, and, almost immediately,
gone abroad. The China War and then Lady Cawthrey had
taken him out of Sophie's life for almost four years. When he
had later renewed his spasmodic attentions, Sophie had ignored her mother's remarks about his mercenary motives but
had welcomed him warmly without any pretense of anger or
indifference. Spoiled from birth, she had never doubted that in
the end her childhood passion for Clinton would be gratified.
Though she could swoon in the most ladylike manner, when
her mind was fixed upon a given object, Sophie could be as
tenacious as any terrier. If Clinton did not love her when they
married, she was confident that in time she could make him. A
month ago her mother had threatened to refuse to receive Clinton unless he made his intentions clear. In the last letter Sophie

had written to him in Ireland, she had told him this. For this reason alone, his imminent arrival had a significance far beyond that of any of his previous visits.

When four o'clock came and Clinton had still not arrived, Sophie was feverish with anticipation. Time seemed to pass in fits and starts as she waited on the verge of happiness or great sorrow. One moment she was aware of everything she did and every detail in the room around her, and the next, minutes slipped by unnoticed as she sat in a waking dream. If he did not come, what could she do? How face the days and weeks to come? When she went downstairs and talked to her mother and father, she was amazed that she could speak normally. The next moment she could not remember what she had said. Her thoughts were as incoherent as a swirling mist. And still he did not come.

As the phaeton drew up in the carriage sweep in front of the austere and elegant Palladian façade of Ammering Court, Clinton experienced the same conflicting emotions of a flank marker during a cavalry charge. Until almost the last moment they could still sheer away and pass to the side of the waiting infantry square. A few words to the driver and he could be speeding away again through the deer park towards the tall gates with their heraldic greyhounds. With bowed head he started resolutely up the broad steps, a small figure under the shadow of the lofty pediment.

The proper order of events was very clear to him. Until he proposed to the girl, nothing could be said about the purpose of his visit by either of her parents. If she accepted, she would tell her mother, who in turn would inform her father, who would then wait for Clinton to come to him to ask for his daughter's hand. But courtesy demanded refreshment after his journey, and so he was shortly drinking tea with Mr. and Mrs. Lucas in a magnificently paneled room, decorated with elaborate festoons of fruit and flowers carved by Grinling Gibbons. Among cabinets of buhl and ormolu, seated on chairs worked in Gobelin needlework, Clinton talked about Ireland and listened to his host's sparse theories on the subject. William Lucas, related by marriage to the Gurneys, Norfolk's most famous banking family, was a stout white-haired man, whose height enabled him to carry his corpulence with dignity. His nose was sharp and his eyebrows thick and bushy like little wigs. His wife, who had once been pretty, still retained a girl's silvery voice and manners to match, though now her face was slack and puffy and her figure as solid as her husband's. Both husband and wife were subdued and sad. Though Clinton was titled, his father had made the family notorious in the county, and the Danvers's poverty was widely known. Sophie could have been expected to have made a better match. But neither parent had been able to stand against the tears and tantrums which had greeted their earlier opposition.

Since Mr. Lucas had an idea that people should not talk unless having something worthwhile to say, he said little, and what he did say was so marvelously to the point that further comment was usually superfluous. This, coupled with Mrs. Lucas's excessive politeness, which conveyed her resentment more plainly than open hostility would have done, made conversation a difficult matter. In fact, Sophie's arrival, which Clinton had dreaded, actually came as a relief. Mrs. Lucas's sudden remarks about the pleasantness of the day and the beauties of the garden would have made her purpose obvious to a man possessing a fraction of Clinton's intelligence.

He smiled at Sophie. "A turn in the garden, Miss Lucas?"

The gardens on the south side of Ammering Court were laid out in a series of wide stone-walled terraces connected by balustraded steps. The upper terrace was a long lawn geometrically patterned with clipped box hedges, but below were rose gardens and less formal walks between homely borders of delphiniums, columbine, and foxgloves. Down such a walk, flanked on one side by a pergola heavy with honeysuckle and climbing roses, Clinton and Sophie walked together. Looking at the pale drawn face of the girl beside him, with her black hair and expectant eyes, Clinton felt a dreamlike sense of unreality. Around them the fragrant air and the gentle humming of bees.

"How lucky you are to be able to walk here every day," he murmured.

"Perhaps I'll take root like that Latin lady who turned into a tree."

Clinton's lips felt very dry, and light tremors of agitation made his breathing uneven. Ask her now? Or at that corner by the rustic bench? Or wait till they reached the gate to the rose garden?

"I've become the leading light of the Ladies' Sick Visitation Committee."

"Which you think a worthless activity?" he asked, recognizing her ironic tone.

"Little better than my music or my drawing."

"You draw very well."

"I have a lot of time to practice."

Though the tension and sadness in her voice reproached him, he still could not say the words. Her red merino blouse with its dark braiding suited her perfectly, complementing her mass of black hair and showing off her pearl-like complexion. Pretty hands, a mouth with soft inviting lips, and her delightfully serious way of listening to whatever was said to her, however trivial, all pleased Clinton. But the untouched youthfulness of her face woke nothing in him.

He stared as though in a trance at some butterflies fluttering around a flowering buddleia. Ever since he had seen Markenfield through the shimmering haze, everything happening to him had seemed like some inexplicable nightmare. Could he really marry, change his whole life, solely to avoid selling a house which now seemed more remote than his own boyhood? Even the memories which had given it clearest form were ephemeral: fire buckets, torn wallpaper, the pumping house in the woods where he had kept a tame owl. His father had once said that if a man owns land, the land owns him, and Clinton had accepted this as a fact needing no proof. What was an aristocrat without his acres?

And yet today, looking across the valley at his childhood home, he had found out something else, at first without realizing that he had done so. Markenfield had always been a region in his mind, as well as a physical place. And in ownership of such a house, that inner vision of it, a kind of intangible affinity, mattered as much as title deeds. Markenfield was not just a building but an idea, the sum of all the impressions of those who had lived in it—the servants too. The horses, the dogs, even the trees all played a part. One generation planted what another generation saw reach maturity; the animals overlapped the generations, just as individual servants might have first come in their teens to serve a father, and finally stayed on to serve his grandson. Stories of the family and the house were stored over the years in so many minds. This was the true meaning of being owned by what one held—to be inextricably part of the continuity it embodied.

But when Markenfield had been let, the old servants had left, adding to the void left by Clinton's father's sudden death and his own departure. The chain had been broken. The idea, the real bond, was something *remembered* now, but no longer living. He had come to Norfolk certain that there were no choices left—that Markenfield was sacrosanct and marriage inescapable. Only now, at the moment of decision, did he know consciously what he had half sensed by the roadside an hour ago. His father was wrong; a nobleman's land did not always outweigh all else. The choice was still there to be made: to sell his inheritance and not himself.

And beside him, the girl still watched his every expression, waiting, hoping, making him ashamed that he had needed to be pushed to the very brink before knowing his mind. He longed in some way to make amends for the pain he was about to cause her. Perhaps if he could explain about the married lives of the officers at his club. But why should this sheltered girl ever believe him?

When they reached the end of the border walk, he took Sophie's arm and said gently,

"Have you ever heard that cynical bachelors have a catch phrase about marrying for money and loving for pleasure?"

She looked up at him with a brave attempt at lightheartedness. "I daresay they often come to love their rich wives in spite of their cynicism." She turned away as if about to cry, but when she met his gaze, her eyes were bright with anger. "Do you think I ever thought you loved me? I'm not a fool. If people only married for love, how many marriages would there be?"

"I can't marry you," he whispered, dreading that she would weep and scream at him for having allowed her to hope.

Instead she said in an insistent voice,

"Why can't you?"

"It would dishonor us."

"Only if you love someone else. Do you, Clinton?"

He shook his head, amazed by her calmness. "If I gave you a dozen reasons," he murmured, "they'd only be poor attempts to justify what I want to do."

"So you reject me without a word?"

He tried to take her hands, but she moved away at once. "Ask yourself," he said, "how long can any woman live without bitterness, when every day brings her fresh proofs that her love isn't returned?"

"Do you think I care about bitterness?" she cried. "Would bitterness be worse than never to see your face or hear your voice? Is bitterness more cruel than the misery of life without the one person who makes it possible? I don't care who you've loved or who you'll love. If you'd be faithful even for a year, I'd pay any price. I'd barter my soul for it."

The hint of hysteria in her voice horrified him. "I'm not worth your devotion. I never was. I'm nothing like the person you think you love."

She stood rocking her weight from heel to toe with a faint twisted smile on her face, an absorbed introspective look. "All that time you used to spend with the farm people—how I hated you for that, preferring the company of those dolts to mine. Then going out with the fishermen at Overstrand, your fool of a father letting you in any weather. I used to pray for you." She suddenly touched his arm and looked into his eyes. "I could find the tree where you stripped off the bark in your embarrassment when I first told you I loved you . . . can say what you said when we watched the flocks of starlings over the village the week before you left Markenfield. I used to walk alone to the spot where you'd caught perch as a boy . . . sit where you'd sat." She fell silent and covered her face with her hands. "I shan't give you up, Clinton. I'll never do that. Never."

She stifled a small choking sob and pressed his hands between hers. Before he could think of any words of comfort, she had swung away from him and was running down the long strip of green between the borders towards the terrace steps, her blouse a vivid splash of color against the softer blues and whites of the flowers.

CHAPTER SIX

Sunday morning, church bells ringing, and in the wide squires and cresents between Brompton and Knightsbridge well-dressed families hurrying to church, some walking, others in carriages. Almost impossible to believe it, but a mere decade earlier the whole of this spacious suburb of South Kensington had been largely a district of farms and market gardens. As Clinton walked towards Esmond's square, he watched the broughams, barouches, and victorias carrying the churchgoers to their various destinations, neo-classical, neo-gothic, the sun catching on wheel hubs, curb chains, and carriage lamps. Under a pale blue sky stippled with light mackerel clouds, the white stucco of the houses and the recently watered streets looked as fresh and laundered as the white gloves and breeches of the coachmen and grooms. The slums and rookeries of Lambeth and Seven Dials were as remote as another continent, shut out from this Eden by the ornamented gates and railings, which now closed off the best residential streets from the public highway. A hundred yards from Esmond's house a uniformed gatekeeper with a cockaded hat kept away the street musicians, hawkers, and beggars whose presence was prohibited by notices on the gates.

Informed by the butler that Mr. Danvers was at church, Clinton once more prepared to wait, this time at his own request in his brother's library, among the leather chairs and the glass-fronted bookcases containing rows of creamy vellum, antique brown calf, and dull red morocco. Through the half-open windows came the twitter of sparrows and the distant clamor of the bells; in the room the stately ticking of a Louis Quinze clock. Clinton was idly examining the spines of the books, quite expecting to see some rare Decameron or Caxton Bible, when he heard the rustle of a dress. A soft low voice.

"Lord Ardmore?"

He turned and saw Theresa watching him. "Not at church, Miss Simmonds?"

She passed through a square of sunlight on the polished floor and gestured vaguely with a hand. "Religion to me is more an aspiration than a matter of formal observance."

As at the theater, he had no idea whether she was speaking sincerely. He nodded as if in agreement. "I've nothing against the deity myself; it's some of his followers I find it harder to get along with."

She sat down on the chesterfield in the window, the sunlit panes haloing her auburn hair with wisps of smoky gold. Her dress was plain gray silk, tight-waisted, with a high collar and a loose black velvet bow at the neck. Having himself decided against marriage, Clinton no longer had any interest in Theresa's motives for keeping Esmond waiting. And with the urgent matter of the sale of Markenfield preoccupying him, he was not pleased by the prospect of making polite conversation while waiting to break to Esmond what would undoubtedly be most unwelcome news. But, even in these circumstances, he could not help recognizing the woman's unusual beauty. Her face was composed and secretive, with a hint of a smile playing about her lips and eyes.

"So we meet again after all, my lord."

"Indeed," he replied crisply, vexed by her smile, certain that she would have told Esmond about his visit to the theater. Inevitably Esmond would have mentioned Sophie. If she thought she was going to have more fun at his expense, Clinton was determined to make her think again. He carried on blandly:

"I daresay my brother told you why I'd be returning so soon?"

"I know he advises your trustees."

"He said nothing about my business in the country?"

"Nothing about business anywhere, Lord Ardmore."

"But that's too bad, Miss Simmonds." He sounded both sympathetic and surprised. "You mean he never told you I went to Norfolk to get a wife? I was never half so secretive with my mistresses." He grinned at her. "Esmond's going to be delighted with me. He gets a heap of money when I marry." He caught her look of bewilderment. "You don't mean that's something else he never mentioned?" He clicked his tongue. "He can be a dark one, that brother of mine. There's nothing very secret about it. We can carve up the trust as soon as I marry a lady of substance."

"Should I offer my congratualtions?"

Her unsmiling face pleased Clinton. Of course Esmond had never said a word about the money to her.

"Certainly you should," he replied brightly. "Miss Lucas will have a dozen bridesmaids, six in white and six in blue. You've seen wax dolls at charity fairs? Just so. A mitered bishop to do the honors. St George's, Hanover Square, has the right tone, and is most conveniently placed. I shall insist that you're invited, Miss Simmonds."

"Would that be quite proper, Lord Ardmore?"

Clinton raised a hand to his brow. "I see what you mean. Awkward." He paused. "Perhaps it would be better if you and Esmond didn't come in the same carriage. Absurd of course." He saw the slight tightening of her lips. "Actually," he went on reflectively, "I can't help finding hypocrisy rather touching. It's only a kind of modesty to set such store by other people's opinions." He sat back in his chair and crossed his legs. His affable expression turned to listlessness. Stifling a yawn, he picked a hair from the sleeve of his dark green morning coat and murmured, "Do you disapprove of me, Miss Simmonds?"

"I hardly know you well enough to say."

He smiled at her knowingly. "Rather prim for an actress. Frankly I think we've a lot in common. The workhouse may be the gate of heaven for saints, but we sinners prefer an easier passage."

"I'm flattered you think us so alike. I'm afraid I don't deserve the comparison."

"Very deftly done" Clinton laughed, clapping as though in the theater.

She looked at him with the unswerving directness that had been his undoing in her dressing room. "Is it fun ridiculing people?"

"I often think so," he replied, smiling.

Theresa left her sofa and strolled across the room as far as the long glass-fronted bookcase. "Could Esmond have helped you?"

"Ask him if you're interested." Clinton hid his amusement. He had puzzled and disquieted her. Esmond would not enjoy the sort of questions she was likely to ask.

An hour after Clinton had left the house, Theresa was facing Esmond across the luncheon table. Because she was sure that Clinton would have described their conversation, she decided to make no secret of it. "Your brother's business went well, I hear," she remarked neutrally.

Esmond looked up sharply, spilling some wine on the cloth. "I'm not in a mood for jokes, Theresa."

"You wanted him to marry, didn't you?" she asked with confusion.

Esmond sat motionless in his chair; his unnatural stillness emphasizing his pent-up anger.

Theresa felt confused. "You're surely not angry I spoke to him?"

"I meant no reproach for that," he said impatiently. "I merely expected that you might have had the taste and sense to—" He broke off helplessly, letting his hands fall to his sides. The fury in his eyes was now all addressed to his absent brother. "I'd swear he went there knowing what he was going to do. He knew all along. How he expects me to face the girl's father after it . . . quite apart from the total disregard for her feelings."

Theresa gazed at him, dumfounded. "He turned her down?"

"What else do you think I'm talking about?" moaned Esmond.

As Theresa started to laugh, he jumped up, overturning his

chair, and strode from the room. Had Theresa understood the reason for Esmond's anger, she would undoubtedly have been less amused. But, since she assumed that he was only suffering from indignation at the cavalier way in which his brother had once more turned a blind eye to necessity, Theresa was not unduly alarmed.

When Esmond slammed his study door and sat down at his desk, his face, though calmer, gave no better indication of his true feelings than before. Though open with Theresa in other ways, Esmond's hard schooling in the City had taught him to draw a veil over important financial matters, especially over reverses. The worst monetary crises could usually be survived if they remained quietly hidden in ledgers and not shouted about. The last course Esmond ever contemplated in times of difficulty was to reduce his personal expenditure. To do so would be to invite speculation about the soundness of his business. The City's confidence was as important to a bill broker as coal and iron to a foundry owner.

Though his discount house was doing more business than ever and its profits were substantial, Esmond had been drawn into another area, which, even when he had first met Theresa, had been causing him anxious nights. Had Clinton ever discovered Esmond's principal reason for trying to force him into marriage, it would have astonished him far more than the revelation of his brother's passion for an actress. Esmond had done his level best to promote Miss Lucas's cause because he too needed his share of capital from the trust. His failure had damaged much more than his pride.

For some time, because of the expansion of his business, and more recently because of his involvement with Theresa, Esmond had delegated more and more of the lengthy but vitally important work of examining the securities of those seeking advances. One of his managers had made a disastrous error in assessing the creditworthiness of a shipping line. When the Greek & Oriental Navigation Company failed to meet the bills which his house had discounted, Esmond had bailed out the line with a loan of £60,000 secured against its ships. He had hoped to save face in the City and protect his original loan. But since then it had become steadily more apparent that he would only recover his capital by replacing the company's oldest steamships. Unless he could now find funds far in excess of the regular requirements of his business, Esmond faced the certain prospect of losing all his earlier loans. Quite unintentionally, he had become the owner in all but name of an insolvent shipping line, which he could not allow to fail without ruining himself. Staring at the papers on his desk, he knew that he would be prepared to take considerable risks to restore his position.

Over the years, especially at times when credit had been tight, Esmond had given more than passing thought to ways of freeing his trust capital, but had always shrunk from positive action for fear that the necessary legal sleight of hand might later come to light and be represented as fraud. But as he sat in his study that Sunday afternoon, the gravity of his situation and the shock of Clinton's capricious and entirely unlooked for volte-face with Sophie brought a decisive shift in his thinking. For the first time he began to see breaking the trust as more than a subject for self-indulgent speculation.

In many ways the present moment seemed remarkably auspicious for preparatory work on such a venture. Clinton had asked him to begin negotiations with the principal mortgagees of the Markenfield estate for a sale at the end of the current lease, so Esmond expected to be meeting the trustees quite frequently in the next few months. He could hardly hope to get a better opportunity for winning their unquestioning confidence. From his occasional dealings with them in his capacity of unpaid adviser on trust investment, Esmond considered the trustees financial innocents. Nevertheless, in spite of his growing optimism, Esmond could not avoid all misgivings about proceedings which, if successful, would link Clinton's future fortunes, as well as his own, to the survival of an ailing shipping line. But as he had learned at times of crisis in the City, the only dependable maxim in extremis was *Sauve qui peut.* Nothing in their shared past made him feel that he owed Clinton any special immunity.

CHAPTER SEVEN

Esmond made his first serious mistake with Theresa in the last week of August and knew at once what a damaging one it was. For some years now, in the early autumn it had been his habit to spend a few days with his mother at Kilkreen, the family's small estate in the west of Ireland. He had first told Theresa about this annual event some months before, hinting obliquely that he would like her to come with him. Then later he had been unable to resist the temptation of asking her directly.

Her refusal had been immediate and vehement. How could he possibly think of taking a mistress to stay with his mother? The idea was insulting and absurd. Esmond had done his best to mollify her. His mother's elopement and broken marriage had left her not merely indifferent to convention but positively hostile to genteel respectability. If he chose to bring a milliner or shopgirl to Kilkreen, she would be treated with as much respect as a peeress. But nothing he had said had in any way softened the antipathy of Theresa's original response; and after his solitary attempt to justify himself, Esmond had not tried again.

The real reason for Theresa's resentment, though she never said so, had been obvious to him without any need of words.

His invitation had been a violation in spirit of the three months' respite he had promised to give her before pressing for a final decision about marriage. Had she agreed to be his mother's guest, Theresa would virtually have acknowledged herself his fiancée. The fact that he had understood this before asking her, and yet through overconfidence had pressed ahead, did not make it any easier for Esmond to live with his miscalculation. Like a cautious chess player who had concentrated hard and long to achieve a winning position, only to lose it by a single impatient move, he endured the bitterest regret of all— the kind that allows the sufferer no chance to place the blame anywhere but on his own poor aching shoulders.

Acceptance of his invitation would have banished every anxiety; refusal made him fear that in spite of many contradictory signs she might yet reject him. And though he hid his dejection, knowing how little he himself liked displays of self-pity and defeatism in others, the effort cost him reserves of composure he could ill afford to lose with another crisis fast approaching.

In mid-September, *Masks and Faces* was due to close, and Esmond knew that he would have to decide whether to try to influence her against taking another engagement or leave her free to make her own choice. Dangers seemed to lie in either course, but intuitively he felt that the worst risk lay in the line of least resistance. By not making his preference known, he would merely be postponing a clash which could have deadlier consequences nearer the time of her more important decision about marriage. To face the issue bravely now as a matter of choice might win him back some of the respect he had lost over the Kilkreen episode. Gentle but unyielding firmness had served him well in the past, and he did not intend to fall victim to nervous vacillation at the very moment when resolution was needed as never before.

Esmond very rarely collected Theresa from the theater except on a Saturday night. Only on that particular evening, with the prospect of a whole day to come, unmarred either by his early departure for the City or her daily expedition to the theater, did he feel entirely carefree. For this reason he was convinced that Saturday would be the right day for broaching the delicate subject of her theatrical intentions. After any disagreement, there would be the whole of Sunday for reconciliation.

Sitting in his landau, concealed by the raised hood, Esmond lowered the window and watched the departing audience milling on the pavements, waiting for carriages, or competing for the dozen or so cabs in sight. The night was still and warm, and Esmond was aware of the distinctive exhalation of well-cared-for and scented bodies gently perspiring in the sultry air. Beneath the babble of talk and rumble of wheels he sometimes caught a softer sound like a thin breeze—the whisper of scores of silk and muslin dresses as their owners moved.

It would be ten minutes at least till Theresa emerged from the stage door, and for the moment Esmond felt calm and clear-headed. He started to think ahead. Before Theresa took her bath, they would sit together and drink chilled wine in the garden arbor. He closed his eyes, imagining. Scent of flowers, quietness after the clamor of the theater, seclusion after public scrutiny, peace and gentleness. He would say that before meeting her his life had not been worth much, that he had stumbled from day to day pleased if he was not anxious or sad; sure that the not quite painful tedium of his existence was the common lot—the inescapable way of the world. Then he had learned from her what happiness could be, and from that moment of discovery had been ready to give up society and reputation, had gladly risked loss of business and broken connections in the City. He would speak without regret, lightly; but because he had never before spoken of his sacrifices, she would be the more affected by them. Instead of letting her reproach herself, he would quickly add that such losses were nothing to him beside the necessity of loving her. In love and in marriage, wasn't it always essential to choose what mattered most and let the rest go to the devil? Could one ever realistically expect to get what one wanted most as well as the next best thing? And slowly he would lead her to acknowledge the need to abandon secondary aims and ambitions in the interests of a greater good. Even if she refused to accept this, and he finally conceded, his generosity would deepen her sense of obligation.

All this was very clear to him until Theresa appeared at the stage door. She was clutching a number of packages that kept slipping as she laughed with several members of the cast before looking around for the landau. After she got in, the groom handed in her parcels and shut the door. Moments later the horses were heading homewards at a spirited trot with traces flying.

Theresa waved to her friends and then kissed Esmond on the cheek. She sat back briefly before resting a gloved hand on his arm. "Why don't we go to Giraudier's or Quinn's? We haven't been anywhere for weeks."

"I didn't think you wanted to," he replied, seeing their conversation in the arbor receding. Recently her moods had been far more changeable than usual. "I'd rather get back," he murmured.

"Don't be so staid. I need to do something amusing." Beneath the brim of her black tulle hat, her eyes glittered in the back-glow of the carriage lamps.

"How about dancing at the 'Gyll?" he asked in a lightly ironic voice.

"Splendid." She laughed and glanced in the coachman's direction. "Aren't you going to tell him?"

"What do you think?" he replied, keeping the reproachfulness out of his voice. The thought of dancing with Theresa in the Argyll Rooms was deeply repugnant to him. The mirrors might be opulently gilded and the band famous for its sentimental dance music, but the place was still little better than a vast public assignation house, where maids and shopgirls vied with professional whores to take what they could from the young toffs who went there. In his youth Esmond had not been above going, but now memories of the hot frenzy that had driven him there left a strong aftertaste of disgust. And yet he had loved the smaller vaudeville halls or any dimly lit cellar full of outlandish goings-on: nude tableaux vivants, bawdy songs and acts, but never quite without guilt. These were the places his father had liked, places where men forgot their obligations to wives and families, where adulterated drink was sold and inexperienced gamblers were mercilessly fleeced. As he had grown older, his new professional gravity and the City's demands on his time and energies had made him turn his back on questionable pleasures. Yet how dull at times he had felt without that seductive glitter of gaiety, no matter what foul pools its bright surface hid. Even now this ambiguity remained, attracting and repelling.

There was something of this in his love for Theresa, a quality he scarcely dared admit, not just the lure of her profession or her beauty, but a sense in which she shared the demimonde's dangerous freedom from the conventional scruples which restrained him and his kind. She did not need to argue against prejudices, she simply walked through them as if they did not exist. She would not have minded dancing in the Argyll Rooms or being seen there. He knew that she had occasionally got up on the dais at Evans's Supper Rooms to sing or to parody the regular entertainers. And while he admired this absence of reserve, it scared him, making him feel self-conscious and wooden by comparison—a middle-aged man who had never known how to let go.

Because she could also be gentle and subtly responsive, he had deliberately emphasized this milder, more ladylike side of her nature, as if by doing so he could somehow damp down those wilder impulses that captivated him but made him jealously mistrustful.

Theresa twisted round sinuously and stretched her legs across his knees, her graceful slender ankles just showing beneath her skirt. Leaning back against the side of the carriage, she watched him with benevolent amusement. "When I was young and just married," she said wistfully, "I used to dream of riding in carriages like this. The whole night ahead of us . . . money to go anywhere."

"Fine. We'll go to Giraudier's."

She thought a moment, then shook her head. "We'll go to Cremorne."

"We won't get there till past midnight."

Her mouth rounded and her eyebrows went up. "I love it when you scold me and look straight into my eyes. Please, love, look straighter. Now tell me how wicked it is to go to Cremorne at night."

He smiled in spite of himself. "Not wicked. Just depressing."

"Depressing? Chinese lanterns in the trees, ferneries, grottoes, dancing out of doors."

"Drinking fictitious Moët."

"There may be fireworks." She hung her head. "Perhaps we're too old for pleasure gardens."

They were not too old; but Esmond did find the place quite as depressing as he had expected, in spite of the welcome breeze from the river and the operatic selections fading, swelling under the massive elms. As they walked along the narrow lamplit paths between the geranium beds and the brightly painted refeshment boxes, he saw, as he had known he would, that most of the men were young and well dressed and the women invariably tarts of the class to be met with in the Strand. On the "crystal circle," the largest dance platform, the band drowned not animated talk but thick silence, as the sexes eyed each other warily, assessing possibilities carnal and financial. The contrast between the bubbling gaiety of the music and the calculating lustful faces of the dancers amused Theresa but struck Esmond as grotesque. When seated, they overheard a drawling diminutive youth at another side table abusing a waitress for bringing him too small a glass of brandy. She returned contemptuously with a larger one.

"Careful you don't fall in and drown yourself."

He made a lunging attempt to pinch her retreating backside, but missed and spilled his drink down his pleated shirtfront. The girl laughed stridently and flounced away. After drinking hot negus, Theresa and Esmond left the more frequented parts of the gardens and crossed the deserted bowling greens in the direction of the Thames. Looked at from the banks, the lights in the trees, the glowing rotunda, and the distant music created an effect of fairyland. On the dark river two barges were slipping downstream on the tide, their sails and hulls jet black against the brilliant reflections in the water. Eastwards, above the City, the sky was tinged with coral.

"You see," she murmured, slipping her fingers between his, knitting them together.

"Like most old harlots, Cremorne looks best from a distance in the dark."

"You're not sorry we came?"

"I'm never sorry to go anywhere with you." He smiled at her tenderly. "Unless a gang of desperadoes spring out and rob us."

"But, Esmond, I'll look after you. I've one of the best screams in the business."

"If they take no notice?"

"I'm ready for that," she whispered, reaching up and producing a villainous hatpin.

Esmond looked at it gravely. She laughed and then took his chin between thumb and fingers and, standing on tiptoe, kissed him twice on the forehead. As the band began a polka, she danced ahead of him on the way back to the carriage, pretending to push away the hands of an indecently amorous partner as she went.

Speeding towards Brompton, she asked him what he remembered best. He mentioned the young man with his spilled drink.

"My God, Esmond, I believe you're sorry for him."

"Maybe I am," he replied softly. For all his firms intentions of two hours ago, Esmond found himself no nearer to saying what he had meant to. His eyes strayed over her parcels lying on the carriage floor and rested on the hem of her dress. As the trim villas and building plots gave way to streets and crescents, he tried to think of a fresh approach but he was tired, and the horses' hoofs drummed insistently in his skull. Not far to go now.

The sleepy porter opened the door for them, then shuffled away to put out the lights. Upstairs Theresa's maid had fallen asleep in a chair, having waited up to undress her. Theresa sent the girl to bed at once and sank down on the low ottoman in front of the heavily curtained window. Everything in the room was bathed in the soft opal light of glass-shaded candles: exquisite carpets, tapestried walls, and the gauze draperies hanging from the bed's gilded tester. The heavy scent of flowers made the atmosphere oppressive. After the open vistas of Cremorne, the house closed in around them like a luxurious cocoon.

"I wish they wouldn't stay up like that," she said, taking off her hat and letting her pelisse slip to the ground.

"It's their job."

"It makes me feel even more like a pampered convalescent than having a footman carry my parcels from the shops." She broke off, remembering. "I left them in the carriage." About to ring the bell, she grimaced and left the room to bring up her afternoon's purchases herself; but the porter had forestalled her and they were lined up outside the door.

Esmond watched as she carelessly unwrapped a bizarre assortment: a fan of white ostrich feathers, a jade monkey, a Bristol vase, some scent bottles, and an Indian shawl. She glanced about the room as if seeking a place for the vase; then she shrugged and turned her back on the ornaments.

"Trifles to fill an idle afternoon!" she exclaimed. As she caught Esmond's eye, he did not smile. She moved closer and said with sudden urgency, "But what *do* they do, these ladies without half the world to call on, or guests to dinner every other night? I wish I knew, Esmond. It can't always be needlework and salon pieces on the piano." She stripped off her gloves thoughtfully. "I wonder if those worthy brokers and bankers of yours will ever accept a mistress turned wife. I doubt if their wives ever will."

He faced her stiffly. "If anyone offends you, they won't get a second chance under this roof."

"And if that leaves us on our own?"

"It won't."

"How can you be sure?"

"I think I can." He hesitated and raised his eyes slowly, ". . . If you leave the theater."

"To appease their envious little minds?" Although she spoke mildly, she pulled fiercely at the fingers of her gloves. "I wonder what they think we do all day in the theater. Drink and debauch each other?"

"My love, it isn't that at all."

"They haven't an idea how we work. Gestures and interpretation just come without thought—"

"I think they do know it's not easy; I think they dislike the way they suppose actors live."

She slapped her gloves lightly against the palm of her free

hand and let out her breath. "Yet mistresses are almost always treated better than wives, simply because they can leave if they choose."

"Of course there are bad marriages, full of restraints and fears, with none of its dignity, none of its warmth and protection." His voice was thick and slightly blurred.

She looked at him with perfect candor. "And how does one get the better kind?"

"By honest acknowledgment of faith and intention. By absolute loyalty."

"Perhaps you really mean obedience."

"I meant fidelity, the sort that can't abide the smallest betrayal. When man and wife both know that to betray each other once is never to have been faithful at all." He spoke solemnly with great confidence.

"But I've been married, Esmond," she replied softly. "At times any trivial thing can seem a betrayal."

"Broken faith can never be trivial. I only meant things that matter. Causing deliberate pain by selfishness. Expecting every kind of gain without being prepared to make an equal sacrifice."

"My profession?"

He bent nearer her, his face strained and waxen. "How many times," he asked imploringly, "have you complained of overcrowded dressing rooms and rotting lodgings in provincial towns? Of maulings by leading men . . . separations from Louise?"

"There was companionship too. Courage. Jokes instead of self-pity. The generosity of people with very little to give. Even when he was dying, John refused to pay off the company and end the tour." She picked up the ostrich feather fan and opened it without thinking what she was doing. "When his lungs were very bad, he worked out a way of getting things sent over from the shops without having to go up or down the stairs. A boot hung in the window was for more coal; a white shirt meant a pork chop. He made up a whole code—trousers, socks, hats. There were others like him. Esprit de corps perhaps." She put down the fan in the long silence that followed.

92

here her old self had gone, and how this sweet gui
n girl had surreptitiously taken her place.
few days before leaving for Kilkreen, a conversatio
ch only weeks earlier would have had no adverse effect o
had underlined her uncertainty with special emphasis
en Esmond had mentioned in passing that Clinton woul
obably be spending a few days at Kilkreen while they wer
ere, she had lost her temper. Hadn't she made it sufficiently
lear to him that the man had insulted her during both their
previous meetings? Taken aback, Esmond had gently reminded
her that she had seemed amused rather than irritated, and had
actually said she wanted to meet Clinton properly. In any case
he was only going to stay a day or two at most. It would have
been absurd to have asked him to come all the way to London
to discuss the latest offers for Markenfield, when this could be
done in Ireland without any inconvenience. Nothing would
please him more than to be able to forget Clinton's problems,
but, since before a sale the mortgages on the place would have
to be redeemed by pledges against the trust, he was involved
whether he liked it or not.

In a patient, almost apologetic voice, Esmond had gone on to
his main concern. He had recently been worried by Clinton's
threats to put in a new agent at Kilkreen; and, since their
mother had only a life interest in the estate, Clinton, as legal
owner, had every right to try to end the wastage and force the
tenants to pay their arrears. Because the Fenians were murdering landlords for less, Esmond had not needed to dwell on why
he wanted to make sure that Clinton's next stay at Kilkreen
coincided with his own. Surely she saw he owed it to his
mother?

Yet explanation had not made Theresa feel any better.
Plagued by increasing misgivings about marriage, the small
additional burden of having to deal with a man so strikingly
different from Esmond in almost every way, at this critical
time, had been enough to agitate her out of all proportion to
the likely problems his presence might cause.

In the event, she was not actually aware that Lord Ardmore
had come, until the morning after his arrival when, walking

With a faint shrug Esmond said flatly, "He was still unfaithful to you."

"Some husbands always are."

"Wasn't it just the theater?" he asked, "The same reason you
didn't remarry when he died but took lovers instead. Did you
love many?"

"Three isn't many." She paused. "I suppose I did for a time."

"Before you betrayed them."

"Or they left me. I felt warmly or not at all."

"Don't blame your nature," he said sharply. "The theater's to
blame. You know just why it encourages passing fancies. Uncertainty about the future. No decent privacy, plays always
turning on love, young men wanting experience. Could any
woman stay virtuous for long—tempted like that every day?"

"I did when I was married. I could again." She faced him.
"Doesn't your loyalty include trust? I can't survive on my own
in this house without activity, without friends. Can't you share
with me and not insist on everything for yourself?" Her hair
was pinned up, and as she turned away, the nape of her neck
was very white and exposed-looking.

He stood for a while like a man supporting a crushing
weight, then with a low sigh he stepped forward and kissed her
neck. "You must do what you have to. I accept it."

"Without resentment?"

"I hope so."

"You must think hard about it, my love."

"I don't need to. It's not much harder than deciding whether
to go on breathing."

"You can be very generous, Esmond."

"Yes," he murmured, faintly smiling. "Perhaps if I can't have
rights, you'll grant me privileges."

"Any number." She opened her arms to him and held him.
Later, stepping out of her skirt, she paused. "I think I've
changed my mind about something. Can I come to Ireland
with you?"

He stroked his long chin thoughtfully. "I shouldn't be surprised." The words were dry, but his voice still trembled with
emotion.

CHAPTER EIGHT

The country around Kilkreen was wilder and more remote than anything Theresa had envisaged. Set in small fields, the mud cabins of the peasants crouched in insignificance under the great brown shoulders of the neighboring mountains. From the beech woods near the gates of the domain park, glimpses could be caught of a rocky bay, and within its gray curve the jagged outline of two small islands. The local people wore the short frieze coats and misshapen caubeen hats which Theresa had previously considered the sole property of stage Irishmen.

Lady Ardmore too had her theatrical qualities: carrying on the tradition of the old landlords with sublime indifference to the fate of so many of that anachronistic breed swept away by insolvency after the famine. According to Esmond, flitches of bacon and plump hams found their way from the house to the village almost daily. Sheep were also slaughtered at a rate out of all proportion to the household's needs, and the butler regularly charged the estate office for wines that had never been bought, or if they had been, had gone the way of the sheep. There were gardeners in plenty at Kilkreen, but the borders were overgrown with briers and the fish pond was choked with

weed. The whole estate seemed plu
peaceful that nothing merited reproof

Queen over this slow decay was her
even than her servants, she liked to tak
wheelchair pulled by a footman, with a m
parasol over her if the sun shone. It pleased
pretend that any exertion or excess of heat or
moment prove fatal. Her puffy fingers were h
and bracelets puckered the skin at her wrists. F
rouged cheeks, and the fur trimmings of her v
reminded Theresa of some exotic bird. When she v
ing or playing cards, her face often took on a deathly
ity. But, as Esmond had predicted, she treated Ther
courtesy, though never with warmth. She spoke as if s
come a long way from wherever she had been in her min
could not spare much time before returning. In spite o
Esmond's efforts to put Theresa at her ease, Lady Ardmor
manner and the all-pervading atmosphere of decaying gran
deur made Theresa's first days at Kilkreen an unnerving experience. Nor could she escape the place even briefly, since
Esmond considered it unsafe to drive anywhere outside the
domain while there were Fenians in the county.

But in truth, the eccentricities of her hostess and the strangeness of the house only marginally contributed to Theresa's unease. Even before their departure for Ireland, she had keenly
regretted her sudden impulse to come with Esmond. Within
days of his acknowledgment that her career would continue,
Theresa had ceased to view this concession with the same
bright optimism. What had at first seemed to remove the single
greatest obstacle to their future happiness had soon appeared
to her in a truer light. Whatever he might say, Esmond would
always resent her need for a life that he could not wholly control. And because he would be sure to suffer in honorable silence, Theresa knew that her guilt would grow until eventually
she would feel obliged to offer him some new forfeit—just as
she had offered to come to Ireland as an atoning act of gratitude. Whether he knew it or not, from a semblance of weakness
Esmond had fashioned a weapon more subtly undermining
than naked strength. Already at times she had started to won-

with Louise, she saw a man near the stables wearing cavalry overalls and a forage cap. Without waiting for permission, Louise went up to him and asked where his master was.

"Gone here and there" was the laconic reply. Under foxy eyebrows, his blue inquisitive eyes moved from Louise to her mother. He had been sitting on the grass whittling a stick, but at Theresa's approach, jumped up and clicked his heels together. "Corporal Harris, at your service, ma'am."

"You're most kind," she murmured dryly. The soldier's brash and confident manner grated slightly. She had always found it mildly depressing the way servants took their personal importance from the rank of their masters. She was turning when Louise, curious as ever, asked him if he had been Lord Ardmore's servant for long.

"Since I fished a bloke out of a river," he answered with a grin.

"He chose you because you saved a man's life?" asked Theresa with some skepticism.

"Tried to, ma'am. He was dead and done for."

"Drowned?" Louise murmured faintly.

"Hit in the head, miss," said Harris, pointing to his forehead. "One of them Fenians."

Louise shuddered. "A Fenian shot him?"

"No, miss. One of our lads."

An hour later on the bumpy croquet lawn, Louise was still chattering indignantly about shooting men in rivers. Theresa suggested that the Irishman might have tried to shoot first, but Louise was not convinced. Who'd ever heard of anyone going swimming with a gun? It was therefore unfortunate that the child's first glimpse of Clinton, shortly afterwards, should be of him carrying a gun and a game bag bulging with snipe. Theresa had just hitched up her dress so she could take a proper swing to get her ball through the last hoop. As she succeeded, she heard a cry of "Bravo" from the terrace and looked up to see Lord Ardmore raising his gun, wide-awake in salute.

Pleased by a good morning's shooting, Clinton loped down the stone steps to the lawn, smiling to himself as he recalled Theresa's primness during their last conversation in London. The woman really was a superb hypocrite—pretending to be so righteous and yet having the barefaced audacity to come to Kilkreen quite openly as Esmond's mistress. In a fur boa and feathered Tyrolean hat, with red leather boots showing under her skirt, she looked a wildly improbable figure against the somber ivy-covered walls and mullioned windows. Seeing the child moving away towards the house, Clinton called to her not to stop the game, but she did not turn back.

A few yards from Theresa, he dropped his game ·bag and picked up Louise's mallet. "Favor me with a game, Miss Simmonds?"

"I've just finished one, Lord Ardmore."

He stood in silence for a moment, watching a squirrel searching for food among the fallen leaves on the far side of the lawn. He sniffed the air with evident satisfaction.

"Marvelous these autumn days. Mist and woodsmoke . . . golden light." She was looking at him doubtfully from beneath the brim of her hat. "Damn it," he muttered, as if suddenly remembering something. "I owe you an apology, Miss Simmonds. Wasn't right to say I was getting married." He stared hard at his muddy boots. "Fact is . . . it's not easy to admit to being turned down. Damned painful." He caught a movement of her lips. "Now you're laughing at me."

"On the contrary, sir. I'm grieved for you."

"You would be if you knew the things she said to me."

Theresa laughed unexpectedly. "Your acting's much better, Lord Ardmore; though I think I can guess what she said."

Clinton frowned. "Can't think how you intend to do that, madam."

"A knowledge of melodrama quite as extensive as your lordship's." He raised a hand to acknowledge the thrust. His expression was encouraging. "As you took her hand, she cried, 'Unhand me, fiend!' "

Clinton gasped. "Her very words. Uncanny, that's what I'd call it, Miss Simmonds. Tell me what I said after that, and I'm your slave for life."

"That's easily done." She paused. "My voice isn't the right pitch, you understand?"

"I'll try to overlook it."

" 'Rage on my beauty; your scorn but adds to your perfection, maddens me. You shall be mine.'" She smiled apologetically. "After that I think you owe me her reply, in character, of course."

"My cue," he replied solemnly.

"'You shall be mine.'"

He clasped his mallet handle and quavered in ladylike falsetto, "'Rather would I die a thousand deaths than submit to such bondage. Trifle not with a woman's jewel, her chastity.'" He chuckled to himself. "It's a damned shame that kind of thing always gets burlesqued nowadays. I used to love it. 'Come we must fly; all is discovered; your husband is in hot pursuit. I have a pork pie and a blunderbuss.' No wonder real life's such a disappointment." He sighed as he picked up his game bag. "I must prepare myself for battle."

"Battle, my lord?"

"Nothing so dignified, I fear. My mother's half-witted agent is lunching with us."

In the brief silence before he raised his hat to her and turned to go, Theresa was surprised to feel a flutter of nervousness. Anticipation of the unexpected had become a habit for her when talking to him—as if at a moment's notice, charm and levity might snap like ice, as on the last occasion at Esmond's house. Watching him walk away, she still could not quite believe that they had parted on amicable terms. For the first time good humor seemed to have masked no sting. She was therefore surprised by Esmond's warning, just before they went in to luncheon, not to involve herself in any argument that might develop.

The dining room at Kilkreen was in the Jacobean part of the house, which formed a single flank of the three-sided court and connected the medieval gatehouse with the larger eighteenth-century wing. Under an ornately carved ceiling, studded with a profusion of knobs and bosses like stalactites, was a table long enough to accommodate many times the number of the present company. Clinton and his mother were at opposite ends, at a distance which made them inaudible to each other unless they raised their voices. Esmond and Theresa sat side by side to Clinton's right, and to his left was Mr. Wright, the agent.

Theresa noticed nothing ominous in the conversation until dessert; and even then, Clinton sounded quite affable as he asked Wright what steps had been taken against tenants who had defaulted for over a year. He was a few years younger than Clinton, and evidently in awe of him; and Wright's restless eyes betrayed his nervousness—his gaze frequently leaving Clinton's face to light on the stuffed birds ranged in cases along the walls.

When Clinton had finished, the agent said diffidently, "If we evict, nobody else will dare rent the same farms. The Fenians have seen to that."

Clinton looked at him with weary patience. "That's why I'm asking for rent rather than evictions. Have you impounded the worst offenders' animals?"

Wright studied his plate awkwardly. "It's not an easy matter, my lord. They drive their beasts into a neighbor's field as soon as they get wind of anything."

"Then you must act with greater secrecy."

Lady Ardmore, who had been fastidiously cutting the ripest grapes from a bunch on her plate, suddenly put down her fruit scissors. "They'll drive our sheep into the sea if we touch theirs. It happened at the Elliotts'. I won't have it here, Clinton."

Clinton laughed harshly. "So we leave them to pay if they feel like it?"

Theresa had seen Esmond's fingers drumming on the table and was not deceived by his light conciliatory manner. He drained his glass and smiled at Clinton. "Surely things aren't so bad. This is Ireland after all. Better get what rent you can than risk worse trouble. If you lived here, it'd be a different matter; but as it is, we have to think of Mother on her own."

"There's no safety in weakness," said Clinton sharply. "They don't only murder exacting landlords. Anyone who surrenders basic property rights without a fight is well on the way to losing everything."

Esmond shook his head sadly. "You're ignoring the root of the problem. Why won't they pay? Isn't it because they're renting uncultivated land instead of established farms?"

"Of course they are. That's why the rents are so low."

"No other reasons?" asked Esmond innocently.

With a faint shrug Esmond said flatly, "He was still unfaithful to you."

"Some husbands always are."

"Wasn't it just the theater?" he asked, "The same reason you didn't remarry when he died but took lovers instead. Did you love many?"

"Three isn't many." She paused. "I suppose I did for a time."

"Before you betrayed them."

"Or they left me. I felt warmly or not at all."

"Don't blame your nature," he said sharply. "The theater's to blame. You know just why it encourages passing fancies. Uncertainty about the future. No decent privacy, plays always turning on love, young men wanting experience. Could any woman stay virtuous for long—tempted like that every day?"

"I did when I was married. I could again." She faced him. "Doesn't your loyalty include trust? I can't survive on my own in this house without activity, without friends. Can't you share with me and not insist on everything for yourself?" Her hair was pinned up, and as she turned away, the nape of her neck was very white and exposed-looking.

He stood for a while like a man supporting a crushing weight, then with a low sigh he stepped forward and kissed her neck. "You must do what you have to. I accept it."

"Without resentment?"

"I hope so."

"You must think hard about it, my love."

"I don't need to. It's not much harder than deciding whether to go on breathing."

"You can be very generous, Esmond."

"Yes," he murmured, faintly smiling. "Perhaps if I can't have rights, you'll grant me privileges."

"Any number." She opened her arms to him and held him. Later, stepping out of her skirt, she paused. "I think I've changed my mind about something. Can I come to Ireland with you?"

He stroked his long chin thoughtfully. "I shouldn't be surprised." The words were dry, but his voice still trembled with emotion.

The country around Kilkreen was wilder and more remote than anything Theresa had envisaged. Set in small fields, the mud cabins of the peasants crouched in insignificance under the great brown shoulders of the neighboring mountains. From the beech woods near the gates of the domain park, glimpses could be caught of a rocky bay, and within its gray curve the jagged outline of two small islands. The local people wore the short frieze coats and misshapen caubeen hats which Theresa had previously considered the sole property of stage Irishmen.

Lady Ardmore too had her theatrical qualities: carrying on the tradition of the old landlords with sublime indifference to the fate of so many of that anachronistic breed swept away by insolvency after the famine. According to Esmond, flitches of bacon and plump hams found their way from the house to the village almost daily. Sheep were also slaughtered at a rate out of all proportion to the household's needs, and the butler regularly charged the estate office for wines that had never been bought, or if they had been, had gone the way of the sheep. There were gardeners in plenty at Kilkreen, but the borders were overgrown with briers and the fish pond was choked with weed. The whole estate seemed plunged in a deep slumber, so peaceful that nothing merited reproof or change.

Queen over this slow decay was her ladyship. More indolent even than her servants, she liked to take the air in a wicker wheelchair pulled by a footman, with a maid at hand to hold a parasol over her if the sun shone. It pleased Lady Ardmore to pretend that any exertion or excess of heat or cold might at any moment prove fatal. Her puffy fingers were heavy with rings, and bracelets puckered the skin at her wrists. Her sharp nose, rouged cheeks, and the fur trimmings of her velvet mantles reminded Theresa of some exotic bird. When she was not eating or playing cards, her face often took on a deathly immobility. But, as Esmond had predicted, she treated Theresa with courtesy, though never with warmth. She spoke as if she had come a long way from wherever she had been in her mind and could not spare much time before returning. In spite of all Esmond's efforts to put Theresa at her ease, Lady Ardmore's manner and the all-pervading atmosphere of decaying grandeur made Theresa's first days at Kilkreen an unnerving experience. Nor could she escape the place even briefly, since Esmond considered it unsafe to drive anywhere outside the domain while there were Fenians in the county.

But in truth, the eccentricities of her hostess and the strangeness of the house only marginally contributed to Theresa's unease. Even before their departure for Ireland, she had keenly regretted her sudden impulse to come with Esmond. Within days of his acknowledgment that her career would continue, Theresa had ceased to view this concession with the same bright optimism. What had at first seemed to remove the single greatest obstacle to their future happiness had soon appeared to her in a truer light. Whatever he might say, Esmond would always resent her need for a life that he could not wholly control. And because he would be sure to suffer in honorable silence, Theresa knew that her guilt would grow until eventually she would feel obliged to offer him some new forfeit—just as she had offered to come to Ireland as an atoning act of gratitude. Whether he knew it or not, from a semblance of weakness Esmond had fashioned a weapon more subtly undermining than naked strength. Already at times she had started to wonder where her old self had gone, and how this sweet guilt-ridden girl had surreptitiously taken her place.

A few days before leaving for Kilkreen, a conversation, which only weeks earlier would have had no adverse effect on her, had underlined her uncertainty with special emphasis. When Esmond had mentioned in passing that Clinton would probably be spending a few days at Kilkreen while they were there, she had lost her temper. Hadn't she made it sufficiently clear to him that the man had insulted her during both their previous meetings? Taken aback, Esmond had gently reminded her that she had seemed amused rather than irritated, and had actually said she wanted to meet Clinton properly. In any case he was only going to stay a day or two at most. It would have been absurd to have asked him to come all the way to London to discuss the latest offers for Markenfield, when this could be done in Ireland without any inconvenience. Nothing would please him more than to be able to forget Clinton's problems, but, since before a sale the mortgages on the place would have to be redeemed by pledges against the trust, he was involved whether he liked it or not.

In a patient, almost apologetic voice, Esmond had gone on to his main concern. He had recently been worried by Clinton's threats to put in a new agent at Kilkreen; and, since their mother had only a life interest in the estate, Clinton, as legal owner, had every right to try to end the wastage and force the tenants to pay their arrears. Because the Fenians were murdering landlords for less, Esmond had not needed to dwell on why he wanted to make sure that Clinton's next stay at Kilkreen coincided with his own. Surely she saw he owed it to his mother?

Yet explanation had not made Theresa feel any better. Plagued by increasing misgivings about marriage, the small additional burden of having to deal with a man so strikingly different from Esmond in almost every way, at this critical time, had been enough to agitate her out of all proportion to the likely problems his presence might cause.

In the event, she was not actually aware that Lord Ardmore had come, until the morning after his arrival when, walking with Louise, she saw a man near the stables wearing cavalry overalls and a forage cap. Without waiting for permission, Louise went up to him and asked where his master was.

"Gone here and there" was the laconic reply. Under foxy eyebrows, his blue inquisitive eyes moved from Louise to her mother. He had been sitting on the grass whittling a stick, but at Theresa's approach, jumped up and clicked his heels together. "Corporal Harris, at your service, ma'am."

"You're most kind," she murmured dryly. The soldier's brash and confident manner grated slightly. She had always found it mildly depressing the way servants took their personal importance from the rank of their masters. She was turning when Louise, curious as ever, asked him if he had been Lord Ardmore's servant for long.

"Since I fished a bloke out of a river," he answered with a grin.

"He chose you because you saved a man's life?" asked Theresa with some skepticism.

"Tried to, ma'am. He was dead and done for."

"Drowned?" Louise murmured faintly.

"Hit in the head, miss," said Harris, pointing to his forehead. "One of them Fenians."

Louise shuddered. "A Fenian shot him?"

"No, miss. One of our lads."

An hour later on the bumpy croquet lawn, Louise was still chattering indignantly about shooting men in rivers. Theresa suggested that the Irishman might have tried to shoot first, but Louise was not convinced. Who'd ever heard of anyone going swimming with a gun? It was therefore unfortunate that the child's first glimpse of Clinton, shortly afterwards, should be of him carrying a gun and a game bag bulging with snipe. Theresa had just hitched up her dress so she could take a proper swing to get her ball through the last hoop. As she succeeded, she heard a cry of "Bravo" from the terrace and looked up to see Lord Ardmore raising his gun, wide-awake in salute.

Pleased by a good morning's shooting, Clinton loped down the stone steps to the lawn, smiling to himself as he recalled Theresa's primness during their last conversation in London. The woman really was a superb hypocrite—pretending to be so righteous and yet having the barefaced audacity to come to Kilkreen quite openly as Esmond's mistress. In a fur boa and feathered Tyrolean hat, with red leather boots showing under her skirt, she looked a wildly improbable figure against the somber ivy-covered walls and mullioned windows. Seeing the child moving away towards the house, Clinton called to her not to stop the game, but she did not turn back.

A few yards from Theresa, he dropped his game bag and picked up Louise's mallet. "Favor me with a game, Miss Simmonds?"

"I've just finished one, Lord Ardmore."

He stood in silence for a moment, watching a squirrel searching for food among the fallen leaves on the far side of the lawn. He sniffed the air with evident satisfaction.

"Marvelous these autumn days. Mist and woodsmoke . . . golden light." She was looking at him doubtfully from beneath the brim of her hat. "Damn it," he muttered, as if suddenly remembering something. "I owe you an apology, Miss Simmonds. Wasn't right to say I was getting married." He stared hard at his muddy boots. "Fact is . . . it's not easy to admit to being turned down. Damned painful." He caught a movement of her lips. "Now you're laughing at me."

"On the contrary, sir. I'm grieved for you."

"You would be if you knew the things she said to me."

Theresa laughed unexpectedly. "Your acting's much better, Lord Ardmore; though I think I can guess what she said."

Clinton frowned. "Can't think how you intend to do that, madam."

"A knowledge of melodrama quite as extensive as your lordship's." He raised a hand to acknowledge the thrust. His expression was encouraging. "As you took her hand, she cried, 'Unhand me, fiend!' "

Clinton gasped. "Her very words. Uncanny, that's what I'd call it, Miss Simmonds. Tell me what I said after that, and I'm your slave for life."

"That's easily done." She paused. "My voice isn't the right pitch, you understand?"

"I'll try to overlook it."

" 'Rage on my beauty; your scorn but adds to your perfection, maddens me. You shall be mine.'" She smiled apologetically. "After that I think you owe me her reply, in character, of course."

"My cue," he replied solemnly.

"'You shall be mine.'"

He clasped his mallet handle and quavered in ladylike falsetto, "'Rather would I die a thousand deaths than submit to such bondage. Trifle not with a woman's jewel, her chastity.'" He chuckled to himself. "It's a damned shame that kind of thing always gets burlesqued nowadays. I used to love it. 'Come we must fly; all is discovered; your husband is in hot pursuit. I have a pork pie and a blunderbuss.' No wonder real life's such a disappointment." He sighed as he picked up his game bag. "I must prepare myself for battle."

"Battle, my lord?"

"Nothing so dignified, I fear. My mother's half-witted agent is lunching with us."

In the brief silence before he raised his hat to her and turned to go, Theresa was surprised to feel a flutter of nervousness. Anticipation of the unexpected had become a habit for her when talking to him—as if at a moment's notice, charm and levity might snap like ice, as on the last occasion at Esmond's house. Watching him walk away, she still could not quite believe that they had parted on amicable terms. For the first time good humor seemed to have masked no sting. She was therefore surprised by Esmond's warning, just before they went in to luncheon, not to involve herself in any argument that might develop.

The dining room at Kilkreen was in the Jacobean part of the house, which formed a single flank of the three-sided court and connected the medieval gatehouse with the larger eighteenth-century wing. Under an ornately carved ceiling, studded with a profusion of knobs and bosses like stalactites, was a table long enough to accommodate many times the number of the present company. Clinton and his mother were at opposite ends, at a distance which made them inaudible to each other unless they raised their voices. Esmond and Theresa sat side by side to Clinton's right, and to his left was Mr. Wright, the agent.

Theresa noticed nothing ominous in the conversation until dessert; and even then, Clinton sounded quite affable as he asked Wright what steps had been taken against tenants who had defaulted for over a year. He was a few years younger than Clinton, and evidently in awe of him; and Wright's restless eyes betrayed his nervousness—his gaze frequently leaving Clinton's face to light on the stuffed birds ranged in cases along the walls.

When Clinton had finished, the agent said diffidently, "If we evict, nobody else will dare rent the same farms. The Fenians have seen to that."

Clinton looked at him with weary patience. "That's why I'm asking for rent rather than evictions. Have you impounded the worst offenders' animals?"

Wright studied his plate awkwardly. "It's not an easy matter, my lord. They drive their beasts into a neighbor's field as soon as they get wind of anything."

"Then you must act with greater secrecy."

Lady Ardmore, who had been fastidiously cutting the ripest grapes from a bunch on her plate, suddenly put down her fruit scissors. "They'll drive our sheep into the sea if we touch theirs. It happened at the Elliotts'. I won't have it here, Clinton."

Clinton laughed harshly. "So we leave them to pay if they feel like it?"

Theresa had seen Esmond's fingers drumming on the table and was not deceived by his light conciliatory manner. He drained his glass and smiled at Clinton. "Surely things aren't so bad. This is Ireland after all. Better get what rent you can than risk worse trouble. If you lived here, it'd be a different matter; but as it is, we have to think of Mother on her own."

"There's no safety in weakness," said Clinton sharply. "They don't only murder exacting landlords. Anyone who surrenders basic property rights without a fight is well on the way to losing everything."

Esmond shook his head sadly. "You're ignoring the root of the problem. Why won't they pay? Isn't it because they're renting uncultivated land instead of established farms?"

"Of course they are. That's why the rents are so low."

"No other reasons?" asked Esmond innocently.

Clinton inclined his head with mocking deference. "I'll let you sort them out, Esmond. When you've stopped the Irish drinking like fish and breeding like rabbits, I'll talk them into giving up grazing for a bit of honest cultivation. Since that's going to take us a few centuries, I'll squeeze some rent out of them in the meantime." He turned a jovial face to the agent. "Isn't that so, Mr. Wright?"

"We can try, my lord."

"Hear that, Esmond?" Clinton laughed. "The man's a tiger."

"I'm sure you'll find his funeral most amusing." Esmond paused, his pale features and clenched hands bizarrely at odds with his quiet ironic voice. "Maybe you recall the gallant nobleman who told his tenants they wouldn't intimidate him by killing his agent."

Clinton pushed back his chair, parodying outrage. "Do I detect a slight on my honor? Actually, I'm going to strike the blow; then Wright can go in and take prisoners. Break the ringleaders, and the rest will pay up on the nail."

Esmond nodded with taunting gravity. "Shoot them, you mean?"

Clinton looked at him reproachfully. "You always underestimate my brutality."

A slight shiver passed through Theresa as she watched the two men face each other in silence. Nothing about their manner was as it seemed, Esmond's elder-brother calm superiority being as much a mask as Clinton's insulting gaiety. Lady Ardmore too, for all her outward composure, was no more able than they to break the shadowy threads that bound them to their past. For what was this argument about land and rents, Theresa asked herself, but a thin pretext for renewing a deeper conflict, dormant at times but never extinguished or resolved?

Then suddenly the menace she had felt so palpably seemed absurd and fanciful. Clinton was pouring more wine in her glass, his expression so warm and candid that she could not help smiling back. When he began asking Wright more mundane questions about methods of getting payment, she believed that if there had been a crisis, it had passed.

Wright was silent a moment and then said in reply to a question about bailiffs, "I did offer a premium of fifty pounds to any man who'd bring in the worst of the lot. Nobody was prepared to earn it. The man's said he'll kill anyone who tries to arrest him. He carries a loaded horse pistol with him everywhere. I've seen the handle sticking out of his coat."

"How long till we could get the constabulary to evict?"

"Under an ordinary notice to quit?" Wright pursed his lips. "At least a year at present."

Clinton sipped his claret reflectively. "And lose another thousand in the meantime. I think not." He touched Wright on the arm. "You reckon this one's responsible for the rest not paying?"

"Most of them anyway."

Clinton nodded. "Excellent. I'd better talk to him. Draw me a map of where he lives. If I have to ask questions on the way, someone's sure to warn him."

The casualness of Clinton's voice took Wright by surprise and it was a moment before he seemed to realize what had been said. "He lives up by Rathkenny. McMahon's his name." The agent's voice shook a little. "Hadn't I better come with you, Lord Ardmore?"

"He'd recognize you. I don't want a fight."

"What do you want?" shouted Esmond, past caring how he sounded.

Lady Ardmore got up from her chair, face flushed and lips trembling. "There isn't enough trouble for him in Carrick-feeney, so he comes here to make more. He won't be the one who has to crouch behind iron shutters at night. That'll be my pleasure when he's gone."

"You can't feel safe with your tenants wandering about with guns under their coats." Clinton met her eyes calmly. "What would you do if he came here and demanded every gun in the place? It happens, you know, when landlords allow their rights to be trampled on."

"Rights?" cried Esmond, making Theresa start. "Spare us your cant about upholding the law. You want more money out of the estate and you'll risk her life to get it."

She had seldom heard Esmond raise his voice before, so now the fixed flame in his narrowing pupils and the sneering edge he gave his words chilled Theresa to the heart.

Clinton stood up slowly. "I do need money, Esmond. But I'll risk no life but my own."

"Has it crossed your mind that you may have to kill this man in self-defense?"

"Certainly not."

"Then just consider the consequences."

Clinton smiled blandly. "I've no intention of taking a loaded weapon." He walked to the door and looked back. "Come along, Mr. Wright. That map of yours."

The agent rose at once and followed Clinton out.

As soon as they had gone, Lady Ardmore sank into her chair and slumped forward with her head in her hands. Her widow's cap had slipped down over her forehead and she was trembling, whether with grief or anger Theresa could not tell. She herself felt dazed and slightly sick. She watched Esmond rise and lay a hand on his mother's shoulder, their bond of close sympathy repelling her.

The old woman looked up at him pathetically. "You swore you'd prevent this."

Esmond sighed heavily. "I didn't know he'd take blackmail so far."

"Blackmail?" echoed Theresa, in amazement.

Esmond said slowly, as if to a child, "I refused to lend him money. This is his reply: Give me what I want, or I'll make our mother's life such misery you'll be forced to give in to me."

"But it wasn't a threat," she stammered. "He's going, Esmond."

"Not a threat?" He groaned, jerking back his head in exasperation. "Let's call it a taste of what he may do later—replace Wright, serve writs by the dozen, start evicting. That's what he's telling us."

"Why couldn't you talk to him reasonably?"

"You think he was reasonable to me?"

"You patronized him, so he went further than he intended. I'm sure he never meant to—"

"You know nothing about him," snapped Lady Ardmore. "Some men need to risk their necks, the way others need strong drink at breakfast."

The woman's derision shocked Theresa less than her lack of

all concern. "Isn't either of you worried about him?" she whispered.

Lady Ardmore glanced at Esmond before turning back to Theresa. "My dear," she said silkily, "you really shouldn't insult Lord Ardmore until you know him better. I can assure you he'll be more than a match for any wretched one-horse grazier. It's the ruffian's numerous companions I feel less sanguine about."

"If the man's such a poor fool, why won't anyone go near him for any money?" Theresa replied hotly.

Esmond raised a propitiating hand. "Of course if he was utterly contemptible, you wouldn't catch Clinton demeaning himself. He enjoys a challenge."

Theresa murmured urgently, "Ride part of the way with him, Esmond. Be there to fetch help if he doesn't come back."

"If he wanted my help he'd ask for it. I'm not going to try to steal his thunder."

"Is bravery so laughable?" she asked, wounded by his scoffing tone.

"It's evidently made a better impression on you," he replied with a bitter little smile on his lips.

"All I wanted was to be left in peace, that was all," moaned Lady Ardmore.

"Shall I help you to your room, Mother?"

Without speaking Lady Ardmore rose and held out her arm for Esmond to take.

A little later a maid came into the dining room to clear the table, but seeing Theresa still seated, she went away. Theresa stared aimlessly at the decanter in front of her; shafts of light from the window made the dark red wine glow and sparkle, its color refracted and intensified by the many-faceted glass. Without thinking, she reached forward and poured herself some more wine, but her hand shook and she spilled some drops on the cloth. Like blood, she thought, dark stains on a white shirt. She heard Clinton's laughter on the croquet lawn and shuddered. Her forehead was hot and she was gripped by a hateful feeling of suspense as if a tightly wound spring were about to uncoil with sudden violence.

How could it have been unnatural for her to show fear and apprehension? Used only to Esmond's intuitive understanding, the memory of his grim-faced hostility struck her with the chill impact of revelation. Never, until seeing him goading Clinton, had she thought him joyless and bitter, as if his brother's youthful animation drained him. Now too Theresa thought she knew why she hated his complicity with his mother; their bond seemed to owe as much to shared antipathy to Clinton as to love for each other. And through every exchange between them, Theresa had felt the helplessness of absolute exclusion. A family's hatred, no less than its love, had the power to create an inexorably closed world.

Through the small thick panes of glass, Theresa saw the somber outline of the surrounding hills and imagined the rooks flying high above the house in never-ending circles. With a sudden throb of panic, she wondered how she would endure more days at Kilkreen. Seconds later Clinton came in, and with his presence everything that had seemed ominous and dark in the silent air seemed to leave it.

"I wanted a word with Esmond before I went."

"He's with your mother."

"A most devoted son, Miss Simmonds," he replied, smiling at her brooding face.

As he moved to the door, she called after him with a vehemence that surprised her, "Why are you going?"

"Questions like that, and I won't know whether to start with my right foot or my left." He looked at her kindly and flicked at his riding boots with his whip. "Don't we all do what we want, and dress it up with words like duty?"

"You must be frightened," she murmured after a brief silence.

"Too little imagination. Hasn't Esmond told you?"

She did not smile, but said quietly, "He may refuse to pay anything; he may not be able to."

The anxiety in her voice drew from him a tenderness of expression she had never seen before. "I only want to persuade the man not to harass tenants who would otherwise pay their rent. Nothing very alarming in that."

The gentle reassurance of his tone contrasted so strangely with the masculine jut of his jaw and the almost arrogantly authoritative way he held himself that she was bemused by a

sudden sense of his accessibility, a feeling that for the first time
there was no barrier between them and that if she chose to talk
more to him he would reply without the constraint and tension
she had become used to. And yet how unconsciously proud he
seemed of his healthy young blood and the vitality that surrounded him like an aura. Illness, death, and old age only
happened to ordinary people; but, like a god in a cloud, he was
invulnerable. His serene confidence both exasperated and
touched her. Suddenly he laughed, and she wondered why
until then she had never noticed how irresistible his laughter
was.

"I was thinking," he said, "of my aunt's remark after a performance of *King Lear*: 'What a tiresomely disagreeable family
those Lears must have been.' " He smiled. "You mustn't take us
so seriously, Miss Simmonds. It's not good. It's my worst fault,
so I ought to know."

Then, with a slight inclination of the head, he turned and
was gone. Unspoken sentences raced through her mind and
dispersed like swirling smoke, leaving only a confused sense of
loss. For several seconds she could not remember a word he
had said. The same tension she had felt earlier returned with
greater force. For an instant she saw Clinton with uncanny
clearness: the cut of his nostrils, the curve of his cheeks, still
glowing after his morning in the open air, the golden hairs on
the back of his hands, a slight scar above his left eye—details
she had observed unaware and was now astonished to possess.
A treacherous warm tide of emotion bewildered and scared
her. She thought of bullets lodging in his body and felt a spasm
of giddiness. With a shock she realized that Esmond had come
in.

"I didn't think you'd still be here."

"Did he find you?"

Esmond nodded and sat down next to her.

"Did you manage to dissuade him?"

The lines deepened at the corners of his mouth and his pale
eyes mocked her. "Would you like to see me turn water into
wine?"

He ran a hand wearily through his graying hair and stared
vacantly at the table. "Please, Theresa," he murmured, reach-

106

ing out blindly to her, "Don't judge me too harshly by today. Perhaps you think I envy him. Maybe I do. If I were his age, we might understand each other better. If he'd struggled as I have . . . if, if." He looked more like his old self—rueful, ironic. "A man like Clinton really doesn't have to be brave; he simply couldn't conceive of this Irishman or anyone else standing against him. I don't pretend it's just youth or arrogance." His face relaxed and the furrowed frown left it. "Anyway you'll be glad to hear I found him in the gun room loading a revolver. It's not untypical, believe me." He noticed her lips curving upwards and looked away. "Is that funny, my love?"

"I suppose it must be since I want to laugh."

But instead of laughter coming, her throat felt tight and choked, and when Esmond asked her what was wrong, she could not look at him or answer.

Clinton rode through the beech woods bordering the domain park, over ground thick with fallen leaves, and on into rougher country where the bracken was russet and golden. Ahead of him a pheasant darted away in a jerky undignified rush. From a misty sky the sun was shining now with a fainter warmth. He was nervous about the coming encounter, but the feeling did not displease him—just a gentle flutter under the diaphragm and no parched mouth and shaking hands. Elation mingled with the faster beating of his heart.

Since his arrival at the house late the previous evening, Clinton had deliberately checked his natural desire to press Esmond about the sale price which Markenfield now seemed likely to realize as a result of his preliminary negotiations with the mortgagees. And to remove any possible temptation, Clinton had absented himself for the entire morning. But now that he had given Esmond so clear an indication of what he might do to raise funds if the estimated price were to prove low, Clinton felt confident that Esmond would return to London considerably more eager to bargain hard before reaching a final agreement. Clinton would have preferred to safeguard his interests in a less dramatic fashion, but, since Esmond in all their past dealings had only done his best for him when given a clear incentive, Clinton had made up his mind to provide one.

Trotting his horse along a rutted lane between hedges bright with rose hips, he savored the gratifying and entirely unlooked for effect his behavior had seemed to have on Miss Simmonds. It was extraordinary how even the most experienced and canny women were often swayed by male recklessness into an almost maternal solicitude. To pass the time, and take his mind off McMahon, Clinton allowed himself to wonder what he might do were she to give him any more positive signs of being attracted. She was an intriguing woman certainly, and unnervingly forthright. It was his clear recollection of this quality which made the possibility unexpectedly disquieting. With a measure of regret painful enough to surprise him, he reluctantly accepted that anything short of active discouragement would be unthinkable.

When the straggling village of Rathkenny came in sight, he was not sorry to concentrate all his attention on his map. After a short distance he left the main track and struck out across the fields to avoid exciting attention. Hardly any of the farms he was now passing were larger than five acres; most being split among children who ought to have moved away. The numerous untilled fields testified to the fatal Irish theory that animals ought to grow fat on the pasture provided by nature rather than on winter crops. In consequence few farmers were able to keep more than a handful of beasts on their exhausted land.

The Kilkreen estate, as Clinton well appreciated, was a fine example of another Irish vicious circle. Landlords could not afford to drain and bring new land under cultivation unless rents were paid in full, and this in turn would never happen until more acres were farmed. Even if the present rent strike were broken, and Clinton did not believe it would be, others would soon arise unless massive land reclamation were begun. Yet even this would fail without the simultaneous merging of numerous smallholdings into areas large enough to become viable mixed farms. And when that day came, in spite of his efforts to persuade Esmond otherwise, Clinton knew he would never be prepared to bring on his mother the odium of the necessary mass evictions.

After passing a tract of stonier country, Clinton came to a group of cabins nestling by a narrow strip of potato ridges. An overturned cart, with one wheel off and some loose sticks and furze stuck into the gaps like a barricade, served as a shared gateway. A few geese were scrabbling about in the muddy front patch among the weeds and thistles, and a large mastiff jerked at his chain and started barking. Clinton tethered his horse and walked up to the central, most solidly built cabin, avoiding a manure heap in his path. Rags had been stuffed into broken windowpanes and the roof was patched with turf.

Breathing deeply to steady himself, Clinton knocked loudly with the bone handle of his riding crop. After a short interval a man wearing a dirty moleskin waistcoat came to a window and asked him what he wanted.

"To come in," replied Clinton.

"You can't get in here" was the sharp and suspicious reply.

"You must be Joe McMahon," said Clinton with a smile.

"What if I am?"

"You're the man I want to speak to."

Evidently taken aback by Clinton's friendly tone, McMahon eyed him warily for several seconds. "And what'd you be after doing then?"

"I can't tell you until you let me in." The man said nothing; his eyes all the time scanning the track and the hedges for concealed bailiffs. "Do you know who I am?" Clinton went on.

"If you were the pope himself I'd not give a rap."

"So you won't care that I'm Lord Ardmore."

"If it's yer lordship right enough, you'll still not come in."

Clinton shrugged his shoulders. "You can't be McMahon," he said dismissively. "He wouldn't be scared of one man on his own. Come out and see for yourself if you don't believe me."

"I'm not a fool entirely."

"But you're a coward for all that."

With a sudden snort of disgust McMahon slammed the window shut and soon Clinton heard the sound of bolts being withdrawn. The man bowed to him with deference bordering on mockery. "Walk in, your honor, walk in."

McMahon led him into a room furnished with a table, a dresser, and a few three-legged stools. In the grate a turf fire was smoldering, and behind some hen coops on the far side of the room next to a stack of oats was a crude wooden bed frame covered with straw laid across wattles. A young woman with a sallow face stood by the fire, her fingers pulling at the edges of her black shawl; probably in her early twenties, she looked ten years older. Clinton noticed her apprehension and at once guessed that she was far more frightened of what her husband might do than anything a mere stranger might attempt. Though smaller than Clinton, McMahon was thickset with muscles like knotted ropes in his broad forearms. Beneath a lock of straw-colored hair, his blue eyes were watchful rather than belligerent. Seeing a bill hook resting against the wall by the window, Clinton placed himself between McMahon and this weapon.

"So you're the terror of the countryside, McMahon, and nobody dares take you?"

At these words the man made a quick uneasy movement towards the door, as though expecting Clinton to signal to people outside the window. "No one will take me," he growled.

"How will it end?" asked Clinton quietly. "You owe two years' rent, and now you're frightening your neighbors out of paying. I'm told you've sworn to shoot any process man who tries to serve a writ."

McMahon unexpectedly grinned and went over to a greatcoat hanging on a nail by the dresser; turning the coat a little, he exposed the large brass-mounted handle of a horse pistol. Clinton, whose right hand was already in his pocket, cocked his revolver the moment McMahon touched the pistol. McMahon heard the click and threw down his gun with a harsh laugh. Clinton looked down and saw that the Irishman's weapon had neither lock nor barrel.

"Your honor has a fine set of bailiffs to be afraid of that," McMahon said scornfully.

When Clinton laughed, the woman smiled with relief and seemed more at ease. Though amused by the thought of the terror this broken gun had inspired, Clinton was also saddened. The reality of this isolated man holding out against the bailiffs was very different from the picture painted by Wright. But perhaps there were other firearms hidden in the house.

After a pause, Clinton said, "I'm going to have to make you

pay rent, McMahon. Until you go to the agent's office nobody round here will dare settle with him."

"I can't pay."

"You must pay something."

Clinton saw the muscles in the man's neck knit and tighten.

"I'm glad it's your lordship says so. Sure, if ye were Mr. Wright, I'd have you out soon enough."

"If you resist personal service of a writ, I'll apply for an order of substitution from the courts. The notice could be stuck up on any wall in the village and you couldn't help that."

The woman made a move towards her husband, but his expression was so menacing that she backed away. "They'd still have to take me," he snarled.

"Certainly."

"I've planted every stick and raised every stone on this place and I'll not part with it."

Surprised by McMahon's sudden frenzy, and seeing his eyes fixed on the bill hook, Clinton decided to be conciliatory. "I said nothing about eviction, only that you must pay off some of your arrears."

"I tell you I can't," he shouted, clenching his fists.

"Then drive your cattle to the pound and I'll release them for a token."

McMahon stared at him uncomprehending, his eyes glittering with anger. "Is it myself to be first to break the pledge? I'd die first."

For a moment the tension of the man's nerves seemed so great that Clinton thought he was gathering himself to spring at him. But, as if on a sudden impulse, he flung open the door and dashed out of the room.

The woman screamed after him, "No, Joe. No, d'ye hear?" She turned hysterically to Clinton. "He'll murder you, sir." She flung open the window and looked at him imploringly, but he stood where he was and took out his revolver; her gaze fastened on the dull wink of the barrel and she began to scream. As McMahon kicked open the door, she flung herself at him, almost knocking the blunderbuss from his hands. In the second it took him to brush her aside with the butt, Clinton hurled himself forward. As both men fell to the ground the gun went off with a detonation like a cannon, lighting the room with a sheeting orange flash. Blinded by a thick pall of acrid-smelling powder smoke, Clinton could not see if either of the others had been hurt. The woman was moaning now, but when McMahon lifted her she ran behind the hen coops. The dresser was pitted with small shot, and McMahon was bleeding from a wound in the arm. Since the gun was a muzzle-loader and both barrels had been discharged, Clinton dusted himself and put away his revolver; his ribs ached where he had come up against the corner of a stool. McMahon looked in astonishment at the dark blood welling from his arm. The smoke was starting to disperse through the open window. Clinton picked up the blunderbuss and walked past McMahon to the door. Though the man was losing blood, Clinton was sure that the pellets of sparrow hail had caused no serious injury. Shaken and angry, his first thought was to ride to the nearest magistrate, but if the man were to be charged with attempted murder on his word alone, the rent strike would probably be strengthened. The wife might well perjure herself, and because McMahon had been the only one hurt, local people might even believe that the landlord had himself provoked the attack.

McMahon followed Clinton out of the house, his damaged arm clasped to his chest. His eyes were glazed with shock and his breath came in gasps. "What'll your honor do?"

"See a magistrate," said Clinton slowly, noting the man's look of despair. "Or you can come to the agent's office tomorrow."

McMahon stood in silence for a few seconds with bowed head and then nodded.

"You'll come?"

"I will." He sighed, turning away.

Crossing the yard, Clinton came to a rock and, grasping the blunderbuss by the butt, brought down the barrel with all his strength on the lump of limestone. On the second blow the metal snapped away from the stock and fell cracked and twisted to the ground.

Riding back in the direction of Rathkenny, Clinton felt little satisfaction. Only the woman's action had saved him from having to shoot the man or face being shot by him. Luck rather than judgment had brought him victory, if such it could be called. Around him the barren amphitheater of rocks and hills stretched away without relief except where streamers of mist lay in the bog hollows among the stones and heather. A little later the hidden sun pierced the bank of low clouds above the village, sweeping the brown hills with moving beams of silver.

Shortly before half past three that afternoon, Esmond knocked at his mother's door to ask whether she was ready. At about this time on most fine days Lady Ardmore went out for a short carriage ride. During the morning it had been agreed that today Esmond and Theresa should accompany her.

Dressed in a heavy fur-lined pelisse and an old-fashioned bonnet with puffs of tulle and muslin flowers sewn inside the brim, Lady Ardmore sat in a tall-backed chair among the étagères and whatnots, which, with her large half-tester bed, occupied almost every foot of the floor. Since she rarely used any of the downstairs sitting rooms, she had filled her bedroom with a chaotic collection of treasured things: blue knotted Dresden candlesticks, a fragile Wedgwood tea service, silver card cases, Pompadour fans, and screens in crewel work. Esmond threaded his way across the room and sat down next to her on a small cane chair.

She looked at him anxiously and sighed. "I wish I knew what to talk about with her."

"Anything you like," he reassured her.

The long sad lines which ran down from her nose to the corners of her mouth, making her look sour and discontented, filled him with pity. He had shared with her the years that had done most to etch those lines: the agonizing period before his father had finally rejected them both. Neither her rouged cheeks nor the ridiculous flowers inside her bonnet had any power to arouse his criticism or mockery. In truth, her weaknesses deepened his affection for her, contrasting so poignantly with the image of her he had preserved from childhood as the guardian angel who could do no wrong. Now she could sleep only with the help of laudanum and suffered the cruel indignity of indigestion that would sometimes bring a foam of bubbles to her lips in spite of heroic efforts to prevent this. Often he thought that her love for him was all that connected her with the world; her interest in his doings was her only hold on reality. She was pulling at one of her rings and seemed worried.

"It's so hard," she said, "to ask her anything at all without appearing to be prying into her past. You do see that, don't you, Esmond?"

"Of course," he replied gently.

His mother raised her gold-rimmed lorgnette and gazed at him with a wistful smile. "I'm afraid she hasn't made you happy, my poor boy."

The fierce tenderness of her voice touched and yet disturbed him. If anything could bring her contentment, it would be his own happy marriage.

"There's no carpet for us over the stones as the Irish say," he said lightly.

"I can't help feeling—"

"She'll be waiting, Mother."

Lady Ardmore made an impatient gesture. "Let her wait. You shouldn't let her dominate you. That was my mistake with your father." She paused and thrust her hands into the fur muff on her knees. "The way she almost told you how you ought to feel towards Clinton. I could have hit her. I'm sorry but it's true. Let an actress get the whip hand, and you're sure to be humiliated." She withdrew a hand from the muff and laid it on one of Esmond's. "Promise me," she whispered emotionally, "Promise to take a firm line. If she still won't agree to marry you in a month, tell her to go. You should never have let her stay; you're too sensitive to understand women like her."

"She's not at all how you think she is."

Lady Ardmore made a slight clicking noise with her tongue and got up. "And when I know her better, I suppose she'll make a fool of me too?"

"She wins over everybody in the end."

"I hope so, Esmond; really I do," she murmured, clutching his arm.

When they reached the hall, Esmond could see the old olive green barouche standing on the carriage sweep and could not help recalling with a throb of emotion how smart he had thought it when it had arrived from Dublin shortly after he and his mother had first come to Kilkreen. The horses had once been dappled grays, but neglect and age had changed their coats into a slatey hue marked with light smudges like lime or whitewash. The harness looked cracked and hard and in danger of breaking if the tongue of any buckle were to be thrust into an unaccustomed strap hole. The coachman wore a dirty stained greatcoat, and a woolen muffler like a London hansom driver. His face was almost hidden under a broad-brimmed hat slouched down over his eyes. Every time Esmond came to Kilkreen, he longed to stop the servants' exploitation of their mistress, but she had told him so emphatically that she liked everything as it was that he had accepted conditions which he would not have tolerated for five minutes in his own house. Having helped his mother into the faded silk-lined interior of the carriage, he returned to the hall, expecting to find that Theresa had come down. Since he could see no sign of her, he ran upstairs to her room.

Opening the door, he was surprised to see her lying on the bed. "Have you forgotten?"

"Please go without me," she replied, her back still turned to him.

"But why, Theresa?"

"I feel ill."

He came and sat down on the edge of the four-poster. "Badly, my love?"

"My head hurts a little, that's all."

He bent forward and, gently brushing aside her hair, kissed her tenderly on the neck, longing to turn her face and kiss her mouth. Her stillness afterwards filled him with a familiar mixture of desire and humiliation, sharpened by his recollection of what his mother had just said.

"Mightn't it be wise," he said quietly, "to send to Westport for Dr. Finney? My mother swears by him."

She rolled over and faced him. "Drag a doctor twelve miles for a slight headache?"

"If he had to come twelve hundred, I'd send for him if you asked."

"But I didn't, Esmond."

He looked down at the patchwork counterpane and nodded.

After a pause she said, "I wouldn't like to think of your mother being kept waiting."

She lay on her back staring up at the canopy above the bed, with her hands behind her head; the white skin of her throat, the slight undulation of her breasts, and the tightness of the silk across her thighs made the room seem vague around her, so tense was his concentration on her. The inaccessibility of her expression wounded him. He knew she was not ill but could not bring himself to say so.

"Why not go?" she murmured with a hint of pleading.

"Because I don't choose to yet."

"I do know when you're angry." He sat silently, head bent, brows drawn stiffly. "Shall I tell you why?"

"I think I know my own mind," he replied softly, her words stirring his anger. "You prefer to stay here thinking about my heroic brother. You should go shooting with him; it might allay your anxiety." He got up and paced over to the window. "Why do you make me say angry things, when all I want to tell you is how I love you? When I kissed you, it might have been some fly bumping against you." He came to her and knelt beside the bed. "Kiss me now," he whispered.

She raised herself and brushed his forehead lightly with her lips. The next moment he had seized her and was forcing his lips against hers, straining his body against her. She pulled away, but he got onto the bed, pinioning her shoulders with his hands.

"Please don't tear my clothes; I'd rather take them off myself." Her detached voice sobered him like the cut of a whip.

As she began to unfasten the back of her bodice, he hid his face. "Do you think I only want your body?" he asked in a tight rasping voice. "I could buy women for that. I want the whole of you—heart and mind. I'd rather be refused than have you give yourself like this. I'd sooner embrace a corpse. If you ever know the pain of being alone in a lover's arms, know how it is to feel grasping when all you wanted was to *give* . . . I'll pity you."

She leaned forward and embraced him, her eyes soft with sorrow, yet to him as empty as a sky without stars. The shadow of dependence lay heavily on his heart. When he felt her cheeks wet against his, he still knew no certainty; there could be a thousand reasons for grief, and love was only one. He walked away from the bed and left the room without speaking.

His mother glanced at him with questioning eyes as he sat down beside her in the carriage.

"A headache," he murmured. "She said another day. Was sorry." He shrugged his shoulders and attempted a smile, which scarcely moved his lips.

Lady Ardmore looked away as the barouche lumbered into motion. Her face was as impassive as before her son had entered the carriage. Inside her muff, her hands were squeezed together. A headache, she thought derisively, and Esmond had sucked it in, probably scared of brain fever. At night she herself sometimes woke from her drugged sleep with pains in her chest, her skin clammy with sweat, breath coming in shallow gasps. But what did Esmond care about that, when a girl's headache could make him look like death? As they rumbled into the beech woods, she laughed softly to herself.

"Something to amuse you," she said abruptly. "That girl's fool of a governess. O'Flaherty took her into Westport to buy wool, and she saw a boy running after the dog cart naked except for his jacket. She asked O'Flaherty whether the lad had no other clothes. 'Ma'am,' said he, 'that boy could have clothes enough if he chose, but he's so wonderful ticklesome he never could stand to let a tailor take his measure for a pair of breeches.' "

Esmond smiled but did not laugh. His mother looked at him for a moment with feigned disappointment and then gazed through the dirty window at the falling leaves. If things went on like this she would have to talk to Miss Simmonds before she left and tell her a few things that would give her more than a headache.

Long after Esmond had gone, Theresa still felt angry and ashamed. Was it her fault he made himself responsive to her slightest smile or frown? He had woven her so closely into the web of his emotions that he could no longer recognize the true causes of her moods, but always with a lover's egotism took upon himself the blame or credit for her every shift. Unable to remain idle any longer, she went in search of her daughter. Still apprehensive about Clinton, she badly wanted the distraction of Louise's company.

The child was not in the library, her temporary schoolroom, nor in her bedroom. Theresa walked through dark rooms where shafts of light picked out curved legs of cabinets and dim tapestries. She passed the assortment of potted palms, sticks, and pruning knives in the hall and continued into the less frequented part of the house, where, the day before, Esmond had shown her matchless Catherine of Braganza chairs shrouded under brown hollands. In a small unused sitting room, her eye took in wax flowers under a glass dome and a blue Chinese vase on a marble chiffonnier. From here she entered a servants' passage and found a door leading into the stableyard.

High up, on the back of a large black mare, Louise was being led round the yard by Corporal Harris. The radiant pleasure of Louise's face brought a lump to Theresa's throat. The child's expression was full of the trustingness Theresa remembered so well from the time when Louise had been a little girl of five or six. How contented and pleased with everything she had been then—before her father's death and the more extravagant expectations of her new life had changed her. On the child's head was a cavalry forage cap and in her hand a crop held up like a sword.

Harris was saying in a gruff parody of a military voice, "So when you comes level with the trough, on the command 'Eyes right,' you brings down your sword to the salute."

Louise nodded solemnly, and, as Theresa heard Harris say, "Eyes right," she saw Clinton step out from the shadow cast by the door of a loose box. A moment after raising his hand in salute to Louise, he came forward smiling and patted the horse's neck.

"Nothing to it, was there? If you can manage the march past by squadrons at review, we'll soon have you leading a troop."

Moving back a little to remain out of sight, Theresa felt relief so intense that for a moment she had to lean against the wall. Not even hurt, he was standing there as calmly as if he had just returned from a walk through the gardens. Just seeing him, as he lifted Louise down, made Theresa incredulous that she had ever imagined he could come to any harm. His coming seemed as inevitable as the sun's rising or the rooks return to the elms at nightfall. The early-evening sunshine filled the yard with dancing motes and gilded the pools of water between the cobbles. Harris drew the bridle over the horse's head, loosened the buckles of the girth, and lifted off the saddle; then he covered it with a blanket and led it into a loose box.

Looking at Clinton, Theresa was overwhelmed by a feeling both frightening and exhilarating, a slow yielding of the heart like a plant's inclination to the sun. Afraid to move in case she should speak either with the forced gaiety of a juvenile lead or the incoherence of a flustered child, she stayed hidden a little longer. He's just another man, she told herself lightheadedly, at the same time wanting to laugh at such absurdity. In a score of plays she had kissed so many men without awareness of their sex, but with everything Clinton said or did, she sensed his maleness. And because of this, the aura of remoteness she had clothed him in fell away, and she felt able to treat with him on terms that made birth and position irrelevant. And yet Louise, Esmond, the future? Was she never again to be free and irresponsible, never know the heedless courage able to seize the moment at whatever cost? And suddenly her fear was greater than her elation. Through a mist of doubts she heard him speak her name.

He said that Louise wanted to see his horse being groomed. She was aware of the rattle of a pail and a metal shoe ringing on the cobbles.

"Of course," she murmured.

When she had followed Clinton into the stable, the mare was eating wisps of hay, while Harris washed the hocks, shaggy with their passage through the undergrowth. The man was patiently looking for thorns and scratches with a small bull's-eye lantern; and as he worked, he explained to Louise what he would do next. The air was warm and damp, filled with the soft noise of horses feeding.

After a brief silence, Clinton said, "I'll show you the saddle room; it ought to be opened as a museum of an age before saddle soap."

She followed him past some empty stalls to a large room lit

by a smoking lamp, where the saddles, hung high on rusty nails, cast brown shadows on the peeling walls, and bridles dangled like creepers in a conservatory. On the far side of the room she saw some dusty carriage lamps and a cracked dashboard piled up near a heap of shafts and springs. He took down a bridle and with a sharp tug pulled it apart.

"As well my mother's riding days are over, or they very soon would be."

She stared down at the broken strip of leather where he had let it drop and looked up at him. "Why have you brought me here?"

He laughed easily. "I'd better tell you I'm a clergyman and married; this should assure you it cannot be my intention to do you the wrong you may expect."

"Where did that come from?" she asked with a faint smile.

"God knows. A play with a marvelous vicar who couldn't stop trying to save fallen women. I can't remember the title."

"What happened with the Irishman?" she whispered.

"He's coming to pay his rent. With some help from his wife, he turned out quite amenable."

"Like everybody else?" she asked with sudden bitterness.

As she turned her face to him, Clinton was confused by her unexpected anger. He had wanted to talk to her, away from Harris and the girl, but without any clear idea of what he would say. He had come to enjoy the uncertainties and needling undertones in their brief conversations.

"I don't understand," he said softly. "Would you like me to go?" And at once, seeing the subdued fire in her eyes, he felt the tension in the air around them, dense as the lamp smoke. As though he had been running, he drew breath, and with effort sufficient for a great leap, moved back a single step. At last, averting his eyes, he said with harshness strange to him, "You play at your profession on the stage to keep your talents for real life."

"Do what?" she asked faintly, from a distance, like one in pain. The pale light from the windows and the lamp cast soft shadows on her face. "Are conquests worthless to you unless fought for through every trick of false pride and modesty?"

As she pushed past him, he caught her hand in a grasp at once rough and delicate.

"I want no kindness, no superior sympathy," she said.

"Believe me," he whispered, raising her hand to his lips and kissing her palm and then her fingers; no longer trying to look away, he met her eyes with a sadness she had not seen till then.

"Oh God," she said softly, hesitantly. "Was it because . . . because a man who refuses is crushed by satire? That modesty in men is . . .?"

He shook his head and for answer embraced her and kissed her lips, his hands moving down the length of her arms to her waist, with so firm a pressure that they seemed to mold rather than caress her body. After the pain of hesitation, their joined lips brought respite as much as desire. A warm long kiss, neither tranquil nor devouring, which brought a shiver to her spine and slow waves of warmth, a suspension of time and thought behind closed eyes. They parted breathing heavily, their eyes soft and misty. For minutes afterwards Theresa could still feel the pressure of his hands.

As they walked back between the stalls towards the loose box where they had left Louise and Harris, Theresa's desire to reach out and touch him changed to incredulity at what had happened.

Watching Harris at work on the mare with a brush and currycomb, Clinton smiled at Louise. "Do you see what it means not to turn a hair?"

And Theresa, seeing the other meaning to his words, resolved that, whatever might be said or done, she would keep their secret. Minutes later, as the old green coach rattled into the yard, she felt the first sharp pangs of fear, and a dread of the future which made her knees shake, but she walked on towards the house at the same unhurried pace, smiling at Louise chattering by her side.

When Theresa and Louise had left the stables, Clinton leaned against the manger, absently watching each evidence of the understanding between mare and groom; the way the horse inclined its head to the man as he brushed vigorously at the little valleys and folds where the ears grew from the skull. When Harris put down the brush and picked up his comb again to start on the mane, the mare curved its long neck and nibbled him fondly on the shoulder.

As if he had been drinking, Clinton tried to reassemble his thoughts with ponderous deliberation, but, like the fragments of a brittle dream, they split apart, leaving him bemused. Everything around him—stables, horses, every familiar sight and sound—seemed distanced and unreal.

CHAPTER NINE

After dinner Clinton and Esmond stayed on in the dining room for cigars and port, while Lady Ardmore and Theresa retired to the only large reception room still in regular use. Since there was no piped gas at Kilkreen, at night the house was lit entirely by oil lamps and candles, which left dark pools of shadow in the corners of rooms as cavernous as the cedar drawing room, in spite of two massive Waterford chandeliers.

While Theresa waited for Lady Ardmore to sit down in one of the tall-backed Carolean chairs by the fire, she glanced at a hanging to the right of the carved marble fireplace: a piece of fraying embroidery richly decorated with birds, fishes, and plants. In a central rectangular panel was a hand holding a pruning knife against the stem of a vine and under it a Latin maxim on a scroll: *"Virescit vulnere virtus."*

"The Danvers motto," murmured Lady Ardmore, who had been watching her attentively. "Shall I translate it for you?"

" 'Courage grows stronger through a wound,' " replied Theresa after only momentary hesitation. The old woman nodded as if surprised by Theresa's erudition.

"Our version is 'Virtue flourishes by a wound.' I'm not so sure myself. The weak often grow weaker in adversity." She paused. "Do many actresses know Latin, Mrs. Barr?"

While Clinton always called Theresa by the maiden name she retained for the stage, Lady Ardmore invariably used her married name.

"I spent six years at a convent in Boulogne. Latin and French were almost the only subjects."

"Your parents liked France?" asked her ladyship, her raised brows expressing suspicious disapproval of a country popularly associated with libertinism and scandalous novels.

"My father lived there to escape his creditors."

"So you were brought up a Catholic?"

"Yes. As a child I was very devout."

"Too little to eat and too much to swallow," muttered Lady Ardmore; but Theresa did not bother to comment on this much quoted description of Catholicism. She could feel the woman's hostility in the air around her almost as a physical presence, not directly from what she said, but rather from the stiff unyielding way she sat in her high-necked black velvet dress, her hands tightly encircling the handle of her ivory cane. On her head she wore two strips of velvet matching her dress as a bandeau, from which gray strands of hair fell over her temples like straws escaping from a nest. The skin around her lips was slightly puckered, as though she had recently bitten into an acid fruit. She said at last, "Most mothers pretend their sons' mistresses don't exist. Don't you wonder why I agreed to receive you here?"

"I assumed your fondness for Esmond—"

Lady Ardmore shook her head impatiently, and the sharpness of her voice contrasted strangely with her dispassionate gaze. "Why d'you stay with him? Money, I suppose?"

"No."

"Then why didn't you clear out when you turned him down? Waiting for somebody else, I daresay."

"Would he like you to ask these questions?"

"He'd hate it. Will you tell him?"

"I don't think so."

Silence for a while except for the cracking of burning logs in the grate. Lady Ardmore lowered her head. "I suppose he begged you to stay?"

Theresa shook her head. "I wanted time to make up my mind. He was generous enough to agree."

"He's a fool then, and you're no better. If you don't know to start with, you're never going to. All you do is make your refusal ten times worse."

"He may refuse me."

Lady Ardmore looked at her derisively. "If you're nasty the whole time. But the moment you're civil, he'll be keen as mustard again. . . . Hope's an absurdly healthy plant in our family." She sighed, and Theresa was surprised by a sudden change in her face, its aquiline features and hollow cheeks no longer hardened by lack of feeling. "He may seem hardheaded to you, but in many ways he's naïve and far too trusting for his own good. Even when his father sent us here, he still didn't think ill of him. Even blamed himself. When something's too painful to face for what it is, he usually pretends it's something else."

From the darkness of the garden came the sudden raucous screech of a peacock. Lady Ardmore unexpectedly got up and came and sat down on a low chair next to Theresa. "I wanted you to come here so we could talk to each other. You're not at all the little minx of a vaudeville trouper I expected, smoking cigars and wandering round in Arabic trousers singing yodeling songs. Or perhaps you're on your best behavior." She smiled at Theresa for the first time; a fleeting, nervous little smile, which for a few seconds hinted at the beauty she had once possessed. "It'd be so easy to set him free, my dear, so very easy. Invite some actor to the house and let yourself be discovered, sell one of his precious things, let him find a letter from another man. The best cures are the sharpest. Perhaps our motto isn't a bad one after all. But instead of wielding the knife, you prefer to feed his infatuation."

"That isn't true."

"Then prove it isn't. Accept him now." After a brief pause, she said with a wry twist of her lips, "I thought so. In that case, I wonder if I can help you to be cruel, Mrs. Barr?"

"You mean you've made some sort of plan?" asked Theresa faintly.

"You could get to Westport in the trap by early morning, be

on the first post coach to Dublin before anybody knew you had gone. Just wait till he's asleep and go. The servants will do anything I say to help."

"But he'd come after me. It's absurd, like some play. . . . And what could I tell my daughter? She's fond of him." Theresa tried to sound amused.

Lady Ardmore spread out her fingers on the arms of her chair and went on as if she had not heard Theresa's response. "Tell your daughter the truth. She can't have led a sheltered life. I can give you money, unless the idea offends you. Far better he should be with me after you've gone, and not in London on his own."

"Perhaps I don't want to go," replied Theresa affably, as if politely tolerating a tasteless joke. She smiled archly. "Could you stop him pursuing me?"

"Nothing easier, Mrs. Barr. All you need do is leave a letter." Again the same bland delivery, her tone as soft as silk or a moth's wing; but all the time in the old woman's eyes was an almost inhuman coldness of penetration, as though she saw Theresa merely as a construction of flesh and bones, an object to be molded to her will, rather than an independent being. An expression inconceivable except in a woman who had spent many years alone harboring past resentments.

"And what would your ladyship have me write?" asked Theresa, still smiling.

"What he would least like to hear." Again the slight hint of movement at the corners of Lady Ardmore's lips. "What do you think that might be?"

"I'm better at charades than riddles, your ladyship," said Theresa, barely maintaining her pretense of humoring her. Her cheeks were burning as she formed a clear presentiment of what Lady Ardmore meant. "I don't think," she added caustically, "that he's ever likely to think *that* of me."

"He is not unaware of his brother's attractiveness to the sex, Mrs. Barr. I fail to see why such a lie would be so very terrible. You could claim to be fleeing from an impulse which would otherwise . . ." She paused and raised her ringed hands in an ambiguous gesture, suggesting that Theresa's profession should leave her well versed in the sort of lines to be written. "No blame need attach to Lord Ardmore if you claim all the odium for yourself."

With a twinge of fear, Theresa rose and glanced back apprehensively at Lady Ardmore. Impossible that she could suspect anything. Impossible, yet why that unfathomable assurance in her eyes?

As Theresa moved towards the door, Lady Ardmore murmured, "Another indisposition, Mrs. Barr?" She leaned forward in her chair with a suddenly contrite expression. "Please . . . you must forgive me. I never dreamed that I could shock a woman whose experience of life's vicissitudes must have . . ." She paused and looked rapidly at Theresa, as if frightened that she was still offending her. "You see what an innocent my lonely life has made me, always thinking people worse or better than they are, not knowing whether directness will seem indelicate, or a desire to help unpardonable interference. And now I've made an enemy of the one person I could least afford to offend." She broke off and got up awkwardly, dropping her cane and moving hesitantly towards Theresa with outstretched hands. "Don't make him hate me. Please don't do that. I ask nothing else." Her anxiety was so real in appearance that Theresa could hardly believe that, moments before, the same face had expressed sly mockery and domineering confidence.

"I shan't say anything," she said slowly, hearing her own voice with surprise, reassured by its normality. The fear she had felt seemed unreal now, as if she had been tricked by a skillful illusionist. All along she had had the power and had failed to see it. Or was this merely what she was intended to believe?

Looking at his brother's pale chiseled face in the lamplit dining room across the dead-sea surface of mahogany between them, Clinton tried to shake off the oppressive no man's land of consciousness which had engulfed him ever since he had left the stables. His brother's presence made him feel both guilt and anger. How could he be so complacent and spineless as to let the woman play with him? To save him from such obvious self-delusion would almost be a kindness. Yet neither flippancy nor false detachment removed Clinton's itch of shame.

When Esmond began to talk about the sale of Markenfield, Clinton welcomed the chance it offered him to escape his present dilemma and vent his resentment in another form. Yet as soon as Esmond had outlined the terms offered by the mortgagees, there was no pretense about Clinton's involvement.

"Five thousand pounds—only that?" he cried, bringing down a clenched fist on the table, making the glasses tinkle and ring.

Ignoring the violence of this gesture, Esmond fingered his watch chain and then picked up a cigar cutter. "Aren't you forgetting the balance payable on completion of the sale?" he asked mildly.

"I can't complete for three years, until the end of the lease. What the hell do I do in the meantime?"

Esmond shrugged his shoulders and chose a cigar from the box beside the decanter in front of him. "Make the best of the five thousand. Frankly, since the mortgagees won't press you to redeem any of the mortgages before completion, I think they're being remarkably helpful offering this sort of deposit so far in advance of gaining possession." Cutting the end from his cigar, Esmond leaned forward and lit it from the nearest candelabrum. Puffing slowly to make sure it burned evenly, he seemed entirely unconcerned. "I have to admit," he went on, "being rather puzzled by your surprise. The situation was perfectly clear before you turned down Miss Lucas."

"We never discussed selling Markenfield then. Of course I thought I'd get more on agreeing to a sale."

"I hope you're not blaming me for not warning you."

"Is that all you're worried about?" shouted Clinton. "The only point in selling the place is to give me enough money to survive on till the trust's wound up. I need three years. That money won't even cover mortgage interest for half that time. With my other expenses, the result's clear as day. I'll have to pledge every penny of my trust money to get by. *Then* where will I be in three years?"

Esmond watched the ascending coils of his cigar smoke and frowned. "How large a deposit did you think you'd get?"

"Ten thousand at least."

Esmond poured himself more port and sighed. "I'm very sorry. Of course you could talk to the mortgagees yourself, but I can't see anything coming of it." He paused and sucked thoughtfully at his cigar. "I know the idea won't appeal to you, but if you went cap in hand to your uncle, he might be prepared to help."

"We tried hard enough there when father died, and much good did it do us. My only long-term hope of solvency is inheriting from him. Do you think I'd jeopardize that to get through a few years? Better the debtors' prison than that."

"I have a feeling," murmured Esmond, "that Uncle Richard would hardly appreciate his heir——"

"So help me, Esmond," burst out Clinton, jumping to his feet, "if you don't make me a loan secured against the final balance on Markenfield, I'll wring every last farthing of arrears owing on this estate, and no power on earth can stop me."

"A Fenian bullet might when you start evicting."

Clinton sat down on the edge of the table and looked down at his brother with a mocking smile. "Shall I go to Mother now and tell her what I intend to do and why? Explain that I'm forced to make her life a misery because her sweet Esmond won't show me the same favor he'd grant to any mangy manufacturer with a wallet of dog-eared bills?"

Flicking some ash from the silk lapel of his evening coat, Esmond looked at him through half-closed eyes. "I'd never expected blackmail from you, Clinton."

"Surprises give life much of its relish."

"Oh yes," murmured Esmond, with a smile which Clinton did not like. "Apart from those threats of yours, can you think of a single reason why I should be willing to help you?"

Clinton looked at him candidly. "Because you enjoy having a financial hold over me."

"I think you flatter yourself," Esmond remarked coolly.

"Not at all. In your place I'd enjoy it too. I'd find it wonderfully satisfying to toss largesse to someone who began life with most of the advantages I thought should have belonged to me."

"Like throwing twigs to a drowning man?" asked Esmond, with straight-faced interest.

Clinton smiled wryly. "I'd hoped for something a little larger. I'm sure you'd agree, there's no more fun to be had from a man's struggles when he's gone down for the last time."

Esmond folded his arms and regarded his brother with the patient sufferance of a disappointed schoolmaster. "I intend to help you, Clinton—in spite of your insults. Not because I've the smallest desire to hold you under any obligation. You made your point very clearly this afternoon, and I don't mean to let you have any excuse for distressing Mother like that again. And frankly, as you're well aware, it wouldn't help my reputation in the City if you found your way into the Bankruptcy Commissioners' Court."

"May I ask what I can expect?"

"Indeed you may." Esmond inclined his head and then looked up abruptly. "Nothing . . . unless your expenditure remains at last year's level for the next six months. If it does, I'll accommodate you when the deposit's exhausted. Perhaps you'd like this in writing?"

"Your word will do very well, Esmond."

"You have it," replied Esmond curtly, leaning across the table to take his brother's hand.

Leaving the room, Clinton realized very clearly the price he would now have to pay for any indiscretion on Theresa's part. One thing was certain anyway—that little escapade would go no further. A kiss, he thought bitterly, only the touch of a woman's lips. Enough perhaps to turn an adolescent's head, but hardly a cause for much repining to a man of the world. But self-mockery did not salve his pride, or the stinging resentment he felt. The wisest course would be to leave without another word to her. A coward's exit: leaving her to think what she chose. He imagined himself penning a note begging her to forgive his ungentlemanly "insult," and to forget an incident he now deplored. To hell with that too. She deserved an honest explanation and would get one.

Alone in the dining room, Esmond imagined Clinton's amazement were he ever to guess the real reason why he was being forced to wait six months for a loan. The plain answer was that before then Esmond did not expect to have any disposable money. In recent months Esmond's difficulties with the Greek & Oriental Navigation Company had led him to investigate and reject a number of ways of breaking the trust. Then a sudden worsening in the shipping line's position had unexpectedly thrown up a straightforward solution.

Before ever contemplating trust breaking, Esmond had thought of advising the trustees to buy Greek & Oriental stock on Clinton's behalf. But at the time he had been doubtful whether such cautious men would agree to make a very large investment in a single company. Nothing short of £20,000 would make any appreciable difference to the shipping line's depleted reserves.

A few days before coming to Ireland, Esmond had at last accepted that the line's creditors would force the company to liquidate unless he publicly declared his support. Although understandably reluctant to guarantee the line's credit, Esmond had seen that this inescapable eventuality would at least give the trustees unlimited confidence in the Greek & Oriental. When they knew that his discount house was standing surety for the company, Esmond was certain that the trustees would finally overcome their prejudice against heavy investment in a single stock and would act on his advice to convert the greater part of Clinton's capital into Greek & Oriental shares. The company's problems would continue, but the purchase would provide two or three months' invaluable respite.

At the end of a harrowing day, Esmond found it satisfying to reflect that when Clinton got his loan, his own capital would have been largely responsible for his benefactor's ability to lend to him. If Clinton left Kilkreen feeling that he had achieved what he had set out to, Esmond had no intention of denying him that pleasant delusion.

CHAPTER TEN

 The following morning, wanting only to be done with his final interview with Theresa, Clinton was disappointed not to see her at breakfast. But he was comforted by the knowledge that Esmond and his mother would later be lunching at neighboring Killaloe Park.

Not really expecting to find Theresa alone yet, he looked into the morning room. Esmond and his mother were there. Unable to retreat quickly enough, Clinton was obliged to obey his mother's beckoning hand.

"We were talking about marriage," she announced firmly, as if to anticipate any argument.

Clinton nodded agreeably. "The one I didn't make?"

"Certainly not." Lady Ardmore eyed the door to see that it was closed. "I was thinking about Esmond."

"It's not a subject I care to discuss with Clinton," remarked Esmond, shifting in his chair.

"I second that," said Clinton, moving to the window and looking out at the heavy rain clouds. A few sparrows with puffed-out feathers were hopping on the wet terrace steps.

He heard his mother say calmly, "In some matters Clinton's views are worth listening to."

Esmond cast his eyes upward and turned to Clinton. "In spite of her experiences with Father, our dear mother still seems to believe that women need horsewhipping to make them amenable."

"They respect firmness." Lady Ardmore rapped on the floor with her cane. "Do stop staring out of the window, Clinton." He faced her with reluctance. "Well, would *you* think much of your chances with a woman who thought she could twist you round her little finger?"

"That would depend on whether she was right."

"Quite true," said Esmond. "The French have a saying: *On recule pour mieux sauter.*"

"Trust the French to be such fools," snorted his mother. "Start reculing and you may not be able to stop; that's my saying." She looked to Clinton for approval, but he merely shrugged his shoulders.

Esmond looked at him gratefully. "It's no good, Mother. Clinton's not a model of decisiveness either. Take the way he dithered over the Lucas girl."

"Stuff," said Lady Ardmore. "The girl did the dithering there —letting him blow hot and cold instead of telling him to clear off unless." She sniffed loudly and sat back more comfortably in her chair. "Anyway, I've just been reading about a far more resourceful lady. She married her footman, got bored with him, and sent him packing. A lesson to the Miss Lucases of this world."

"But how much did she have to settle on the footman?" asked Esmond, plainly relieved by the change of subject.

"Not a farthing. That's the whole point. Did either of you know it's against the law here for a Catholic priest to marry a couple if one of them's a Protestant?" Esmond shook his head. "I'm not surprised you don't. There can't be more than a handful of priests in the country who'd sanction a mixed marriage, whatever the law might say."

"But if she was a Protestant," asked Esmond, "How did she get a priest to do the necessary?"

"How do you think? By saying she was a Catholic of course."

"Did the footman sue when she turned him out?"

"Course he did. But when she told the court she'd been a Protestant all along, the judge ruled against the marriage."

"Must have been in the Dark Ages," Esmond laughed.

"Only twenty years ago." She turned to Clinton, who had taken no apparent interest in what had been said. "Perhaps you can tell us something more amusing, Clinton?"

"I don't think so."

Lady Ardmore smiled reflectively. "What about the time Sir John Markham found you in his wife's room?"

"Pure hearsay."

"Didn't you tell him you'd come to investigate a smell of burning?"

"I may have done."

"I heard you left the following day."

Clinton looked back from the doorway. "I'd meant to. Just as I mean to leave here tomorrow—or maybe sooner. All good things come to an end." He bowed respectfully to her and left the room.

Shortly after eleven o'clock, with his mother and Esmond safely on their way to Killaloe, Clinton sent a maid to tell Miss Simmonds that Lord Ardmore wished to see her in the cedar drawing room.

As Theresa came in, he noticed with a familiar sinking of the heart that, even in the brief interval since he had last seen her, she seemed changed to him. A difference in the light, he told himself without conviction, knowing the sensation too well to be deceived. Wasn't it always like this? The nervous comparison of an ideal image with a real face? Her look was lightly challenging; the initiative was all his. Moments before, he had known quite clearly what he would say, but already simply by her presence the context had shifted.

"Because I leave tomorrow," he began awkwardly, "I had to see you to say how much I regret—"

"What do you regret?" she asked, scarcely above a whisper.

"My weakness."

"For encouraging a poor innocent and then overwhelming her with passion? How I struggled to save my virtue."

"Most women's virtue comes down to cowardice or self-interest in the end."

"A consoling thought for all rejected men," she replied, unsmiling.

"It's easy to make fun of a man who's trying to be serious. What you choose to see as cynicism I intended as a compliment."

She shivered slightly and hugged her astrakhan mantle more tightly round her. "Your mother should warn her guests to bring a sack of coal with them." She smiled. "I never want to see or smell another peat fire again. Do they have coal fires at your barracks?"

He moved towards her, his handsome face drawn and miserable. "Was it so little to you?" he murmured. "Why are you acting with me?"

"The best performances are often given to an audience of one."

"Tell me why you're so angry?"

She tossed back her hair and looked at him with sadness devoid of all pretense. "Because I know what you're going to say."

"Tell me."

She walked across to the fireplace and picked up a poker which she tucked under her arm like a cutting whip; then, leaning back against the mantelpiece like some languid youth, she looked at him with a parody of male complacency. "Great personal respect . . . in any other circumstances goes without saying . . . but family considerations . . . heat of the moment, don't you know, acted like a perfect bloody fool . . . damned attractive woman, no denying it, pretty as a picture . . . no intention of raising false hopes . . . but no hard feelings eh? Better cut now instead of hurting anybody later. Damn near breaks my heart—or what's left of it. Never forget you . . . treasured memory."

She broke off, dropped the poker on the carpet, and resumed not in her stage parody of a silly-ass cavalry officer, but in her ordinary voice. "Then exit both in opposite directions, with consciences as clear as summer skies."

After a long silence he said stiffly, "I'm afraid I was vain enough to think that you cared a little for me."

She shrugged her shoulders. "It must be a great relief to find yourself mistaken." For a few seconds she endured his reproachful eyes, then burst out: "Would it please you better if I wept . . . said we were cowards? That we'd spend our lives regretting what wouldn't come again?"

"Yes," he murmured at last, "I would like that better."

Thinking him about to embrace her, the memory of their first kiss burned Theresa like a great thirst. She held out her hands to him, but he paced restlessly to the window.

"This house . . . it's like being at the bottom of a river."

"Let's leave it for a while."

He took her arm eagerly. "There's a trap in the stables. Let's hope the wheels stay on.

Hurrying after him, Theresa no longer even remembered the resolution she had so lamentably failed to carry through.

Sitting perched next to Theresa in the high two-wheeler with the reins in his hands, Clinton relished their aloneness. The bare hills by their very isolation seemed to bring them closer, their smallness shared under the gray immensity of the sky. His eyes strayed from the curve of her cheek to a fold in the hills that repeated it, from the red ribbon of her hat to the scarlet rose hips in the hedges.

Through the sleeve of her coat, he could feel the shape of her arm linked through his; and there, resting just above his wrist, was her neat chamois leather glove. He stared with resigned astonishment at this very ordinary glove, as if unable to understand how it came to be placed on his arm, and then put his own hand over it. Again and again in her company he had an uncanny sense of the suspension of normal time and logic, as though he had arrived at a point ahead of where he expected to be.

She smiled at him and said, " 'If from a glove you take the letter G,/Then glove is love, and that I send to thee.' "

He laughed. "Am I supposed to reply in verse?"

"Heavens no. A few months ago I was sent a glove with that message—by an elderly man called Page who used to drive me mad by coming to watch me every night in the same box. Poor man. 'If from Page you take the letter P,/Then page is age, and that won't do for me.' "

"You sent him that?"

"Of course. Wouldn't you if you'd thought of it?"

"Who wouldn't?"

"I sent the glove back too. I never keep anything, though with rings it's tempting. I once had one that came with a note saying that if I wore it on my right hand during the first act, the sender would know that I'd meet him afterwards."

"So you wore it on the left?"

"I changed it from hand to hand." She looked across the fields at some cows sheltering from the wind under the lee of a leafless hedge. "I can't think why I told you that. I'm usually very kind. Pure nervousness."

"You nervous?"

"If you only knew," she murmured, her words barely audible above the creak of the springs and the thud of the horse's hoofs.

Had they not at that moment been approaching a man and a woman carrying bundles of hay on their backs, he would have stopped the trap and kissed her. Then a little later they passed a girl driving a dozen or so geese ahead of her towards the town of Clonmore.

"Must be market day," said Clinton as they came up with more people on the road: an old woman with a single pig and a barefooted boy driving two heifers.

"Could we go there?" she asked.

"It's not much of a place."

But her eagerness overcame his slight misgivings. There had been few reports of trouble in this part of Mayo.

At first when they reached the small town, Clinton was glad that they had come. Fairs, markets, and local races were the only diversions which brought a little life to places usually devoid of any interest. By the statue of O'Connell, a juggler was performing, varying his act by breaking stones against his chest. Men stood in groups outside the doors of spirits and grocery shops, talking, laughing, arguing. In a number of pens in the center of the square, sheep and cows were being bought and sold, the farmers prodding them with sticks and haggling with each other. The wind was thick with tobacco smoke and the smell of fresh dung. All around the edges of the square were carts and donkeys.

They left the horse and trap with a boy outside the one hotel in the town and then set out on foot to look around. Very soon

Theresa was disconcerted by the covert looks directed at them: a mixture of curiosity, deference, and hostility. Though she was sure that Clinton was perfectly aware of these eddies of resentment, he seemed utterly indifferent to them, talking to her as unconcernedly as if they were walking down Bond Street or St. James's. Though Clinton was wearing an old riding coat, its cut, and the sheen on his top boots, as well as the clearness of his complexion, made him look like a man from another planet among this crowd of weather-worn faces and coats of frieze and corduroy. As though describing the habits of Africans, Clinton told her why the people sold their calves early instead of keeping them through the winter to get a better price in the spring. Because of the number of their own children, they often could not afford to spare enough milk to feed the new calves. He showed her blocks of the coarse bread made with Indian corn which they ate until the new crop of potatoes, and pointed out some women buying this corn in exchange for eggs.

"But why," she asked, "don't they eat the eggs themselves?"

"For a week's supply of eggs, they can buy enough corn to last three."

"How awful," she murmured, "not to be able to eat their own eggs."

"They should grow more corn," he replied with a brusqueness that shocked her a little, but then she was unaware that, since reaching the center of the square, Clinton had sensed that they were being shadowed. Neither wanting to scare Theresa, nor let anyone else know he was alarmed, he assumed an air of indifference. But he stopped deliberately at the corn merchant's window to be able to look back as if unsuspecting; and then he was no longer in any doubt. One of the men, as he had at first guessed, was McMahon; and from the way his companions were walking, it was clear that they were drunk. To avenge his recent loss of face, McMahon would very likely have been spreading rumors about a new campaign of evictions.

Being reasonably sure that McMahon and his cronies were still the only people in the square to know his identity, Clinton was determined to leave before they shared their knowledge with many others. To get back to the trap without being seen would involve doubling behind the stalls on the far side of the square and running; and though this might take McMahon by surprise, it would undoubtedly attract other attention. Without telling Theresa that anything was wrong, Clinton suggested that they should be getting back. Then taking her by the arm, he walked straight towards the small group of pursuers.

With a few yards dividing them, McMahon suddenly knelt down and shouted, "Down on your knees, boys, when his lordship passes."

Without turning his head to see whether the rest had followed McMahon's inflammatory example, Clinton walked past, tightening his hold on Theresa's arm.

"Who are these men?" she asked shakily.

"Keep walking" was all he said.

No effort was made to stop their reaching the trap, but when they were both seated in the vehicle, Clinton saw that McMahon and a dozen others stood spread out in a semicircle some ten yards away. With a shout to Theresa to get behind the dashboard, Clinton brought down his whip and launched the trap at the waiting men. As one jumped forward to seize the bridle, Clinton lashed out with the whip. Theresa screamed as she saw the plaited leather curl round the man's bare arm tearing away the skin. She hid her face and a second later heard another sharp crack and a roar of pain. The light carriage was swaying and jolting terrifyingly, and she was deafened by angry shouts. A stone struck the tailboard and another crashed against the back of the box, but when she raised her head she could see across the horse's haunches that the way was clear. A few people scattered, dropping baskets and packages, but Clinton did nothing to slacken the horse's pace. Dazed with shock and bruised where she had beeen flung against the dashboard, Theresa was amazed to hear Clinton laughing.

When they were clear of the streets, she turned on him furiously. "You're mad. We might have been killed."

"Nothing of the sort," he replied, checking the horse's pace to a brisk trot. "We might have been knocked about a bit if we'd stayed."

"You treated them like animals."

"You think I should have tried gentle persuasion?"

"Yes," she cried, "I do."

"The discussion might have been rather one-sided."

Again he was smiling, more with relief than amusement, but Theresa was in no mood to draw distinctions. "What if you'd blinded one of them? Or crushed a man under the wheels?"

He tried to take her hand, but she pulled it away. He said softly, "The one who knelt down—remember him? He tried to shoot me the day I went to—"

"Shoot you?" she stammered. "You never as much as . . ." She broke off in confusion. "He should be arrested."

"And tried at the next assizes?" asked Clinton with a wry smile. "On my evidence alone? Imagine my mother's joy. If most of her tenants weren't Fenians when the trial started, they would be by the time it finished."

After a silence she said in a low unhappy voice. "He might try again."

"Not a chance. I made a mull of things and he lost his head."

"And just now?"

"Drunken bravado. Imagine you'd been humiliated, and suddenly out of the blue comes the man who did it to you. You're with some friends so you put on a show." He sighed and twisted the reins in his hands. "I was mad to have agreed to go there. People come twenty miles to a market, and McMahon lives just over the hill. I wasn't thinking."

His sudden contrition dismayed her; in all probability his speed of reaction had saved them from a gruesome ordeal, but far from thanking him or showing any relief at their escape, she had made him regret the whole expedition, turning what might have been the bond of a shared adventure into cause for dissension and reproach. A bank of low dark cloud was sweeping in from the west, submerging the whole landscape in shadow. The shrill cry of the redshank overhead and the sound of the wind in the thin-leaved poplars filled her with sadness. She felt that if they were to speak to each other now, it would merely be for something to say: courtesies exchanged between strangers. He would return to his barracks and his men, and she to her old life, with or without Esmond. Perhaps all the time she had been reaching for something beyond her: happiness, that old delusion, forever slipping away into the blue distance. She thought of the flippant anecdotes she had told him before they went to Clonmore. Small wonder if he thought her an empty flirtatious woman. She wished she had told him about her childhood, her marriage, anything but what she had said.

A little later when it started to rain, she was surprised that he took the trouble to cover her with a rug. The drops were at first isolated, driven hard by the gusting wind, but soon settling into a downpour of dense slanting rain that made the road ahead glisten and raised clouds of steam from the panting horse's back. They drove on another half-mile till Clinton saw some farm buildings and swung the trap into the muddy yard. He jumped down and banged on the door of the cabin, intending to ask if they could shelter there till the rain slackened. Getting no answer, he tried the door, which proved to be locked. Leaving the horse under the partial shelter of an oak, he ran with Theresa to the nearest barn. As they entered, some hens ran squawking past them out into the sheeting rain. Inside it was dark and smelled of hay and dung. Theresa could hear the rain trickling through the thatch; outside it came down with a steady hissing sound, forming large puddles in the yard. She was cold from the tips of her fingers to the pit of her stomach. His silence made her want to scream; it might rain for hours, and all that time would she have to endure this silence?

He was leaning against the wall of the barn with his hands on his hips and a lock of wet hair across his forehead, a picture of debonair insouciance, but young, so young in the pale white light that slanted through the long opening between the barn doors. To a girl of twenty he would seem perfect in his maturity. Looking at him, Theresa found it hard to believe that he had lashed out savagely with his whip so short a time before.

When she had resigned herself to his absorbed contemplation of the rain, he turned to her sadly. "Was it because I laughed? Did that make you angry?"

"Laughed?" she asked, not understanding him at all. Amazed by a submissive note in his voice.

"Laughed when we'd driven through those fools. You

thought me brutal. Don't you ever laugh without knowing why? Hadn't we got away? And their faces—didn't you see them? The way one of them crossed himself as if he'd seen the devil." Her silence baffled him.

"In China," he said harshly, "they tied our hands together with wetted cords which tightened as they dried—stopping the flow of blood, making fingers split and blacken. When they searched me, they didn't take my signet ring. My jailer saw it and wanted it, but my fingers were too swollen. He cut off my cords to restore the circulation and rubbed my fingers till he could get the thing off. That's why I'm here; the rest in that cell got gangrene in their hands. Weeks later I laughed about that."

"I was never angry," she murmured.

"Then why treat me like this?" he shouted. "Could I help what happened? If you answer me with clever words and lowered lids . . . Instead you look at me with amazement. What do you feel, if you feel at all?" He came towards her and roughly took her hand, forcing open the fingers and placing her palm under his coat against the heart. The fast thumping beat made her feel faint. When he kissed her on the lips, her body seemed to become as flowing and amenable as rain. He tipped back her hat where the brim got in his way, and kissed her again with soft light kisses on her eyelids, cheeks, and throat, as though to verify what he had seen with his eyes. Feeling his arms tighten around her shoulders, she let her head tilt back with a shuddering sigh. Her lips resisted a little until his tongue parted them. Her mouth imperceptibly molded itself to his, spreading through her whole body a voluptuous glow of pleasure—docile at first, but soon sharpening to desire, catching her breath, drawing her fingers to his hair and neck; and all the time their bodies were pressing harder together. His hands moved to her breasts and then round her waist, seeking to unlace her bodice, which she did for him, shivering at the cold damp air.

Lying beside him on the damp hay, kissing again while his hands searched under her clothes, she helped him, lifting her skirts, not caring what was torn under them. He had loosened his trousers and she could see his erect member and his flat stomach as he leaned across her to place his coat under her head; she touched it with her cold hands as he parted her thighs; his hands were icy too against her skin, but desire made her shiver more than any cold. A frenzied longing swept her: to possess and be possessed. As he entered her, she cared only for the wonder of that moment when she felt him moving in her; his face was buried in her neck, yet she seemed to see him standing aloofly against the barn wall as the first sharp cries of pleasure broke from her.

"Kiss me, my love. Kiss me," she moaned, pulling his face to her, as he thrust for the last time, gripping her hips, and then slipping down on an elbow at her side, breathing hard, pressing her to him. And still it rained, but more softly now, the sky a pale white through the doors, spreading its light in wan rays like a gentle fan.

As they drove back to Kilkreen across the wet countryside, torn rags of blue appeared in the pewter sky. The sun shone briefly as they passed a roofless hovel with one of its walls burnt black where the hearth had been. The horse's hoofs threw up lumps of mud that thudded heavily against the dashboard. Though Clinton's arm was round her waist, she sensed his apprehension.

"I expected nothing from you," she said gently. "Nothing afterwards." She felt his arm tighten round her.

"But I want you to. I want that very much," he replied without moving his eyes from the road ahead.

"Want me to?"

"Want you to know I'll suffer when I leave here." On his face the same brooding unhappiness.

"Are you ashamed?" she asked hesitantly. "Because if you'd thought me a lady . . . ?"

"I loved a baronet's wife. We didn't hold hands together when we were alone. I'd be ashamed to compromise an unmarried girl. But what's that to us?" He studied the handle of his whip. "If you leave Esmond because of me, I'll make what restitution I can."

"I didn't mean that," she cried. "I didn't want you to feel guilt. That was all. You owe me no obligation."

"If you love me, how can you say that?"

"Esmond loves me, and see how I treat that obligation." She looked at him beseechingly. "Don't speak of obligations—*your* duties to *my* love. What about *my* duties? *Your* love?"

"What should I do to prove it? Esmond can ruin me. Isn't that enough?"

"Say it to me. I want no other proof."

"I love you," he murmured, "want you with me, want you . . ." Pulling on the reins, he stopped the trap and kissed her fiercely, pressing his palms against her cheeks.

"Dear God," she moaned, breathing heavily as they parted. "You tell me this and you're going."

"There's no help for it."

"Would they shoot you if you stayed away a few days more? Would your men die of grief?"

"Do you think I'd stay to see you with him? I couldn't."

"Not one more day?"

"If there was some woman with me, would you say the same?"

She shook her head and looked down at the rain-flattened grass by the roadside. "What can I do?"

"Love me. Be patient. My regiment moves to Dublin in two months. I'll take a house there."

"Don't promise anything—not yet." She felt that if she let herself go in the least, she would cry.

"You might change your mind?" he asked tensely.

"Me do that? Me? You fool, Lord Ardmore." She smiled. "Do you know, I've only ever called you that?"

When they swung into the stableyard, Corporal Harris came out from the harness room and helped them down from the trap. In his master's presence he was quiet and unobtrusive. But Theresa blushed crimson when the servant whispered something to Clinton, who, soon afterwards, brushed some wisps of hay from her dress.

Walking back to the house she said quietly, "Is it one of his regular duties to notice such things?"

The face Clinton turned to her was so anguished that she could only stammer incoherent words before tears choked her. He drew her to him gently, and held her a little before they left the shadow of the paddock hedge and walked on in silence across the open lawn.

When Theresa had changed out of her wet clothes, she rang for a maid and told her to bring a tray to her room. Eating the unappetizing cold collation that eventually arrived, she remembered that it was the governess's afternoon off and that Louise would therefore be spending the rest of the day with her. By the time the child came to her room, it was raining again, and so Theresa suggested playing consequences or forfeits.

Louise looked doubtful. "There's no point when you always let me win."

"What about riddles? You're better at them than me."

"Only because Miss Lane's got a book."

"Try me."

Louise sat down heavily and shrugged. "How do I get myself through a keyhole?" Theresa thought for a few seconds and then shook her head. "By writing 'myself' on a piece of paper and pushing it through. Silly, isn't it?"

"I think it's ingenious."

"The trouble is," said Louise with a frown, "you either know them or you don't." She stared gloomily at the rain-streaked window. "I think it's awful here. I wish we could go home."

The weight of affection she gave the word made Theresa blanch. She had often been acutely concerned about Louise's attachment to the trappings of their life with Esmond, but never with the distress she now felt. She noticed how closely Louise was watching her.

"Why did you go out with Lord Ardmore?"

"Because he asked me to."

"You didn't have to."

"It would have been rather rude to refuse."

Louise thought about this with narrowed eyes. Her thin face was unusually pale and angular in the gray light. She looked up abruptly. "Did he tell you the secret?"

"The secret?"

"Why Esmond doesn't like him, of course. I know he doesn't, so don't pretend."

"He didn't mention Esmond."

"But you must think Esmond's in the wrong."

"Why on earth should I?" asked Theresa, confused by Louise's insistent tone.

"Because if you thought he was right, you wouldn't have gone out this morning." Louise's voice had become increasingly shrill and impatient.

"But darling," murmured Theresa gently, "why are you so upset?" She took Louise's hand. "It can't possibly affect you."

"We live with Esmond," said Louise in a small shocked voice. "Both of us. We ought to side with him. If you love people you ought to take their part."

"But that doesn't mean pushing one's way into their private quarrels."

"And it doesn't mean going out with people they don't like. You know it doesn't."

Theresa did not know what to say as Louise stared at the floor in accusing silence.

At last Louise said quietly, "I don't believe you love him any more."

Suddenly Theresa knew that she was not going to lie. To girls of Louise's age, love or its absence explained every otherwise inexplicable contradiction in adult behavior.

"I did think I loved him. And I'm still fond of him."

Louise was staring at her with sympathy and disbelief. "But couldn't you tell—about loving him? I know who I love. Why don't you know? It's easy."

"I wish it was," said Theresa after a long silence.

Louise seemed disillusioned rather than hostile. "It must be awful to be grown-up—not to know things like that. To live years and years with parents, loving them, then to meet a man and not know, and afterwards be with him all the time, even at night. I'll never live with a man or marry."

With a shiver of recognition as vivid as a personal memory, Theresa knew what she meant. The sense of being on show during the day, and needing to escape at the end of it to restore oneself. And Theresa remembered too being terrified by the thought that the whole of one's past could be swallowed up by a wrong decision over some unknown man.

"Are you going to tell Esmond?" asked Louise fearfully.

"I think I'll have to."

"Will he be angry?"

"And sad. . . . I expect more sad."

"I'd be angry," Louise replied firmly. "Will we have to live somewhere else?"

"Will that be awful?"

"How do I know?" She bowed her head. "I knew it really—knew we'd have to leave someday, ever since Grandpa told me you hadn't accepted."

Louise's pinched and worried face made Theresa's eyes sting. She remembered her as a small child, delighted by stage jewelry, fussed over by actresses and stagehands, always contented and trusting. And where was that trust now? The child swung her feet to the ground and strolled across to examine a porcelain bowl on the console table behind her mother's chair, almost, thought Theresa, as if she had become bored with emotional concerns.

With a glance at the clock, Louise said calmly, "Perhaps we ought to play somthing."

"What would you like?"

"The Grand Mufti," replied Louise after a short pause. "I'll play if I can be the Mufti. And you must stand on a chair, like we used to do it."

"Must I?" murmured Theresa, not feeling at all like a game, least of all the one suggested. But when Louise insisted, she got on a chair; and when the Grand Mufti told her to put her hands on her head, to stand on one foot, to squint, and do other ridiculous things, Theresa finally laughed and lost the game, as the Grand Mufti's victims invariably did. Louise looked at her sternly one moment longer, and then, when Theresa did not at all expect it, flung her arms around her.

CHAPTER ELEVEN

Not long after Louise left her, Theresa was plagued with a shivering nervousness. In a little while she would have to dine at the same table as Clinton and show him no more than the bland politeness of an acquaintance. The thought of betraying herself made her heart beat wildly. Later, she lit the candles on the dressing table with a spill from the fire and sat down in front of the mirror to brush her hair. The glass was very old and spotted under its dull silvery surface with small brown and gray marks, making her face seem blurred and misty. Only her eyes, liquid and shining in the candlelight, gave her an illusion of depth and clarity. To be in love, she thought, is to see oneself as another sees one and to value only his distorted and ideal image. She moved the candles closer to the glass and leaned forward.

When she dressed for dinner, she chose one of her plainest evening gowns, not through penitence or a desire to look chaste but because her mood demanded it. In front of Esmond, she could not dress herself to attract admiration. The thought of seeing both brothers together scared her.

Just as in the theater she could blind herself to the faces in the pit beyond the footlights, at dinner that evening, facing Clinton, Theresa managed to create a sense of distance. In the drawing room earlier, Esmond had been arguing with Clinton about success and ambition, and now he returned to the task, confidently telling Theresa that, in spite of Clinton's claims, the army was like any other profession.

"Success is the only justification. To win battles, win esteem . . . In the end it's not the thing itself that counts but what others think of the result."

"Do you agree, Miss Simmonds?" asked Clinton.

"I'm not a soldier, my lord."

"But you do battle with your audiences."

"They must be wooed, not crushed."

"Quite so," murmured Clinton. "And wooing can take many forms." How confident he is in me, she thought with pride. "You can delight them by bad acting just as you can by good. The applause may be the same, but it won't please you unless you've pleased yourself."

"So?" asked Esmond.

"So you're wrong." Clinton laughed. "The performance matters more than what people think of it. The thing itself is more important than success."

"We weren't talking about the theater," said Esmond, concealing his irritation.

"It's the same with a cavalry action. Skill's always more satisfying than brute force." He smiled at Theresa with a hint of apology. "I fear soldiers always seem purely concerned with results, but battles are really more often won by numbers frightened than numbers killed. The good commander masks his intentions till the last moment, does everything he can to confuse the enemy, moves men here and there, uses the ground to advantage. The enemy must expect duplicity even when he moves in earnest. A feint and an unexpected wheel can force a squadron to change direction before coming to the charge—leaving gaps in his formation as wide as streets. He's beaten before a blow's been struck."

Esmond waited impatiently for the footman to remove plates and bring in others.

"That's only saying that the best means to an end succeed best and are praised most. Of course you employ them to get your result. But success is still the only justification."

"I admire intentions as well as achievements," replied Clinton mildly. "There's nothing shameful about failing against the odds. Failure can be an inspiration."

"To romantics and children."

"If they're the only ones who can do a thing for its own sake, I'll take that as a compliment," replied Clinton.

In the silence that followed, Theresa thought how extraordinary Esmond was to risk appearing odious simply in order to force Clinton into agreement with an idea that he disliked, like putting out one's own eye in order to do the same to an adversary.

When dessert came, Lady Ardmore insisted that Theresa should tell them some theatrical anecdotes. So reluctantly she trotted out tales of pistols that had not gone off when expected, vital letters not placed in pockets where they should have been, and price tags not removed from the new shoes of a stage corpse. She did not mention the bitchery of lines ruined by unscripted business or cues deliberately mistimed. She herself had once switched round Lady Sneerwell's words at the beginning of *The School for Scandal*, changing "Have you inserted those paragraphs, Mr. Snake?" to "Have you inserted those snakes, Mr. Paragraph?" causing the hapless actor to reply with a speech from another play. On numerous occasions she had experienced just such changes put in almost as a game: a test of composure.

As the meal had progressed she had allowed herself to look at Clinton more often, no longer scared of doing so, once she realized how enviably at ease he was. The thought that he would have learned this equanimity from past deceptions did not hurt her. Tomorrow his seat would be empty, tomorrow he was going. This thought alone absorbed her, so that with every casual glance she tried to store up a little more of him against the coming months. Of all love's many pains, the ache of absence was the simplest and most complete. He was with me; he has gone. At that moment she thought herself ready to stoop to any deceit or falsehood that might make him stay.

Shortly after eleven, Theresa was sitting by the fire in her room talking to Esmond, trying to make him understand by indirect hints that she wanted him to go to his own room, but, in spite of all her efforts, he remained impervious. The absorbed patient way he was looking at her told her more clearly than words that he was determined to make love to her. His legs were crossed, and she noticed the little jerks of his raised foot registering the faster beating of his heart. A slight chill passed through her limbs as she thought of his smooth hands touching her as cautiously as they might some rare and fragile ornament. She knew that she had made his love anxious and possessive by her reserve, and that their lovemaking was vital to him now as proof of her affection.

His absolute immobility, except for the little rhythmic movements of his foot, filled her with apprehension. Sitting there in his black dress coat, the circle of lamplight defining his profile in cameo, he looked distinguished, self-possessed. Yet she knew that a word from her could melt that pale ascetic face to tenderness or misery. Her eyes had become fixed on the prominent veins on the back of his hands. Ashamed of her revulsion, she could not master it. Guilt sharpened her distress. She could no more explain the power of her attraction to Clinton than she could justify it. The suddenness of her involvement had scarcely given her opportunity to guess how she would behave with Esmond. With mounting panic, she realized that she could not endure it if he touched her.

The burning peat hissed gently in the hearth; from the landing came the low ticking of a grandfather clock. At the creak of a board, she turned and saw him rise. Even before he moved, he seemed to thrust his face and his eyes forward at her. She jumped up, knocking over a pole screen as she moved behind the table where the lamp stood. He looked at her with surprise and dismay; probably he had thought the silence restful, a token of their harmony.

"It was getting low—the wick," she said rapidly, lifting the porcelain globe, and then replacing it in confusion. The wick was adjusted by turning a wide screw easily accessible without touching either globe or chimney.

"I know you want me to go," he said quietly, placing the tips of his fingers on the table. "Do you wonder why I don't, when you make yourself so clear?" His eyes were sad, but a curious twisted smile curled his lips. "You see I never really expected you to love me; I never saw why you should. I only asked to be allowed to love you. To be with you and love you." He leaned over the lamp, casting a long shadow on the ceiling. "What must I do to regain that privilege?"

The pain in his voice was like acid to her. His words had shocked her and she had lost the sense of them.

"I can't help it," she murmured.

"What can't you help?" He sounded suddenly hopeful. "If I knew what you wanted me to be, if you told me that . . ."

"It's what you are," she cried, appalled by his humility, frightened that he was about to go down on his knees.

Instead he turned away and stood with his head bowed. "You think you're so different from everybody else. Like children do. Won't you ever learn how much alike we all are? You expect the impossible from people."

"I do. I know it," she agreed with shrill vehemence, seeing the surprise on his face turn to suspicion.

"No," he shouted. "You think it an excuse—what I said. I'm worthless, so I say everybody else is too, to make myself feel better. That's what you think."

"I don't care," she moaned. "That's all. You could be a genius or a block of wood, and I still wouldn't care."

"But you came here," he said doggedly, as though he had not heard what she had said but only her strident way of saying it. He seemed to take her anger as a sign of hope. While he could make her angry, she could not be indifferent to him. She knew from her experience of past quarrels that he had already passed the point where indignity could hurt him. So often he had used his humility as a weapon to make her surrender to him. To-night she could not give in. She sensed he knew this from a glint of hard opposition in his eyes, an expression that scared her.

The same look was there as he came towards her with outstretched arms, forcing her back against the heavy oak wardrobe beside the bed.

"Please," she implored as he bent over her so close that she could feel his breath on her cheek. She swayed back, face averted, hearing him murmur endearments, knowing her resistance was inflaming him further, but unable willingly to let him touch her, fighting an impulse to hit out with her hands, to scratch and tear. Just bodies—nothing more. Nothing, nothing. But when he kissed her mouth, she started to sob, though no tears came and only a stifled sound came from her throat.

He backed away, his face deathly pale and his hands trembling. "Why? Tell me why," he said with the choked restraint of a man frightened to release the pent-up flood of his inner rage. She leaned against the wardrobe without answering. How could he look at her so steadily without even blinking? "Tell me," he insisted, his voice no more than a rasping whisper.

"It's me . . . my fault. Not yours."

"Fault?" he snapped, pouncing on the word.

She hung her head, feeling a sickness like vertigo on the brink of a precipice; she both dreaded and longed for the relief of jumping.

"Do you love him?" he asked softly. "Love Clinton?" Again she sensed the effort of his restraint; he had breathed the words with the careful delicacy of a woman threading a needle.

"Can everything only be explained like that? A crumpled letter, furtive infidelity, the shadow of another man?" Her derision rang true, but she was sure he would only accept a direct denial, and she dreaded uttering that simple lie. She dreaded it without knowing why. "Have I the right to ask why you suspect me?" she asked sharply.

"Just now . . . the way you treated me."

"Is that all?"

"My mother," he said reluctantly. "She thought—"

"I shouldn't rely too much on what Lady Ardmore thinks."

"What do you mean?" he asked with an edge of anger that immediately made her regret what she had said. But now it was too late to retract.

"She wanted me to pretend to be captivated. The best way to cure you—that's what she said. I don't expect you to believe it."

Indeed the disbelief on his face was so total that she at once saw the futility of trying to convince him. Already she had dangerously increased his suspicions.

He walked into the deep shadows by the window. "You drove with him today," he said in a dry ironic voice.

"Certainly."

"My mother's maid said you came back without your hat."

"And what about my shoes?" she asked with a forced laugh.

"Without your hat," he repeated coldly.

"It blew off," she said lightly, knowing it must have been left in the barn.

"You didn't stop to pick it up?"

His persistent logic enraged and frightened her. He was watching her, and she could think of no answer. Where he was standing she could not see his face.

"You're being absurd, Esmond."

"As absurd as not retrieving a perfectly good hat?"

"We went to Clonmore," she replied, thinking quickly. "Some people jostled us; it was knocked off. We couldn't go back for it."

He came closer and she saw the same twisted little smile that had already disconcerted her. "You said it blew off. Now it's been knocked off."

"Your brother didn't want me to say that we went to Clonmore. He thought you'd blame him for not anticipating trouble."

"You're very eager to protect him."

"Is a trivial lie so terrible if it stops a stupid quarrel between you?"

She knew by his silence that she had come through unscathed; but as he moved slowly to the fire and leaned against the mantelpiece with his back to her, she felt remorse rather than relief. When he turned, she thought she saw a gleam of moisture on his cheeks.

After a long silence he looked at her. "Jealousy's like madness," he murmured. "At night I sometimes dream you're with other men, saying what you once said to me—the very words." He came closer, and now she could see the tears. "You have to be in love to see betrayal everywhere, to find treachery in any harmless lie. Forgive me."

"There's nothing to forgive."

To see him so bowed down and despairing was agony to her,

but she knew that if she tried to comfort him, he would kiss her again. His bent shoulders and desolate face made her feel a murderess. What had she done to the confident wordly man she remembered? The driving purpose of his work, the order of his life—all shattered by his infatuation.

Suddenly her knees were shaking, but not because of guilt or any distant fears. The idea had come to her with the clarity of a match flaring in a darkened room. Only if I make him hate me, only then, she thought, will he survive my going. All her sensations were concentrated to a single needlepoint of fear, not for what he might do to her, but in case she lacked the courage.

"Esmond," she whispered at last, "Esmond, I do love him."

So very long before he moved, long enough to see in isolation the glow of the fire, a blue vase in a recess, the seals on his watch chain, to hear her heart hammering like a tight fist in her chest.

"And him, does he love you?" He was not looking at her, his eyes deliberately passing her, fixed somewhere beyond her; his voice had pitched on a single note.

"No, he doesn't love me."

"You told him you loved him?" he asked with a ghastly calmness, as though the shock had killed all feeling in him.

"I let him understand it. He told me never to speak of it again. Told me you could ruin him, said I was—"

He cried out suddenly with incoherent pain—the sound a man might make when a tooth is violently drawn. She watched him, fascinated and afraid. Because he had held his eyes so long averted, his direct gaze shocked her. As he came at her, her throat made a small sound, the ghost of a scream, which died before his hand flashed across her mouth, knocking her back against the bed. She lifted a hand to her lips and felt the warm moisture.

He was looking down at her, his face darkened by the blood rising in it. "Is this how you repay me?" he shouted. "You'd like his kisses, would you? Like him undressing you?"

He reached down and tore her dress violently so that it parted at the neck, ripping off the tiny cloth-covered buttons down the front, exposing her chemise. "Like him on you, you whore? I wasn't enough." Again he was tearing at her clothes, as if his words had excited him, clutching at the staylaces, tugging till they broke, indifferent to any pain he caused her.

Numbed with shock, she struggled a little, but knowing herself helpless, let him go on undressing her, driven on by his frenzy to break and humiliate her. A curious ease, almost like the coming of unconsciousness, clouded her mind, though she was trembling uncontrollably. He stood still for a moment as though mesmerized by the sight of her naked skin and the dark cloud between her thighs. With an abrupt movement he pulled her forward so she was sitting on the edge of the bed, and then threw her back, forcing her legs apart. Loosening his trousers, he pulled out his penis, as stiff as the shaft of a broom. Still standing, he forced himself into her, leaning forward a little, supporting himself with extended arms on the bed. Hardly touching her except at the loins, he gazed down with desire and revulsion, his hips bumping against her with each pumping thrust, until a deep spasm seemed to shake him, and with a low shuddering groan he let himself down on her, sobbing as his orgasm broke.

He lay motionless, face downward on the bed, long after she had dragged herself from under him. With a coat pulled round her and a candle in her hand, she left the room and moved purposefully along the corridor towards Lady Ardmore's door.

Esmond blundered across the lawn and stumbled into a clump of laurels as he searched for the steps leading down to the lower terrace. The damp had already penetrated his thin patent leather shoes, and without either a cape or overcoat he was shivering with cold. But anything was better than staying in the house, and when he tripped or knocked his shins against an unexpected object, he was almost grateful for the pain.

Before leaving the house, he had drunk four glasses of brandy. Trees and bushes seemed to swim out of the dim distance, looming suddenly when a gash in the soot black clouds revealed the moon. For brief moments a bit of moss-grown wall, a strangely shaped holly bush, or a skeletal tree would take on a fantastic shape in the fitful light.

By the great dark trunk of a chestnut tree, he stopped to rest, suddenly unable to understand what had happened to him and why he found himself alone in this unfamiliar place with aching limbs and a taste of bitterness in his mouth. Then a glimpse of the distant house brought back the memories he had tried to obliterate. It's the end; there's nothing more, he thought. Nothing more. But what should he have done? Blessed her for ruining his life? A little later he could not believe what had happened. He would return to find everything the same. Alone under the heavy boughs of the chestnut tree, he started to laugh wildly. From the inky sky a freezing drizzle had started to fall. Soon he was shivering so much that he found it hard to walk, but at last he found the level carriage drive and started back in the direction of the house.

CHAPTER TWELVE

 Clinton had planned to set out for Carrickfeeney shortly after breakfast, but, since he was determined not to leave before finding out from Theresa where he could safely write to her, he waited on a full hour longer than he had intended. He had been certain that she would slip some note into his room or contrive a brief meeting, so her failure to come down made him uneasy. Her sangfroid the previous evening, which at the time he had thought so perfect, now troubled him. Perhaps a brief adventure had been all she had wanted. Actresses led such strange lives that comparisons with other women were useless as a guide to their behavior. Quite possibly she might not be prepared to be patient for the two months he had suggested. And, since he had not explained the precise hold Esmond had over him, she might see this delay as evidence of uncertainty—a device for keeping her at bay until he knew more clearly what he felt for her. He would have to make matters plainer before he left.

Becoming increasingly impatient, he went up to his mother's room. Sooner or later he would have to say goodbye to her. From outside her door he was surprised to hear Esmond's raised voice. Clinton could remember very few occasions when he had ever heard Esmond shout at their mother, but with other things on his mind he decided not to try to catch anything that was being said. Instead he knocked and entered. A tense silence greeted him.

At first Esmond had his back to him, but when he turned, Clinton was shocked by his swollen red-rimmed eyes and the sickly pallor of his skin: the sort of face a man might own after several weeks of unrelenting debauchery. As Clinton looked away, he heard a crash and saw that in forcing his way past him to the door, Esmond had knocked over a small table loaded with china figures and ornaments. Without a word of explanation or apology, Esmond slammed the door behind him.

"I intruded?" asked Clinton.

"You make a habit of it," his mother replied wearily. As Clinton sat down near her, he noticed how haggard she looked, the red silk of her brocaded dressing robe making her face seem gray by contrast.

"Surely we can be more amiable. I came to say goodbye, Mother."

"You've no idea what's happened?" she asked sharply.

"Esmond's in a rage. The first time this week I'm not to blame."

He saw a faint smile flicker across his mother's birdlike features.

"She told him, Clinton."

"Told him what?" asked Clinton with as much composure as he could manage.

"That she loves you."

"Do I take it I'm supposed to have encouraged her?" he asked with unfeigned fury. Was this his reward for expecting loyalty and good sense from an actress? He felt that if she had walked in at that moment he could have torn her to pieces.

"She said you rebuffed her."

"How kind," murmured Clinton with scathing irony, doing his best to conceal the overwhelming relief he felt. He was puzzled to see that his mother seemed anxious. He had a strong impression that she considered him blameless but found it difficult to say so.

After a brief silence, she said with studied calmness, "I think you ought to consider what you're going to say to Esmond."

"I don't have to. The whole thing's a preposterous lie."

"I'd rather you didn't say that."

"What?" he shouted. "If you don't understand my position, let me explain."

Lady Ardmore sighed and closed her eyes for a moment. "I was afraid you might take this attitude."

"What attitude would you suggest?" he asked, completely at a loss to understand her intentions.

"I'd like you to support her story—that for once you think of Esmond's interests. Just as she did."

"She's hardly made him jump for joy."

"She knew she had to make him want her to leave him. That's why she invented this . . . lie, story, whatever you want to call it."

Clinton stared at his mother in amazement. Had he been made the victim of a performance that had all along been staged for Esmond's benefit? "She told you this?" he asked weakly.

"Of course. We've talked about it before." She paused and frowned. "I'm afraid I judged her rather harshly. She's really a very fine woman of her sort. I can understand why you're angry, but please accept that she made it very clear that you were in no way to blame. Esmond admitted that to me."

"And you suppose he believes it?" Clinton got up and walked to the door, taking care to avoid the fragments of broken china. "I'm afraid Miss Simmonds is going to have to do a little retracting." He turned in the doorway. "Where is she?"

"On her way to Dublin," Lady Ardmore replied gently.

"You let her go in the middle of night?"

"She asked me to help her to. There was some unpleasantness. There was nothing else to be done. I sent four servants with the carriage." She smiled at him. "I think you'd be unwise to contradict her story. Esmond has a suspicious nature. Too much protesting might . . ." She raised her hands and shrugged. Something about the way she was looking at him disturbed him, a knowing disdainful expression replacing her earlier submissiveness.

"What do you really think?" he asked in a low threatening voice.

"You're your father's son," she replied lightly. "No, I believe the lady." She looked at him with chilling directness. "We all ought to, don't you think?"

Clinton waited a moment, as if about to reply, but then turned on his heel.

Esmond sat on the long Tudor settle in the hall waiting for his brother to come down. His eyes strayed idly from the antlers on the wall, to a suit of armor without a leg, and then to a pile of baskets near his feet: long baskets for flowers, round ones for blackberries, square picnic baskets. The clutter of broken fishing rods, walking sticks, and balls of gardening twine, which usually offended his sense of order, today meant nothing to him. Was there really a world somewhere where people could trouble to pick berries or tie up plants? Though his head and body ached, his mind had reached the strange stage of heightened lucidity, sometimes produced in him for a few hours after a largely sleepless night: a deceptive reprieve before exhaustion came. At whatever cost, by whatever means, he was determined to find out the truth from Clinton; like a man clinging to a single thread across an abyss, Esmond clung to this intention.

As soon as Clinton appeared on the landing, Esmond rose. "A word with you, Clinton."

"I never wanted involvement, and I don't want it now."

"You'll hear me, unless . . ."

The unspoken threat brought a frown to Clinton's face, but when Esmond led him through the disused billiard room to their mother's favorite conservatory, Clinton followed.

"We won't be disturbed here," said Esmond quietly, closing the door.

The air was thick with a musty jungle smell of steam and moss. Late in the year for Lady Ardmore's orchids, there were still a few spots of bright color among the dark leaves. Waxlike fleshy flowers with vivid blotches of red on white, or brown on yellow. In the damp air the pure fragrance of stephanotis mingled with less obtrusive scents. Some baskets of humble fuchsias hung from the capitals of the wrought-iron columns.

"I wanted to ask you a question, Clinton, as a man of the world, a man of experience where women are concerned."

Esmond paused and watched his brother's handsome impassive face. "Have any of your conquests ever declared themselves before you've given some slight indication of interest?"

"When they choose, women can be every bit as direct as men."

"That isn't an answer," whispered Esmond.

"Say what you mean then. You're accusing me of encouraging her."

"Did you?"

"I never meant to."

Esmond smiled sardonically. "Of course that would have been quite unnecessary." He paused, having to check himself, consciously fighting the anger rising in him. "Would it surprise you to hear that after a few hours with you, she couldn't bear me to come near her?"

"I can't see that this is going to—"

"I said, Did it surprise you?" repeated Esmond.

"If you're claiming the same thing never happened before."

"Never in the same way." Clinton's continuing calmness no longer dismayed him, and suddenly Esmond knew what to do. "It's really quite touching," he said with a faint smile. "The way she told me, I mean. You see I'd made my intentions as clear as a man can, and she'd made her reluctance just as obvious. She told me as a last resort—a woman's final appeal against a man's lust. 'I love another.' Come now, Clinton, wasn't that most affecting?"

"You ought to get some sleep, Esmond."

"I shall . . . I'll sleep for years, but not just yet. I want to tell you what happened after she told me what she felt for you. Surely you'd like to hear?"

Clinton pushed forward, but Esmond stood between him and the door. All the time Esmond's eyes never left his brother's face. "I hit her," he said softly, "across the face, split her lip."

"How gallant."

Still the same aloof indifference on Clinton's face, but the lips a little more compressed, the contraction of a muscle in his jaw.

"Surprisingly spontaneous for me. I should have said I hit

her hard enough to knock her down. Some women don't weep easily—Theresa always found it hard—but she wept when I hit her. She was too scared to scream."

Without warning, Clinton flung Esmond aside and strode out into the stone-flagged passage.

Esmond caught up with him in the billiard room. "The best part's to come. You can't want to miss it."

Clinton's head had been bowed, but when he looked up, Esmond saw that his eyes were brimming with tears. His fears confirmed, Esmond gazed with hatred at his brother's suffering face. "I raped her," he shouted. "She struggled a bit . . ."

As he spoke, Clinton's first punch slammed into his ribs, winding him, but he caught hold of the table. "She enjoyed it . . . the whore enjoyed it."

A moment later Esmond was sprawled on the floor, his head a ball of pain, a noise like waves in his ears. He tried to tell Clinton that he was finished, beggared, but no sound came from his lips. For several seconds he wondered if he was dying; his sight was blurred and points of light flared in front of his face. Slowly these dispersed and he realized that he had only been stunned. Raising himself with difficulty, he propped his back against one of the massive legs of the billiard table. The pain in his head had become sharper and he felt he might be sick, but little by little as the physical shock diminished, he was aware of a new feeling: a finality of fatigue and desolation so overwhelming that he could only bow to it. With this surrender came a merciful numbness—a kind of peace.

When Clinton reached the town of Roscommon it had been dark for several hours, and though he had spared his horse as much as he had known how, the animal was very near the end of its strength. Clinton himself felt little better, having spent almost the whole day in the saddle, apart from the periods when he had rested and fed his horse. Being certain that Lady Ardmore's carriage would have brought Theresa to Westport or Castlebar in time for her to transfer to the Dublin post coach, he had ridden to Roscommon, where the coach always remained overnight before traveling the final stage on the following day.

Past a whitewashed chapel and a row of small shops, Clinton turned into the stableyard of Ryan's Hotel, the local posting inn. The clatter of hoofs on the cobbles brought no eager groom to meet him, but a shout eventually roused an ostler from the warmth of the parlor, the opening door bringing a gust of talk and laughter across the silent yard. As the man took the horse's head, Clinton lifted his spurred heel over the withers with a grateful sigh. His knees buckled a little as his feet met the ground. Slapping the horse's neck, he told the man to give him some hay and oats before grooming him.

In the shabby hall, which smelled of old clothes and tobacco smoke, he picked up the handbell and rang it vigorously.

"The coach is in?" he asked as the landlord came out from the dining room.

"Two hours since," the man replied, looking at Clinton's well-cut clothes with an avaricious eye—a gentleman who would take one of the best rooms and not question his bill. Yes, there had been a woman and a child; and Mr. Grealey, the lawyer from Westport, and his wife; and Mr. O'Flaherty, the biggest cattle dealer in Claremorris.

"The lady with the child—I want to talk to her."

"You'll be the lady's husband? It's a dacent house we keep here, you understand." The man paused. "You'll be taking supper?"

"After I've seen her."

"What name?"

"Mr. Higgs," replied Clinton. To have told his real name might have been to command immediate acquiescence; but, as Clinton knew, it would also burden him with offers of every kind of service, from a stringy duck to a bottle of undrinkable claret, and the best, meaning the largest and coldest, room in the hotel. After a pause the landlord called a maid and told her to ask whether the lady would see a visitor. Without waiting for any assent, Clinton followed the broad-hipped girl, cursing as he tripped on a loose stair rod, his heart already beating faster as he imagined telling her he knew what had happened. He would take her in his arms, consoling, begging forgiveness for making her his mistress before being able to protect her. Her long day's traveling after a sleepless night and then this drab hotel at the end of it all brought an emotional tightness to his throat.

The girl stopped at a door and knocked, but before any answer came, Clinton pushed past her and entered the room. He stood dazed and motionless for a moment before stumbling back into the passage and closing the door. In a chair by the fire had sat not Theresa but a sharp-faced woman nursing a baby in her arms.

"There was no other?" he blurted out to the astonished maid. "No woman with a girl?"

"No, sir."

He walked slowly down the stairs, leaning heavily on the banisters, his sense of disappointment as sharp as a blow inflicted by Theresa herself. For a moment he thought that she might have stopped at Claremorris when the horses were changed, too tired to go on, but he knew in his heart that she would not have extended her journey another whole day for the sake of a few hours' respite. She must have known she might be followed and had therefore chosen the longer way home by the road to Limerick and then to Cork or Waterford. She had fled not just from Esmond but from him too. How else could he construe it? The servants at Kilkreen had told him that the carriage had left on the Westport road. Either she had bribed them to lie or had told the coachman to change direction when they had left the estate. Grief laced with self-pity choked him as he walked blindly into the empty street. He felt the dull fury of a man who had subjected himself to needless bathos and made himself ridiculous. But no anger or pretense could hide from him the fact of his loneliness, this sudden ripping out of hope. From the hotel parlor he could hear the sound of a fiddle and voices raised in song. With her by his side, the music would have pleased him; instead it seemed only a senseless noise in the night air. But he did not long bemoan his helplessness. Whatever time it took, however hard the search, he would find her, and then let her dare say to his face that what had passed between them had been nothing. Let her dare.

PART TWO

CHAPTER THIRTEEN

 Deacon's Place was a neglected cul-de-sac of eighteenth-century cottages leading off a mews, dwarfed and overlooked by the unadorned backs of a stately crescent. A few such fossilized survivals of an earlier rural period remained hidden away behind the broad formal streets of Belgravia, hemmed in by livery stables, garden walls, and tradesmen's entrances. Now, apart from the grass growing between the paving stones, there was little rustic about Deacon's Place; the neighboring mews resounded day and night to the clash of hoofs and the grating carriage wheels, and the Two Chairmen on the corner was a public house much frequented by the younger servants from the surrounding mansions. The residents of the cul-de-sac, though living in such close proximity to the titled and rich, were less exalted—a retired butler, an engraver and his family, a lawyer's clerk, and Major Simmonds, widower, late of the Bombay Rifles, later still auctioneer, theater manager, and bankrupt, at present living on a small annuity.

Arthur Simmonds was a gentleman by birth, and though for years he had lacked the means to live like one, even at the age of sixty-one he could not resign himself to the indignity of his situation. He pretended to be indifferent to the opinion of others, but was in fact extremely sensitive to it. When he went out, he did not go to his old club or call at the houses where he might expect to meet associates from his more prosperous days. Instead he frequented chop houses and oyster bars where he still felt superior to the average clientele. In such places he sometimes behaved with embarrassing rudeness, but, just as often, he treated those he met with exaggerated civility; by these extremes proving, to himself at least, that he naturally belonged in a different and more exclusive milieu.

With fellow unfortunates he was usually indulgent, enjoying comparing past misfortunes and sharing wishful dreams of what might have been. Being well aware of his own shortcomings, he could be exceptionally tolerant of weaknesses in others. But, like many men who felt that fate had treated them unfairly, he also had periods of prolonged ill-humor, taking the form of obstinate pride or ironic buffoonery; in both conditions he would deliberately make the worst of everything, as though to revenge himself for the humiliations of a life that had thwarted his ambitions.

Like so much else in his life, his relationship with his only daughter was bedeviled by disappointed expectations. Though he loved Theresa with a demonstrative fondness unusual in most fathers for their grown-up children, her mode of existence made him cruelly aware of his personal failure. His time as theater lessee and manager had been the happiest in his life; the isolation of the stage from other walks of life and its air of illusion had been a welcome escape from the scant social rewards of colonial soldiering and the later stigma of trade. But never had he thought to involve his daughter in that particular world. His one ambition for Theresa had been a splendid marriage; her beauty and accomplishment deserved no less. In no other way could she enjoy the rightful privileges of her sex and know the indispensable comforts and many satisfactions of living as a lady.

His wife's death when Theresa was twenty had been a grave setback to the major's matrimonial plans for his daughter, since the mother's natural matchmaking role would have to be discharged by him; and hard though he had tried, not one of the young gentlemen he unearthed had impressed Theresa. Instead she had promptly fallen in love with an actor in the company and after many months of bitter arguments had forced her father to consent to her marrying him. She had already shown some dramatic talent on the few occasions when she had managed to bludgeon her father into allowing her minor roles, so her choice of marriage partner had made her future career inevitable; even had she wished to discontinue it, the birth of Louise and her husband's early death had made such a course impossible, especially since these events had coincided with her father's professional decline. At the time when Theresa had most needed help, Major Simmonds had been least able to provide it. Alternately blaming her for having brought about her own hardships, and torturing himself for being unable to alleviate them, he had later been incapable of enjoying any successes she achieved.

The arrival of Esmond Danvers in both their lives had seemed to the major the final fulfillment of an impossible dream; and though his mind had later turned to possible advantages for himself, at first his delight and relief had been for Theresa alone. That she should have turned down a marriage proposal was incomprehensible to him. Only an actress could have behaved with such malign perversity. Esmond's wealth had tantalized Simmonds. Eventually most financiers could be relied upon to buy a country place, and the major had passed many idle hours contemplating his own residence in a comfortable dower house on the estate. He would fish and shoot, and, for the first time since his Indian army days, lead something approaching the life of an English gentleman. No longer burdened by fears for his daughter and granddaughter, he had imagined his last decade passing in perfect peace of mind.

While Theresa had stayed on with Esmond, the major had continued to nurse his hopes. In fact he had seen their trip to Ireland as a distinctly promising sign. His daughter's sudden return therefore struck him with the force of all unexpected disasters. Only her undisguised misery had enabled him to hold back the full tide of his resentment. But at times during her first week as his reluctant guest, he could not contain his anger. If her decision had brought her contentment, he might have been able to reconcile himself to what she had done, but her unhappiness only underlined for him the madness of her proceedings.

Every day since her arrival at Deacon's Place, Theresa had been out for hours at a time making the rounds of agents and managers, returning late in the afternoon, tired and dispirited. Her obvious eagerness to get work at once appalled her father. An actress who appeared desperate would end up being offered a smaller salary than if she seemed to be pondering engagements at her leisure. Because the revival of *Masks and Faces* had been a success, he knew that Theresa ought to take particular care not to accept anything that might be seen as a downward step. Before his ruinous ventures into extravaganzas at the Lyceum, Arthur Simmonds had been a successful manager with very few failures among the long string of adapted French farces he had mounted at the Strand Theatre. He knew he was well qualified to give advice, and so suffered the more for being ignored.

Hurt and perplexed, he consoled himself with Louise, taking the child for walks in Hyde Park to see the carriages and riders in Rotten Row and along the Lady's Mile. If the weather had been warmer, he would have liked to have gone with her to the open-air tea gardens near the Regent's Canal or taken her on the river by penny steamer to Greenwich. Instead he bought her presents he could not afford: a straw hat with ribbons, a silver bracelet, an inlaid sewing box. He also treated her to performances of his numerous imitations: extraordinarily accurate mimicry of various animals' cries, the sounds of an orchestra tuning up, street vendors' calls. His favorite was a tour de force of railway travel, starting with the approach of a puffing engine, its progress through a tunnel, accompanied by whistles, stopping at a station, with the porter calling out the place, and then the final departure of the train with gradually accelerating puffs and hisses. By making his granddaughter laugh, he felt he was doing something to soften the impact of her altered circumstances.

One morning during Theresa's second week in Deacon's Place, Major Simmonds thought he detected a change in his daughter's manner. All that day because of Louise's presence he could not ask anything openly, but after supper when the child was in bed, and he was sitting with Theresa in the small ground-floor sitting room, he began to question her. She had said that two London managers had spoken vaguely of an engagement in the near future, had she heard any more?

Theresa looked down at the rucked-up tiger skin rug in front of the fire. "I've accepted an offer."

"May I ask where?" he asked, fingering the eyeglass he always wore on a black ribbon round his neck.

"York."

"York?" he repeated in amazement. "You must refuse. You can't possibly take anything with a stock company until you've waited longer."

"I don't want to wait. I can't."

"You can sell some of the jewelry he gave you . . . . I'll do what I can."

"It isn't a matter of money," she replied quietly.

"Then what is it a matter of?"

"I need to work. That's all."

He stared past her at the litter of cigar boxes, papers, and unwashed glasses on the table. "If you must go to the provinces, why not to Manchester or Liverpool? But York . . . You know those third-rate stock companies—the costumes of ladies of fashion straight out of the theater rag bag, the leading lady decked out in crumpled satin, the dowager in Lady Macbeth's cast-off velvets. You'll play opposite a jeune premier who'd be more at home behind a muslin counter than on the stage."

"And only a harp and one violin in the orchestra?" she replied with a faint smile. "You're exaggerating as always. It's only for six weeks and the parts are good."

"And Louise?"

"Can't she stay here? It isn't for long. I may be able to find a day school to take her at short notice."

The major got up and stopped in front of the cracked barometer by the door. "I don't understand," he murmured. "Can you explain it to me?"

"Not in any way that would satisfy you."

Later when she was getting into bed in the cluttered room which her father usually used as his study, Theresa was disturbed by the memory of his kindly puzzled eyes. She had known that he was right all the time, but, since leaving Clinton, she had found unoccupied days intolerable. At first she had thought everything burned out and finished for her by Esmond's despair, but time had proved her wrong.

Now, though every emotional part of her revolted against the way in which she had run away, she still could not bring herself to write to Clinton. What happiness could there ever be for them, when so much conspired against it—his family, his debts, his regiment? Her child and her career? Ahead of them, all she could foresee was the pain of separations, of meetings snatched at too eagerly, of broken plans. Her fear seemed a betrayal, but she could not escape its many forms—fear of dependence, of loving more than she was loved, and worst of all, fear that were they to meet again, she would submit regardless to whatever he might ask. Only work, she believed, could restore to her the woman she had been before knowing him.

CHAPTER FOURTEEN

 For a week after his return to England, Esmond remained at home incapable of attending to business, unable to think of anything outside the confines of his own misery. He had locked Theresa's boudoir and the bedroom they had once shared, and now slept and spent all his time in his dressing room. For hours he would pace about this small room, disinclined to read a book, just looking at the prints on the wall, or picking up a newspaper, reading at random advertisements for carriages or pianos, requests for a French governess or pedigree pointer dog—any paragraph his eye fell upon. He glanced at the paper's date. Yesterday? The day before? A year ago? A strange illusion held him, that he was entirely alone, trapped in a lost pocket of time, like a stick floating in the revolving eddies at a river's bend, circling, but not progressing with the wider stream. Others were working, loving, going to theaters, living lives that moved, their days in step with the greater world's. But to him that active world was as distant as a half-remembered dream; the slow merging of his own empty days and nights had become reality.

Unable to sleep at night unless half drunk, he dozed during the day, amazing his servants by the sudden abandonment of long-established routines. The landau stayed all day in the stables; his valet was sent away when he came in the morning with clothes and hot water for shaving.

In a huddle outside his door, valet, butler, and housekeeper conferred about the advisability of sending for the doctor; fear of dismissal dissuaded them. Instead they patiently tolerated every new and eccentric demand. At four in the morning he might ring for prawns and radishes with a bottle of sauterne, or oysters and iced punch. One evening the first footman was alarmed by smoke on the landing outside his room and came down to find his master, poker in hand, burning a woman's dress on the fire; beside him was a heap of taffeta, striped satins, muslin, and shot silk.

Every day a clerk came from the City with papers for his urgent attention, but, in spite of the man's pleas, Esmond never went down to see him and the papers remained unread. He seemed to be in a dazed state of convalescence, utterly remote, yet violently irritated by any intrusion.

Sometimes, when he was very tired, he fancied he heard Theresa's light tread on the stairs as he had done in reality whenever she had come back late from the theater. Several times he threw open his door, only to find a maid returning to her room after putting out the lights.

But slowly, like a man blundering through mist towards a dim light, he forced himself to think of a future beyond the boundaries of his present misery. In time he would have to find out what he still refused entirely to accept. Just as a bereaved person may need to see the corpse to understand his loss, Esmond sensed that he would have to learn whether Theresa was with Clinton. Again and again he had put off making the discovery which alone could destroy the half-admitted hope, which alternately sustained and tormented him.

If Clinton had let her down, as he had other women in the past, one day—probably not soon, perhaps only after many months—might she not come back?

Every day Esmond told himself that he would to go Deacon's Place the following morning. If she was not there, her father would know where she had gone and why. Yet every time he braced himself to call the coachman, his pulse began to race and he could hardly breathe. The bellpull in his hand seemed as deadly as the trigger of a loaded pistol. Never in his life had he felt such dread in the face of what logic and reason cried out had to be done.

On a gray and blustery morning, when the wind shook the window frames and tore the last leaves from the trees in the square, Esmond's valet knocked and told his master that his chief clerk was in the hall and refused to leave until he had spoken to him. After a long silence, Esmond pulled on his brocaded dressing gown and told his servant to show the visitor up.

George Herriot had worked for five years for Esmond with a meticulous attention to detail almost equal to his employer's. Usually dapper and constrained, today Herriot was agitated and flustered. His thin wispy hair, normally glued to his scalp with macassar oil, was wild and unruly, and instead of his invariable black silk cravat, a miracle of geometric folds, he wore a made-up octagon scarf. When Esmond admitted to his chief clerk that he had read none of the papers sent from Lombard Street, Herriot's mouth sagged at the corners and he sat down heavily in the wing chair by the fire.

"The Greek and Oriental's credit can't last another week, and you haven't read those papers?" His voice ended on a faltering gasp. "You know how we're placed if the company suspends payment?"

"Our losses will become public."

"Destroying the confidence of the banks," cried Herriot, flinging out his arms with the jerky suddenness of a clumsily animated puppet. Suddenly he started to sob, sniffing at first but then without restraint. Esmond waited for him to recover, shocked out of his indifference.

"Every day I'm asked when you'll be in; every day more excuses. I can't go on. I've no authority to buy bills over five thousand or to renew. Have some pity, Mr. Danvers. The clerks have all got children. I've three sons. At present discount rates, we can't absorb the Greek and Oriental's losses. Martell and Hennessy have given the preference to General Steam in the Charente brandy trade. That's six steamers idle. We're being bled to death."

"Can't we cut our rate on the Charente service?"

"Below twenty shillings a ton with ten per cent primage?"

"Perhaps not. In six weeks we'll have the new steamers on the Black Sea service. I'll call a conference with the line's major creditors."

Herriot's face was instantly transformed. "Can I telegraph the Liverpool office?"

Esmond nodded, his mind already calculating possibilities. The thought of the chain of failures that would follow his own had been made real by Herriot's tears. His life was not in isolation; his fortunes were linked to those of hundreds of others. Even before Herriot left, Esmond found himself considering remedies: using the wine ports merely as a call on outward voyages to Brazil; reducing the Levantine trade. But his mind kept returning to the worst difficulty of all—the problem of immediate credit, and capital to pay for the new steamers. For the first time since returning from Ireland he thought of the trust and remembered what he had intended to do. Esmond clapped his hands.

Next week he would meet the creditors and agree to secure all outstanding liabilities. Then he would go to the trustees and advise them to take up as much stock as possible in the Greek & Oriental while the shares were undervalued. He had given good advice in the past, and they would hardly doubt him now when they knew his highly respectable discount house was financing the company.

If the line failed, Esmond knew that he would be ruined. The prospect seemed less disturbing now that he was confident of involving Clinton in the same fate. Nevertheless, when Herriot left the house, Esmond gave no more attention to his brother or the trust. The time had come to pay another call. An hour later Esmond was in his landau on the way to Deacon's Place.

CHAPTER FIFTEEN

On a November morning, several weeks after her arrival in York, Theresa received, with a letter from her father, a sealed enclosure in Esmond's hand.

My dearest,

At your insistence, your father refuses to disclose your address but promises to forward this with his next. If you are secretly with Clinton, or refuse to see him for fear of any sword of Damocles you may think I hold over him, dismiss this fear. However he has wronged me, I will not hurt you by withholding the help I promised him.

I miss and love you, and regret more than I can express the manner of our parting.

I remain, dearest Theresa, your still loving,

Esmond

Suspecting Esmond's purpose was either to find out whether she was seeing Clinton, or to hurt her by seeming forgiving, Theresa did not reply, although it did occur to her that she might be wronging him. But having decided not to make any attempt to contact Clinton, she felt no guilt for her continuing longings. Separated from Clinton, Theresa's mind seemed as clearly marked by him as wax, recording every scratch and line from a vanished seal.

Gone were her old fears of future unhappiness with Clinton; these now influenced her feelings as little as remorse over Esmond's sufferings. But while she still derided herself for running away, she could not bring herself to write to him. It had become a matter of pride and principle with her that Clinton should do the seeking. And since she was sure that any inquiry agent, armed with a list of theatrical agents could find her in hours rather than days, she did not mean to offer help. If Clinton made no effort to trace her, it would prove the inequality of their need and the futility of further meetings. Though her heart rebelled, the days passed and Theresa did not weaken.

From the start of her engagement at the Theatre Royal, very little had gone right. The manager, considering himself lucky to have bought the services of an established actress for the salary he could afford to pay, had decided not to trouble her with more than two rehearsals of the first play: one to explain the business and stage positions, the other to run through the lines. For the regular members of the company, drilled in their parts almost like soldiers, the experience of performing with an actress who gave more attention to response and feeling than to prompt-book instructions was as unnerving as it was novel. And Theresa's precautionary habit of pinning up bits of her part on the backs of chairs and on vases bred other fears. But on the opening night she was not only word perfect but able to give a performance that unfortunately exposed the inadequacies of the rest of the cast.

Several times walking the narrow streets, under the overhanging eaves of the timbered houses, Theresa had been drawn to the ugly modern Catholic church in Duncombe Place. One day she did not walk past, as she usually did, but went in and knelt down in the dark interior. The little huddle of people outside the confessional made her think despondently of the well-being she had always felt after receiving absolution. Never having been prepared, while living with Esmond, to confess week after week to a sin she would repeat, Theresa had not been to confession for over a year. In the silence of the church, the glow of candles and the smell of incense filled her with a chill sense of exclusion and loss. Wanting Clinton, and knowing that she would continue to, without any desire to amend, she was still separated from the offices of her church. Memories of her convent schooling haunted her: the purple palls on the statues on Passion Sunday, the white veils at confirmation, the tinkling bell at sanctus. Sadness far greater than nostalgia weighed upon her as she rose to leave.

A week after the opening of *The Patrician's Daughter*—Theresa's last play with the York company—the manager changed the musical interludes in the final act. In a break during the rehearsal called to alter cues and the timing of business, Theresa walked out into the spacious entrance hall with its sweeping double staircase leading to the circle and upper tiers. Twenty years ago, before the railway had lured the local gentry to London for their pleasures, the Theatre Royal had been a fashionable resort. Now, only the faded flock wallpaper, the dusty chandeliers, and the gilded plasterwork recalled days when the manager had stood nightly in silk stockings and tails by the doors to welcome his eminent patrons.

While she was considering whether to go out, Theresa heard her name spoken from inside the box office. Through the small window she could see, bent over a ledger, the woman who took the money and issued tickets. She was old and fat and wore men's boots, and had seen too many actresses come and go to take much notice of them. Her little den was lit by an oil lamp. A long-haired tabby lay on her broad knees.

"A man came with a letter for you."

"A gentleman?" asked Theresa, taking the envelope thrust out at her across the hollow worn in the wood by countless coins.

"Servant," the old woman replied curtly. "A sight too pleased with hisself too. Said you was to have it there and then and damn rehearsals."

Theresa opened the envelope without much interest, supposing it would be another improper invitation from a prosperous corn factor or shopowner. Suddenly her heart was fluttering like a caged bird, and she longed to escape where no eyes could see her while she read. But though her hands shook, she could not tear her eyes from the paper.

Lord Ardmore's compliments to Miss Simmonds. His lordship humbly requests the pleasure of Miss Simmonds's company at the Black Swan, Coney Street, after tonight's performance. A refusal will excite his lordship's profoundest regrets. In short, Theresa, I won't stand it. You have dragged me across the Irish Sea and half England like a monkey on a chain, put my man to the trouble of grubbing his way through the greasy offices and anterooms of every posturing theatrical agent in London. If you think I'm as easily cast off as the old gentleman with the glove whose discomfort you so much enjoyed, then think again. You said you loved and trusted me. Agreed to come to Dublin. You changed your mind, which is every woman's privilege. Mine is to know why. If need be I will break the heads of more actors, doormen and stagehands than there are seats in your lamentable playhouse, before I leave this place without seeing you. This requires no answer except your presence at the time and place I ask.

When she had finished, Theresa sat down on the bottom step of the staircase and rocked herself gently. From the auditorium she heard pizzicato notes on the violins. The callboy came out to say that they were starting again. She nodded as if she understood but remained sitting where she was, absorbed and yet animated. She rose and then walked rapidly to the street door, where she paused as if suddenly dazed. She stood a moment, her hand resting on the brass handle; then she turned it abruptly and stepped out into the winter sunshine. Crossing the street, she walked swiftly in the direction of Clinton's hotel, her eyes fixed ahead of her, her lips slightly compressed. A coster's cart and a dray loaded with barrels lumbered past. The sun flashed on the thick panes of glass in bow-fronted windows and made the colored bottles in an apothecary's shop glow like stained glass. After the darkness in the theater, everything was sharp and bright: women's clothes, jars of preserved fruit, a striped barber's pole.

As though the street were a bridge that might part in the

center and leave her stranded on the nearest side, she hurried on into St. Helen's Square under the shadow of the Mansion House and past the line of waiting hackneys. Shops and doorways seemed to slide by as if she were borne on by water. With an urgency close to fear, she was reaching forward, always forward to each new moment, as though any hesitation might drag her back into the treacherous currents of the past. With a sensation like falling, she entered Coney Street and saw, beyond the church of Martin-le-Grand, the large black wooden swan nesting on the porch of the hotel.

Turning, she saw her reflection in the window of a dusty corner shop: a strange little general store selling Dutch dolls, squares of yellow soap, and rickety kites. Her hair was disheveled and she realized that, beneath her cashmere shawl, she had on the dark gray woolen day dress she only wore in the theater. Next door was a milliner's with numerous hats on stands: Glengarry caps, and bergère bonnets. She went in, hardly hearing the tinkling of the bell. Anything would do to hide her hair. Looking at herself in a cheval glass, she thought that the cold had made her nose pink. A veil—a hat with a black veil. She chose a leghorn with a pronounced forward tilt. The girl who served her was infuriatingly attentive, offering other choices, latest styles; the Rubens hat was very fashionable in London. Theresa snapped at her.

"I'm sorry, Miss Simmonds," the girl stammered.

"You've no call to be. I'm in a hurry."

Theresa felt that she ought to make up for her bad temper by asking whether the girl had enjoyed the play, but as soon as she had paid, she left the shop.

At the desk in the entrance hall of the hotel she was dimly aware of a painting of a horse and some yellowing framed timetables of the defunct York to London coach service. When the landlord's wife came in answer to her ring, Theresa told her whom she wanted.

"Lord Ardmore?" the woman repeated sourly. "We've no lords here, nor baronets neither, and won't have till the races, if I know aught."

Theresa felt her cheeks glow. Why should he have decided to meet her somewhere other than the hotel where he was staying? In case Esmond was having her watched? If he was scared in York, how much worse would he be in London or Dublin? Yet he had seemed so utterly devoid of caution. Bitterly disappointed not to see him, yet also confused, she walked out into the street. A crossing sweeper was shoveling dung, carriages passed. Slowly she started back towards the theater.

Her performance that evening was nervous and tentative. Afterwards the manager came to her dressing room and asked if she was unwell, but she sent him away with a brightness belying her nervousness. The more she thought about it, the more extraordinary it seemed to her that Clinton had not offered to come to the theater. The aggressive tone of his note, which had at first amused her, now struck her in a different light. Was it possible that he had not wanted to be seen calling on an actress well known in the town? She dismissed the thought as ridiculous, and yet the confusion she had felt in the hotel remained. Why had he waited so long before coming to her, when he must have found out why she had left Kilkreen so suddenly? The gas hissed loudly in the mantel over her mirror; from the dressing room above came the gurgle of water. The room was quite warm, but she found herself shivering. She sat down on the lumpy chesterfield by the window and tried to calm herself.

After very little time, she knew that she would not go to the Black Swan. He would have to come to the theater. The matter had become more important to her than a gesture or a desire to score a petty triumph. Various phrases in his letter stung her now, however facetiously they had been meant. The idea that she had inconvenienced his valet, for some reason hurt her particularly. Her head ached slightly and her skin prickled with a strange heat. She removed her makeup and then tried to wrestle with the complicated hooks and laces at the back of her dress, but could not manage it. She had sent away her dresser earlier, and when she rang for her again, discovered that the woman had gone home. Her heart had started to beat fast with the thought that he might be angry with her for not coming to the place he had indicated. And if he was angry, what would she think of him? Suddenly she wondered whether she knew him at all. She always kept some brandy in her dressing room and now poured herself a large measure into a cup. Perhaps she ought to have gone to the hotel. Perhaps he had had a perfectly good reason for asking her to go there. She found his letter and read it again; this time not knowing what to think. At the end of a quarter of an hour her uncertainty and nervousness were as bad as ever, but, though wanting to change her mind and go to the Black Swan after all, she now feared that he might have left and be on his way to the theater. She would wait.

Hours later, or so it seemed to her, she heard knocking at the door. She did not look up as Clinton entered, though she saw from the corner of her eye the heavy folds of an Inverness cape. He closed the door gently.

"Look at me," he whispered in a low hoarse voice. Expecting anger, Theresa saw pain and incredulity in his eyes. He looked tired—older than she remembered. A lock of hair had fallen across his forehead. "I wanted to protect you; that's why I wanted you to come to the place I asked."

"I went there," she murmured. "Why didn't they know your name?"

"If it's known that I'm a nobleman," he replied gently, "do you think the first maid or waiter who sees Miss Simmonds of the Theatre Royal go to my room will draw breath before running to the editor of the local scandal sheet to claim his guinea? Do you want clerks and shopkeepers ogling you each evening not for your acting but for that?"

"I don't care how they look at me."

"But I care," he said quietly. "I know these provincial towns. I couldn't bear to harm your reputation."

"*My* reputation?" she echoed faintly, feeling her eyes fill.

As he took her in his arms, in her relief every fear and misgiving fell away. She could not understand how she had doubted him. When he kissed her lips and then held her, she longed to stay forever with her head pressed against his throat and her fingers in his hair. Nothing in the world, it seemed, would ever hurt or trouble her so long as he held her like this. But when he stepped back to look at her, she saw the tension still there in his face and suddenly felt scared.

"Don't tell me how long you can stay—not tonight. Tomorrow you can tell me, but not now." Then she held him with all the strength of her arms, seeing the gentle smile on his lips, feeling her heart hurting her with a pain that was also joy to her.

She did not bother to change her stage dress but threw a mantle over it. On the way to the stage door, they passed behind the scenery flats and the numerous ropes which were used to lower the drops. Seeing what looked like a cannon ball, Clinton stopped and picked it up.

"They're used for thunder," she said. "Half a dozen rolled up and down that wooden trough."

He bent down and lifted the end of the long sloping trough, sending the metal balls racing away with a loud roar that reverberated and echoed through the theater.

"Good God, it works," he shouted above the din.

"We can make lightning too, and rain. We can do anything," she said with a laugh that caught in her throat and escaped as a sob.

"Thunder's good enough for me," he said, "thunder and love."

Theresa was too absorbed by the simple fact of walking beside him to think about where they were going. She saw buildings and lighted windows in isolation, her eyes taking in random details with fragmentary clarity—at the end of a long alley the river shone like polished ebony; in a silversmith's barred window candlesticks and tankards gleamed palely. Far from distressing her, Clinton's silence seemed to affirm their new confidence in each other. What emptiness could there be in silence for minds filled with the constant murmur of unspoken thoughts? When she looked at his face, she saw a subdued radiance—the mirror image of her own contentment.

Suddenly her fingers tightened on his. They were approaching the Black Swan.

"I don't want us to be Mr. and Mrs. Danvers."

"If my title's impossible, the best I can do is use my family name."

"Yes, *your* name," she said urgently. "If you're real, then I'm a sort of mirage. I want you to make up a name for us. I want us both to be the same. I won't be mythical on my own."

"But you are mythical. You can't help it. Any other woman would have said, 'I don't want to pretend to be your wife.' " He smiled, that slow irresistible smile she remembered from Ireland. "You won't be Mrs. Danvers, and I can't be Mr. Simmonds. If I can't take your name, I can take your profession. How about Mr. and Mrs. Garrick? Mythical enough for you?"

"Too mythical," she murmured.

"Dramatists are less public?" he suggested.

"Congreve," she said, "I like Congreve." But as soon as she thought of some of the cynically witty lines that used to make her laugh, she suddenly found them sad and bitter. Her earlier reservations about posing as his wife seemed less important. She told him she would not mind being Mrs. Danvers. A silly scruple was not worth going to another hotel. He seemed surprised by her volte-face but did not question it. Entering the hotel, Theresa felt the euphoria that had carried her along since leaving the theater begin to wane. Fears that she would disappoint him nagged her. Too often bathos followed joy.

Above them, a flaking rococo ceiling: crumbling cherubs and clusters of vine leaves. Faded red damask on the walls and a mustiness about the room in spite of a generous log fire. She sat down in a chintz-covered chair and hid her face in her hands. A little later she felt his lips gently touching the backs of her fingers.

"What are you thinking?" she asked.

"That I know what it's like to be a shot bird—winged, but not knowing it. Flying on for a bit and then dropping without knowing why."

She lowered her hands and looked at him with amazement. "You feel that?"

"Perhaps I shouldn't have said so. Lovers oughtn't to say too much. Not to start with."

"It gives them time to think?" she asked with a faint smile.

"Time to become cautious and scared."

"Is it safer to do things first and think about them later?" She intended no mockery but saw his face darken.

"Do you suppose I had no time to think after you'd gone? No time when I tried to follow you? While I waited to hear where you were? I'm done with thinking."

She gazed at him in silence, as if till that moment she had been blind, his passionate suffering face scattering her doubts like the blast of a cannon. Again she felt the overpowering weight of physical attraction that had knocked her sideways in the theater. She pressed herself against him and felt the deep throb of his heart.

"Kiss me." She sighed, and the touch of his lips sent a tingling shiver under her skin and a warmth of relief that was like homecoming. Her hands, stiff and awkward a moment ago, were soft now and warm, her whole body striving to mold itself to his.

She felt his fingers at her back, trying to loosen her dress, and knew that he would not succeed without help. She tried to assist without parting their lips but could not do it.

"It's terrible," she said, "all broken laces and bent hooks and eyes. I die in the last act. Heroines always have to die in white, and this thing's so full of whalebone that it holds me up even when I try to fall down."

To her relief, he laughed, and she no longer felt awkward when with his aid she finally stepped out of the dress, wearing only a thin chemise and petticoat. They had both needed to laugh.

"Why do you die?" he asked, still smiling.

"I'm a faithless wife," she whispered sorrowfully. "Impure heroines always have to die if they can't marry their repentant seducers. It's a very moral play."

"It sounds vile."

"It's quite jolly to start with. The trouble comes later. The fiend casts me adrift."

"He must be mad," said Clinton, lifting her up like a child and carrying her into the bedroom. She lay back on the bed watching him undress, impatiently tugging at his watch chain until a link parted, strewing his clothes on the floor. Before taking off his long woolen undergarments, he undid her chemise and cradled her breasts in the palms of his hands, breathing faster.

"I want to look at you," he murmured in an intense but faraway voice. She got up and slipped off her petticoat and drawers, standing naked in front of him without moving. He stared at her avidly, eyes following the flowing line of her flanks, moving from the auburn warmth of her hair to the whiteness of breasts tipped with coral pink. Looking down, she saw that the dress had left marks and indentations on her skin. She covered them with her hands, but he came to her and kissed these places tenderly.

"My left shoulder's a little higher than the right. When I was little, I wore a sort of steel and leather thing to improve my posture. It didn't work." She found herself blushing.

"I'm glad it didn't. I love your shoulders. I'd hate them to be different."

"Hold me. It's lonely being looked at."

He came to her and kissed her shoulders, then pressed his cheek against her breasts. When he held her, she could feel the hard lump of his penis through his drawers and reached down to touch it. He stripped off his remaining garments and they lay hugging each other, caressing and stroking, limbs intertwined, his hands deftly exploring, sliding between her thighs as Esmond's had never done, arousing her as Esmond had never done. His mouth strayed from her lips to her nipples and back again, kissing her throat and the lobes of her ears, until she ached for him.

"Please, my love," she gasped, guiding him, raising her hips, moaning with pleasure as he entered her. She did not care how he had learned what he knew, did not think of it at all, but gave herself totally, her body responding to his rhythm as if they had been lovers for years. Never had she known such instinctive understanding of the flesh; her hands and fingers were stroking his hair, tightening on his back, pressing down on him.

Afterwards, searching his face for pride of possession, she saw nothing but tender astonishment.

"You weren't acting with me?" he asked with sudden doubt, moving from her.

"Do that? You couldn't think it."

"You never will?"

"How could I ever need to?"

He lay back and closed his eyes, his relaxed lips and long lashes making him look as if he were smiling.

Later he mentioned his regiment's engagement with the Fenians in Tipperary, and her heart grew cold.

"It's nothing yet," he said, sensing her alarm. "A few brave men against regular troops; it's butchery, not fighting."

"And if there's a rebellion?"

"We'd welcome it, believe me. It's only the small groups that can't be dealt with easily. But a large gathering—a battery of horse artillery. Just one battery. It's kinder not to think about it. I hope I won't be there."

"You could be shot in the street."

"If they start that game, they'll try for the Chief Secretary or the Lord Lieutenant."

"But you'll be careful?"

"Boredom's the only thing I'll die of over there. That and missing you."

She stroked the hairs in the central hollow of his chest and kissed him. Lying back, she watched the pale flickering reflections of the fire on the ceiling, listening to the slower pace of his breathing, until, imperceptibly, sleep came.

Because Theresa had not wanted to eat lunch in the hotel, they had gone to a chop house in Stonegate, which Harris had previously learned was reputed the best in town. Afterwards they walked through the labyrinth of alleys around Monk Bar, looking at strange little shops that were open without it seeming possible that they would ever do any business: key shops filled with thousands of rusty keys, sweet-stuff shops with farthing and halfpenny literature hung on strings in the window, herb shops selling preserved tapeworms and calves' stomachs. For the first time since coming to York, Theresa no longer found the narrow streets and grass-grown courts sad and oppressive. Nor did the cries of the knife grinders and wandering sellers of matches and penny toys jar on her nerves as before. She enjoyed the bustle and activity in the streets, sharing with Clinton anything worth remarking upon: a woman in an absurd poke bonnet, the multiplicity of different objects in a pawnbroker's window.

At last they came past half-timbered St. William's College to the Minster, and stood looking up at the towering mass of masonry, the broad expanses of glass and jutting pinnacles and gargoyles. Inside, the light was dim silver-gray, beating down softly from the cold clerestory. The tall columns rose like an avenue of immense trees, their branches the ribs of the fan-vaulted roof. Beyond the chancel screen, the east window glowed with ruby, sapphire, and topaz. In the aisles behind the choir stalls, they looked at the mural monuments and brasses. A Jacobean husband and wife knelt under an elaborate marble canopy, not facing one another but with the woman looking at the man's back.

"How awful to be like that forever," she whispered, squeezing his arm, and the remark made him long to kiss her. Other things she said also touched him. The sadness of being as terribly old as the niched statues in the screen, to suffer the slow loss of noses, arms, and fingers through the centuries, as if smitten by some never-ending leprosy. She was wearing a dark green Zouave jacket, frogged with braid like a hussar's uniform, which he thought delightful, because it enhanced by contrast a new softness he sensed in her—the indefinable beauty which comes with happiness and love, as subtle as a flower's scent or the bloom on fruit.

They looked at the Zouche chantry chapel and the chapter house, and returned to the nave in time to see a genteel congregation assembling for evensong. Respectable tradesmen and professional men with their wives, soberly dressed in black and gray. Normally not caring a jot about such people, Clinton was surprised to feel uneasy at their appearance. The idea that they would scarcely condescend to look at Theresa if they knew she was his mistress made him feel sick. One code on their lips, another in their hearts. Thwarted in their ambitions, under-nourished in their pleasures, of course they would be venomous.

The little procession of canons, headed by a black-robed verger with a silver wand, and the pure-faced choristers in their surplices epitomized that well-regulated and morally certain world which would unhesitatingly condemn his liaison as dishonorable. If Theresa ever agreed to live with him, though he would still be received in the same places as before, her existence would be denied, even where it was perfectly well known. She would be considered a person unfit to mix with virtuous women and, as such, the victim of every social slight and insult. That he would be powerless to alter this increased his indignation but also made him ashamed. She had attempted to escape him and had done her best to end their relationship, but he had come after her, and by doing so had bound himself in honor to protect her. He felt in his bones that he owed her something more than assurance of his love. Yet equally he realized that any offer of support would offend her. Though on the surface happy, these doubts gnawed at him unseen. He had not yet told her that he would only be able to stay one more full day before returning to Ireland. Several times he had been on the point of breaking the news, but had dreaded ruining for her the little time they had together.

On the way back to the hotel, they passed a mantua maker's, and Clinton stopped, seeing something in the window which he wanted to buy for her. He told her to go on ahead, promising not to be long. Theresa waited for him in their rooms, noticing that in their absence Harris had cleared away his master's clothes. On the mantelpiece were some coins, a box of lucifers, a cigar cutter, and several crumpled letters, evidently taken from the pockets of the coat he had worn the day before. With unashamed curiosity she picked up one of the envelopes and took out the folded paper.

My Lord,

While we appreciate that your lordship expects to receive more than sufficient funds from the sale of your country estate to replace your overdraft and provide for your future requirements, we must with regret advise your lordship that the payments which have recently been made on your account in the bank's books have occasioned an overdraft thereon of £983 at the close of business yesterday.

In the circumstances, we think it reasonable that pending the aforementioned sale, your lordship should either give a proper security for the debt or pay it off by installments. Under this conviction, we request your lordship will favor us with the name of your solicitor in London that we may communicate with him on the subject.

We have the honor to be your lordship's obedient servants,
Messrs Drummonds

She replaced the letter, feeling suddenly faint. Esmond had always told her that Clinton would never sell Markenfield and yet here was evidence that he was doing just that. Worse still, this information had not been enough to satisfy his bankers about his future credit. Perhaps the letter Esmond had written to her had been a calculated lie. The thought that Clinton's love for her could ruin him had been nebulous before; now it had become real.

He came in smiling, holding a long cylindrical package in his hand. He gave it to her.

"Don't you want to see what it is? A telescope? A gun?" Seeing tears in her eyes, he embraced her. "What is it, my love?"

"Nothing."

She stripped away the paper and took out a shot silk parasol with a beautifully carved ivory handle.

"For the summer," he said. "I want to see you use it in the summer." He held her in his arms and murmured softly, "You'll come to Dublin in January—you and your daughter. I told you I'd take a house. I can rent it by the month. There'd be no obligation. If you wanted to go, I wouldn't try to stop you; I'd only want you while you wanted to be with me."

"I read the letter from your bank," she said in a dead voice.

She saw the anger in his eyes and the tightnesses around his lips.

"I'm going to talk to them; they've misunderstood my position over Markenfield." He looked at her steadily. "Of course we can give up now because the world's too hard and cruel for us, because we can't face consequences. And what would that prove? That we'd done ourselves more harm than the world outside, that we'd prefer a kind of suicide to risking any suffering later on. Is that what you want?"

She walked over to the window and looked out at the darkening street, then she snapped open the parasol and twirled it over her head. "What do you think, my lord?"

"That you'll come."

"It was never in doubt since the moment you came here." She dropped the parasol and threw her arms round his neck, kissing him fiercely. "How could you doubt me?" she moaned. "How?"

Her words brought a sharp pang to his heart, and he could think of no way to answer her except with his body, to wipe out the sense of their separateness, to forget that he was going. Taking her hand, he led her to the bedroom, time dying as he moved. No time at all, he was racing to undress and yet everything was so slow, as if he were moving through water. Only when he felt the smoothness of her skin against his, when she was in his arms and he was entering her, did the straining in his heart cease. Her half-closed eyes and ecstatic face filled him with thankfulness.

CHAPTER SIXTEEN

Clinton walked through the large hall of business where the routine bills of regular clients were discounted, and entered the clerks' room. Here Esmond's minions worked at a dozen sloping ledger desks separated from each other by mahogany partitions. On the far wall were numerous pigeonholes for delivering and receiving bills, stock receipts, and checks. Every now and then one of the frock-coated figures would rise and remove something from one niche, only to return to place the same papers or some others in a similar compartment. Other documents, clipped together and hung on a row of pegs near the door, were from time to time collected and taken to some other part of the building. Clinton watched this activity for a minute or two with the surprised attention of a naturalist confronted by the bizarre rituals of a species he rarely encountered. That men of some education, who had once had the choice of other occupations, should accept such a life was beyond him. Attracting the attention of a clerk, he explained who he was, and without delay was shown to Esmond's office.

As Clinton entered, his brother's back was to him, and the clerk was reluctant to interrupt his employer in the middle of dictating a memorandum.

"Since it is common knowledge," Esmond was saying, "that ships make more freight at a lower draft of water by filling with jute, hides, and other light goods than with grain, seeds, and so forth (which occupy the same space and weigh more), why are our agents taking on present quantities of grain from Galatz? I wish to know the minimum that must be carried as deadweight. . . ." His tone had been belligerent, but, as he turned and saw Clinton standing in the doorway, his expression froze.

When they were alone together, Esmond stared at his brother with a look that was hostile and yet somehow beseeching. Clinton guessed from Esmond's agitation that he had heard nothing from Theresa. Clinton lowered his eyes. "I've behaved as badly to you as your worst enemy could wish, and I acknowledge it."

Esmond had turned away and was facing a bookcase filled with registers and directories. Clinton could see from the movement of his shoulders that he was breathing deeply as if bracing himself. "So you're seeing her?" he said in a thick, scarcely audible voice.

"Yes."

Esmond spun round, blanched and trembling. "And being a man of honor, you thought it right to say so to my face—to square your conscience. A pity you didn't think of what was honorable before you seduced her."

"She'd have left you anyway."

"You offer that as an excuse?" yelled Esmond.

"As a statement of fact."

Esmond sat down on the edge of the table, calming himself with a great effort of will. His lips curled into a sneering smile. "I'll give you another statement of fact. I wanted to spend my life with a woman whom you'll use for a month or two."

"I came here to correct that impression."

"You mean she may last a year? I'm overwhelmed. You love her as honorably as man ever loved woman. You thought I'd take that sort of cant from you—from you, Clinton, of all people?"

Somebody knocked at the door, but Esmond shouted at him to go away.

"You have every right to say that," murmured Clnton, moving towards his brother. "But it isn't cant." He paused momentarily. "I'm going to ask her to marry me."

The quietness of his words did not diminish their ghastly impact. A tree might have fallen between them or a man run in and shot himself to produce the same effect on Esmond.

Clinton took his arm and said gently, "If I'd never set eyes on her, she'd still not have stayed with you. I know it sounds cruel, but it's true. What's happened makes no difference to what would have—"

"That *you* should have the only woman I ever wanted—no difference?"

Revulsion and hatred Clinton had expected and almost hoped for, but not this dreadful pain. Since childhood, Clinton had never seen him weep, and he was horrified when Esmond pressed his knuckles to his eyes and began to sob in short rasping spasms. Because Clinton could not himself conceive of a love made sharper by humiliation and betrayal, he found his brother's collapse the more shocking. With a sharp pang of remorse, Clinton realized that grief, rather than vengeance, had lain behind Esmond's taunting confession of what he had done to Theresa at Kilkreen.

"I never meant . . ." Clinton began hesitantly, at once losing the thread of what he had intended to say.

"Go," shouted Esmond, picking up a heavy glass paperweight. "Get out."

As Clinton reached the door, a clerk entered awkwardly. "I'm sorry, Mr. Danvers. Sir Robert's been waiting since three in the partners' room."

With a roar, Esmond hurled the rounded glass into the grate. As the clerk swiftly closed the door, Esmond threw himself into a leather armchair, sending it crashing back against the iron safe by his desk. Clinton watched him helplessly.

"You're worried. Think I might . . ." Esmond jerked his head in the direction of the window. "Wouldn't like that on your conscience. Not nice to think of when you're in her bed." He seemed suddenly calmer as he said in the scathing tone Clinton knew so well, "Perhaps I'd better save that for your wedding day." He looked down at the Turkey carpet and shook his head. "You're a strange man, Clinton. Because you did me the worst turn one man can do another, you'll save your honor by marrying her and ruining your life."

"Mock me by all means," murmured Clinton, "but just consider how easily I could have kept it all from you in order to get that loan. You think that would have been better than telling you the truth? At any rate, that's what I came to do."

Esmond glanced at him with a ghost of a smile. "The worst murderers often die best, but I don't like them better for it. You stabbed me in the back. Am I supposed to applaud you for stabbing yourself too? Honor, ha ha."

"I love her."

"You'll be screaming that when you hate the sight of her." Esmond leaned forward across the table. "Have you asked her yet?"

"No, and I don't intend to either, until enough time's passed to convince her I'm not acting on the kind of impulse you suggested."

When Clinton had gone, Esmond remained bent over the table for several minutes. But then he drew himself up and walked purposefully to the door. In the passage his chief clerk came after him, protesting about something, but Esmond brushed him aside, and walked out grim-faced into the street.

He hailed a hansom, gave Deacon's Place as his destination, and sat back on the worn leather seat. A single thought obsessed him: to see Theresa as soon as it was humanly possible. Unless Clinton had lied about delaying his proposal, he could still be stopped. Who else but Clinton would ever have the arrogance to suppose that simply because he had made up his mind to marry, weeks or months could pass and he would be accepted just the same, regardless of anything that might happen in the meantime? But, in spite of Clinton's claim to be in no hurry, Esmond knew how easily such resolutions could crumble. For this reason he thought it vital to see Theresa even before Clinton's next meeting with her.

When Esmond had last visited Theresa's father to try to find out her whereabouts, the old man had been resolute in his refusal to disclose anything, but since he had agreed to send on any letters, Esmond had not tried to trace her by other means.

It was an omission he now regretted. Since inquiry agents invariably worked slowly, Major Simmonds represented Esmond's only chance of finding Theresa in anything under a week. The thought of a second failure with the old man made Esmond's stomach turn. Everything in him rebelled against the possibility that Clinton should casually gain the one objective that he himself had striven so hard for and had wanted above all else.

The light was already fading by the time Esmond raised his cane and rapped on the major's peeling door. As he waited, little eddies of dust and dead leaves swirled about his feet. Just as he had expected, he was welcomed with the major's usual blend of irony and effusiveness. With his expansive shirtfront and elaborate necktie, against the background of a room filled with framed playbills, collapsing furniture, and dusty Indian trinkets, the major seemed a figure more suggestive of high comedy than real life. Given the importance Esmond placed upon his visit, this was not a comforting observation. Simmonds had an uncanny gift for making perfectly mundane occasions farcical.

The old man glanced apologetically around him. "They say an old dog gets the kennel he deserves. No sentiment these days. None at all." He sniffed, and advanced to take Esmond's coat—a favor which Esmond did not hesitate to refuse. The fire was meager and drawing badly, and the room felt damp. "A glass of port wine?" Esmond shook his head. "That whole business." The major paused. "My dear fellow, I can't express how badly I feel about it all. Believe me, it wasn't for the want of a few paternal remarks on your behalf."

"You could still help me. I don't mean getting back the past. I want to see her once more, to set my mind straight on certain—"

"Can't be done."

"I think it can."

"Revive painful memories. No point in it."

"Have I ever asked you any other favor?"

The major pursed his lips and frowned. "She asked me not to tell you where she is. That's the fact. Made me give my word. No more to be said."

The old man's combination of facetious servility with rock-like stubbornness confounded Esmond. Across the room on the open flap of a warped bureau he could see a mess of papers and old cigar boxes. Somewhere there would be letters from her.

Simmonds smothered a cough. "Pity Louise isn't back from school. She'll be vexed to miss you."

Esmond nodded, trying to think of another approach. "Can't you see, I'd never tell her you'd told me anything?"

"Course you wouldn't. Word of a gentleman."

"So you feel able to rely on me?"

"Absolutely rely on you."

"So it's settled?"

The major looked at him sorrowfully. "It's the principle, my dear fellow."

"You didn't mind her being my mistress. What was so principled about that?"

"Nothing at all. Didn't enter into it."

"What didn't?" asked Esmond, close to losing his temper.

"Principles. Neither of you promised anything, so no promises were broken. If you'd offered her marriage first and then cut and run, that would have been a very different sort of fish. Keep faith. That's the thing."

Esmond looked at him coldly, fighting his anger. "You're going to force me to say some unpleasant things."

"What I didn't hear in the army, I heard in the theater."

"Very well then. Return all the jewelry I gave her and the money you had from me."

Without speaking, Simmonds walked to the desk and began shuffling through a heap of papers. At last he handed Esmond a check already written out. "Should have sent it." He thrust it out and sighed. "I nearly did." When Esmond tore it in two and dropped the pieces, the major looked no happier. "She asked me to return the things you gave her. I didn't. Gifts, you understand. Ah well, she was right, and I was wrong. I'll get them."

As soon as he had left the room, Esmond began feverishly to hunt through the bills, letters, and other papers in the bureau, knowing that he would recognize her writing as soon as he saw it. He did not stop searching even when he heard the old man's tread on the stairs. What did it matter what he thought of him if he could only find the address he was looking for? But Esmond could not put his hand on what he so badly wanted. From the corner of his eye he could see the major watching him sadly, a leather box in his hands.

"Keep the stuff," he groaned. "If she won't let you, give it to Louise. I'm sorry. I'm afraid there aren't too many principles where love's concerned."

Dreading that Simmonds would either be sympathetic or try to force him to take the box, Esmond hurried out, astonished that he had failed so lamentably with a man he had always derided.

He had asked the hansom driver to wait in the neighboring mews and was walking there blindly when he heard his name.

He looked up. "Louise," he stammered, seeing her staring at him curiously.

"You weren't looking where you were going."

Beside the child stood the major's elderly maid of all work.

"Sometimes I don't," he replied with a smile; the sight of the girl reminded him painfully of her mother, but he had to show some pleasure. Louise might even miss him, for all he knew. Or hate him; he had no idea what Theresa might have said to her to explain their sudden departure from Kilkreen. "How is your mother?" he asked lamely, unable to think of anything else to say, thankful that the girl seemed to consider the question perfectly natural.

"Hating the theater and just about everything. Her letters to me are quite jolly. The ones to Grandpa aren't such fun."

"Manchester isn't much fun," he said casually, his chest tightening as he waited for her to contradict his guess.

"It's ever so much worse. You should have heard what Grandpa said about York. A theater that's simply dreadful and . . ."

Esmond heard nothing as he fumbled in his pockets for a sovereign. Finding a few florins, he pressed them into Louise's hand, kissed her, and to her astonishment ran towards the hansom.

"King's Cross Station," he shouted to the driver, and then, sinking back against the leather, he felt for the first time in many weeks a glow of emotion which he might once have described as happiness.

She came next morning, in answer to his summons, to the Railway Hotel, her face half hidden by a veil, and stood opposite him in the private sitting room he had engaged. She said nothing, and the veil and the silence made her seem ghostly to him in the gray light. Ghostly and insubstantial, as if he had never held or touched her, never felt the softness of her lips or the warmth of her breath. For all his determination to behave with icy impassivity, resentment stirred in him like acid, tightening his chest, making him grip the brim of his hat till his fingers ached. The martyred dignity of her silence—something about the way she stood, head slightly bowed—insulted him, as if the wrong had all been his, and she was now reproaching him for the cruelty of forcing on her a futile and distasteful meeting.

His tight lips formed an artificial smile. "Since you have nothing to say to me, let me tell you something which may please you." He moved closer. "My brother means to ask for your hand." The slight intake of breath and stiffening of her body goaded him. "I see I have your interest now."

"I don't believe you," she whispered, with an agitated movement of the hands.

"You'll find out soon enough," he replied quietly. "Do I find you speechless for joy?"

She raised her veil and looked at him in incredulity. "Why should he have told you—*you* of all people?"

"In a word, honor—misguided of course, but the real thing just the same." He met her gaze easily, as if unaware of the nerve-racked entreaty of her expression. "He knew just how vilely he'd behaved; I daresay he felt he had to prove that he hadn't betrayed me just to indulge a casual whim. And of course he realized he'd lost you a husband—dishonored you, in fact; so naturally he wanted to do the chivalrous thing by you." He smiled through scarcely parted lips. "That's what's so odd about men of honor—they're as hard as nails in almost every respect, but they can't abide a bad conscience." He let out his breath in a long sigh. "You know I was going to lend him a good deal of money? His pride wouldn't suffer that after the way he'd treated me. Extraordinary how men can get so much moral satisfaction out of throwing away what they desperately need."

The blood had risen to Theresa's cheeks. "What will happen to him without that money?" she asked in a choking voice.

Esmond shrugged his shoulders and frowned, as if considering a subject that bored him. "He'll have to leave the army. After that . . . maybe what he gets from Markenfield will last him a year, perhaps a bit longer. I shouldn't think he'll survive till he gets his trust money."

She had listened with apparent meekness, but as he finished, she faced him furiously. "Is your punishment to ruin him?"

"My dear Theresa, are you suggesting I ought to lend him money after what he's done?"

"Tell me your terms," she said sharply.

"You misunderstand me. I won't blackmail you to abandon him. Even if you never see him again, I wouldn't raise a finger to help him."

"Then why have you come?" she cried, twisting the fingers of her gloves.

"I wanted you to know the consequences of accepting him. His future's in your hands, not mine." The slightest tremor of anger ruffled the polished surface of his words. "He stands to inherit his uncle's fortune. More money than his father ever squandered, or I'll ever have. His entire future hangs on whether he gets it." He met her eyes blandly. "I'm not talking about trifles like keeping his career. Without that money, he'll be bankrupt by the time he's thirty-five. Nothing more from Markenfield, the trust capital gone, no hope of survival except that inheritance." He paused and sat down nonchalantly on an arm of the sofa. "There's just one problem. Clinton won't get as much as a bent pin from his uncle if he marries you."

"Are you telling me Clinton's unaware of this?"

He met her defiance with a smile. "He's an incurable optimist. He thinks he'll get round the man. Of course he hasn't a chance."

"Shouldn't he be the judge of that?" she asked fiercely, her hands trembling.

"You don't know Richard Danvers," he said gently. "He married money, so he deplores everyone who doesn't do the same. But you're not just poor. You're an actress too—a kind of courtesan in his eyes. Then you're a Catholic. I'm afraid that's a particular bête noire of his." He brought his fingers together and rested his chin on them. "How would you rate his lordship's chances of persuasion?"

"Tell me this, Esmond," she asked with flashing eyes, "how do ordinary people marry? Do they need fortunes? Do they grovel to their relatives and beg permission?"

The suddenness of her attack surprised Esmond and cut through the façade of civility he had imposed on his raw emotions. "You think a man used to spending two thousand a year on his career ordinary? A man who's half dead unless he's occupied? You think love in a cottage would suit his temperament?" His voice had risen, and he could no longer suppress the harsh and biting edge he now recognized. "You think he'd insult himself by letting you stay on the stage—by giving you anything but an establishment fitting your rank? And when he's beggared himself for love, and love's gone, don't expect him to thank you for what you've cost him."

He had hoped to convince her rationally of the disservice she would do Clinton by marrying him. Now with each new proof of her determination to deny his arguments, Esmond wanted to crush and humiliate her. "Have you asked yourself what he sees in you?" She stepped swiftly to his right, but he blocked her path to the door. "I waited three months at your convenience, Theresa. You'll pay me the courtesy of a few minutes now." He leaned his back against the door and met her outraged eyes. "Won't you answer my question?"

"Why he loves me? I'm sure he could answer better." Though her voice was level her eyes were filling.

"You ran away. Just what he likes—the ones who are hard to break. He loves risks and dangers. The fact you were my mistress—now *that* was spice to him, far better than seducing any other man's wife. He's used to easy success, but you denied him that, making him press harder. But wait till he's sure of you. When you're married and the diet's unchanging from day to day, see how long you hold him then."

"Isn't that what you wanted for yourself," she blurted out, "the person you loved with you all the time?"

"I'm touched that you remember. But there are small differences between us. Ask for a list of his women. Ask what he said to them, what he promised."

She covered her face with her hands and stifled a moan. A moment later when she moved hesitantly towards the door, he no longer had the heart to detain her. Instead he stepped aside. After she had gone, he longed to have the chance again, to talk to her gently, reasonably, with dignity. But that opportunity would not come a second time. He had been so confident to start with, so sure he could dissuade her, that when she had resisted he had lost his head. Now he had not the least idea whether he had succeeded.

In the station, amid clash of couplings and hiss of steam, he scarcely noticed people pushing past him to the waiting train. But later, among the fringed antimacassars and shaded lamps of a first-class carriage, he began to feel less despondent. Perhaps he had not, after all, entirely lost to Clinton; even if he married her, there could still be other ways to bring him down. As the train sped on under its long banner of smoke, this thought alone was comfort to him in his bitterness.

CHAPTER SEVENTEEN

Clinton's regiment was sent to quell outbreaks of rioting in Cork and Killarney during December, so he did not see Theresa in Dublin at the date they had previously arranged. By the first days of January, he was at last stationed in the Irish capital, and less than a week remained before Theresa's long-awaited arrival.

Yet Clinton was neither jubilant nor carefree as he crossed the deserted parade ground three evenings before he was due to meet her at Kingstown harbor. Returning a sentry's salute, he glimpsed through the dark entrance arch the forlorn ill-lit streets sloping down towards the Liffey. After the babble of voices at the mess table and the bright gleam of gold lace and silver, the surrounding city seemed silent and ghostly under its overhanging pall of smoke. In his quarters, Clinton lit an oil lamp and opened his brassbound writing desk. He took out an envelope, sat down by the fire, and pulled out the letter he had received from Theresa two days earlier—a day which had ended all his certainties. Now once again he glanced through the humorous opening that gave so little indication of what was to come.

My dearest Lord,
    If this sounds like the beginning of a revivalist hymn, forgive

me. You see, though I love its possessor, I have never liked the name Clinton. It sounds like a family name masquerading as a Christian one. Like Scrope and de Vere, it makes me think of Burke's Peerage, orders of precedence, dates of creation, and all the other aristocratic accoutrements that seem to keep me at arm's length . . .

He skipped a page and came once more to the first piece of information that had badly shaken him.

Darling—the most wonderful news, and so soon after the winter of my discontent in York. I have been offered Beatrice at the Prince of Wales. I know I need not tell you what this may do for my career. A classic role and one almost made for my talents. I can hardly believe my good fortune. My one regret, and it is not a small one, is that I will only be able to spend a week with you in Dublin. And for several months after that I will be quite unable to get away. But they will surely give you leave before the spring? You know the theater, so all you will need do is whistle and I'll come to you, my lad. You know the rest of that verse I am sure. I often wish there were vivandières in our army like in the French regiments. Then my profession would keep me near you.

Not for the first time since rereading this, Clinton cursed himself for not proposing to her in York. But at the time it had seemed beyond argument to him that any proposal would gain force if it were delayed, since then it would seem properly considered. To have rushed in then would have been to risk appearing too hopelessly smitten to be able to think about consequences. And Clinton had heard too many tales of women panicked into refusal by premature offers to care to take that chance.

Now his regret at not having hazarded everything in York was sharpened by the calm way she wrote about not seeing each other till the spring after her one brief Irish visit. Nor did he suppose that if he waited patiently, while every evening brought in new suitors, his chances would improve as the months passed. And yet the letter also contained tender passages.

Sometimes you seem almost a myth to me—a pet phantom of mine, as hard to believe in as the Emperor of All the Russias. Clinton, I do so need to pull you down from the pedestal in my imagination and know you better. I don't mean know about your past loves or what you feel ashamed of. I want to find the secret springs of your character. Does your heart expand on summer mornings when you hear the wind in the trees? Do pebbles on a beach or woodland shades have hidden meanings for you? What moves you to tears? Is this uncommon language to use to a soldier? I hope you will not think it sentiment or gush, because we must share everything we feel. Darling, my finger ends tingle to touch you. Every inch of me from the top of my head downwards is burning for you. Every single hair of my head longs to be stroked. My eyes yearn to see you, my ears to hear your voice. I want you, want you, want you.

But this passage came just before another that to Clinton seemed worse even than the earlier intimation of the overriding priority she gave her career.

A very strange thing happened before I left York. Our manager proposed marriage, without for a moment asking himself whether the life would suit me. Though earning his living from the stage, he would not have allowed me to do the same. He believes actresses degrade their husbands if they stay on the stage. Yet how he could expect a complete change in me is incomprehensible. Think of the absurdity of hoping to turn me into a prim and proper stay-at-home person. But on top of that he never gave a thought to Louise, who does not know him or like the little she does. Heigh-ho, I daresay he won't be the first to ask a woman to give up career and occupation in the hope that she will be able to embroider over the gaps. One of the dangers of people living together in idleness is that they spend too much time together and exhaust in so many months what might otherwise have lasted years. "Perdrix, toujours perdrix," as that old sinner Louis XV remarked. I think it a great shame one cannot go on trial with marriage as with other things. It is a formidable affair for life. Enough of it. For us it will never raise a problem, being impossible. Since I am no lover of convention, I like getting off the beaten track and am proud rather than ashamed that we cannot do what others can or follow rules to the letter. What cannot be got straight has to be enjoyed crookedly.

The bluntly expressed opinion that marriage between them was impossible, following hard on the heels of so many statements that could apply to him just as appropriately as to the wretched theater manager, was clear enough warning what he could expect if he proposed. In fact, Clinton strongly suspected she had invented the incident with the one intention of discouraging any mention of marriage. But it would make no difference to what he did. He knew that long ago he had passed the point where he could pull back; already his whole life seemed suspended in anticipation of something that would have to be gone through before he could continue with it. He would propose, regardless of his chances, because he had to; because until that obstacle was cleared, he would know no peace or happiness. Whatever the likely outcome, he would not throw in his hand until he had played it to the last card.

They came through the early-evening darkness along the coast road from Kingstown to Dublin in a closed landau, seeing through the rain-flecked carriage windows the wide bay, and close in, under the dark outline of the hill of Howth, a few sails, caught for a moment in the wandering beam of a distant lighthouse. Passing a row of seaside villas, Clinton placed a steadying hand under her chin and kissed her lips, laughing when the swaying carriage made them bump noses. After a mile or so, he asked her what she was thinking.

Theresa squeezed his hand and smiled. "Only how pleasant it is to be freed from the trouble of thinking."

"I've never heard a better way to stop a man's mouth before he has time to open it."

"And this?" she murmured, kissing him firmly, so that no movement of the creaking springs could part them until she drew away. "When you close your eyes, your eyelids make you look as if you're smiling. Did anyone tell you that before?"

"Do you usually kiss with your eyes open?"

"I take little looks from time to time. I love looking at you."

She sat back and leaned her head against his shoulder. "I was thinking how wonderful when everything's still quite new, when even my silences seem mysterious, and you find it better than a play just to sit beside me. That was before you asked what I was thinking, and then I wondered if I ought to say this or that, but instead I said what I did. And now I'm thinking that I'm lucky to be coming to a strange town where I won't have to find the theater and lodgings, and argue about lumpy beds or whether I paid for a large jug of hot water in the morning or a small one, and why, when every room in the place except mine was empty, I had to be put next to a screaming baby and a woman who snored. Don't you think silence is less commonplace?"

"Not when you're breaking it. I'd never given a thought to snoring babies and women in lumpy beds."

"Until I made such poetry with them. Oh la, for shame, sir, to take advantage of a poor country girl with your flattering phrases." She heard him sigh and wished that she could be calmer with him; but again and again she found herself over-taken by a bubbling gaiety, a kind of intoxication that she could not help. "You make me so happy," she murmured, "like some sudden legacy or a chimney pot on the head—everything unexpected."

This time he laughed, but she still sensed that she had hurt him and should have been more serious so soon after their reunion. Yet in another way she was glad to have begun like this. If her letter had not already persuaded him that his pur-suit had placed him under no obligation, she would have to show him by her manner that though she loved him, she did not want the proposal which Esmond's arguments had made her dread.

The carriage came to a lurching halt among a press of ve-hicles drawn up outside the Shelbourne Hotel in St. Stephen's Green. At once two porters were volubly competing for the privilege of carrying Theresa's battered valise and hatboxes. Clinton peremptorily awarded the task to one of them and, taking Theresa's arm, led her into the crowded hall. The scene to her was an extraordinary one: women and young girls in ball dresses with long trains and aigrettes of diamonds in their hair, and men outlandishly decked out in tight silk stockings and blue velvet coats with silver buttons; most seemed much taken up with the effort of not tripping over their swords.

"Isn't this court dress?" murmured Theresa.

"It's the Lord Lieutenant's Drawing Room at the Castle to-night."

"Oughtn't you to be going?"

Clinton laughed as they pushed their way to the desk. Shouts went up around them that Lady Somebody's carriage had arrived.

"I'm not a debutante," he replied above the hubbub, causing titters of laughter from some young women standing nearby. When he returned with a maid to direct them to the rooms he had engaged, Theresa saw him accosted by a distinguished elderly man in court dress with the ribbon and cross of some order round his neck. Clinton at once introduced her as Mrs. Barr. She caught the name Lord Roxborough and felt her cheeks flush as she was asked whether this was her first Castle season.

"The Court of St. James's is more Mrs. Barr's territory," answered Clinton lightly.

The old peer looked at him quizzically. "Not going tonight, Ardmore? It's the young men they need for the dancing."

"Yesterday's levee was quite enough."

At the foot of the stairs Clinton was stopped by another acquaintance, this time an officer in full-dress uniform. After an introduction the officer asked Theresa if she was any relation of the Warwickshire Barrs.

"No, only the prison Barrs," she replied curtly, mortified with Clinton for not having warned her that he had taken rooms in the town's most exclusive hotel on what was evidently one of the busiest nights of the season. The soldier seemed uncertain whether to be amused or offended and was still pondering this when Clinton nodded to him and moved on up the stairs. On the first landing was a little winter garden with a fountain splashing in the midst of ferns and stone frogs. A crowd of housemaids and waiters were looking down over the banisters at the animated scene below, and a group of cigar-smoking billiard players, with cues in their hands, were commenting on the looks of various of the debutantes.

"If that one—"

"Which one?"

"Girl with a green sash. If she isn't a vixen, she ought to take an action against her face."

Their laughter merged with the shouts of the head porter announcing the arrival of more carriages.

When the maid had left Clinton and Theresa in their rooms, and the porter who had brought up the luggage had departed with his tip, Clinton looked at her admiringly. "Poor old Archie Daventry's going to be wondering what he did wrong for days. He'll think there's been some awful scandal with the family he mentioned. One of them in prison."

"Don't be absurd."

"I'm not." He shook his head with sudden vexation. "Damn. I should have told old Roxborough you were going to spend six weeks at the Prince of Wales's. He'd have been frothing away to everybody about meeting a delightful creature—friend of the heir apparent, constant dinner guest at Marlborough House."

Theresa said quietly, "Isn't it just possible he's heard of the Prince of Wales Theatre?"

"What on earth's the matter?" he asked.

"Why are we here, Clinton?"

"It's the best hotel in Dublin. No lumpy beds or snoring brats."

She came up to him and took his hands, fixing his eyes with a look of tender exasperation. "You know very well what I meant. Remember your concern for my reputation in York? What about yours here? Why didn't you ask me before making noble gestures on my behalf?"

"We had to consider your audiences in York."

"Don't you have to consider your brother officers? And the court occasions at the Castle?"

"I wouldn't care a rap if I was scratched off the Chamberlain's list tomorrow."

"But I'd care," she cried. "I'd care a lot if it was because of me."

"My love, it isn't worth a thought. Of all Ireland's shams, the Castle season takes the prize. Most of the Irish nobility live in England. Imagine a court without a resident aristocracy."

"Who were all those people then?"

He took off his chesterfield overcoat and threw it over the back of a chair. "Can't we talk about you?" he implored. "I'm really not interested in them." Seeing that she was still insistent, he went on rapidly: "They're the richer sort of tradespeople, doctors, lawyers, the odd squireen—all scrambling over each other to marry their daughters to the sprinkling of peers who turn up."

"Stop being so condescending."

He threw back his head as if appealing to heaven to justify him. "*You* try not to be, with people who insist on licking your boots without giving you time to stop them. Deference breeds condescension as often as the other way round." He frowned and gave the fire a few vicious stabs with the poker. "The worst of all the grinning and fawning is that really they'd love to see us in the mud."

A moment before, his arrogance had chilled her, but now the sight of his sad proud face filled her with remorse. Of course he would feel bound to mock and treat as insignificant the world he intended to give up for her.

"Aren't you giving them their chance by bringing me here? Feeding their hate?" He gazed into her troubled eyes and ran his fingers down the line of her cheek. "Please answer me," she murmured.

"What they feed on is their affair. I owe them no duty." He paused and moved away impatiently. "So they can have their balls and Drawing Rooms, I went to Killarney—"

With a sudden movement he drew back a curtain. "Come here." Standing beside him, she looked down into the street and saw a silent crowd of ragged men and boys waiting in the rain, watching the departing carriages and the silks and knee breeches. He let the curtain fall back into place. Without moving, he said softly, "Why aren't they at home knitting socks or mending their roofs? I don't know. Because their landlords are abroad, must they live with their pigs and leave a dunghill by the door? They could build a shed and dig a drain. They're

generous. There's scarcely any pitch of misery they've not endured. They love their children as few people do; they murder
without mercy or remorse, and often the very landlords who
tried to improve their lives. I don't like or understand them."
He smiled bitterly. "You saw them down there. How dare they
for the sake of a little poverty go out begging and interrupt
gentlefolks in their pleasure?" He sat down next to her on an
ottoman and stared at the fire. "When I'm sent out to fight the
likes of them"—he gestured in the direction of the window—
"to protect that flummery at the Castle, I tell you I'd rather
. . ." He checked himself with a deep breath and went on more
calmly: "I'd rather face any ignominy than be dictated to by
such people."

"You mustn't ever be," she whispered fiercely, "never, my
love."

"I won't be," he replied in a small hard voice. "I'm getting
out."

"Selling your commission?" she murmured faintly, with a
depth of dismay that astonished him.

"It's not the end of the world. I knew it ages ago. Ireland
only makes it easier."

"Don't lie to me," she begged him. "I know I cost you Esmond's help."

"I lost it for myself."

"No," she cried. "If you'd promised to give me up, he would
have—"

"You think I should have pleaded with him?" he asked bitterly.

"Didn't you sell Markenfield to save your career? I know
what it means to you." She looked at him fearfully. "Don't give
up anything because of me. Don't hold that over me."

"I give you my word it would have happened anyway." Her
distress had started to alarm him. She had come horrifyingly
close to saying that he ought to abandon her and make his
peace with Esmond. He slipped an arm round her waist and
said calmly, "I've told you the truth and you must believe it."

She turned away and shook her head back and forth. "I don't
know what I believe, Clinton."

"Listen," he murmured intently, "you can help me."

Her obvious fear as she swung round to face him, made him catch his breath.

"I only meant that you could soften the blow," he added quickly.

"In what way?" she faltered.

"Why are you so pale?"

He tried to turn her face to him, but she drew back. "How can I help you?" she asked beseechingly, as if begging him to end some unendurable suspense. As though a bolt had been shot back in his brain, he sensed that she had thought him about to propose and had been in terror of it.

"By coming to the barracks," he replied flatly. "Watch church parade, riding school. It would be easier for me to leave if you'd seen it all."

"Of course I'll come," she returned with an eagerness that appalled him, since it spoke so clearly of her relief that he had meant no more than this. He sat next to her mutely staring, clasping his hands until he could trust himself not to show his bitterness. At first all he wanted was to speak the words and be done with it. Like a man in a rage set to unravel a knotted rope, he longed to tear it free by force. Then slowly, like a pulse of lost feeling, resolution grew in him. He had time to wait his moment, and if that was his only asset, he would not throw it away. Whatever her reservations about marriage, he did not doubt that she loved him. Should he ultimately succeed in changing her mind, it would not be the first time love had worked such a change.

She had been looking at him with deep concern. "What will you do," she asked, "when you've left the army?"

He shrugged his shoulders and smiled, determined to lift the gloom. "What would *you* do if you left the theater?"

"Eat precious little." She stroked his hair fondly. "You're very generous to think our positions comparable." She smiled. "If they really were, I probably wouldn't love you."

"Do I always make my rank so obvious? In China the mandarins have special little buttons and drive different-colored carts."

"That's not the point at all." She laughed with the low, slightly hoarse note he loved. "You don't need the buttons. You are what you are. Nothing could be more plain. Of course rank means nothing to you. People only get excited over what they haven't got."

He took her wrist firmly, as if threatening to turn it. "Tell me you love me only for myself."

"I can't tell you that. Your rank is part of you. Acting's part of me." She looked at him with gentle mockery. "Do you love me because I'm an actress?"

Without warning, he swung her to her feet and lifted her up until her head nearly touched the ceiling. Taking no notice of her cries to be put down, he shouted up to her, "I love you in spite of what you are."

"I'm not an acrobat," she implored as he raised her still higher, holding her only by the knees.

"I have you in my power."

"Monster!"

"Angel!"

Moving his hands to her waist, he tipped her upside down, her skirts and petticoats muffling her cries. When he put her down, they faced one another breathing hard, she trying to look angry, he doing his best to seem contrite, until they both burst into laughter that died as suddenly as a squall of wind, leaving them dazed. With the softness of an almost indiscernible caress, he laid his hand against her flushed cheek. The strain and tension she had felt ebbed from her in a slow sigh of relaxation as she leaned against him. The men with their little swords, the beggars in the rain, and all her fears became no more than driftwood in the sweep of an incoming tide. At the first touch of his lips, she burrowed deeper into his shoulder, pressing against him. No words now, only incredulity that they had ever spoken when there could be this urgency of wanting.

Yet for Clinton there was no such loss of cares. Her earlier reaction, confirming the fears her letter had started, convinced him that unless he could bind her by a coup de main before their long separation began, he would lose her irretrievably. The ease with which she yielded her body to him was scant comfort when he thought how soon she would be returning to the stage. He would have little time to work in, perhaps too little.

CHAPTER EIGHTEEN

Early next morning, when the mist and fog still hung in the streets, Clinton left St. Stephen's Green and headed down York Street in the direction of the Liberties. He had told Theresa that he had to spend the morning presiding at battalion orderly room, which was in part true, since he would be on duty there after eleven. But now it was barely nine and he was in a part of town nowhere near his barracks.

Long into the night, Clinton had weighed the options open to him, and it had occurred to him that even if he persuaded her to accept his proposal, her immediate departure and the long delay dictated by her career would provide ample opportunity for her present doubts to reassert themselves. If she were to have a great success with Beatrice, if Louise were to take against him before a wedding could be arranged, if Theresa should realize that his leaving the army would indeed be brought about by the loss of Esmond's assistance—then any one of these possibilities might persuade her to go back on her word. And the more he had thought about these problems, the more he had come to believe that his only sure way of keeping her was to marry her before she left Ireland. Even if he got over the highest hurdle of all and won her consent, there would be a daunting number of other obstacles to clear; and they would have to be dealt with first.

Not the least of these was the need for the ceremony to be kept secret. Since Clinton was certain that his uncle would disinherit him if he learned about the marriage, the utmost discretion would be essential. Because Theresa was a Catholic, and her church did not recognize civil contracts, a priest would have to be found willing to condone a secret marriage. Though Clinton remembered his mother's claim that marriages between Papists and Protestants were invalid if celebrated in Ireland by Catholic priests, he found it hard to believe that such archaic laws could still be in force. To the best of his recollection, the events of his mother's story had taken place upwards of twenty years ago. What alarmed him more was a strong premonition that most priests—for no better reason than straightforward religious bigotry—would be extremely reluctant to marry any man or woman who had not been baptized a Catholic. Though he had no intention of taking one priest's refusal as final, Clinton was still acutely nervous about the outcome of his first encounter.

Skirting the gray walls of St. Patrick's Cathedral, he crossed the squalid ghetto of Patrick's Close with its booths and rag stalls spilling out across the sloping street. Here, old women, mothers with babies, and barefooted boys picked their way through piles of soiled bedding, blackened cooking pots, and cracked china, as though searching for hidden treasure. His mind fixed on other things, Clinton eyed them absently, only briefly perplexed that such objects could be of service to anyone.

Looking to right and left down the narrow side streets off the Coombe, Clinton at last saw a church and rapidly made his way to the door. At the far end of the nave near the altar a single pale light was glowing; closer at hand, clusters of candles lit a crudely painted statue of the Virgin. Over the chancel arch hung a massive crucifix, Christ's twisted body running with blood as luridly red as the heart on the Virgin's breast. A young woman dipped her fingers in the holy water, crossed herself, and genuflected before moving to a pew. Although he did not share his uncle's prejudices against Catholics, their rituals were alien to Clinton and struck him as extravagant and faintly distasteful. The reverential mutterings of the handful of black-shawled figures increased his unease.

A woman with a broom came out of a small door in the wall to the right of the sanctuary. Clinton asked her in a low voice where he could find the priest.

"In the presbytery," she replied brusquely, moving away to brush the carpet within the altar rails. Not knowing whether the presbytery was the priest's house or some room within the church like the vestry or sacristy, he pursued her and asked her to explain.

"He'll be here soon enough" was the curt reply.

Ten long minutes passed, and then, through the door used by the cleaning woman, came the priest. He was a small man with a bald skull and gray comblike fringes of hair above his ears. Beneath unruly eyebrows, his deep-set eyes were intelligent but strangely impassive.

Clinton rose at once. "May I speak to you, Father?" The priest inclined his head in silent encouragement. "I want to marry," murmured Clinton, looking at the stout-soled shoes sticking out beneath the frayed hem of the priest's soutane. He continued softly: "The wedding must be kept from my family."

"Banns must be read, my son."

"Is there no way to avoid that?"

"In certain circumstances." He looked at Clinton closely. "You're not of this parish?"

"Nor of any other."

"Why is that?"

"I'm a soldier."

The priest, who was holding a heavy bunch of keys, moved them from hand to hand, as if weighing them in his palms. "You attend Mass wherever you're stationed?"

"I'm not a religious man."

The priest looked at him with the same immobility of expression, the merest hint of disparagement and pity momentarily apparent in a slight movement of his hands. "But you're a Catholic?"

The hint of questioning was so faint that Clinton for a second thought the remark was simply one of reproach. He gazed at the row of cloth-covered buttons down the front of the soutane, then looked up and knew from the man's watchful and expectant face that he would have to give a direct answer. His heart was beating faster.

"I have no religion," he whispered, meeting a suddenly cold and unsympathetic gaze.

The woman in the sanctuary was still vigorously sweeping. The muttering of prayers was very faint now, as though all ears in the church were attentive to this muted conversation between priest and petitioner.

"Were you baptized a Catholic?" Clinton shook his head. "Were you baptized into any other church?"

"I was christened but not confirmed. I'm no Protestant."

The priest looked at him steadily, as if some unpleasant doubt had finally been resolved. He seemed relieved. "There's no priest will marry you."

"An infant has no choice in baptism. I've never been an Anglican communicant."

"That makes no kind of difference at all. You're a Protestant in my eyes. Apostasy from your church makes no odds." He paused and thrust the keys into the deep pocket of his cassock.

Masking his anger and cruel disappointment, Clinton said calmly, "The woman's a Catholic. Would you have her live sinfully and her children grow up heathens?"

In the dim light, Clinton thought he caught a shadow of doubt in the priest's downcast eyes. He said rapidly, "If you wish to be received into the church and place yourself under instruction . . ." Seeing the almost imperceptible negative movement of Clinton's head, he broke off and began to move towards the sanctuary rails.

"Wait, Father. If I become a Catholic, what would I have to do to have the banns waived?"

The man moved with a gesture of impatience. "Wait till you've been received, my son." He turned his back with finality and opened the wooden gate in the rails.

An hour later, in the colonel's absence, Clinton, as adjutant, was presiding at morning battalion orderly room. From the square he heard the sergeant major's commands, the usual wearisome routine.

"Escort and prisoners, halt! Front turn! Fall in the evidences. First man, cap off! Escort and prisoners, right turn . . . left wheel . . . quick march. Left, right, left, right."

Clinton looked up from the baize-covered table as the first man halted inside the door between the fixed bayonets of the escort.

As the orderly officer handed Clinton the charge sheet, the sergeant major barked out, "Number 432, Trooper Williams, C Troop. Neglect of duty when orderly man and making an improper reply to a noncommissioned officer, Corporal Wilson. State your evidence, Corporal."

While Clinton listened with half an ear to why and in what manner the trooper had refused to clean a ration tin, he was thinking of quite different words spoken in the dim interior of a church and what they meant to him.

The corporal was rambling to the end of his evidence: ". . . and he said if it wasn't clean enough for me, sir, I could do the other thing."

"Which was what?" asked Clinton gravely.

"It was obscene, sir."

"His exact words please, Corporal."

"Stuff it up your arse, you cockeyed bastard, sir."

Clinton nodded and raised an eyebrow. "Your vision is normal, Corporal?"

"Yes, sir."

"And you are legitimate?"

"Yes, sir."

Clinton looked at the prisoner. "Do you wish to be tried by court-martial or be dealt with by me? I give you the choice because you'd been drinking."

"By you, sir."

"Your remark was slanderous and you disobeyed an order personally given by a superior." He paused. "Two months' imprisonment with hard labor and ten days confined to barracks after that. March out."

The seven other cases he dealt with at a similar pace, handing out the routine punishments for the usual crimes. Once he had found it hard not to smile sometimes during the reading of the charges, but now he could hear anything without moving a muscle.

When the others had gone, Dick Lambert, that week's orderly officer, grinned at him. "Weren't you a bit soft with the first one?"

"Justice with mercy, Dick." He frowned and unhitched his sword slings from the side of his chair. "Do you love Kate?" he asked abruptly.

Lambert looked at him in astonishment and then laughed. "I sometimes think so."

Dick had lived with his shopgirl mistress for two years in England, and on coming to Dublin had immediately taken a villa for her a few miles south of the town at Blackrock.

Clinton stood up and sighed. "What'd you do if Kate wanted to come here? Asked to see a parade or riding school?"

"Tell her not to be a bloody idiot."

"It must be hard for her."

Lambert looked puzzled. "You been drinking, Clinton? If I brought her here, what the hell would Lady Spencer say to Mrs. Hanbury? Talk about being cut in the mess—I'd be hacked to bits. Old Spencer would bust a blood vessel."

"Does she mind being hidden away?"

"What the hell's the alternative? When in Rome . . . don't you know?"

Clinton smiled briefly and moved to the door. "Rules of the game," he murmured lightly and walked out onto the square. A mistress would expect her existence to be denied, but it would be a very hard thing for a wife not to be able to avow her marriage in public. Yet if she accepted him, he would have to ask that of Theresa.

Ever since leaving the church, it had become more and more apparent to Clinton that the sudden marriage, which now obsessed him, would prove impossible unless he lied about his religion to a priest. As he entered the mess anteroom, his thoughts were hopelessly divided. When noon came—the time he had asked Theresa to come to the barracks—and the brisk chimes of the stable's clock rang out across the parade ground, he was still undecided what he would do.

Theresa climbed down from the outside car and paid the driver. Outside the gates a sentry was marching to and fro, stoically ignoring the jeers of a couple of small boys scampering ahead of him. In the gray shabby street his neat yellow-corded uniform and brilliantly burnished scabbard looked bizarrely out of place.

As instructed by Clinton, she walked under the arch and told the sentry outside the guardroom that Lord Ardmore was expecting her. The man clicked his spurred heels together and went inside. Moments later another soldier emerged and set off across the gravel barrack square towards the mess. The buildings were stark and unembellished save for the royal coat of arms in the center of the pediment above the stables. Everywhere a soulless neatness: scrubbed brickwork, whitewashed stones marking the perimeter of the square. At first she did not recognize the uniformed figure approaching from the far side of the parade ground, and when she did, she had no time to feel emotion; at that moment she started violently as the sergeant of the guard roared out behind her, "Guard, turn out!"

She watched with a mixture of perplexity and interest as men tumbled out from the guardroom, buckling on sword belts and fastening buttons as they ran, completing these tasks while forming two ranks.

"Guard, open order march. Ranks, right dress. Eyes front."

The stamping of feet and jingle of spurs distracted her, and she was surprised that Clinton was already only yards away. As she moved forward with a smile on her lips, she was frozen by another deafening shout: "Guard, present arms!"

With a clash of boots, the hussars brought up their carbines, hands slapping hard against the stocks in unison.

Clinton raised a hand to his forehead, and waited a moment for the sergeant to bellow, "Guard, right turn. Dismiss," before shaking Theresa's hand and murmuring, "Welcome to Richmond Barracks."

"How often does all that happen?" she asked with a flicker of amusement.

"Whenever an officer passes the guardroom, or a troop comes in or out."

"I'd think twice before walking about if I caused all that trouble."

"Rubbish. Guards like a little exercise to break the tedium." He saw her looking at his plain black frogged braid and pillbox forage cap with what he took to be disappointment. "You'll see us in full dress on Sunday parade. Plumes and sabretaches. No end of frippery and toggery."

"It looks gorgeous and you know it."

He gave an ironic shrug and smiled. "A thing like a lady's muff on one's head with something like a red jelly bag at the side. Enough plumes to make an undertaker's horses look naked. Yes, it's gorgeous. Like a dress rehearsal for Waterloo."

He returned the salute of a passing trooper. Across the square near the riding school, a column of defaulters were being marched up and down, turned and halted, brought to the double, and set to mark time with an arbitrary speed of command that struck Theresa as positively sadistic.

After one order, not a man moved, and Clinton nodded appreciatively. "That's good drill."

"Oh?"

"The order was deliberately wrong."

In the riding school the recruits were being put over a brushwood jump, their stirrups crossed in front of their saddles and their arms folded so they could not reach for the reins. As one man was pitched over his horse's head, Theresa looked away.

Clinton kicked at the soft tan on the ground with the toe of his boot. "He'll be fine."

The riding master, a spare, wiry little man, helped the trooper to his feet. "Sit further back, lad, and you'll get a longer ride."

As the next man cantered up to the jump, the master yelled, "Grip with those thighs. You're not in a circus."

By clutching the horse's mane, the rider somehow contrived to stay in the saddle. As the next man was flung to the ground,

Theresa turned on Clinton angrily. "Why can't they be taught more first?"

"I'll show you," he said, before going across to the riding master and having a few words with him. A broad grin creased the master's leathery face.

"It's your lucky day, lads. You attend to his lordship."

Not knowing quite what to expect, Theresa watched Clinton mount the master's broad-backed cob and, employing both reins and stirrups, ride at the jump. Just as the horse rose, Clinton leaned out ludicrously to one side across the animal's neck, so that it seemed certain he would be thrown as the horse landed, but by dexterous use of the reins he saved himself amidst loud laughter. Theresa felt her cheeks burn with anger and humiliation.

The riding master shook his head sadly at the recruits. "Lord Ardmore has just controlled his horse to keep his seat. His lordship will now use his seat to control his horse." He cleared his throat and went on with the weary pedantry of a school-master with a class of halfwits: "As the horse rises, you will see the adjutant lean forward from the hips, taking his weight off the quarters and keeping his own position vertical. When the horse lands, you'll observe his lordship lean back, taking his weight off the forelegs and keeping his own balance." He paused and sucked in his cheeks. "And just for the lads who laughed, I'll lay some coins between the adjutant's knees and the saddle . . . and, lads, I'll give you each a guinea if one of those coins comes adrift."

The master crossed the stirrups in front of Clinton and in-serted the coins. Flexing his thighs and with a touch from his hand before folding his arms, Clinton set the horse at the jump. The perfect ease and unity of horse and rider over the hurdle brought a strange tingling to Theresa's cheeks. In dead silence the riding master walked up to the horse and removed the coins. As Theresa and Clinton were leaving the school, they heard him pouring abuse on his pupils; if he ever heard any man laugh at an officer of the 15th, by God, he'd . . . By then Clinton and Theresa were out in the square, and Clinton patted his thigh with his whip.

"The jump makes them use these. A good seat comes first;

without it they'd never survive two minutes in a melee. Imagine relying on reins for balance while making pirouettes and fighting with a sword. If they're rising in the stirrups, they won't carry the horse's weight into their cuts."

Behind the school was a six-acre walled field covered with sparse grass. Here troopers with pointing swords were galloping down a course lined on each side with a mixed lot of dummies, some upright, others prone, representing crouching or lying men. The rapid thud of hoofs, the snorting of the horses, and the sharp cries of command sent a shudder down Theresa's spine. The glint of flashing steel and the power of the stretched muscles under glistening coats held her fascinated. Within a couple of minutes three men had lost their swords and one had sprained his wrist before completing the course.

Clinton nodded in the direction of the man nursing his wrist. "He timed a point badly; they've got to be delivered at a precise moment in closing." He grinned at her. "Yours isn't the only profession where timing matters."

Seeing the alertness and animation in Clinton's face as he watched the riders, Theresa came close to tears. The sights and sounds around them—flying tails, wildly distended nostrils, the display of power and control, and the tense concentration and pride in effort—overwhelmed her.

At the approach of riders, noncommissioned officers standing by the various dummies, yelled out, "Engage . . . point . . . withdraw."

The words formed a continuous chant against the background of the thundering hoofs.

"In time it becomes instinctive," remarked Clinton, pointing down the course with his whip. "The next lot starting are better. They'll just get warnings of infantry right or left and judge their own distances."

Some of the dummies were so close together that the speed of reflex needed not to miss one out was exceptional.

After a long silence, Theresa asked, "When do you need to do this?"

"In pursuit of broken infantry. Stops them re-forming. The sensible ones lie down and try to shoot us in the back when we've gone past."

A sudden vision of these straw-stuffed dummies as men, and the steel biting into living flesh and bone made her wince.

"Safer to kill them first," she murmured.

"Much," he replied lightly, and Theresa recalled Louise's question those months ago about the number of Chinamen Clinton had killed.

She glanced up the course. "Would *you* miss any of these?"

He laughed good-humoredly and guided her arm for a moment. "Come over here."

A hundred yards to the left, the regiment's subalterns were tent pegging: charging down in threes, leaning low in their saddles, trying to carry away the small pegs on the points of their swords. Only one threesome out of the six they watched managed to lift all three pegs from the ground.

"That isn't so easy."

"It looks impossible at that speed."

"It is to start with."

Before leaving, they saw a half-troop charging. The closeness of the riders to each other puzzled Theresa; it not only looked dangerous, but the men scarcely had space to swing their swords.

"Their knees are almost touching."

"That's how cavalry charges. Imagine closing with an enemy squadron as disciplined as your own." He smiled ruefully. "It's so terrifying that if there are any gaps in your line, men are going to try to turn or pull round. They mustn't ever be given enough room to succeed."

"How can they use their swords?"

"They won't need to till the melee. The weapon that takes them through is the horse's weight and speed—and the compactness of the line. Like a solid nine-foot wall moving at ten yards a second." He jabbed at the ground with his whip. "Each horse and rider weighs about a thousand pounds."

The deliberate prosaicness of his description surprised her.

Passing the back of the officers' mess on the way to the coach house, he apologized for not being able to take her inside.

"Do women ever go in?" she asked.

"Only officers' wives on Christmas night."

"That's all?"

"Unless the regiment holds a ball." He seemed suddenly dispirited and weary. From behind closed windows in the main troop-room block, they heard the band practicing minor scales: a sound as mournfully evocative as muted organ music in an empty church.

As the landau rattled through the streets of north Dublin, Clinton's grim mood persisted.

She took his hand. "You'll miss the life dreadfully."

"Perhaps sometimes. It's often duller than death. Training, and more training, and at the end of it all . . . Ireland." He stared absently out of the window at the decaying and spectral mansions in Mountjoy Square. I'll only really miss the possibility of proper fighting."

"Do you enjoy war?" she asked neutrally, but he could see her incomprehension and it saddened him.

"I love it," he murmured in a low, almost passionate voice. "Only large infantry battles are vile—long hours of killing until one side's had enough. A cavalry charge takes minutes, melees and pursuits a few more. Surprise and skill with steel weapons is a thing apart. . . . Can't you understand?" After a brief silence she nodded slowly. "Armies are great lumbering things, blind and deaf without us—the light cavalry. We're an army's eyes and ears—patrolling in darkness up to the enemy's lines, taking a prisoner or two if we can. And in battle—You've seen hawks and kestrels hovering. We do too—wait and watch. We'll charge to relieve breaking infantry, to guard a flank or break a square. We'll protect a retreat and see that a beaten enemy never saves his guns."

She smiled. "An army's natural aristocrats. And none of you ever hurt or killed."

"Not many if the moment's right. And if it is—" He broke off bitterly, eyes dark with frustration. "I can't describe it." He paused and then leaned towards her intently. "Everything's so fast, and choices so simple and real. I don't know what it is—a kind of joy takes you by the throat, every second singing in the blood, hearts hammering with the hoofs, and the world rolls under one."

"And it's terrifying."

"Has to be, but it's not real death one faces when every sense is burning. Not like the horror of a slow disease when the end is certain and the mind fixed on it. Who's ever more alive than when in danger? Life's loved far less in peace; time limps and young men babble about suicide and skulls. In China we loved the sky and the stars, the mist in the morning and the coolness before the sun rose high. We ate hungrily and slept deep by bivouac fires and never thought beyond the next day."

"And then they took you prisoner."

"I was talking about fighting."

"Not what follows?"

"I'm here to tell the tale."

"You never have, Clinton."

"I will. But not today."

They were passing down stately Sackville Street, past Gresham's Hotel, and speeding on towards the Nelson Pillar and Ormond Bridge. Elegant carriages drove by in front of smart drapers' shops and the lofty classical façades of public buildings. An orderly clattered past on a sleek-groomed horse, probably on his way from the Castle to the General Post Office.

"I'll tell you about the day we came back to the depot. There were large crowds and women running out across the street grabbing at stirrups, weeping. I remember the cottage gardens, a child in a pinafore leaning over a gate, pink geraniums in a window, and everywhere people tumbling out to look at us and cheer. There was delirium that evening. No discipline at all, dancing in the barrack square . . . and such drinking. I've seen some too. And later, men and women writhing together in the corn bins in the stables, and others watching. Some splashing naked in the horse troughs."

"Why did you choose to tell me that now?" She sounded curious rather than disapproving.

"It came to mind."

"A reproach?"

"I don't know." He paused and struck a clenched fist against the carriage seat. "You can be so damned dispassionate. You make my past seem—" He stopped, unable to find the right word. "You wrote about wanting to be a vivandière, a simple woman. You wrote as an actress."

"I'd have run out and grabbed your stirrups."

"Like an actress."

"Like a woman who loves you."

"Who takes off her modesty with her skirt. Only when we're in bed—" He broke off and covered his face with his hands. "Why did you write what you did?"

"Because I'm scared. Do you know that word's meaning? I'm like the cowards who'd pull round if they could. And all the time you're trying to force me on. I *want* to give everything; but I'm not like you. Sometimes, yes, I can be impulsive; but I can't afford the luxury of your simple choices. If you had a child, you'd understand fear better. If you'd struggled, seen somebody you loved slowly crushed. Seen that other death, when the cut's not clean but the cords fray away one by one— sight, touch, speech—and the heart strives vainly to reach across a gulf that only widens." She looked at him imploringly. "You want so much, Clinton."

As she finished speaking, the landau came to a stop outside a narrow bow-fronted house with a small painted sign above the door: DRESSMAKER & COSTUMIER. Clinton bowed his head and then shouted to the coachman to drive on to the hotel.

"Why did we stop there?" she asked.

"It's of no account."

"Please."

"I wanted to take you to a Castle ball. I thought it might amuse you. I made a mistake." He had spoken harshly but turned to her with sudden tenderness. "I wanted to dance with you, be seen with you, do everything we can before you go. I fixed your invitation with the State Steward."

"Please take me."

He nodded absently, as if he could no longer understand why the subject had been mentioned. "Help me to understand you," he whispered.

"Perhaps we only love what can't be understood, what's always changing." She kissed him. "Take me back to the dressmaker's. I want you to help me choose."

He shook his head, distressed to be reminded. "I looked at some pictures. The woman knows the one I liked. White . . . it made me think of York."

"I do love you, Clinton."

"Then marry me."

Afterwards she felt that he had dropped the words into a space between seconds, as softly as falling feathers, so that they did not reach her till later. Panic tightened about her heart leaving her dazed and trembling.

"I can't answer you," she stammered. "Don't press me, Clinton. I beg you not to press me."

"I'm sorry I distressed you," he murmured, looking out at the passing buildings, his face remote and closed.

She stared at him as if he had hit her. Her words came in a breathless rush. "You showed me your regiment—the life you live for, the life you lose unless you make your peace with Esmond."

"I can't make my peace with him," he replied quietly, "so don't continue using that against me." He leaned closer, his eyes burning into her; she stared stupidly at the gold lace around his cap as her heart beat like a fist in her chest. "Very well," he went on in a resonant whisper, "you won't answer me. A refusal might end a pleasant liaison while you're still in love. I sympathize." He let out his breath and gazed ahead of him. "I only ask you to understand this: If I ever ask again, I must have your answer." He had spoken so gently that his words had only just been audible above the noise of the wheels.

Theresa did not reply as Grafton Street ended and they swung left into St. Stephen's Green. Though his face did not show it, Clinton was inexpressibly relieved. He had taken a very great risk and come through unscathed. She had not rejected him, but her determined evasion had finally blasted all the scruples and misgivings that had shackled him. She had allowed him a second chance, and when he took it, Clinton intended to be ready. At last he was certain he knew what he had to do.

A little later, as if nothing of significance had happened, Clinton suggested that they return to the dressmaker's.

CHAPTER NINETEEN

 On Theresa's third morning in Dublin, Clinton told her that he would have to spend the day attending to military duties; but in fact he traveled some forty miles out of town on the Southern & Western Railway to Portarlington, where he hired an outside car and told the driver to head north.

Though the sun was shining in a clear pale sky, the track was rutted hard with frost, and the wind was cold enough to make Clinton's eyes water. The carman held the reins loosely in his mittened hands, letting the mare trot or walk as she pleased, and this, combined with the old man's soft melancholy singing, irritated Clinton considerably. When he remonstrated, the driver replied that he had to "keep the baste in humor with a song."

"Then keep her in motion with a touch of the whip."

With a shrug, the man struck the mare lightly with the ends of the reins, and she trotted briskly up the next hill before ambling again. On either side were scanty fields drifting from thin grass to bog and back again, a pattern repeated as far as the distant rim of wandering hills. A shimmering lake with rushes around it provided momentary diversion from the monotony, as did a group of well-kept cabins, but Clinton was tense and restlessly impatient to reach the next village. The country was desolate and bare, yet beautiful in the winter sunlight.

"Everyone's leaving the country." The old man sighed, dropping his chin into the layers of frieze round his wrinkled neck, like a tortoise preparing to withdraw its head into its shell.

Ballygowan began in broken pavements and dirty thatched cottages, and straggled loosely up a low hill towards a main street lined with naked trees and boasting a single building of consequence: a whitewashed convent set in a large garden. The scores of broken windows, invariable donkey carts, and familiar crooked lettering above the windows of the shops reminded Clinton of a hundred other villages. There was no hotel, only a place that was half inn, half whiskey shop. Clinton told the driver to stop there. Apart from a few women buying bullocks' hearts and other scraps of meat from a stall, and three men trying to force a large sow into a cart, the place was deserted.

Clinton entered the inn, hoping to find a farmer or two who might talk a bit after a few drinks about the local priests, but the only inmates were a couple of women behind the bar, dandling a baby boy and crooning to him. Clinton went out again and beckoned to his driver. A carman was as likely to know all the local gossip as anybody else.

"Come and have a whiskey negus."

The old man looked at him suspiciously. "Is it making a fool of me you are, sorr?"

"Get down and come in."

By the time they reached the bar, the younger of the two women had slipped down her dress and was suckling the child.

"Shame on you, Mary Skully," said the old man in his thin peevish voice. "Making a show of yourself before strangers."

"And shame on you too, you old fool."

"If you were my daughter—"

"I'd be on the streets with the rest," she replied without rancor.

The old man spat into the turf fire and sat down on a bench by the window while Clinton asked for their drinks.

"I'll have to be heating the water for negus, and we've no lemon," said the older woman.

"Then bring the whiskey neat."

As they drank together, Clinton saw his companion's lined face slowly softening. He jerked his head in the direction of the women. "The devil a bit of use talking to the likes of them," he muttered and drained his glass. When Clinton called for another, he said, "More power to your honor. May your heart never stop beating."

After talking about horses and the hard life of a carman in winter, Clinton's driver became more confiding and spoke of the wife and six children he had to support.

"On seven shillings a week, your honor. Just that to keep 'em all and put dacent clothes on me back for driving gintry like yourself. No wonder I'm only the wreck of the man I was."

But in spite of the weary maudlin voice, Clinton detected a gleam of cunning in the old hooded eyes. Gentlemen did not buy drinks for carmen and talk to them without good reason. Clinton folded his arms and said, without wasting further time, "I want to find a priest who'd dispense with marriage banns for a consideration."

"And would your honor be considering an old man with devil a shilling to lay by for his childer?"

"Your children must have left home years ago."

"As God's my witness, I married late in life."

Clinton did not bother to reply but took two sovereigns from his pocket and placed them by his glass.

The man eyed them with eager longing, and cried out excitedly to the girl, "Haven't I six childer, Mary?"

"And six cows beside," she said lightly, taking her nipple from the child's gums.

The old man leaped up and clenched his fleshless hands. His lips were drawn back in a snarl, and he shook his shriveled head from side to side.

Clinton took his arm firmly. "I don't care if you've six or sixty children. Find me a priest who likes money as well as you, and you'll get what you want." Clinton swept up the coins and returned them to his pocket.

The girl, who had evidently been listening to the conversation, hitched up her dress and came over to them. "Father Phelan's your man, sir," she said, patting the baby's back.

"You keep to your own," shouted the old man, clutching the edge of the table.

Ignoring him, Clinton looked attentively at the dark-skinned girl. "Would he marry a couple without many questions?"

"Saving the fee, your honor," she replied, smiling as the infant burped loudly.

"Enough," roared the carman.

"Why isn't he particular?" asked Clinton.

"He wouldn't marry Kate Deacy to Colm Higgins for a pound. Three pounds or nothing, says he. So they went against him and lived under the one roof, and Colm blamed their sin on him, so he had to marry them for a pound, and now never a soul in the parish will pay a penny more than Colm. And his reverence's power over the people is gone from him entirely."

The old man drew himself up and laughed derisively into his glass. "As true a priest as any in Ireland. Now Father Maguire, there's the man for your honor." He thumped the table and faced the woman, stabbing the air with a crooked finger. "Isn't his church roof fallen in and the builders gone with it half mended? Wasn't he selling indulgences and scapulars and still not enough money to finish it? And the plaster's off the walls with the wet, and the people all going to Lisnama for Mass because of God's curse on their church and the cold in it." The old man looked at Clinton triumphantly. "What does your honor say to that?"

Clinton did not reply but took out a penny, making it plain that he was going to toss it.

"Let the woman call," jeered the carman, hiding his tension.

As Clinton flipped up the coin, the woman called out, "Heads."

The old man bent low over the stained table, watching in agony as the coin hit the wood, wobbled, tilted, and finally fell.

"Tails it is," screamed the carman, dancing a few shuffling steps in his large hobnailed boots. "The darling," he cried, raising the coin to his lips and handing it back to Clinton.

"If you're wrong, we'll try the other."

"Never a fear of it." The old man chuckled. "Never a fear."

It was four miles from Ballygowan to Father Maguire's church at Rathnagar, but Clinton did not resent the slow and bumpy ride. He felt well pleased with his morning's work. His guess that he would fare better in the country than in Dublin already seemed likely to prove correct. Here in the villages, where congregations were smaller and poorer, the priests would take less door money after Mass and receive lower fees for their offices. Whether some would therefore be more helpfully disposed towards rich strangers than were their better-provided colleagues in the city remained to be seen. Though Clinton had not said any more to Theresa about marriage, he was determined not to be taken by surprise if she accepted him. It was not his intention to allow her time for further reflection.

There was a silence in the room while the priest stood thinking. From the window of Father Maguire's parlor, the west end of the church was only a dozen yards away, hemmed about with wooden scaffolding. Clinton looked from the gilt paper cope round a saint's effigy on the mantelpiece to the priest's ruddy face. Wiry hairs sprouted from his ears and nostrils, and the backs of his muscular hands were well covered with a thick black fuzz. He crossed the room and sat down, resting his arms on the breviary on his writing desk.

"The bishop can dispense with the banns right enough, but it's a special favor he'd be conferring." He looked searchingly at Clinton. "He'd only do it if you invoke the prayers of the poor by way of an offering."

"Would five pounds see to it?"

"You must show yourself worthy by a real sacrifice."

"Tell me the normal fee."

"You'll know the story of the widow's mite?" Maguire paused, wrinkling his bushy eyebrows, which reminded Clinton of furry caterpillars. "Will you say why you come here to be married?"

"My family consider the lady unsuitable. She has no fortune. I have to keep it dark."

"Your family are Protestants?"

"I'm no Protestant myself. My mother's mother was converted to Catholicism. I've some Catholic cousins. The lady I want to marry is a Catholic." Clinton stopped, afraid that he had appeared overanxious.

"You'd agree to any children being brought up Catholics?"

"Yes."

"There must be extenuation in that," murmured the priest, as if to reassure himself. Until then, Clinton had felt apprehensive, but this remark made him more confident. The priest cupped his heavy chin in the palm of a hand. "It's a great hindrance you can't declare yourself a Catholic."

"Won't you help me otherwise?"

Maguire sighed and closed his eyes for a moment. "I'd marry you myself as happy as you like, but there's a legal difficulty." His thick eyebrows came together. "Isn't that why you came to an out-of-the-way place?"

Clinton shook his head. "I knew I'd have trouble anywhere if I didn't say I was a Catholic. I thought a country priest might be more sympathetic."

"It's more than sympathy you're wanting. It's a felony I'm guilty of if I marry a Protestant to a Catholic. I'm thinking you knew that, sir."

After a silence, Clinton said, "I'd heard that used to be so. I honestly thought those sorts of laws had been changed years ago." The priest said nothing. Very close to giving up, Clinton made a last effort. "I told you I'm not a Protestant. I've not been to church for years. So how can the law apply?"

"I can't be taking the risk."

"I wouldn't expect you to make an entry in your register." He smiled at the man's troubled face. "You can't think you'd be unfrocked."

Maguire laughed gloomily. "Unfrocked is it? There's not a stitch of clothing they'd leave on me if you turn out a Protestant. You could walk out on your wife and the law wouldn't stop you. A convenient sort of marriage for scoundrels."

"But if I say I'm a Catholic, that exonerates you?"

The priest remained silent, evidently weighing various considerations. At last he met Clinton's eyes. "I'd renew a previous consent for you."

"What does that mean?"

"If you've been to the register office with her, I'll renew the consent you gave there."

"Will your ceremony take the form of a church marriage?"

"Sure it will."

Clinton frowned. "How can a previous ceremony add anything to a wedding in church? A marriage is a marriage in my view."

"That's my opinion too," replied Maguire blandly.

"Then why bother with anything else?"

"To protect myself."

"How?"

"If there's trouble later, I can say I gave a blessing to a marriage already entered into. For the lady's peace of mind, you understand." The priest lowered his head and then looked at Clinton gravely. "Did you make a civil contract with the lady?"

Clinton hesitated. Yet how could the lie be worth the name when the man was actually inviting it? Vows spoken in church in perfect faith could not be affected by such petty quibbles. He folded his arms. "I made a civil contract."

"Would you say you did before a witness?" Clinton shook his head, watching the priest tensely. A long silence passed. Maguire gazed out of the window and then rose abruptly. "Very well. I'll trust you. When are you planning on coming?"

"Is three days too soon?"

"If it's Sunday you're coming on, you'd best not be later than an hour before Mass. I'd be obliged if you'd pay the fee now. You can make it twenty pounds." The priest spoke rapidly as if eager to be done with the matter in case his doubts returned. Sensing this, Clinton counted the notes without argument and placed them on the mantelpiece. A new thought set his conscience at rest. The law could be no threat, since the only possible reason for invoking it would be a desire on his part to renege on the marriage, a course, he told himself, he would die before contemplating. Leaving the house, he laughed suddenly. The interview he had just undergone would seem pretty stupid if she turned him down. His smile died a moment later, and with a set expression he stepped out into the sunshine.

238

As the carman ran up eagerly, Clinton dipped into his pockets and, without further ado, slapped the sovereigns into his hand. The old man crossed himself and dropped the coins into his waistcoat pocket. Then beaming with happiness, he struck his chest two mighty blows with his fists and danced round Clinton with sudden little steps.

" 'Twas God sent you," he shouted, "for saving the church and helping a poor man. Three cheers for the bride. Hurrah!" He stopped dancing and, sweeping off his battered hat, bowed ceremoniously to Clinton as he stepped up into the car. Then with the agility of a man of twenty, he leaped up onto the box and whipped up the horse to a canter, so that Clinton had to hold on with all his might to avoid being jolted out onto the rutted track.

CHAPTER TWENTY

After the darkness and the long wait in the packed procession of carriages crawling up Cork Hill to the Castle gates, the brilliance of light and color at the foot of the grand staircase was dazzling. Divested of wraps and cloaks, naked female shoulders shone white as ivory under the blazing gaslight of opulently twisted candelabra. High on the white paneled walls, the burnished blades of hundreds of swords, arranged in star patterns, flashed as brightly as the chandeliers. Like tall statues ranged facing each other all the way up the staircase were uniformed guardsmen, whose dripping faces under their bearskins matched the scarlet of their coats. Footmen in powdered wigs and purple livery tailcoats stood on every landing, watching the ascending wave of humanity with expressionless eyes, indifferent alike to aigrettes and epaulettes.

"Don't introduce me to anybody unless it would be rude not to," murmured Theresa as they reached the foot of the stairs. Clinton made no reply but looked around him with the eye of a man surprised suddenly to find himself mixing with the cast of a pantomime. "And no cynicism," she said, emphasizing her point with a swift touch of her elbow. She had never been to a court ball, and her lover's gold-braided uniform and campaign medals filled her with pride and an emotional tightness in the throat. Certain that such an evening would never be repeated, she wanted to be able to look back on it with simple wonder. Yet even before they reached St. Patrick's Hall, she read the sadness and envy on young girls' faces and the silent determination stamped on the features of their mothers. Strangest of all was the sight of women, some older than herself, meekly submitting to the guiding nudges of chaperones, as if numbed into inanity by memories of past failures on the Castle's waxed and polished floors. The fashion for sleeveless low-cut dresses was merciless to bony shoulders, and mandatory long white gloves tortured those with fat arms. The fight for eligible marriage partners was not a struggle that favored the faint-hearted.

Since Clinton had first asked her to marry him, so unconcerned had he seemed about all serious matters that at times she could scarcely believe that the subject had ever been raised. Yet she knew him well enough to recognize his hallmark. Too proud to show resentment, disdainful of bargaining or compromise, he would remain silent until presenting her with a final choice. When that time came, he would not spare her. Knowing what answer she ought to give, it still terrified her that her will might break. It had been to achieve just this that he had let her know in advance that if she would not give everything, then he would accept nothing. And every day that he maintained his nonchalance, and she dared not broach the subject, a few more threads of resolution frayed and parted.

As they passed a panting dowager, squeezed by a miracle of tight lacing into a dress that seemed made for a woman half her size, Clinton said quietly with the easy humor that had now become his mask, "the survival of the fattest by unnatural adaptation." Theresa looked at him reprovingly, but he only laughed. "It really is like Darwin's theory. Only the strong survive the struggle; the female's never more vulnerable than when guarding her young."

"And never more dangerous," whispered Theresa as they entered a long drawing room where the Louis XV furniture had been pushed back against the walls, providing seats for the weary but not impeding the passing throng. Clinton had been looking for somebody, and at last hailed an officer in a uniform identical to his own. Approaching at a leisurely pace, the soldier inclined his head slightly to Theresa.

Clinton turned to her formally. "Mrs. Barr, permit me to introduce Captain Lambert." They shook hands, and Lambert looked at Theresa appraisingly. Clinton continued: "If duty calls, Dick, could you . . . ?" He glanced at Theresa.

"I should be delighted, milord."

"Do I need a chaperone?" asked Theresa, a smile masking real irritation.

"Captain Lambert has a fund of entertaining anecdotes." The two men smiled at one another, and Clinton asked in a stage whisper, "Have you danced with our colonel's lady?"

"I have, and her hoofs have lost none of their power."

"Have you never trodden on toes?" asked Theresa.

Lambert grinned affably. "Figuratively, Mrs. Barr, but not physically."

A debutante and her mother came up to them and greeted Lambert, who made the necessary introductions. The girl was fingering her dance card anxiously, eyes liquid with invitation.

"Perhaps I might have the honor of your next waltz, Miss Tyne?" asked Lambert with a hesitance owing more, Theresa guessed, to reluctance than to bashfulness.

"Yes indeed." The young lady flushed as she looked at the few scribbled names on her card. "Oh dear, I'm afraid it's already promised. Perhaps the . . . ." She caught her mother's eye and looked down miserably.

Lambert gave a convincing show of disappointment. "The one after is a polka, I seem to recall from the program. A shame my only dances are the waltz and the galop."

"Not the quadrille?" asked the slighted mother with an arch smile.

"Alas, a prior engagement." Lambert sighed, slicing away the last frail threads of their net; but he walked on with the disconsolate pair, chatting to them as they made for St. Patrick's Hall. Clinton and Theresa followed them at a distance.

"Why does he come if he won't dance?"

Clinton shrugged. "To look around. The Castle aides-de-camp dance with the ones who are left out. That's their job."

"The girls must love dancing with them."

"They dance very well, I'm told."

"You know what I meant, Clinton."

Threading their way through the crush on the edge of the dance floor, Clinton was cornered and obliged to promise later dances to two officers' wives. On either side of the whirling sea of tulle and muslin were little gilded chairs, and at the far end of the immense hall a red dais supported the empty thrones of the viceroy and his consort. In the gallery, behind a screen of palms and evergreen, a hidden orchestra played tirelessly, only ceasing for short periods between the dances.

As a waltz began, Clinton turned to Theresa with eyes suddenly grown serious. "Will you do me the honor, Miss Simmonds?"

He offered her his arm, and they set off towards the center of the floor, where the circling of the dancers was slower. He drew her close to him, and they moved off carefully at first, because of the press of couples, but soon they felt the rhythm and their bodies seemed to soften and mold together as they glided and turned, quickening as one when the tempo changed. She raised her eyes to his and felt the same tremor in her breast that was always there before they kissed. And it was like loving, this feeling that she was slipping away from herself, the room swimming vague about her, while at the center they seemed quite still, held steady in each other's arms as everything else revolved around them—chandeliers, iridescence of silk and satin, curling side whiskers, dark dress coats. The sad girls and predatory matrons had spun away and tilted far beneath the horizon of their circling world; and she was absorbed totally by the illusion that his movements had become hers and that his warmth and strength flowed through her with the pulse of the melody, bearing her up, carrying her like seaweed in the curve of a wave.

Next came a polka and then a galop, sweeping the whole floor with dashing exuberance, bringing boisterous laughter and apologies as breathless couples collided, legs tangling with skirts. Clinton kissed Theresa's triumphant happy face as they were swept together, his cheek brushing straying curls. Her movements were light and fast, and her eyes flashed with confidence and vitality. Her lovely oval face and parted lips, her auburn hair, glowing warm above the dead white of her dress, drew admiration to her as she danced; eyes followed them as they merged and separated from the living swell of shapes and figures.

Later, Clinton reluctantly left Theresa talking to Lambert while he himself returned to the dance floor to fulfill his two promises. Between the the first and second was an interval of three dances. He was leaving the floor, intending to return to Theresa during this respite, when he felt a light touch on his back. A pair of dark doelike eyes were scrutinizing him from a pale, serious face.

"I'm not a ghost," the young woman said coldly, "though I had to make myself ill before Mama would agree to come here." The music had started again and people were pushing past them onto the floor. Without speaking, Clinton led the way to the quieter dining room, where refreshments were being served from a long horseshoe table.

"An ice, Miss Lucas?" he murmured as they sat down at one of the small candlelit side tables.

"You may call me Sophie, Clinton."

"Champagne or claret cup?" he asked after a silence.

"Neither." She forced a brittle smile. "If Mahomet won't come to the mountain . . . Isn't it lucky my uncle's comptroller of the household? I was sent ever so many bouquets before the ball."

"And which lucky man's flowers did you bring?"

"I threw them all away." Her expression was precariously poised between irony and tears. "Why aren't you attending any private dances or dinners?"

"I don't care for society here."

"No sauntering down Grafton Street or skating on the viceregal pond?"

He looked down at her mother-of-pearl fan. "If you came here to see me—"

"I succeeded. I told you I wouldn't give you up. Did you think I'd stop existing when you left Ammering? That's how you're looking at me now. What right has she got to be here? Why didn't she die or fade away when I turned my back? That's what you're thinking." She gazed at him with sudden intentness. "All those months and you couldn't decide. Or was it just mindless cruelty to let me hope for so long?"

"Of course I wasn't sure."

She leaned forward with a nervous eagerness that horrified him. "Then why should I assume you're so certain now? If Mama hadn't tried to press you—"

"It's history, Sophie."

"I'll tell you some more history. I wrote to your brother, asked his opinion before coming here."

"His opinion about what?"

"Whether you intended to marry somebody else."

"You'd have done better to see a fortuneteller. What was his guess?"

"That you had no immediate intentions."

Her tenacity both impressed and repelled him as he met her eyes. Looking away at the jeweled comb in her black hair, he though of the fierce fight she would have had with her parents to make them consent to this last vain effort. Very few girls would have had the courage and the will.

"He said there was an attachment—some actress." The scorn and bitterness in her voice wounded him. "Were you dancing with her? I watched you both. I thought I was going to be sick." She paused, her anger passing. "I didn't know I'd dare say as much. It's strange, suddenly finding oneself much stronger than one ever expected."

"I've nothing to add to what I said at your parents' house."

"But I have, Clinton. I said then that if we were married, I wouldn't mind what happened if you were faithful for a few years. I've learned a lot since then. Do you remember Alice Clayton? Within a month of her marriage to Miles Claremont, she found out he'd kept on his old mistresses."

"Poor girl."

"No," she cried, "the whole point is that she doesn't care. At first she was horribly upset." Sophie blushed and lowered her eyes. "Men and women are very different. Apparently Claremont was too passionate, quite brutal, in fact. I can't tell you. But don't you see? She's not sorry at all that there are other women. None of the poor creatures seem to last long, and they make him quite tolerable to live with. She likes his company, loves him in other ways, and she has ever so much to attend to. A large house, entertaining. She's perfectly happy."

"Like a hundred other self-deceiving wives."

"You haven't understood. Only a woman who loves a man for her own sake rather than his can't accept his weaknesses."

"Alice sounds clever," said Clinton with a faint smile.

Sophie was staring at him with fixed bright eyes. "It's true though." Her voice was shaking. "*I* could be as tolerant as that, Clinton. Dear God, I've tried to love other men . . . the humiliation of it. But now I've done with pretending. I don't care about pride." Seeing tears brimming, he rose, not knowing what to say, amazed that a girl so carefully brought up could have made this proposition. He shook his head and stepped back. "Am I so repulsive?" she whispered.

"No, no. You deserve a man who loves you, not some squalid travesty of a marriage."

He was returning to the blue drawing room, still shaken by this encounter, when he saw a large florid-faced woman detach herself from a group and come towards him; she was his colonel's wife.

"Just in time for the quadrille, Lord Ardmore. I thought I'd been forgotten."

"On the contrary, Mrs. Hammond."

Her shimmery blue dress was wreathed with silver gauze and studded here and there with large frosted water lilies.

"Who else is in our set?" he asked, noticing that there were lily buds in her thickly coiled hair. The effect was grotesque.

"Sir Charles and Lady Spencer."

"Splendid," replied Clinton, though he cordially detested his brigade commander and his wife.

While waiting for Clinton, Theresa decided that she did not like Richard Lambert with his bright confident smile and inquisitive eyes. He would choose a general subject to talk about and then pass effortlessly to himself, his views on life and this and that; and though he could laugh at his own expense, she felt that all the time he was judging the effect he was having on her. She found particularly distasteful a kind of knowingness of expression, as if to say, You're an artful woman to have managed to snare such an exceptional and normally dispassionate man as Lord Ardmore. When he spoke about Clinton's merits as a soldier, these remarks took on for her the coloring of a reproach, while Lambert's occasional polite inquiries about her own profession seemed tinged with condescension.

When a striking debutante came up to them, Theresa was relieved and sat back, glad of the diversion which Lambert's efforts to extricate himself would provide. Perhaps he might not want to disappoint this particular young lady, whose dark eloquent eyes and flawless skin made her undeniably lovely. The girl's dress, with its exquisitely worked pattern of birds and butterflies on the lace overskirt, was the most perfect creation she had seen that evening.

Strangely, the girl ignored Lambert completely and, to Theresa's astonishment, stood motionless in front of her, gazing with a peculiar glitter of hostility in her eyes. Then she turned abruptly to Lambert. "Perhaps, sir, you'll be kind enough to introduce me to the lady."

Lambert got up with slightly elevated brows. "If I was acquainted with you, madam, I'd have no difficulty."

"Miss Lucas. Sir George Lucas is my uncle, so don't trouble yourself about my suitability."

Lambert looked at Theresa helplessly. She ended his uncertainty by holding out her hand.

"How do you do, Miss Lucas. Theresa Barr. Miss Lucas, allow me to introduce Captain Lambert."

"I'd like to talk to you, Miss Barr."

"Mrs. Barr," interposed Lambert.

"Can you excuse us, sir?" said Sophie sharply.

"I'm not sure that I can."

"Are you under orders, Captain? Don't worry, Lord Ardmore's an old friend. I'll ask him to forgive you."

"I'm most obliged. He should be back soon."

"I'm quite happy to talk to you," said Theresa.

"As you please," murmured Lambert, bowing ironically to her, before walking rapidly towards St. Patrick's Hall.

"Gone to tell his master," said Sophie. "I'm the sad little country thing he might have married. Did you guess?"

She sat down next to Theresa on the small sofa. Though her voice had been controlled, Theresa saw Sophie's hands trembling in her lap. She was gripping her white kid gloves so tightly round her fan that now and then her hands gave a little shudder.

Theresa said softly, "If you think I had anything to do with—"

"I don't care whether you did or didn't. Sophie hesitated, as if about to weep. "I'd have done anything for him. More than you could ever guess."

"If I was rich—"

"So you talked about me," cried Sophie with sudden fury.

"Lord Ardmore's brother mentioned you."

"Lord Ardmore? Is that what you call him? A nice ring to it. Haven't you some charming personal name for him?"

"Don't try to trade insults with me. If you've anything to say, say it."

"Very well. When men want to get rid of their mistresses, they buy them off. I'd like to buy you off, Mrs. Barr."

"I'm afraid I'm not for sale."

"When he's a beggar, you may regret it."

The girl's pale angry face and arrogant voice had stung Theresa, but now, as if a glass shutter had slid down across her mind, she could not think how to respond. This innocent-looking skim-milk miss was trying to corrupt her; without being able to help it, she laughed in Sophie's face.

"How much would you pay, Miss Lucas?" she asked, doing her best not to laugh again. But once more the girl's burning eyes reached her, killing her amusement, confusing her, so that she no longer knew whether she felt pity or anger.

Sophie said rapidly, "Do you love him enough to be ready to—" She broke off as she saw Clinton looking down at her.

"Go on, Sophie," he said.

"Don't look at me like that." She covered her face with her gloved hands, dropping her fan; then she let out a long slow breath. "I don't care, Clinton. I'd rather be hated than forgotten." In spite of herself, Theresa was moved by Sophie's defiance. In the distance she could see Captain Lambert leaning elegantly against a column and thought she saw a sardonic smile. She felt Sophie's hand on her arm. The girl said, "If he ever needed me, I wouldn't try to stop him seeing you. That's how much I love him—not for my sake but for his—to save his career, to help him to be the great man I know he could be with an unselfish woman's support."

"All right, Sophie, you've said your piece." Clinton checked himself as if on the point of shouting at her. Theresa had never seen him as angry, and yet when he spoke his voice was soft and low. "Do you think fame and a million of money would please a man long if he had them only on condition he walked everywhere with a thorn in his shoe?"

Sophie made no reply but looked at him as though he had hit her across the face. She remained very still, and Theresa was stunned to see not anger or self-pity on her face but a look of humility and undiminished adoration. A moment later she walked away towards the laughter and the music.

CHAPTER TWENTY-ONE

The sky was tinged with orange, darkening to copper where scarves of freezing mist obscured the sun; and already the light was dwindling to dusk among the nearer trees. From the carriage windows flocks of starlings seemed suddenly to dip into sight out of nowhere and vanish as mysteriously. Hedges made ghostly white by crystals of hoar frost slid gently past as the landau rolled on.

When Clinton had suggested to Theresa that they spend her last two days out of Dublin in the country, he had offered her no better reason than being sick of the town—his real intention being, she suspected, to give her no opportunity to run away at once if she decided to refuse him. An issue of such gravity would not be allowed to rest upon the outcome of a single skirmish. A few days earlier, Theresa knew that she would have raised difficulties; but her meeting with Sophie Lucas had produced a deep change in her. In spite of her real fears of a lasting break with Clinton, so sure had she been of his love for her that she had hardly given thought to the possibility of being supplanted soon afterwards by an actual rival. But the jealousy and determination in Sophie's eyes had revealed more to Theresa than her own fierce possessiveness. To give up Clinton for his own sake appeared in a very different light, now that the alternatives open to him had become so starkly clear. The idea of this young girl taking her place burned Theresa with a depth of revulsion that blurred all her previous misgivings, making them seem as futile as a swimmer's struggles against the currents of a river in full flood.

Since Clinton had decided to dispense with the services of a coachman and drive himself, Theresa had chosen to sit next to him on the box rather than enjoy the comparative warmth of the carriage's interior. Though swathed in rugs, the cold still reached her as darkness fell, but she had no desire to leave his side. Around them in the dim wastes, she saw the dull red glow of hearth fires through cabin windows and once, etched black in a low doorway, the motionless figure of a man. The sky above was jeweled with a multitude of stars, uncannily brilliant in the chill night air. Looking up at them, while the carriage swayed gently under her, Theresa felt as if she were floating; their journey no longer earthbound but through the gliding panorama of the stars into realms of boundless space. She turned to Clinton as he gazed at her, and for a moment his eyes seemed to share the sky's secret, penetrating far beneath the surface of her thoughts, ages down into her beyond the limits of her own life and birth.

"Look at the stars," she whispered.

"They make me think of death." He paused, sensing her disappointment. "I prefer the infinite in smaller doses—a grain of sand or a blade of grass."

"Do you feel no mystery?"

"What you asked in your letter. Does my heart expand under the trees?"

"Why be ironic? You love life."

"Too much to abandon reality for its shadow."

Ahead of them, the carriage lamps cast soft pools of yellow light on the road.

She touched his arm. "What is it in us feels pleasure? Our hands, eyes, ears? Don't we know truth with our hearts as well as our minds? Love's proof of that—proof of what can't be seen or understood. I want more in you than I can touch."

"My soul?"

"Why not? I'm not trying to prove God's existence. While I

can feel and see, I've no need to explain him. When I think of leaving you, the pain's no simple physical hurt, but a deeper wound—a bleeding of the spirit. Don't you understand?"

"Yes, and I love *you* for it, nothing else." He was silent a long time. "When people without hope or consolation can sit down and weigh scruples, still cling to some soiled rag of pride in defeat or facing death, I kneel to them. To thank God for their courage robs them and us." He twisted the reins in his hands and sighed. "Perhaps I'd do better to agree with you. But I need more in my own way than I can touch. I don't want you to love some phantom of me. I want you to love me as I am." At the top of a steep hill he applied the brake and checked the horses. "I want to be loved for the worst in me as well as the best. You think I'm a sort of chivalrous savage—self-sacrificing to a fault. It's not so. Whoever makes sacrifices wants something for them."

Approaching a wood, he lifted a shotgun from behind the dash.

"Why are we traveling in darkness?" she asked.

"I had things to do in town. We're too near the Curragh Camp to meet any Fenians." He patted the stock of the gun. "Better safe than sorry. In the south or west we'd have been tempting providence."

"Why no servants? I've never known you go anywhere without a valet."

"Don't you like it better being alone?"

"But you don't care what they hear or know; you never did in the past. And leaving so late . . ."

"I'm not going to murder you," he replied, laughing. But though she asked him no further questions, he sensed that she was still dissatisfied. He was angry with himself for not having explained matters to her before they left. The trouble with waiting for inevitable moments to say certain things, was that these perfect occasions had a habit of slipping into the future; and since Father Maguire would be waiting for them the following day, there was precious little future left.

The best hotel in Portarlington displayed the usual Irish genius for dilapidation: armchairs leaking stuffing, candlesticks with only the faintest evidence of having once been plated, a peevish waiter flicking scraps of food from the dining tables with a dirty napkin. After a dinner of undercooked duck and disintegrating peas, they went up to their bedroom to escape the melancholy music of a piper in the bar and the thick turf smoke issuing from the kitchen. Since Theresa was still cold, Clinton sent for more logs and demanded a bath filled with water that was hot and not merely lukewarm.

When the last jugs had been brought up, he looked down at the square through a gap in the curtains. The roofs and pavements were rimed with frost, glinting in the starlight as if sprinkled with powdered glass. Behind him, a dented copper hip bath steamed in front of the fire. He remained at the window for several minutes, and when he turned, Theresa was already almost naked. The unembarrassed way in which she loosened drawstrings and slipped off petticoats with a cheerful ease and absent-minded immodesty roused him more powerfully than any conscious coquetry had ever done. She tested the water with a cautious foot and then let herself down into it with a luxurious sigh. The logs cracked and hissed, spurting out thin blue and green tongues of flame where the red heat reached veins of moist sap.

The glisten of reflected firelight on her wet limbs and her lazy movements as she soaped herself, made Clinton's skin tingle as though a warm wind were ruffling every light hair on his body. As she lay back, knees breaking the water's surface, he tried to recall the expression on her face under the stars—another woman, another world. How much did he ever see? How much imagine? Out of a million movements of a face, only a few poor frozen images remained of so much subtlety. Never to be without her, always to have another morning and another day in which to store up more of her—only that would bring him peace.

He knelt down next to the bath, kissing her wet lips, drawing her arms around him, oblivious of the water slopping over the sides onto his waistcoat and trousers. Then with sudden restlessness he got up.

"Don't you think," he began hesitantly, "that there are certain cases when the choice is either giving up or not reasoning at all? Hasn't that been true for us almost from the start?" He kicked at a rucked-up corner of a rug and swore quietly. "And that isn't what I meant—more how I'd like things to be, how I feel—" He broke off and came closer to her again. "I should have said it before, like a dozen other things. I can't marry you openly. The reason's money. I spent the morning writing down the whys and wherefores." He pulled an envelope from his pocket and ripped it open. "I was going to hand it to you, walk around for an hour or two, and then ask if you'd marry me on my terms. It seemed quite logical until we came here."

"Marriage is marriage on any terms."

"If you can't tell your daughter or your father?"

"They'd keep any secret."

"I can't accept that risk. I know you've lived with poverty; perhaps you despise me, but if you'd always lived in a certain way . . . They say it's a virtue to know one's limitations. I'd be a bad pauper, and that's the truth of it. To ruin myself would do you no service, married to me or not. The worst losses are things one takes for granted."

"I know how you've lived." She stood up and reached for the towel on the fender. As she wrapped it round her, he watched her in agonized suspense.

Unable to bear her silence, he burst out, "I know how little a secret marriage holds for you—that people will think you no more than a mistress. Do you think I'm not ashamed to say I can't acknowledge you? It cuts me to the heart, but what's to be done? If I lose my uncle's fortune, I'm ruined." He moved closer, his eyes pleading and yet burning with frustration. "I don't exaggerate. If you want proof . . ."

She put on a flannel gown and met his gaze. "You're selling your commission. What other proof should I need?" She held out her hands in a gesture of solemn appeal. "Is it so you can support me? Unless you tell me, I won't answer you."

"I might have stayed another year."

"And with Esmond's help?" she insisted in a voice that shook.

"All right," he cried in desperation, "I don't deny it. I could have saved my career if I'd given you up. But think what I'm asking you." He paused and stared into the fire. "I ask you to deny your name in public—my name. I bind you by a secret marriage and swear you to silence till my uncle dies. Should I make no sacrifice for you when I ask so much?"

She looked at him with misting eyes. "You owe *me* sacrifices?" she faltered. "You deny yourself marriage to others who could have brought you riches—could have saved your career and ended all your worries."

"Your answer," he shouted, striding to her and grasping her shoulders. "I love you, can't endure to be without you. Isn't that enough?"

"Yes, yes," she whispered, her voice throbbing between tears and joy. "What you've just said . . . Don't you know why I was scared before? I thought you *would* marry me openly—would risk everything."

"Then marry me tomorrow," he blurted out, pressing her to him. "You wrote that marriage was impossible, wouldn't answer me before. Do you think I'll let you run off again?"

"Tomorrow?" she gasped in amazement. "How can we? What about banns?"

"I've found a priest who'll dispense with them."

"You did this before knowing my answer?"

"I can't lose you, Theresa. I wasn't confident enough to be patient. I'll never forget what I went through when you left Kilkreen. I didn't presume on your answer." When she said nothing, but still looked at him in incredulity, he broke away from her impatiently. "Will you? What should I think if you refuse?"

"I won't refuse," she murmured. She kissed him gently and smiled. "Did you even buy a ring?" He nodded and she started laughing. "You say you weren't confident. Darling, you're the most insufferably confident man I've ever met."

"Never with you."

Later, when they were lying in bed after making love, he opened his eyes and saw that she was studying his face.

"Do you mind being married by a Papist priest?" she asked.

He smiled at her and shook his head. "I'm sure God's above quibbling over a few differences in ceremonial."

"Please, Clinton."

"I don't much care for the crossings and mutterings, but it

doesn't worry me." He closed his eyes. "You know in Scotland you can just read the marriage service in front of a witness and no priest need come into it. I believe we bind ourselves by our vows. The rest doesn't matter to me."

She seemed about to answer him, but instead laid her head on his shoulder and was silent. The candle by the bed had started to gutter, but when it burned out neither of them moved to replace it. Moments later he heard her crying in the darkness.

"What is it, love?"

"I thought of you seeing a priest, not knowing what I'd say. Poor Clinton."

"Not now."

"I'll be a good wife to you."

"I know. I've never felt surer of anything."

"And you're happy, my love?"

"Very."

From somewhere behind the hotel came the faint cackle of geese and from farther off the mournful howling of a dog. Between the curtains the stars shone with the same brittle and unearthly clarity.

CHAPTER TWENTY-TWO

Because it was Sunday, and Father Maguire had been insistent that they arrive early, Clinton had aimed to reach Rathnagar with time in hand to be married and leave the village before the people began setting out for Mass; but a wrong turning outside Ballygowan, followed a little later by some disastrously bad directions from a farm laborer, delayed them by almost an hour, so that there were already small groups of villagers huddled in the street outside the church when they drew up.

The doors were locked, and when they had knocked and been admitted by the priest, he looked at Clinton reproachfully. "If it's secrecy you're wanting, sir, you'd have done best to come at the time I asked. I had the witnesses come all the way from Lisnama so there'd be no talk in the village. I had to send them away when the people started gathering."

"You sent them away?" echoed Clinton, in fear that the man would now refuse to marry them.

"Would you have wanted them to walk out in front of the people when the doors had been closed and none but themselves and the two of you in here? A couple of strangers like themselves? They'd have been asked questions right enough.

And wouldn't they just have seen your two names in the book when they signed their own?"

"But people will see the lady leaving with me."

Maguire looked at him wearily. "I suppose they'll question gentlefolk like yourselves? Of course they won't." He gave a little cough and looked at them more sympathetically. "You needn't be worrying yourselves. It's not the witnesses that make a marriage but your own consents given before myself in God's house."

When Theresa asked Maguire to hear her confession before marrying them, the priest at once moved towards the confessional, though Clinton could tell how reluctant he was to lose more time. While he waited for them to come out of the box, Clinton reproached himself for having allowed his preoccupation with secrecy to blind him to any accurate imaginings of how things would be. The shabby little church and the hole-and-corner furtiveness of everything dismayed him far more than any doubts about the validity of the proceedings. Before proposing to Theresa, Clinton had carefully reviewed his earlier conversation with Maguire, and had found no reason for feeling qualms of conscience. The priest had made his position plain. He would celebrate a marriage in the proper form, and would never claim that he had done anything but marry them, unless challenged at a later date with having married a Protestant. In that single unlikely eventuality, he would excuse himself on the grounds that he had understood that a civil marriage had already taken place, and would say that he had gone through the church service merely as a blessing on that existing union—his desire being to satisfy the lady's Catholic conscience. Since Clinton believed that he himself would rather die than ever attempt to escape the effect of his vows, he saw no possibility of the marriage being called in question. Even so, he had made up his mind to tell Theresa about the Irish Marriage Act and to undergo a civil ceremony placing the matter beyond doubt. But he could see no way of doing this for several months, since to tell her within days, or even weeks, might be to cause her unnecessary pain while the ceremony itself remained a powerful emotional memory. Anything seeming to detract from it should not be spoken of in haste.

A few minutes later, Maguire led them to the altar, where they knelt and spoke their vows at his prompting. The priest's hurried utterance upset Clinton, but in Theresa's face he saw only happiness and serenity, and wished that he too could distance himself from their surroundings and give himself as entirely to the meaning of the words. But the creak of the priest's boots and the broken veins in his cheeks and other details kept intruding, and he was badly distressed that the ring he had purchased the day before in Dublin was too small to slide over her knuckle. Later, when the correct moment had passed, he took off his own signet ring and placed it on her hand with the seal facing inwards. After Maguire had pronounced the final blessing, he led them to the vestry, where he asked them to sign what he described as his private register. As soon as Clinton had handed over his fee, the priest apologized to them and hurried away to admit the villagers for Mass. They were left alone to leave by the vestry door.

Walking out after Theresa, Clinton dreaded seeing evidence of disappointment in her face. But when he looked at her, he saw the same soft calm light in her eyes that he had observed in the church. A gust of wind lifted her veil, and she smiled as she caught at it. Rough gray-bellied clouds swept across the sky. He saw Theresa point to a clump of snowdrops in the rough grass between the tombstones; he bent down and picked some for her. As the chapel bell began to toll with a harsh clanging noise, he took her hand.

"Even the bell's an insult," he groaned.

"Remember those lies you once told me about the wedding you were going to have at Hanover Square? The frills and ribbons. Wasn't this better?" He did not answer her as the bell clanged on. "But you said it yourself," she cried, "only the vows matter. I wouldn't feel more truly married if a cardinal in all his glory had held the service."

"That dismal black cassock of his." Clinton sighed.

She smiled. "You wouldn't have thought much of his precautions if he'd welcomed his flock in wedding vestments."

"You didn't mind about the furtiveness—the witnesses sent away like thieves, the private register?"

"Why should I have? I knew you wanted secrecy." She

squeezed his hand. "*I'm married to you;* what else could matter to me?"

He gazed at her in silent gratitude before walking on. When they turned the corner into the chapel yard, bare-legged women in blue cloaks and their men decked out in suits of baggy tweed and frieze were going in at the west door.

Theresa stopped Clinton and looked up at him. "I'd like to go to Mass on my wedding day. Come with me this once. They can't know who we are."

Though wanting to go away at once, Clinton agreed. The thought of the priest's creaking shoes, the empty faces of the plaster angels, and the words he would not understand weighed upon him. But when he had got used to the coughing and the sour smell of unwashed bodies, and he saw the un-affected piety of the people, his depression lifted. Their concentration on the prayers and their fervent responses moved him in a way the placid Protestant rituals of his boyhood had never done. Soon he could not understand how so many trivial things had worried him during their wedding. He remembered Theresa's clear soft voice—"To love and to cherish, if holy church will permit, according to God's holy ordinance, and thereto I pledge thee my troth"—and his heart was filled with tenderness. It had been years since he had been to any church, except with his men, and even longer since he had prayed. Now, watching Theresa's closed eyes and slightly moving lips, he felt that she was praying for them both. Memories of his father's disdainful bearing in church still made Clinton feel awkward when he knelt, but he did so with the rest, listening to the words of the Kyrie and later to the Sanctus bell.

"*Hoc est enim Corpus . . .*" The bell again, and the priest holding up the wafer. "*Hic est enim Calix Sanguinis . . .*" Another bell, and then the repeated "*Domine non sum dignus,*" as the congregation moved to the communion rail, Theresa with them—a viscountess with these peasants, about to drink from the same cup. He felt an instinctive shudder, a feeling more powerful than difference of caste, for contained in it was a barbed jealousy that these men and women could share with her an experience from which he was excluded.

When she returned to his side, her presence soothed him; she completed him, as if till then he had been a man with no center, rootless. Never to be without her, he thought with a light shock, to live with her, be happy, quarrel, be amused, bored, enchanted. Everything, and time, so much time together, so that no disappointment or reverse need ever last or part them. Always days ahead of them for reconciliation, always—until the last of them had come and gone. As the responses began again, he felt an enveloping humility which sprang from no process of the mind, but from spontaneous joy in all that was most elusive and incommunicable in his love for her.

PART THREE

CHAPTER TWENTY-THREE

The state of Clinton's and Theresa's relations remained a mystery to Esmond for the first three months of the New Year. He knew that Clinton had stayed on with his regiment in Ireland till the end of March; and since Theresa had been appearing nightly in *Much Ado About Nothing* from late January till the beginning of April, it had struck him as unlikely that they were seeing much of each other at this time. Although he had resisted the temptation of trying to see her, Esmond had been unable to suppress a growing optimism and a return to the scarcely admitted hope that one day she might come back to him.

Then in April he had been shocked to learn that Clinton had sold his commission and taken a lease on a house in Lancashire. With the help of an inquiry agent, Esmond discovered that Theresa had joined Clinton there. Her success as Beatrice had been so striking that Esmond thought it unlikely that she would suddenly have agreed to live in the country unless Clinton had given her good reason. And what could that be but marriage?

With his conviction that Clinton had succeeded with her

came renewal of all Esmond's old hatred. The thought of their happiness was agony to him, made worse by a grudging recognition that Clinton was behaving sensibly. Living in London with Theresa, Clinton would have been plagued by being within sight and sound of the social life he could not share with her until able to make public acknowledgment of his marriage. Even in less formal company, he would have had to pretend she was his mistress, in case his uncle learned that he had married—a most humiliating predicament for a man wanting to shield his wife from slights. But in a part of the country where neighbors would be both few and scattered, such embarrassment would be reduced to a minimum. Removed from the temptations of the capital, Clinton might even be able to live within his means.

But Clinton's finances—as Esmond knew very well—were still vulnerable in one vital respect. He would depend entirely on his trust investment income until completion of the Markenfield settlement at the end of the lease—a period of two years, during which all his capital would remain pledged as security for existing debts. Even a brief interruption of current income would place Clinton in a disastrous position.

In February Esmond had at last prevailed upon the family trustees to purchase £30,000 of Greek & Oriental shares on Clinton's behalf. Just three months later, Esmond had not been very much surprised to learn that the shipping line's trading position had become grave enough to dictate the immediate suspension of dividends or liquidation. In either event, Esmond foresaw appalling repercussions for his brother—whose entire trust holding was invested in Greek & Oriental stock.

At an emergency meeting called by the company in June, the shareholders voted in favor of deferring payment of dividends rather than forcing the shipping line to liquidate. This vote—which gave Esmond a final chance to save the company —brought Clinton very close to ruin, ironically at a time when he felt perfectly secure. A few days after the meeting, Esmond wrote to Clinton warning him of his position; he also admitted the gravity of the situation to the trustees. A month passed, and though he wrote again, Esmond still heard nothing from his brother. By now Drummonds would have sent letters asking

Clinton to explain why they had not received the usual quarterly remittance from the trustees. As his own commercial problems mounted, Esmond still found time occasionally to wonder how long Clinton's love would survive the day his bank began dishonoring his checks and notes of hand.

CHAPTER TWENTY-FOUR

On a hot Sunday in late July, Clinton sat on the terrace at Hathenshaw Hall waiting for Theresa and Louise to return from Mass. With his back to the old redstone house, he gazed across sloping lawns and fields to the wooded riverbanks and the fells beyond. Listening to the baaing of sheep drifting up from the hazy valley, he wished that his thoughts mirrored the peace around him. But Theresa was pregnant; and since learning this two weeks earlier, Clinton had been deeply preoccupied. Before she had told him, he had been about to confide to her the possible shortcomings of their Irish marriage and to persuade her to go through a civil ceremony. His intention had been to break this to her before the end of the month; but to do so now, so soon after hearing her news, might make it seem that he was being honest with her only because forced to by doubts about the baby's legitimacy. Deciding to postpone this revelation, Clinton had broached other problems at once.

Although knowing that Louise might be indiscreet with the servants, Clinton had suggested that she ought to be told about the marriage without delay. The hatred the girl might otherwise feel towards him as the baby started to grow had overcome his reservations—particularly since her behavior to him was already unpredictable enough to change from abject admiration to hostility in the space of a single conversation. But Theresa had flatly refused to tell her, in case she in turn told her grandfather. Although the old man would understand the need for secrecy, Theresa warned Clinton that he might well consider the birth of a child an event overriding all else. Rather than allow anyone to think the baby illegitimate, the major could quite easily take it into his head to blow the marriage open. When Clinton had said he was still prepared to take the risk, Theresa had implored him not to make her responsible through her family for jeopardizing his prospects with his uncle. Though persuaded to give up the idea of telling Louise, thoughts of what she and her grandfather would think of him in the months to come troubled Clinton long after this conversation.

By contrast, Clinton had felt an unfamiliar sense of financial well-being since coming to Hathenshaw. No longer burdened by military expenses, he was living within his income for the first time in years. He had spent more than he had intended on the house, but a three-year lease had been paid for entirely from the proceeds of his commission. Though his capital was just as tightly hedged as before, this could have no ill effects while his outgoings remained at their present level. Secure in this faith, Clinton had not troubled to open several letters addressed to him in Esmond's hand. His brother would only have written to ask unwelcome questions about his marriage or to raise needless alarms about his future. Esmond's letters had joined a heap of others, including several from his bank, at the bottom of a drawer in the gun room. It still gave Clinton satisfaction to feel able safely to ignore communications which only months ago would have given him no peace until read. Without any deliberate intent to forget the outside world entirely, Clinton found it pleasant to remember its existence only when he felt inclined.

With each day still revealing new aspects of Theresa's personality to admire and love, Clinton very rarely regretted the independent life he had abandoned for her. She too had given up a career. At times, certainly, the tranquility of his present life seemed strange to Clinton, and occasionally he wondered

269

without much urgency whether a year would still find them at Hathenshaw. A legacy of years as active as the past half-dozen gave him no cause to begrudge himself a period of retirement. Later, in weeks or months, he would make plans—a time perhaps in the colonies or in South America, where governments were eager to acquire the services of English officers. And if Theresa disliked the change, they could move on. But thoughts of Louise and the unborn child, as well as Theresa's wishes, clouded even the most tentative predictions. More than ever, he lived for each passing day.

Clinton left the gardens and walked between hedgerows heavy with the scent of elder flower and wild honeysuckle. Above the hum of insects, the notes of a cuckoo lingered drowsily on the warm air. Later they would picnic in the water meadows, and afterwards he hoped to spend the rest of the day alone with Theresa at the deserted mill pond they had recently discovered.

The lichened masonry of the old mill buildings seemed to be slowly merging into the surrounding woods. Brambles grew in the doorways and sycamore saplings thrust skyward between the rafters. Through rotting sluices, the stream trickled into the pond, scarcely moving the light surface film in the center. In the silence, the sudden rise of a fish or the cooing of wood pigeons seemed curiously loud.

As soon as they arrived, Clinton had at once taken off his shirt, but when Theresa had made no move to undress, he paused. "Not coming in?"

"Perhaps later."

He stood looking meditatively at the clear reflection of her dress and parasol in the glassy water until she moved and sat down in the grass among the willow herb. Dragonflies caught the sun, skimming over the water lilies. She smiled at him.

"Would you mind if anyone saw us swimming?"

"Not unless they took our clothes." He chuckled to himself as he pulled off his shoes and loosened his trousers. "It'd give them something new to cackle about. You'd think men never swam naked in the sea."

"Women don't."

"Nobody's going to come here." He kicked off his trousers and kissed her forehead. "A world of our own—like Adam and Eve."

"Remember what happened to them," she murmured, touching his thigh. He laughed aloud.

"Pity Adam wasn't in the cavalry. He could have given the flaming sword brigade a lesson in swordsmanship."

She watched him walk through the long grass to the water's edge where it was deepest, eyes lingering on the clean line of his hips and the tautness of his back as he stood poised to dive. Never at any moment had he expressed regret for their isolated existence, nor spoken of the least misgivings about the ending of his career. Whenever she had tried to get him to talk about the past, so that she could judge whether his happiness was as real in truth as in appearance, he had said little, claiming he hated thinking about the years when they had been nothing to each other. His passionate determination to live for each day captivated but also scared her, as if he were seizing on happiness too eagerly, like a hunter clutching and choking his prey in case it escaped him.

The splash of his dive sent rippling waves chasing each other across the pond and set the lilies bobbing wildly. She followed the white shadow of his body under the green surface until he came up under a patch of duckweed. Blowing a little, he flicked the weed from his shining head and swam a few vigorous strokes before turning over on his back and floating. When his cheek brushed against a yellow water lily, he trod water and sniffed the yellow cuplike flower.

"Ugh! Smells of stale brandy." He tried another. "They all do!" He rolled over on his back again. "I saw a newt under the water. . . . Do come in, Theresa. The sky looks marvelous from here; the reeds are tall as trees. I want to kiss you under water."

"Try the newt," she called back.

He began to swim towards her. "I'll come and get you."

She got up slowly and started to undress, enjoying the warmth of the sun on her skin. Wading into the pond, she shivered as the water reached her waist and then lapped against her breasts; she could feel the mud squeezing up between her toes. The water smelled slightly brackish but not at all unpleasant. She launched herself forward, gasping a little with the cold but soon breathing easily. His hair was much darker wet, and it was sleeked close to his head like a seal's coat. As she came closer to him, he dived and swam under her, brushing her stomach with his back, coming up inches from her face, kissing her lips almost as he surfaced. They embraced, treading water, knees bumping gently,

Feeling herself sinking, she swam away. "I look dreadful with wet hair."

"You sound like Louise."

She sniffed one of the lilies and laughed. "You were right."

"Lie on your back and we can touch toes. I want to look at the sky, touching your toes."

"How silly you are."

Before she could say anything else, he had pulled her under. She rose spluttering, and he tossed her up by the waist, sinking as he did so. Then reaching up with a disembodied hand, he touched her face and emerged, breathing fast.

"Morte d'Arthur. An arm rose up from out the bosom of the lake . . . mystic, wonderful . . ."

She smiled in spite of her hair. The sun flashed on the broken water around them; and nearer to the bank, in smoother water, reflections of trees and clouds dissolved and formed again.

Lying on his back in the grass, Clinton let the hot sun dry him while he watched Theresa toweling herself vigorously, raising a warm flush on her pale skin. The baby had not started to show.

"Please don't," he said, seeing her pick up a petticoat, but she shook her head and began to dress. Often they had made love beside the pond after swimming. Reluctantly he pulled on his trousers. He thought he caught a look of fleeting sadness on her face as she began absently to lace her bodice.

A week ago he had suggested going to London together for a few days. Dick Lambert and two other officers from the 15th would be there. Rather than seem overeager to see his friends, he had told her that he ought also to see his trustees. But, whether because she had felt that she would be competing for his company with Lambert and the others, or because she mistakenly supposed that he would rather go alone, she had refused to consider accompanying him. He had offered not to go at all, but she had been so insistent that he stick to his original plan that he had not opposed her. Remembering York, and her reluctance to pretend to be his wife, he had asked whether she now hated the idea of staying anywhere away from Hathenshaw and having to pretend to be his mistress. But she had laughed at the suggestion.

When she had dressed, she sat next to him, dabbing with a finger at the drops of water still lying between the curling hairs in the hollow of his chest. Then she lay back with her head in the crook of his arm, her wet hair cold against his skin. In three days he would be leaving. Around them the country dozed as if drunk with sunshine, the afternoon air thick with the smell of meadow plants and baking marsh mud. Theresa's hair was already growing paler as it began to dry.

"Come with me to London," he murmured.

"I'd feel obliged to see my father if I did."

"He's probably forgiven you."

"For refusing Esmond, possibly. But not for coming here." She watched him stripping some grass seeds idly with his hand. "He adores Louise, thinks I'm sacrificing her and my acting for an idiot's infatuation." A light squall feathered the surface of the water and murmured in the trees. "Anyway," she went on softly, "a wife's a fool who goes everywhere with her husband. You ought to see your friends on your own."

"But next time you'll come?"

"I expect so." She yawned and lay closer to him. "I love long lashes—the way they define your eyes. Your eyebrows are darker than your hair."

"If they weren't?"

"You wouldn't be so handsome."

"Would you love me less?" he asked lazily, brushing away a fly.

"Perhaps you look like you do because I love you." She touched the little white scar above his left eye and smiled. "I don't remember loving scars before."

An hour later, walking back to Hathenshaw through the cool woods, Clinton asked Theresa if she would mind Dick Lambert's coming back with him from London and staying a couple of days en route for Ireland. She laughed and asked him what possible objection she could have. Their path back to the house took them beside the river for a time, where it meandered through a green tunnel of overhanging boughs. After a long bend in its course, the trees thinned and the water meadows shimmered in open sunlight. In the evening air, the ribbon of bright water twisted as far as the eye could see in perfect clarity. The distant fells formed cliffs of tawny light. They stood in silence as a swallow scooped smooth curves against the cloudless blue.

CHAPTER TWENTY-FIVE

 The long spell of hot dry weather had ended. Now, after a few hours of broken sunshine, the atmosphere would gather oppressively under heavy clouds which hung low over the fells, seeming to promise immediate storms, but often, after a few taunting drops, continuing their brooding presence overhead, sucking at the air and leaving the long afternoons breathless and uncannily still. Even when heavy downpours came, they tended to be brief and brought no real freshness. When the sun shone again, the heat seemed to steam about the fields and meadows, blurring the sky until the evenings stole in with a strange yellow haze and rumbles of muffled thunder.

On a particularly sultry afternoon the post boy from Brows-holme brought a telegram for Theresa. The message was that Clinton would not be returning as planned on Sunday, but two days later. No explanation was given, and Theresa's immediate assumption was that he was enjoying himself and saw no reason to hurry back. Though she told herself she was being absurd, she felt horribly disappointed. At times during the past weeks she had felt the strain of living up to his vision of her and in truth had seen his week away as an opportunity for convalescence: a renewal of strength which she had once drawn from the theater but no longer knew where to find. But as the days had passed, she had found herself longing for his return. She had been determined that, after marrying her, he should still have the freedom to see old friends without having to face the embarrassment of presenting her to them as his mistress. For all her protestations of not minding the lie, she knew that he would always feel humiliated by it until he could acknowledge her. Yet though she knew this was so, and that she ought to be glad he was happy in London, she now wished she had gone with him. In the months ahead, the growing baby might make her unattractive to him and then she would regret every day that she had lost.

She went out into the garden, still holding the telegram. A recent spattering of rain had intensified the smell of earth and roses; drops shone and trembled on the leaves of the ivy which clothed the whole house as high as the strange Dutch gables and little bell tower. Without Clinton, Theresa felt a stranger in the place. What to him, after Markenfield, was a small country house, to her seemed cavernously large, its corridors as wide as rooms, and in the attics, enough accommodation to house a staff three times as numerous as the six who worked for them. Though Clinton joked about the faces in the portraits on the stairs, Theresa was disconcerted by them. The dark oak furniture and cabinets of Oriental porcelain accumulated through the centuries by the landlord's family often made her want to be surrounded by possessions of their own. When the peafowl gathered under the cedars at dusk and the rooks returned cawing to their roosts, Theresa's sense of dislocation was at its strongest, a feeling that the house would rather have lain empty and undisturbed, alone with the fluttering of moths at windows and the wind's rustling among branches.

Theresa had left the formal gardens and was in the azalea walk that ran beside the park when the rain started with a sudden flurry that could only herald a downpour. Without time to get back to the house, she sheltered under the only nearby tree, a light aspen, and watched the house and stables grow faint and misty behind a curtain of falling water. A little later, indistinct flashes of lightning lit the whole sky as if projected from behind it. The thin canopy above her soon let through a stream of drops, so that she saw no point in remaining, but walked back in the direction of the house. The drops were coming down so heavily that they splashed up in little fountains where they hit the ground. Already after very few minutes Theresa's skirt and petticoats clung to her legs, and she knew that her chignon would soon collapse into numerous loose ends like dripping rats' tails. Standing still, she raised her face to the sky, suddenly enjoying the feel of the rain on her face and on her closed eyelids. She even took pleasure in kicking through the puddles. Unaccountably she no longer felt downcast.

As she emerged from the avenue of elms and passed the terracotta lions at the stable gates, she saw the shining hood of a fly in the drive far away across the park. Thinking that Clinton had changed his mind, she started running joyfully towards the carriage sweep, laughing at the shock her appearance would cause him.

Moments later, when the carriage drew up, through the mud-spotted glass her eyes met those of a young man she had never seen before. Realizing how she must look, she retreated into the house. In the hall she beat the gong until Harris and one of the housemaids appeared. At first she told the girl to fetch her lady's maid but then changed her mind; it would take over an hour to dry her hair and to dress again, and in any case the man had seen her. Rather than drip all over the carpets, she decided to receive her visitor in the stone-flagged dining room. She asked Harris to send him in to see her there.

"Shall I bring in his card?"

"No, no." The valet was staring at the pool of water spreading around the hem of her skirt. "It's raining, Harris. Didn't you notice?"

After a brief absence, Harris returned and announced a Mr. Hopkinson. The young man stood at the far end of the table, awkwardly looking down at the crown of the top hat he was holding. "I had hoped to see Lord Ardmore."

"He's in London till next week."

Hopkinson did his best to smile. "How very unfortunate. I've just come from there."

"May I ask why?"

"I'm afraid it's a private matter, madam."

"Are you a personal friend? Surely you can tell me that much?"

Whether in her dealings with the servants, or the local people, or this stranger, Theresa was constantly aware of the falseness of her position. Irritated at first by her visitor's diffident air of propriety, she now sensed his real uneasiness and was alarmed by it.

"I don't often wander about in pouring rain," she said lightly.

He said nothing for a moment, then he murmured, "It's very awkward for me. I don't know who you are."

"Really, you can't take me for the housekeeper or a maid."

"No." Hopkinson looked at her unhappily from behind small gold-framed spectacles that made him look like an erudite schoolboy.

"Perhaps you can think up something for me to tell Lord Ardmore about your visit? He'll be disappointed to hear you came three hundred miles and said nothing except your name. Does he know you?"

"My father was Lord Ardmore's solicitor and the principal trustee under the late Lord Ardmore's will." He paused as if undecided whether to go on, but then said rapidly, "A few weeks before my father died, he told me certain facts about recent trust investments. Frankly, madam, I must speak to Lord Ardmore as soon as possible. Perhaps he told you where he was staying?"

"You can reach him through the Cavalry Club." Theresa looked at him imploringly. His strained and anxious face frightened her. "Since it's obviously important, please leave a letter here in case you miss him in London. Use as much sealing wax as you like."

"It isn't a matter of mistrusting you. I daren't put anything in writing. I have to speak to him."

"He said he'd arranged to see his trustees in London." The man's sympathetic silence exasperated her. "Why are you looking at me like that?"

"Neither of them lives in town. I fear I've worried you quite needlessly."

As he turned to leave, she followed him. "Do you think he can have any idea of what you want to tell him?"

"I couldn't hazard a guess."

When Hopkinson had gone, though Theresa felt shivery in her wet clothes, she did not go up to change but instead hurried to the dressing room where Clinton kept his writing box. Thankful to find it unlocked, she was soon disappointed to discover nothing of any consequence. Her heart beat faster as it occurred to her that he might have hidden letters he did not want her to see. Dazed, she found herself staring at a row of coats in his open wardrobe, their empty arms mocking her. The thought that he might have concealed grave anxieties shocked her. To try to shield her from worries seemed less a noble shouldering of responsibility than a denial of trust. She sat down with a throbbing head. Of course he might know nothing.

When she felt calmer, she rang for Harris and told him that when she had changed she wanted him to drive her into Browsholme. A telegram sent to Clinton's club, warning him not to leave town till he had been contacted by Hopkinson, seemed the best that she could do. But, even while her maid was helping her with her clothes, Theresa's uneasiness returned.

*

CHAPTER TWENTY-SIX

Clinton had not wanted to stay on in town and had only done so because of a loss at billiards playing double or quits. Though irritated with himself for losing money at a game in which practice was essential for success, the size of his loss—barely fifty pounds—would normally have caused him little inconvenience. But it had been late at night and the cashier at his club had gone home; and since it was an unwritten rule that gambling debts should be discharged in cash and not by note of hand, he had reluctantly parted with the money he had set aside to buy presents for Theresa and Louise.

At his bank the following morning, Clinton had been astonished to learn from one of the partners that the regular quarterly payment from the trustees was long overdue. Unwilling to admit his ignorance of the reason for the delay, Clinton had promised a letter explaining matters and had accepted without complaint the bank's decision not to pay out on a check larger than twenty guineas. He brushed aside his failure to reply to the bank's letters by saying that he had been away from home for some weeks.

Convinced that the explanation for what had happened would lie in one of the many unanswered letters at Hathenshaw, Clinton decided against affording Esmond the pleasure of enlightening him. Instead he went to a moneylender's where he had once been a frequent visitor, and could therefore expect to get credit without unseemly wrangling about security. Unfortunately, the master was out of town for several days and his clerk refused to accommodate Clinton in his absence. Much against his will, Clinton had been obliged to await the man's return. When he finally left London, Clinton had borrowed three hundred pounds, signing his acceptance to a bill dated a month hence. By then he was confident that his trust income would be paid. Having bought his presents, Clinton joined Dick Lambert at his house in Hertford Street and went on with him by hansom to Euston Station.

It would later strike Clinton as unfortunate that from the time he sent his telegram to Theresa warning her of his delayed return, he did not go back to his club. Had he done so, he would have found her message for him and another from a Mr. James Hopkinson requesting an urgent meeting.

At Hathenshaw, Clinton was at once aware of a new tenseness in Theresa's manner. Wanting to talk to her alone without delay, he did not like to leave Dick on his own immediately after arriving. After talking about their journey, there was an awkward silence and then Theresa began to question them with forced gaiety about their time in London. Seeming unaware of the edge to Theresa's voice, Dick gave a deliberately heightened account of the inconsequential sort of day young idlers in town were commonly supposed to enjoy: a visit to Tattersalls, watching the riders in the Row, gambling in the evening.

"Not much of a life, day in, day out," he went on, smiling at Clinton. "Remember the morning we met Dudley Glynn? Used to be in the Fifteenth with us," he explained to Theresa. "Rich as Croesus and never did a useful thing in his life except travel around with a hatbox full of bank notes for emergencies. He's dying of boredom. Suggested we go off and buy a hundred rabbits and let them loose at the opera."

"Did you?" Theresa asked with a show of amusement.

Lambert shook his head. "If he'd suggested pigeons . . ." He looked at her apologetically. "In fact we had some good times with him a few years back." Dick then told a story of how Glynn had bet a hundred guineas that nobody dining with him on a particular evening could get himself arrested inside ten minutes without assaulting somebody or doing damage to property. Clinton had given a sovereign to a passing tramp and changed clothes with him; then, dressed as a beggar, he had entered a wine bar and demanded service. When he had offered several of Glynn's spoons in payment for his drink, the landlord had called in a constable.

As Lambert finished the anecdote, Louise came in. Clinton handed over the musical box he had bought for her, and then took out the small gold watch and diamond bow he had chosen for Theresa. After kissing him, she pinned it on her breast. A moment later she left the room, saying she wanted to see it in a mirror. Clinton followed soon afterwards.

"For God's sake tell me," she cried as he came into her boudoir. "My telegram," she said impatiently, when he made no reply.

"I got no telegram."

"Didn't you go to your club yesterday or the day before?"

He shook his head, astonished by her distress. Several minutes later when she had finished telling him about Hopkinson's visit, it took all his control to appear calm. His chest felt suddenly tight and filled with panic.

"You said you were going to see your trustees." The reproach in her voice was agony to him.

"I went to Drummonds instead, spoke to one of the partners. There's nothing to worry about." The lie had been instinctive and spontaneous; but the moment he had spoken, Clinton felt committed to it. What could possibly be gained by frightening her?

"Why did he come here?" she insisted. "It's obvious he thinks something's terribly wrong."

Clinton shrugged. "Maybe he does. I'll write to the trustees tomorrow."

"You will tell me things, Clinton?" she blurted out, coming to him with outstretched arms. "You don't think it wrong for wives . . . ?"

"I won't hide anything from you."

"If there are dangers, I must share them with you. Together we can face anything on earth." Her vehemence moved him deeply.

"I know," he murmured, holding her tightly, feeling a deep sigh of relief pass through her. But though he sensed that this first crisis was over, her strained face when they moved apart told him that she would not let the matter rest for long.

Dinner that evening was a difficult meal. When the cloth had been removed and Harris had placed port and brandy on the table, Theresa rose to leave, but Clinton would not hear of it. "There's nothing Dick and I wouldn't feel able to say in front of you."

"Do you agree, Captain Lambert?"

"Entirely." He stretched out his long legs and chuckled to himself. "Strange thing happened at the station. Did Clinton tell you?" She shook her head. "The porter saw me sticking my hand out of the window and thought I was going to give him an extra tip. Anyway as I stuck out my hand, he reached up expecting a coin and got the hot end of my cigar thrust into his palm. I'd been shaking out the ash. God how he yelled."

The story had not amused Theresa at all, but when in reply she had embarked on an anecdote about Grimaldi, she realized that without having intended it, her story formed a direct rebuke to Dick for his tale. Grimaldi had been in a farce which required him to jump through a window and be caught on the other side by two stagehands. One day he had an argument with one of them, who did not make any effort to break his fall that evening. With two broken ribs the clown went on with his performance, making the audience howl with laughter at his grimaces of pain.

"That's not quite the same," murmured Clinton after a pause.

"Somebody expecting one thing gets something quite different. Isn't that the same joke?"

Lambert looked at her with more amusement than rancor. "Perhaps one can be witty without being nasty. I can see I'm going to have to watch myself."

"I honestly didn't mean it like that."

"Of course not." He laughed. "Don't worry, I like quick-witted women who don't pretend to be anything else."

283

In one way Theresa admired Lambert's bland unruffled tone, in another she was irritated by it. "So you don't mind disagreements, Captain?"

"Don't have any, Mrs. Barr—not with ladies. Does one good to praise what one doesn't agree with."

In spite of herself, Theresa found herself smiling. She turned to Clinton. "Did you ever hear a better justification of insincerity?"

"Dick's always far too hard on himself."

Later, listening to the two men talking about the Fenians' recent ignominious defeat on Tallaght Hill, Theresa was troubled by her instinctive dislike for Clinton's friend. She did not want to be treated by him with the mannered civility he would probably show to women of his own class, but neither did she like the assumption of easy familiarity he obviously thought appropriate for his dealings with a friend's mistress. At times, with a feeling of indignation that astonished her, she wanted to scream at him that she was Lady Ardmore. The idea that he might think her an adventuress, without concern for Clinton's future, was very painful to her. Worst of all was the half-admitted fear that being with Dick might make Clinton regret losing his old way of life.

Several hours after going to bed with Clinton, Theresa woke with a slight start. It was very dark, but even before she reached out, she sensed that he had gone. A faint yellow light showed under the door. In case any of the servants was still up, she put on a peignoir with a shawl over it and went down carrying a lamp. Harris was sitting in the hall in a deep leather chair reading a paper by the light of a candelabrum.

"Why are you waiting here?" she asked as he stood up dutifully.

"To put out the lights. His lordship's not retired yet."

"I'm aware of that. Where is he?"

"In the gun room."

Theresa was aware of Harris's watchful eyes as she brushed past him. His neatly clipped military mustache and cavalry overalls jarred her nerves—constant reminder of Clinton's lost career.

She pushed open the gun-room door, breathing in the bitter smell of oiled metal. Clinton was sitting by the bench where Harris cleaned the guns. A litter of greasy squares of cotton, knotted cords, and percussion caps lay in a heap under the window. A decanter, an empty glass, and several crumpled letters were by Clinton's elbow.

"Why on earth are you in here?"

He looked up in surprise, but quickly recovered. "Looking for some things."

"Did you find them?"

He nodded, thrusting the letters into a pocket as she came up to him. "In the drawer." He gestured. "Couldn't think where I'd put them."

"Weren't they in Esmond's hand?"

"What sharp eyes you have, grandmother." He stood and laid an arm on her shoulder, seeming completely at ease. "He's still doting, I'm afraid. Not that I blame him." He smiled. "Anyway the trust worry's explained. I was a fool not to read his scrawl when it first arrived. Thought he'd just written to wish me with the devil. A moral to everything—never stuff unopened letters in drawers and forget about them."

"What did he say?" she asked quietly.

The lamplight shone dully on gun barrels and lent faint tints of gold to his brown hair. His skin next to the velvet collar of his coat looked very white. He squeezed her shoulder. "My love, the way you're looking at me . . ."

"I only want to know what he wrote. Aren't you going to tell me?"

"It's nothing dramatic. The trustees bought some shipping shares a few months back. They're wrangling over the premium offered. A misunderstanding over the amount. The company's hanging on to the dividends till the thing's settled. Pretty tedious."

"Don't you mean serious?"

"Esmond doesn't seem bothered, and he's got as much to lose as I have."

Climbing the stairs, Theresa asked if she could read the letters. He was ahead of her, and she could not see his face.

"Tomorrow, for God's sake." And though he laughed, his tone rang false to her.

"Do you think it wise to rely on him?"

"There are the trustees. You'll have *me* worried if you go on."

His breath when he kissed her smelled strongly of smoke and brandy. This was the first time she had ever known him to sit drinking by himself late at night. As he leaned over to put out the lamp, he quoted to her, "The bright day's over, dear lady, and we are for the dark." He turned down the wick and reached out a hand to her. "Did I get it right?"

"As near as makes no difference," she replied, feeling a curious shiver at the pit of her stomach.

They lay on their own sides of the bed for a long time without moving, and this time it was Clinton who slept the sooner; and though she longed to, Theresa did not dare risk waking him by getting up and taking the letters from the pocket of his coat.

Clinton left the breakfast table first, and when Theresa followed a few minutes later, she discovered him talking intently to Harris in the hall. As soon as Clinton had finished speaking, Harris walked off hurriedly in the direction of the stables. Suspecting that whatever had passed between master and man had concerned Esmond's letters, Theresa ran up to the bedroom determined to read them at once.

To her dismay, the pile of clothes he had discarded the night before had been removed by the time she reached the bedroom. Clinton never picked up his own clothes, so Harris had evidently taken them to the dressing room while she had been at breakfast. She looked in the drawers of the dressing table and rummaged in the miniature chest of drawers on the table between the fireplace and the door, but found nothing. Suddenly she wondered whether what she had actually seen in the hall was Clinton giving the letters to Harris so that she would not get hold of them. She sat down disconsolately on the bed. Through the window she was aware of the brooding beauty of the beech and chestnut trees at the end of the lawn; no leaves were stirring in the still morning air. A bee was buzzing and bumping against the ceiling. A faint scent of dried lavender came from the drawers she had opened. Her maid came to dress her, but she sent her away.

When Clinton came in, dressed and shaved, she remained gazing out at the trees. "Where was Harris dashing off to?"

"Lancaster," he replied absently. "You ought to get dressed. It's going to be too hot to do anything in an hour or two." He sat down next to her. "I wish you'd change your mind about learning to ride."

She glanced sideways at him. "You can't have forgotten, Clinton." He tossed back his head in consternation. "I'm sure some women do ride in the first months," she went on, "but they know they're not likely to fall off." She laid a hand on the back of one of his. "What's he going to do in Lancaster?"

"Buy a few things."

"Oh?"

"Nothing very exciting. Cigars and cartridges."

He had spoken naturally and without the least hesitation; but, just as earlier she had jumped to the conclusion that Clinton had handed Harris the letters, now she suspected he had really gone to Lancaster to send a telegram to Esmond or perhaps to the trustees. Though she tried to be logical, she could no longer escape the tendrils of mistrust that had fastened upon her during Clinton's absence and had been tightening ever since.

Why had Clinton sent him off so suddenly without bothering to give him other matters to attend to while he was there? The man only went there once or twice a month. She felt angry with herself for questioning Clinton about Harris's mission when she ought to have been direct and asked to see the letters. But, having treated him with open suspicion the night before, and now having started the day with further questions, she felt that this would have to wait. Because she had made it so clear that mutual trust was equivalent in her eyes to a proof of love, she realized with chill misgiving that in future every question that might otherwise have appeared innocent to him would now run the risk of seeming weighted.

Walking in the garden together later in the morning, his drowsy contentment with the warmth and tranquility of the day mocked her for her own inability to share it. The dappled light, falling through the leaves on yellow streamers of laburnum and into blue pools of gentians, only distracted her a little from her fears. Near the entrance to the kitchen garden, a sudden pain low down in her stomach made her stop and lean against him. He looked at her in alarm, but the spasm passed quickly and was not repeated; so that when he asked her whether anything was wrong, she merely shook her head and smiled. They walked on.

"Do you ever worry about disappointing me, Clinton?"

His gaze passed her and fixed upon the raspberry canes under their muslin netting. "Wouldn't do me much good. I can only be myself."

"How lucky you are," she said, "to be so sure."

Far from being put out, he seemed amused. "For somebody as individual as you are, Theresa, you say the most unlikely things." He smiled. "I suppose that's why you do."

Later that morning, while Clinton was out walking with Dick, Theresa made up her mind not to press him about the letters while his friend was at Hathenshaw. Before then, Clinton might show them to her voluntarily; he had promised not to conceal things from her. Remembering this conversation, she felt ashamed of her doubts and told herself they were ridiculous. Shortly before luncheon, Theresa found herself having to sort out one of the violent quarrels which seemed to be becoming commonplace between Louise and her governess. Two days before, the girl had refused to continue reading Chapman's *Iliad*, describing Homer as "a blind old person who wrote a silly rigmarole of battles so badly that nobody knows if it's one poem or lots of odds and ends." Louise had also taken to asking deliberately embarrassing questions about love whenever they read Shakespeare. Since Miss Banks was a spinster who had twice been jilted on the point of marriage, the subject was a difficult one for her. Today the argument had arisen when the woman had apologized for coughing, asking Louise to forgive her "barking." Louise had replied that she could go on all day since she liked dogs.

Though Theresa often found these encounters amusing, it had not been easy to find a suitable governess prepared to work in such a remote place, and she was extremely anxious to prevent the woman's giving notice. Several of those interviewed for the post had turned it down at once when Theresa had been obliged to tell the inevitable lie about not being married to Clinton. Soon Theresa knew that she would have to make arrangements for Louise to go away to school—at any rate before her pregnancy became obvious. The thought of the opposition she would face made Theresa dread breaking the news to her. Since she was also sure that Clinton thought she indulged the child, Theresa was dismayed by thoughts of his probable reaction to the arguments in store for all of them. There was every chance too that Louise would appeal to her grandfather to prevent her being sent away; and since the old man already blamed Clinton for destroying his daughter's prospects of an excellent marriage, and after that an unparalleled opportunity in the theater, his arrival at Hathenshaw as Louise's champion was not an event which Theresa could contemplate with detachment.

In the meantime, Clinton's apparent indifference to the future at times shocked her. Simple misunderstandings, which a few words appeared to set straight for him, left lingering echoes with her. On perhaps some dozen occasions since coming to Hathenshaw, she had given way to sudden outbursts of anger, for which she had soon apologized. But the fact that he was always so easily reassured distressed her almost as much as the tensions in herself. At times she blamed their isolation, at times her pregnancy and the strains of secrecy; but when depressed, no conscious listing of reasons helped her. She was not often unreasonable with him, but when she was, Theresa wished that Clinton would argue the matter out with her. Treating her with chivalrous patience seemed more important to him than understanding her.

During the next few days, though she managed to behave more naturally with Lambert, and even enjoyed winning him over, she could not help sometimes resenting his closeness to Clinton. On Dick's second day, she had been walking past the stables with Louise when they heard the two men laughing together. Clinton had rigged up an improvised shower bath there—an old copper with a perforated bottom, slung between two rafters of the hayloft. To make it work, Harris had to clamber up the loft ladder with buckets of water to tip in. Entertained at first by their shouts of amusement, she had soon felt sad and, though she did not admit it, a little jealous. They shared so much more than this capacity for easy laughter over trifles. The bond of the army, common backgrounds of school and home, set her apart from them in a way born ladies would have accepted as entirely natural, but which to her, with her memories of a theatrical life identical for both sexes, seemed hurtful and strange.

On the day before Lambert was due to leave, Clinton had suggested that the three of them should watch the sheepshearing at Sagar's Farm outside Browsholme. Knowing that they would prefer to ride there, rather than take the carriage, Theresa had decided not to go; but Clinton's disappointment was so obvious that, even before they had left, she regretted her decision. Yet because she had been so positive, she had felt unable to retract in front of Lambert without looking foolish. Later she was amazed that she had not simply made light of the whole matter and gone regardless of anything she had said. No principle had been involved and her sensitivity over something so unimportant now struck her as far more absurd than any change of heart would have been. She wanted to ask Harris to drive her to the farm in the phaeton, but could not help thinking that the servant would suppose she had been left out and was only going after the men to get her revenge. Annoyed with herself for being affected by anything Clinton's valet might think, she still could not bring herself to ring for him. She passed a dull day.

Before leaving, Clinton had been definite about the time they would return and so Theresa asked the cook to have dinner ready by that hour. But when the time came they did not appear, and Theresa was left sitting alone in the dining room. Harris, who since coming to Hathenshaw had doubled as butler and valet, stood waiting to serve her. And still they did not come. The silence in the room and the servant's tactfully averted gaze started to play on her nerves. In less than five minutes she had endured all she could and jumped up and left the room.

On the ride back to Hathenshaw, Lambert's mare had gone lame and the two men had dismounted and led their horses home. They were tired and their faces caked with dust that had dried on sweat; their clothes were covered with strands of wool. Having both tried their hand at shearing, they had given the locals more to laugh about than any traveling circus, especially since they deliberately picked some of the largest rams for their beginners' efforts. Later they had got their own back by getting the shearers to race each other for money.

Knowing they were late, Clinton at once went to Theresa's favorite sitting room and, finding it empty, hurried to the dining room. When Harris told him that Mrs. Barr had gone upstairs, he asked the valet to tell her that he had returned and sent his apologies. Then Clinton went to wash and change. When he returned to the sitting room some minutes later, Theresa had still not come down, but Lambert was there talking to Louise. She was showing him her musical box, which now occupied a place of honor in the room. The child had already eaten with her governess and usually spent some time with Clinton and Theresa at this hour before they dined. Wanting to ask her whether she had just seen her mother, Clinton remained silent when she started the musical box. To the strains of a Mozart minuet, the small and beautifully carved figures of a man and woman set into the lid bowed to each other jerkily and then danced to the tinkling notes.

While the music played, Louise crossed the room at her ease like an accustomed hostess and casually sniffed some roses in a vase near Clinton's chair. "Did you go to a lot of shops for my present?" she asked, looking at him attentively with her green eyes that he had always thought too large for her face.

"Several."

"More than for Mama's watch?"

He composed his face, seeing Lambert smile. "Good musical boxes are always hard to find."

She looked at him with an expression of secret triumph. "I thought so."

"But so are watches," said Lambert.

"That isn't what Lord Ardmore said," the girl answered tartly.

"Come on then, Clinton"—Dick laughed—"which took longer to find?"

"There are some things a man keeps to himself."

Louise considered this with her head on one side. The figures on the box bowed to one another and the music tinkled to a close. "What other things does a man keep to himself?" she asked.

Clinton smiled. "I couldn't keep them to myself if I told you."

"Drinking too much? *I* think it's very vulgar to get drunk."

"What else do you think is vulgar?" asked Dick gravely.

"I think mustaches are rather . . ." She paused, uncertain what word to use.

"Hairy?" asked Lambert.

"Yes," she cried, laughing loudly, as though he had made an extraordinarily funny joke. She turned to Clinton. "Do you know what I think your face looks like when you've just shaved?"

He got up impatiently, beginning to feel worried by Theresa's continuing absence. "I don't know."

"Like polished pumice stone," she announced loudly, clearly pleased by the comparison.

"Isn't it usually gray and full of little holes?" asked Dick.

As Louise began to explain what she had meant, Clinton went out and made for the stairs.

Theresa was reading a book when he entered their bedroom. She looked up at him with ironic surprise. "Why did you send your man up instead of coming yourself?"

"Good God, Theresa, I'd been shearing sheep. I was a dreadful sight."

"You'd have been a welcome one to me an hour earlier."

"Dick's horse went lame." He went to embrace her, but she drew back. "Damn it, Theresa, what's the matter?"

"How do you think I felt with that Harris creature watching over me, as if he knew you'd be late? The faithful retainer who knew his darling master better than any mere mistress." She paused, breathing deeply, her eyes still reproachful.

Her last word made him stiffen. "Do you have any complaint against him?"

"I've never cared for him."

"He's an excellent valet and a first-rate groom."

"There must be others."

"Do you want him dismissed?" he asked quietly.

"Look at me, Clinton," she whispered. "You're almost in tears. I didn't mean it. I felt humiliated. Can't you understand why?"

"I should have come up at once. I'm sorry."

"It isn't just that," she moaned. "You like the man because of your past. It's the same with your friend. I haven't seen you happier for weeks than in these last few days. I don't begrudge it you, so you needn't say it isn't true."

"But I do say that," he replied insistently.

She smiled at him sadly. "My love, it isn't noble to deny what's perfectly obvious." She closed her book and met his eyes. "I miss the theater, so why should you be too proud to admit you miss the army?"

"Because I don't."

Having thought her, a few moody days apart, so perfectly contented with her life, her admission about the theater stunned him. He stared at a painted satinwood chair next to hers and remembered Esmond's saying that she would never adapt herself to a life of social isolation. His brain felt leaden and confused.

She was looking at him closely. "Would you mind if I went back to the theater?"

"What do you think?"

She seemed not to hear the tremor in his voice. "Because Lady Ardmore—even if nobody knows who she is—would insult her husband by acting?"

"No," he cried. "I'd think I'd failed you. You know that very well." She looked straight at him, and he was dazed to see the sudden light of happiness in her eyes like a flame—not exultant but assured, glowing. She came to him and laid her head against his shoulder.

After a silence, she looked up at him with a strange little smile, part rueful and part scared. "Perhaps love wouldn't be worth having if we knew it would go on being the same forever. But that doesn't help at all. It's still the worst fear on earth. There isn't anything to touch the terror of it growing less." She moved away from him and looked back with swiftly assumed jauntiness. "I daresay I'll learn to live with it."

"Me too." He sighed.

"If we talk to each other . . ." She let the words die, was still a moment, and then held out a hand. "We must go down."

Dinner, to Clinton's relief, progressed quite unremarkably until almost over, and Theresa seemed entirely herself again. Then shortly after dessert had been served, Lambert mentioned that the senior subaltern in the 15th had recently married.

"And what about you, Captain?" asked Theresa. "Do you ever think about marriage?"

"Often."

"What discourages you? Perhaps you're too fussy."

Lambert pensively ran a finger along the beveled edge of a wine coaster. "Fussiness isn't the problem. In a way it doesn't matter who one marries. At the end of a month one's sure to find one's married somebody else."

Alarmed by Theresa's sudden tenseness, Clinton could think of no way to end the conversation. Instead he listened helplessly as Theresa said with feigned good humor, "How can bachelors know so much about the changes marriage can make in a woman?"

Lambert laughed softly. "One listens, you know."

Theresa nodded and took an unhurried sip of wine. "It's always seemed strange to me that people who call themselves gentlemen are so ready to moan about their wives in public."

"I daresay the fair sex does its share of grumbling too." Dick frowned. "I've never been too sure what a gentleman is. Far easier to say what he isn't."

Clinton took his chance gladly to keep this new subject alive. "My father used to say a gentleman should be too proud to be useful and too indolent for enterprise. Need I say this qualified him excellently."

"What about noblemen?" asked Theresa, looking coolly at Lambert.

"Ask his lordship."

"You'll succeed to a title, Captain."

Dick raised his hands in a gesture of self-disparagement. "I'm a disgrace to my class. Not nearly ruthless enough. It's a fact. Aristocracies never last unless they murder their rivals. At least the French flung away their privileges in an orgy of depravity. We're losing ours without even enjoying ourselves."

"Is that your experience?" murmured Theresa, turning to Clinton.

"Of course not. I may say that when we're alone together, Dick doesn't spend his time saying things for effect."

Lambert stared hard at the table and colored slightly. "I was trying to make civil conversation in the face of—"

"Of what?" demanded Clinton.

"Exception being taken to every word I say." Lambert rose and inclined his head to Theresa. "Please accept my apologies."

After his friend's departure, Clinton's protracted silence made Theresa want to scream. At last she said thickly, "Why don't you blame me? You'd have been talking quite happily if I'd never joined you." She wanted to stop and say she was sorry, but some other force drove her on. Her bitter voice shocked her, as if she were listening to a stranger—a person utterly unlike herself, consumed with resentment. "How can you love me when you hide things from me? When you destroy letters you promised to show me? Now I'm to blame for offending that cynical man."

He did not move or even raise his eyes. Eventually he said in a low voice, "He happens to be one of the bravest, most generous men alive." Theresa said nothing. "Don't you see?" he murmured. "We were imprisoned together in Peking."

"Isn't that something else you should have told me?"

"I don't say it now to place you in the wrong, which seems to be your attitude. I simply don't like to remember it."

"Isn't modesty about bravery just affectation?"

At last he was angry, his eyes seeming to concentrate the fading light, glinting with the same hard gleam she remembered from his confrontations with Esmond at Kilkreen. "There's a sort of maggot in Chinese jails. It breeds in the earth floors and burrows into wounds. Hundreds are killed by it. My ankles were raw where the iron chafed—a perfect meal for the maggots. Dick risked his life and saved mine. He sucked them out—that cynical man."

"I don't understand," she shouted.

"Why I don't like to think of those months?"

"Why you said nothing."

"If you'd lived as we did—in daily terror of death, foul in our excrement, beaten by our guards. We all have a secret idea of ourselves, something to measure ourselves against. We all fall short, but I lost every shred of faith in what I'd thought I was. I could face brief danger afterward, a few days of it, but not month upon month, when nothing's to be done but see oneself weakening." He looked away, hands clenched tightly. "I'll tell you when I last thought of it—in the gun room with those damned letters you want to share." He pushed back his chair abruptly. "All right; see them now if you like. Esmond's ruined me. That's what they'll tell you." He smiled a curious lopsided smile and got up. "And you think, How can he mean this when he's happy to fool around with his friend as if nothing's changed. I've already told you why. I tried to think it through in the gun room, but I funked it. Esmond said there was still some hope; but I didn't go racing back south again, in case I lost that scrap of comfort, didn't run to my uncle, in case that failed. So I'm waiting, hoping a little while I still can."

When Lambert opened the door a little later, he saw Theresa and Clinton sitting like statues. Her face was wet with tears, while he stared ahead of him as though nothing in the world would ever reach him or change by the smallest fraction the fixity of his expression. Lambert, who had hoped to repair any harm his going might have caused, closed the door softly, leaving them alone like figures suspended in a nightmare.

The day after Dick Lambert left Hathenshaw, Clinton set out for London, intending to see Esmond and the trustees and then to consult his solicitor about possible countermeasures.

On the first night of Clinton's absence, Theresa slept badly, waking at intervals, her heart racing. For hours she did not sleep at all, panic rising in her as she imagined what might happen if Clinton failed to retrieve his position. It would not cause her great distress if they had to leave Hathenshaw, or were forced abroad to escape their creditors. No stranger to poverty, its humiliations were real to her but not impossible to imagine surviving. Yet to a man who had lived as Clinton had done, a life of hand-to-mouth and the dwindling of all choices would come as intolerable and degrading affronts. And if he were forced to suffer them, how long, she wondered, would it be before he turned against the wife who stood between him and reconciliation with his brother? Would he one day fling in her face the marriages he might have made if he had behaved less honorably? Memories floated through her mind, merging and fading with the eerie unreality of a waking dream—Sophie at the Castle, the church at Rathnagar, the day Clinton had come to her in York.

She slept a little before dawn, and woke to hear a thrush singing in the lilac bush under her window. The day ahead of her loomed empty and long. During the morning her thoughts touched on a dilemma unrelated to Clinton's difficulties. In recent weeks she had been worried that without a certificate proving her marriage, there might be problems over the baptism of her unborn child. Two or three times she had come close to raising this with Clinton but had hesitated in case he objected to a church christening on the grounds that it might imperil the secrecy of their marriage. Now that he had so much else to trouble him, she found herself even more reluctant to consider broaching this with him. She told herself that it would be absurd and pointless to argue about such matters until nearer the baby's birth. But strangely, though she was overtly far more anxious about other things, once the thought of the certificate had entered her mind, she could not dismiss it.

Her marriage was a fact to her as plain as her own existence. But, just as had happened when Clinton had last been away, she was plagued by irrational misgivings that she could neither master nor fully understand. Seeing Harris exercising Clinton's stallion, her fears took definite form. If Clinton should die, she thought suddenly, if there was some riding accident, a mishap with a gun . . . ? The priest would still have his private register, but suppose that were lost, or he left Ireland, what else would she have to prove her marriage but the signet ring which still served as her wedding band?

Later she felt slightly ashamed that her spirits had sunk so far that she could yearn to hold a scrap of paper to feel secure. But below the surface, in spite of more serious forebodings about Clinton's trust money, this lesser fear persisted.

It was late the following evening when she finally decided to write to Father Maguire about a certificate, and her head was aching with fatigue. But she went on with her task. Only when she had finished the letter did she feel apprehensive. If Clinton saw an Irish postmark, he would certainly be curious. At Sowerby, where she went to Mass, Theresa had met and talked to the village dressmaker, a Catholic like herself. She added a postscript asking the priest to write to her care of Miss Waller of Sowerby. In time she would tell Clinton about the certificate, just as she would talk to him about the baptism. In a month or two his problems might be over. When the letter had been posted, Theresa still felt the same sharp anxiety about the news Clinton would bring on his return, but one small weight of care had been lifted from her.

CHAPTER TWENTY-SEVEN

"Esmond!" he yelled. "Esmond!" His voice echoing through rooms and corridors, astonishing the servants but bringing no answer. Decorous silence mocked him as his shouts died away, deadened by swagged curtains and Oriental carpets. Clinton passed from landing to landing, flinging open doors, sure that the footman had lied to him about his master's absence; but everywhere Clinton went, only the sightless eyes of statues returned his gaze, and no sound reached him except the unhurried ticking of clocks and his own heart's beating.

Returning to the hall, he sat down on the broad staircase. Below him stood the same footman he had sent chasing after his hat a year ago. Then as now, the tall figure of Ceres dwarfed them both. Above the goddess's head, Clinton saw the upper landings and the banisters through which he had caught his first glimpse of Louise. A year ago—only a year.

"Where would your lordship care to wait?"

"Here."

The footman showed no surprise but, with a slight inclination of the head, murmured, "If your lordship should require anything . . ."

"Just leave me."

After a while Clinton wandered into the principal reception room on the first floor but did not stay there long. In the library, Clinton remembered Theresa, sitting by the sunlit window as the church bells rang. The memory sent a dull ache to his heart. His ironic detachment on that day now seemed remoter than childhood—part of another life.

When his brother entered the library almost an hour later, Clinton ignored the hand he held out to him.

"I'm going to sue the trustees, Esmond."

Esmond made a soft clicking noise with his tongue. "Of course you can prove fraud or gross negligence amounting to a fraud?"

The calmness of Esmond's voice angered Clinton as much as open mockery.

"If it isn't gross negligence for a trustee to authorize investment in an insolvent company, you tell me what is?"

"I'm not a judge. I'd imagine you'd have to show the company was insolvent at the time of the transaction and then prove the trustees had reason to know it was. You can't defraud without intent."

"But *you* knew the company's position, and your intent was plain enough."

Esmond seemed puzzled. "Surely not? I was buying shares for myself at the very time I advised the trustees to do the same on your behalf." He sat down, carefully lifting his coattails to avoid creasing them. "Look," he went on eagerly, as if his one aim was to help his brother, "if they bought those shares and then knowingly misrepresented the fund's condition, that'd be quite another matter." Getting no response from Clinton, he pulled out his gold fob watch. "I'm dining out. It'd be quicker if you read counsel's opinion."

"You took counsel's opinion?"

"It's better to avoid litigation when one can."

"Opinions tend to differ from counsel to counsel."

"A great deal," agreed Esmond, pausing, "at any rate in a complicated action. Happily the law's perfectly clear about the liability of trustees." He snapped down the lid of his watch and returned it to his pocket. "You'd lose." He sat back in his chair and looked at Clinton benignly. "Don't worry; ruined peers always command public sympathy. To hell with the tradesmen they wouldn't pay, the servants they couldn't keep; laugh at the banker who trusted their word." He folded his arms. "It won't come to that anyway. You can reassign the lease on that place in Lancashire and buy a commission in an Indian regiment. I've heard of officers who've managed to live on their pay out there. You'd only have to stay a couple of years till you get the balance on Markenfield. Think of the poor devils there for life."

"There won't be a balance on Markenfield," Clinton shouted. "You know as well as I do that on completion the mortgages were to be redeemed with the trust capital. No trust money means no balance. In the meantime, I've no income and can't borrow a shilling against those worthless shares."

Esmond raised his hands helplessly. "Uncle Richard's got to die someday." He paused. "I hear you saw Miss Lucas in Ireland."

It was no worse than anything Esmond had already said—no worse, Clinton told himself, and yet now he felt such hatred that he believed he could have watched Esmond being tortured without raising a word of protest. On the man's face a faint sardonic smile still lingered at the corners of his mouth.

"You know," Esmond continued, "I'd have been perfectly willing to help you if you'd—"

Clinton leaped up, but Esmond anticipated him, jerking at the bellpull by his chair. He smiled apologetically as they heard hurried steps on the stairs. White-faced, Clinton moved over to the window and gazed out at the peaceful square while Esmond sent away the two footmen. Under the plane trees a nurse was wheeling a perambulator with a white sunshade.

Esmond said, "Since you never actually told me you'd married Theresa, I don't think my remark about Miss Lucas was so very tasteless." He looked at Clinton appraisingly. "I presume I'm right about why you were so angry?" Clinton nodded. "My congratulations to you both. I know you won't believe it, but if you'd asked for help, instead of threatening lawsuits, I might have been more eager to assist."

"Without conditions?" Clinton sneered.

"Just one." His eyes rested absently on an embroidered pole screen, as if his mind had passed on to quite different matters. "Perhaps," he murmured, "I'd be more favorably disposed if she came to do the begging."

Without a word, Clinton turned on his heel, knowing if he stayed he would not be responsible for what he did. On the stairs his gaze fell on the colorless face of the statue of Ceres looming beyond the banister rail. The goddess's features seemed to tremble, giving an illusion of sentience—a calm and distant smile, vanishing as he perceived it. His cheeks were still prickling with anger and his skin felt clammy under his shirt. With a sudden movement he leaned his weight against the statue's shoulder, bracing his knees against the banister. The figure tilted on its massive base but tipped back into place. Heaving again, he rocked it, and then gave a second push, watching it hang at the point of balance and then crash down to the stone floor, smashing a console table and splitting apart across the torso. The detached head rolled away crookedly like a lumpy ball.

The violence of the noise brought servants running. Without speaking or looking at the devastation he had caused, Clinton walked on down the stairs and left the house.

The following day Clinton's solicitor confirmed what Esmond had said about the inadvisability of bringing an action against the trustees. If *intent* to misapply funds could not be proved against them or their agents, there would be no case to answer. Incompetence, unless due to gross negligence or fradulent intent, would not be enough to sustain an action. The lawyer undertook to seek disclosure of all trust documents relating to sale and purchase of securities during the past year, but he held out little hope of incriminating revelations. Intent to defraud was notoriously hard to prove. And negligence, which was easier, often only gained a successful plaintiff derisorily small damages.

Without an income, and unable to raise money on his trust shares, Clinton knew that the balance due to him on Markenfield was also worthless as security because of the unredeemed mortages on the property. Apart from selling the Hathenshaw lease and any chattels not listed as heirlooms in his father's will, he now saw that his chances of survival had been whittled away to one.

An appeal to his uncle's generosity was all that could save him from the bankruptcy which the loss of the trust otherwise made inevitable. But, wanting to keep this last resort in being for as long as possible, Clinton decided against an immediate visit. He would allow himself one more carefree month with Theresa before admitting his true position and groveling to his uncle. To gain this month's respite, Clinton knew there was only one way to acquire the necessary funds without having to wait for them.

In an unpretentious Soho thoroughfare like Pulteney Street, not many houses contained anything of value. One notable exception was a property housing choice pieces of Carolean and William and Mary furniture, also pictures and silver of a quality to delight the eyes of the foremost dealers in the capital. These treasures were disposed not in an auction room but in the floors above a coal merchant's countinghouse. And very strange this would have been if that merchant's business had been concerned exclusively with coal. In fact Jabez Norton's more profitable transactions lay in another commodity.

The numerous unredeemed pledges, ranging from large canvases by Dutch and Italian masters to tiny silver snuffboxes and vinaigrettes, therefore caused Clinton no surprise as he was ushered into the moneylender's parlor. Less than two weeks earlier, he had borrowed three hundred pounds from Norton. He now desperately needed to increase that loan; and since he had drawn from this particular well on at least a dozen occasions, he knew that failure would make his chances of success elsewhere exceptionally slender. But though he was nervous, the heavy interest he had managed to meet in the past, gave him grounds for optimism. This mood received a slight check when he learned that Norton himself was not available and that he would have to be content with the attentions of his chief clerk.

Before proceeding to the business of a more substantial loan, Clinton thought it prudent to dispose of the formality of renewing the bill he had accepted on his previous visit. To leave it till later might serve as an excuse for Norton to add a couple of per cent to the interest on any new loan. To Clinton's alarm, when he lightly introduced the subject of renewing, the clerk said nothing, but went to a fat ledger which he opened, but then abruptly closed as if remembering something. "I'm sorry, Lord Ardmore."

Disbelief, and an unpleasant tightness in the chest, left Clinton speechless. Before leaving Hathenshaw, he had promised Theresa that he would have little difficulty in raising funds to tide him over till the truth about the trust was finally established. The mistrust his earlier reticence had already caused would be made worse were he to return empty-handed. The clerk seemed to be waiting for him to put another proposal; he was a small elderly man with slack jowls and a wen under an eyebrow that depressed the lid, giving the disconcerting impression of a perpetual wink.

"You can't mean that. The bill was only for a month."

"I sold it myself in settlement of another debt. Common practice, my lord."

"With short-term bills?" asked Clinton, staring at the clerk's snuff-stained lapels, doing his best to keep his voice down.

"With every sort of bill. Money can be lent, bills can't." The clerk saw Clinton's gaze shift to an elegantly veneered secretaire. "Now chattels is different. Mr. Norton likes chattels a deal better than paper."

"I was paying fifteen per cent," said Clinton with a mixture of anger and incredulity.

The clerk coughed, showing strong yellow teeth. "And now someone else is paying fifteen per cent on what I got for your bill. More than makes up for the discount I paid on the sale. Paper should circulate—that's Mr. Norton's view."

"I'd better tell you now, I was misled by Norton. I'll default unless you make me another loan."

"On what security?"

"My reputation. I've borrowed from Norton often enough."

"You'll have to see him. I can't make advances without security."

Clinton looked at him severely. "I trust I can rely on you to make my position plain to Mr. Norton over that bill?"

The man's humility seemed to conceal mild amusement. "It's not in his hands, Lord Ardmore."

"He knows who bought it."

"I'll do what I can," he replied grudgingly, before unexpectedly smiling with a genuine air of encouragement. "Of course if Mr. Danvers was to give us some guarantee, I'm sure there'd be no—"

"My debts are not my brother's business," snapped Clinton.

"Pity, that," murmured Norton's minion. "We've a great respect for Mr. Danvers here. He knows what's what where paper's concerned." Ignoring Clinton's anger, he went over to his desk and leafed through some papers before examining one particular sheet which he folded and then handed to Clinton. Half inclined to throw it down, Clinton thrust it into his pocket. "Mr. Danvers's signature to that would more than satisfy," the clerk added in a tactfully muted voice. "Witnessed of course."

A sudden suspicion occurred to Clinton. "Has Norton seen Mr. Danvers recently?"

"Mr. Danvers?" The clerk shook his head with a sad reflective look. "He used to discount some of our best bills." He lowered his voice. "Very distressing to sell in perfect good faith and be let down by the acceptor—a nobleman he was, like yourself. Mr. Danvers recovered on a judgment summons, but since then . . . " He broke off with a wry smile that completely closed his deformed eye. "Stands to reason we'd like to oblige his relatives, put things right."

"Provided he knows it."

"In a nutshell."

Clinton drew himself up. "I'll seek credit elsewhere."

The clerk looked at him blandly. "Messrs Drummonds'?"

"Say that again," shouted Clinton.

"Hard not to hear rumors, my Lord. Only rumors, mind you."

"How many bank clerks does Norton bribe?"

"Your little joke, Lord Ardmore, just between us, eh? Mr. Norton doesn't have my sense of humor. Have to watch my tongue. He's a sensitive man. 'Add-a-naught-on Norton' one client called him. Slander he said. No humor."

Walking briskly towards Piccadilly, Clinton's anger had already given way to leaden depression. Though confident that Norton would pay up on the bill if he defaulted, charging an exorbitant rate of interest until the debt was settled, he now saw that without collateral or a guarantor he would never be able to negotiate any sort of loan, whatever interest he might offer. This being so, he would now have to arrange for the sale of whatever unentailed items of silver and jewelry Drummonds held for him in their vaults. However black the future, he did not intend to change his mind about enjoying one more month at Hathenshaw.

Normally when he walked through crowded streets, he felt a sense of detachment from those around him. Today all that had changed. He remembered Theresa's asking him whether he was ever scared of disillusioning her, and his complacent reply came back to him with cruel irony: He could only be himself— a true patrician's answer. And what would that collection of attributes amount to when their possessor was stripped of everything he had taken for granted? What price an aristocrat's *air* without the means to sustain it?

Never could he remember being more aware of eyes upon him, people's clothes, shops, money changing hands as a hansom driver set down his fare, as a woman dropped a coin into a beggar's hand. Clinton tossed the man a florin. His coat was black with grease and dirt, face bleary, beard matted. In the eyes of most passers-by, Clinton knew that he himself would seem rich. His clothes alone would represent a fortune to a crossing sweeper; his gold-topped cane would support a coster's family for a quarter, his watch sell for as much as a cabman earned in six months. An Irish property came to him on his mother's death; he was heir to a wealthy man's estate. But on neither could he raise a farthing, since a will could be changed, a life tenant could leave behind unsuspected debts and encumbrances. Clinton glimpsed his reflection in a tailor's window. Everything in expectancy, nothing to hand. As he watched the paving stones slide by under his polished shoes, waves of shock reached him, making his legs feel weak.

As clearly as if he were reading them, his debts passed in review—a long cavalacade cantering down an ice-strewn slope towards insolvency: debts to Drummonds and to Norton, with interest and compound interest, sums owed to Lancaster tradesmen, payments outstanding to his mortgagees, unpaid servants' wages, a few hundreds owed here and there—to the coachmaker who had supplied his phaeton, the jeweler from whom he'd bought Theresa's diamond watch, his London wine merchant, his gunsmith.

In a daze he walked on towards his bank, oblivious to propositioning prostitutes, street musicians thrusting their hats at him for a coin, hawkers crying their wares—in every street the same struggle, from Bow to Pimlico, voice against voice, man against man, these goods against those, and in the daily conflict, many victims and few conquerors. Around him on every side were scenes he had witnessed scores of times before without the least involvement, like an idle civilian picking his way across someone else's battlefield.

A gentleman with a silk top hat and elegantly trimmed whiskers favored him with a nod, which Clinton returned. Later he could not help smiling. The man had taken him for a fellow bystander and not for one of the combatants.

CHAPTER TWENTY-EIGHT

Clinton had reached Lancaster too late the previous night to journey further, but he set out early in the morning on a livery stable's hack. In the open country the hazy air was sweet with the smell of dew on freshly mown hay. Most of the meadows were pale stubble now, the grass lying in long gray swathes awaiting the pitchforks and the carts. Tall grasses and cow parsley brushed the legs of his horse with a gentle whispering like ripples along a vessel's side. For moments at a time, the stillness and sunlight seemed to enter his blood, blotting out all memories and feelings unconnected with what lay around him, until, with a sensation like treading empty air, he remembered.

In the past, time had seemed to possess a comforting solidity. Even a bad year had offered the prospect of peaceful days or weeks for renewal, like snug anchorages spaced along a hostile shore. Gales might rage beyond the headland, yet inside all would be well. But coasts could be smooth as marble, and nothing stand to stem the following wind that blew time on.

Absorbed in the future, the present came to him with the fitful inconsequence of lantern slides—a boy eating apples on a gate, a cart like a moving haystack in a field, blue flash of a kingfisher over water.

After dismounting in the stables, Clinton took the short cut to the house through the kitchen yard. A maid was singing as she pounded the hen's feed of meal and potatoes, but as she saw Clinton approach, she dropped the bucket and ran into the kitchen. Disquieted, Clinton quickly followed her. As he entered, she was whispering something to a kitchen maid topping and tailing gooseberries at the table. The cook was slowly stirring the steaming contents of a copper pan. The servants eyed him in embarrassed silence.

"Why did you run in like that?" he said sharply to the girl who had been in the yard. No noise except the bubbling of the pan on the range and the mournful sighing of the knife-cleaning machine in the scullery. The cook went on stirring. "What's the matter with you all?"

"Mistress is ill, sir," murmured the cook, putting down her spoon.

He waited for her to continue, but she merely stood in silence, looking past him at the row of large serving plates on the dresser.

"Tell me," he shouted. Theresa was popular with the servants, and he sensed in their covert looks a veiled hostility, as if he were somehow to blame for whatever had happened.

"Best ask the doctor or her maid," the cook replied gruffly, returning to stirring her pan.

He stood motionless for a moment, legs refusing to move, fear biting at the pit of his stomach. Then, with a sudden movement, as if freeing himself from invisible bonds, he lunged to the door, breaking into a run outside the stillroom.

Louise came out of the yellow morning room as he reached the hall, staring in astonishment as he slithered to a stop at the foot of the stairs.

"What's wrong with her?"

"Nobody tells me anything," the girl answered almost peevishly. "She's my mother, but the doctor . . ."

Without waiting to hear more, Clinton ran up the stairs, not noticing Louise's angry face.

"That's how much I matter," she cried after him. "Don't even say good morning or hello to me."

Theresa was not in their bedroom; he hurried across it to her dressing-room door and went in. She was lying in the narrow bed against the wall. From the corner of his eye he saw her maid knitting in a chair by the window. In the stillness of the room, the blood hammered in his veins from shock and fear.

"Darling," he whispered, going down on his knees beside the bed, kissing her pale worn face. Slowly her lids opened upon vacant eyes. Trembling, he turned to the maid. "What happened?"

"The doctor gave her laudanum. She's still sleepy."

Theresa's eyes were less distant as she touched his hand lying next to hers on the cover. When her fingers closed on his, he was shaken by a suppressed sob of thankfulness. Heavy tears stood in his eyes. With an abrupt gesture he dismissed the maid.

"They gave me something that made me tired. . . . I have to rest."

"Why did I ever go?" he groaned, laying his hand against her cheek. Framed by her auburn hair, her face looked as white as the pillow under her head. "Are you in pain?"

She turned her head with a slight but definite gesture of negation. "At first it was no worse than a normal menses—except there was more blood. It happened once before, after two or three months. I was upset—terribly—but not frightened. Later I got up and went down. I felt all right. In the evening, going upstairs, I had a sudden pain—a sort of wrenching. I'd put something on, but I could feel the blood on my legs and my skirt. So much . . . I never knew I had such a lot in me. I fainted. The bleeding went on for ages. I got very weak."

"How long ago?" he asked, unable to stop his voice shaking.

"Three days . . . maybe four."

"Is the doctor coming today?"

"He seems to be here all the time." Her lips formed a faint smile. "I thought I was dying."

He covered his face with his hands. "I wasn't with you."

"I mightn't have known you." She saw his wet cheeks and said gently, as if reassuring a child, "It's all over now. I'm so much better." She closed her eyes and breathed deeply. "If I wasn't so tired . . . They give me something . . ."

The sun only reached the dressing-room window late in the afternoon. Hours now since she had spoken to Clinton, but he was still with her. Outside she could hear sparrows twittering in the ivy. Golden motes of dust hung in a shaft of sunlight. As she moved, he came up to the bed, looking strained and hollow-eyed, as though days had passed since his homecoming.

"Did you talk to the doctor?" she asked.

"I'm still waiting for him."

"There's no danger now."

Sudden despair swept through her. Terrified of conceiving again, her lost pregnancy haunted her with bitter finality. She had held such high hopes of the child, not simply as the living fulfillment of their love, but for the many changes its birth would have made in Clinton. Until a man became a father, he never knew the meaning of fearing for another. Death could take his son or daughter, and no conviction of never-failing strength could survive his helplessness in face of that fact. Never again would he have asked her, even in jest, why she allowed Louise to presume so much on her devotion, when she had done so little to deserve it. In her exhaustion, thoughts of sustaining their life together without the bond of a child seemed beyond her. Out of pride and respect for her feelings, he would go on pretending to be contented, go on telling her he regretted nothing he had given up for her sake. She raised herself on an elbow, sitting up with difficulty.

He hurried forward to place pillows behind her back. Some-how her feet had become entangled in the bedclothes, and the effort to free them made her feel sick and giddy. Her face was burning. She wanted to tell him everything she had felt, but weakness weighed on her like a physical presence, making her head swim.

"More air," she moaned in a voice she hardly recognized.

When he had opened the window, he offered her water to drink, but her throat felt too thick to swallow anything, and a lot splashed down on her peignoir. Her mind was lucid, but she could not articulate her ideas.

"Never pretend," she sobbed, suddenly appalled by the thought of what she must look like.

"Pretend what?" he asked softly.

"Never . . . never . . ." she repeated on a plaintive fixed note.

She turned away, oblivious of his grief. Time passed. "I want a mirror. . . . I want to see myself."

"It doesn't matter. You mustn't—"

"Oh God," she cried. "Can't I have what I want?"

He held up a small silver-backed hand glass for her. She looked at her reflection without speaking. *How can he love me?* she thought. Her eyes seemed enormous and as expressionless as empty holes. Her cheeks were livid patches on dead white. Tears seeped from her eyes, but she made no sound. He bent down and kissed her, but she drew away, staring at him with burning reproach.

"You promised . . ."

He was overwhelmed by the rebuff but did not dare risk aggravating her by admitting that he did not understand. He guessed that she supposed she had said something which she had only thought. He sat down helplessly beside her, cursing the doctor for not coming. He went out onto the landing and called to the maid to confirm the time that he was expected, though he had asked the same question several times before. Little bubbles of panic rose and burst inside him. How could the man know how ill she was and yet go off to spend time with villagers? A wretched country quack. He was amazed at himself for not having sent Harris to Lancaster hours ago to bring back the best physician in town.

Then he saw the doctor's one-horse gig standing in the carriage sweep, and the man himself walking across the hall. Clinton barred his way up the stairs.

"Lord Ardmore?" The doctor had a thick red beard and wore an old Petersham driving coat.

"I wonder that you didn't call in another man," Clinton began brusquely. "In London, in a case of serious illness where there's any doubt about—"

"There isn't. She'll put on strength if she eats and rests."

"Rests? She can hardly move."

"She lost a lot of blood. If I might see my patient, perhaps afterwards we could discuss second opinions?"

Clinton moved out of the way, regretting that he had immediately shown doubts about the man before even listening to him.

He waited impatiently for almost half an hour until the doctor came down and walked out with him into the late-afternoon sunlight.

"Is she better or worse?"

"The bleeding's very slight now." He was a man some twenty years older than Clinton, and he looked at him with guarded admonition. "Calmness is important. She must not be distressed. Worry will only delay her recovery. She must rest for two weeks. That's the only cure. If she sleeps badly, she can have laudanum. If you want powders and potions, go to another physician. Dr. Moncrieffe has the most fashionable practice in Lancaster."

Clinton looked down at the gravel. "Do you suppose that in any future pregnancy . . .?"

"I wouldn't care to predict. Your wife seems healthy in other ways. Many pregnancies end in the first month or two without the woman knowing it. A late menstruum, they may think. I've only known a handful of cases of accompanying hemorrhage." The doctor climbed into the driving seat of the gig.

Clinton frowned. "I daresay," he said awkwardly, "that you intended to be tactful by referring to the lady as my wife."

The man looked confused. "I'd heard rumors, but your daughter denied them most positively to my children." He paused. "I hope you won't consider it an impertinence to have brought them. There are very few large houses near Browsholme."

"Not at all," murmured Clinton absently.

"They played in the garden on the day they came."

"I don't care if they swept the chimneys," Clinton retorted with sudden exasperation. Anger, and guilt for his immediate suspicion that Theresa might have confided in Louise, made him long to get rid of the doctor. "I trust you'll tell your children, or anybody else who may make inquiries, that I am unmarried and mean to remain so." The man sat motionless, the reins limp in his hands. "Shall I settle with you now?"

The doctor looked down at him coldly and lifted the reins. "That won't be necessary."

"Damn your propriety," muttered Clinton, turning on his

heel, angry to have managed matters so badly, but obsessed now with discovering the truth from Louise.

He found her alone in the library, gluing dried flowers into a scrapbook.

"I want an explanation," he said quietly. She glanced from her work with a startled face, her glue brush dripping onto the page of carefully positioned flowers. "Why did you tell lies to Dr. Bradshaw's children?" Her lips moved but no sound came. A deep flush had risen to her cheeks. "Well?"

Though tears glistened in her eyes, she looked defiant. "They said things."

"Tell me."

"That mother was a bad woman . . . that everyone round here knew it and said so."

"Which you knew wasn't true."

For a moment the child looked more amused than fearful. "Of course I do. She's going to confession and Mass. She wouldn't if—"

"If what?" asked Clinton sharply, knowing very well what she had meant but wanting her to say the words so he could deny them.

The child bowed her head. "Ask her yourself."

Her trembling lower lip told Clinton that unless he was more gentle she would start to cry and then he would learn nothing from her. Remembering her inexplicable blushings and exits in the middle of conversations for no apparent reason, and her fury if she thought he was ignoring her, he was well aware of the store she set by everything he said.

He sat down next to her at the table. "Does anything your mother said to you explain what you told those children?" She shook her head emphatically. He said very softly, "Why did you tell them I was your father?"

"They insulted me, called me names. I told them I was Lady Louise Danvers. They're too ignorant to know viscounts' daughters aren't ladies in their own right. I knew I'd be found out, but I couldn't help it. I had to get the better of them."

"By lying?"

"Yes," she shouted, "By lying." She stopped, fighting back sobs. "I was ashamed. They said they'd seen you and mother

. . ." She got up and turned her back. "It's disgusting, horrible. They were going fishing for perch. They said you were there, without a stitch on, by some slimy pond." She was sobbing now, words wrung from her against her will. "They said people had to do *that* . . . to make babies. That a man can kiss a woman and make her do anything." Her voice sank very low. "They said mummy was ill because of a baby." She spun round and faced him. "Is it true?" she whispered, gazing at him in horror.

"Of course not."

"You swear?"

"They lied to you."

She looked at him with such thankfulness that he could have wept. Then, when he was still stunned by her outburst, she ran up and kissed him on the cheek with clumsy violence. The next moment she ran from the room as if terrified by what she had done.

The time of her mother's convalescence was a trying period for Louise. Their walks together ceased, and she spent almost all her time with her governess. But by the middle of August, Theresa was better and Louise had been given a pony chaise by Clinton. It soon became one of her favorite pastimes to drive herself around the estate.

One afternoon she went to the stables to tell Harris to get her chaise ready and harness the pony. She found the servant talking to a boy outside the saddle room. Harris called her over.

"The lad here says he's got a letter for your mother, Miss Louise. Has to give it to her himself. Could you take him while I get Quickstep harnessed?"

Though feeling it rather beneath her dignity to play escort to an errand boy, Louise's curiosity got the better of her.

"Come on then," she said, looking critically at her charge. The boy's face was a mass of freckles under his thatch of butter-colored hair. She noticed that his nose was peeling, and that an immense pair of boots made his legs look like sticks where they showed under his ragged knee-length trousers.

Walking towards the house, she twirled her little parasol

over her head as she took sideways glances at this improbable messenger. The boy's tattered clothes made her feel like a princess, but memories of the scant respect shown her by the doctor's children made her suppress her regal instincts.

"Why can't you let me take the letter?" she asked in a friendly voice. "I could give you a tip you know."

"Keep thy brass. Miss Waller says I'm to gi' it to the lady herself, and I will that."

"Who is this Miss Waller?"

"Dressmaker in Sowerby, miss."

"That's where we go to Mass." Louise looked thoughtful. "Is she small and rather pink?"

"Happen she is."

"I wonder she can't use the post office like anybody else." The boy said nothing, but scuffed his boots on the gravel, kicking up dust. "Don't you think it unusual?"

"Mebbe 'tis. Mebbe 'tain't."

His brusque taciturnity amused Louise. "You don't say much."

"Nowt to say."

Louise smiled at him kindly. "Would you like something to eat in the kitchen? You must be tired." He shook his head and walked on with hunched shoulders. She said sweetly: "Won't you show it me?"

"It's nowt but an envelope, miss."

"I'd still like to see it. Perhaps you haven't got a letter at all. Could be just an excuse to get into the house so you can take something."

They were only yards from the door, and the boy stopped, rigid with anger. "Shut thy gob," he muttered under his breath, pulling a crumpled envelope from his trouser pocket.

Concealing her anger at his rudeness, Louise looked away. "So you brought an envelope," she said quietly. "They're not hard to buy." She turned and met his eyes calmly. "Tell me the name on the letter."

He looked down at his dusty boots, blushing fiercely. "I can't figure it. Lady of the house, I been told."

"Better let me read it then." She held out an unhurried hand, but he stood there stubbornly refusing to relinquish it. His sullen defiance enraged her—an illiterate village boy refusing what she asked and proud of his stupid obstinacy. With a speed of movement that took her adversary completely by surprise, she snatched the envelope away from him and ran as fast as she could towards the door. Hampered by his heavy boots, the boy, though bigger, could not overtake her before she reached the house. Hearing him close behind her, and knowing he would catch her before she could cross the hall, she hit the dinner gong with the handle of her parasol, and turned to defend herself until help came.

"Gi' it back," the boy gasped, coming at her.

"It's for my mother. I'll—"

He lunged forward and she fenced at him with the parasol, catching him in the ribs with the point.

"I told Miss Waller . . . She made me promise." He was desperate rather than angry, and for a moment Louise almost relented, but by now his determination to recover the letter had increased her curiosity to discover what it was.

She saw him surreptitiously move to his right, and she held up the parasol to parry any sudden move. "Do you want Miss Waller to hear how rude and silly you've been?"

The boy grabbed at the end of the parasol. Because the letter was in her right hand, Louise was badly handicapped in the tug of war which followed and was soon disarmed. As he lunged for the letter, she hit him hard across the face, screaming as she cut her knuckles on his teeth. Stunned by pain and by the noise she was making, he hesitated a fatal moment. A second later a maid and a footman came in.

"Put him out," cried Louise.

"She took my letter afore ye came," said the boy, appealing to the footman who was advancing on him.

"It's for my mother. Of course I took it. She'd hardly want to see a village boy."

The footman took the boy's arm and led him firmly to the door.

Louise sat down on her bed and looked at the dirty envelope. Her hand shook a little as she held it up to the light, but the paper was far too thick for her to learn anything about the contents. The memory of the boy's face after she had hit him made her feel horribly guilty, especially since she now had no idea what to do with the letter. She wondered whether he would be sensible and say nothing, or whether next Sunday at Mass, if her mother was well enough to go, Miss Waller would angrily tell her what had happened to her errand boy. Re-examining the envelope to see if she could open it and then glue it again with no damage to the paper, she was horrified to see that she had managed to smear it with blood from her knuckles. She dabbed a handkerchief into the water jug on her washstand and tried to clean away the stain, but the paper was porous and she only succeeded in making the marks worse.

The only remedy would be to use a new envelope and write her mother's name in capital letters. Louise lost no time in opening the old one. To her disappointment, the only enclosure was another sealed envelope, directed to Mrs. Barr, Care of Miss E. Waller, Sowerby, North Lancashire. The postmark intrigued Louise: Ballygowan. She suspected the name was Irish. She turned the envelope over and was relieved to find that the sender had not sealed it with wax. Who could have written to her mother and yet been scared to send it directly to Hathenshaw? Her heart was beating faster as she stared at the cramped handwriting on the envelope; with a shudder of fear and excitement, she hid the letter under her pillow. Already she knew that she was going to open it. Since the servants who had rescued her might tell her mother that she had a note for her, she realized that she would have to be quick.

She left her room and went down to the kitchen by the back stairs. Though a maid was rolling pastry at the table, Louise managed to take one of the large metal ladles from the row of hooks by the dresser without being seen. The servant's back had been turned, and the dresser had helped conceal her. Next Louise took a box of lucifers from the smoking room and returned to her room, once more by the back stairs. Having placed a chair against the door, she took two candles of the same length from the candelabrum on the dressing table, lit one, and dripped two blobs of wax onto the marble top of the washstand. She set the bases of the candles side by side in the warm wax, lit the second one, took the letter from under her pillow, and placed it on the edge of the washstand. When she had half filled the ladle with water, she held it over the candle flames. It took longer than she had expected for the water to get hot, but as soon as it was, she picked up the letter gingerly and proceeded to steam it open.

Inside were two sheets of paper. The first Louise read was headed "The Presbytery, Rathnagar, July 15th, 1867":

Dear Madam,

I had great pleasure in receiving your letter communicating the good news of the expected arrival of a young stranger, and I rejoice that you feel I can be of service in bringing another lamb to the sheepfold. I commend your desire to take your precautions in advance concerning the baptism, and have no hesitation in forwarding to you the enclosed certificate. I must however ask you, in view of my promise to Lord Ardmore to preserve the strictest confidentiality, not to use the enclosed for any purpose other than that mentioned in your letter. Should you wish to, a brief note of assent from his lordship would put all straight with me. Since the object of this little request is to avoid misunderstanding, I trust it will not give offense. Secrecy sometimes places the celebrant upon the horns of a dilemma, especially when communicating with only one of the partners. I need not assure you, madam, that your secret is safe with me. I take great interest in your spiritual welfare, and will again be ready to, should any opportunity occur.

Faithfully, yours in Jesus Christ,
Bernard Maguire.

The second sheet was written more elegantly, as though by a clerk, in copperplate script, the priest's signature being the only part in his hand.

From the book of marriages of the parish church of Rathnagar, in the diocese of Kildare, in Ireland, it appears that Clinton Cairns Danvers, Viscount Ardmore, was joined in matrimony with Theresa Catherine Barr, according to the rites of the Holy Roman Catholic Chuch, on the 6th January 1867, the witnesses being Jane MacDonagh and Mary Brennan. This I testify— Bernard Maguire, P.P. Given at Rathnagar this 15th day of July 1867.

Louise dropped the letters and stood motionless, staring at the white squares of paper on the patterned carpet. At first she was too dumfounded to react; then a surge of happiness swept through her. It was not long before this mood passed. She felt disquieted. There was so much she did not understand. Too much. If they were married, why had Clinton lied to her? And why had her mother said nothing? Not even anything about the baby or her illness. Louise sat down on the bed, feeling suddenly scared. What was the promise Clinton had made the priest swear and what was her mother's secret?

She rolled back on the bed and tried to lie still but could not stop shivering. New thoughts battered her like waves. Esmond had hated Clinton, and her mother had always refused to say why. Why had the priest been afraid to send his letter to Hathenshaw? Still confused, Louise became angry. She had thought her mother trusted her, but all the time these secrets had been kept from her—the child who could be told nothing. She bit her lip to keep back tears. Her eyes returned to the two white squares of paper. At any moment someone might come in. Moving swiftly to her davenport desk, she took out a new envelope and, pausing to steady herself, wrote out her mother's name in large bold letters. Then she carefully replaced the contents of the priest's letter, and with a few spots of glue stuck down the flap. Though feeling herself wronged by Clinton and her mother, Louise could not help experiencing sharp pangs of guilt. She would have been uneasy about opening any letter intended for somebody else; but to have opened one sent by a priest was far worse—perhaps sacrilegious. She knelt down and whispered an Act of Contrition before hiding the ladle under the bed and replacing the candles in the candelabrum.

Afraid to hand the letter to her mother, in case she gave herself away, Louise found her maid and implored her not to give it to her mistress unless she was alone; she also persuaded her to promise she would say she had been given it by a boy from Sowerby. Feeling calmer, Louise returned to her room.

That evening she saw from her window a dull red point of light moving in the darkness on the lawn. On many other nights she had seen Clinton walking alone in the garden, cigar in hand, and had felt reassured and safe. Eyes filling with tears, she turned away and drew the curtains. For hours she lay twisting in bed, longing to confess to her mother, but not daring to. The lie she had asked the maid to tell now scared her. The boy might admit to the dressmaker that he had been tricked out of the letter. In her misery, one thought sustained Louise: If nobody else could be trusted, she could still confide in her grandfather. He would explain everything to her. Reluctant to risk asking a maid to post a letter for her, Louise decided to wait till Harris next took her to Browsholme, where she might manage to elude him long enough to post one herself.

CHAPTER TWENTY-NINE

The arrival of her marriage certificate was soon almost forgotten by Theresa in the press of new events—each one of which seemed more important than the nebulous fears which had first led her to write to the priest. In the past few days, Louise had started to behave with a wayward instability that made her previous shifts seem trifling. Withdrawn for long periods, she would suddenly give way to outbursts of rudeness or tears. Finding herself, just as often as Clinton, the target for her daughter's displeasure, Theresa wondered whether Louise might be infatuated with Clinton and therefore jealous; but she felt no certainty about this. More perplexing to her was the girl's adamant refusal to come to Mass, in spite of other signs of increased piety. But worries about Louise were soon eclipsed by concern for Clinton.

His gentleness and patience during her illness had deepened her love for him, and it caused her poignant pain to see fatalism begin to wear away his old gaiety and nonchalance. When he announced his intention of seeing his uncle before the month ended, he sounded confident of success, but his optimism seemed a shadow of other days and did not hide from her his underlying mood. Too detached to be described as stoical, there was something disdainful about his attitude to his misfortunes: a quality that chillingly reminded her of stories of the French nobility's proud refusal to fight to stay alive in a world they could no longer control. But when the myth of Clinton's invulnerability died for her, Theresa felt not disillusion but relief. If they faced hardships, she would be able to contribute far more to their lives. Used to the sudden shocks of theatrical failure or success, with no intervening hinterland of moderate security, she believed she would not easily be intimidated by anything they might have to face. Her first test came sooner than she thought.

On a gray and windy morning, still several weeks before Clinton was due to see his uncle, Theresa was sitting in the library when Harris burst in without knocking. "There's a sheriff's officer asking for his lordship."

"You saw his warrant?" Though her voice was sharp, Theresa was hard put to master a suffocating wave of faintness.

Harris looked at her with exasperation. "I know what he is. 'Gentleman to see Lord Ardmore.' 'Gentleman?' I says. 'What name?' 'A gentleman,' says he; 'you just fetch him here.' He's a bailiff plain as if he had Queen's Bench stamped on his forehead." Harris came up to her and said gruffly, "You go tell the *gentleman* his lordship's in Lancaster and won't be back today."

Though she was badly shaken, the servant's peremptory manner stung her. "What possible good would that do?"

"Give the master time to meet his debt or make himself scarce till he can. That man's come on a judgment summons or I'm a bleeding bashi-bazouk."

Theresa closed her book and stood up. "If he can meet his debt, he'll meet it. A day or two can't make the least difference."

"Let me be the judge of that. I know what I'm about. Do as I say, and I'll see he steers clear when he gets in from his ride."

The man's urgency was so great that after a moment's thought Theresa nodded silent assent. Though sure that Clinton would have told her if he had had notice of a writ, it was possible that his bank had stopped payment without his knowledge. She left the room in a daze.

Outside the library, Harris hurried away in the direction of the back stairs, while Theresa made for the hall at a more leisurely pace. The sheriff's officer was portly and cheerful-looking; a loose-fitting ulster partly concealed his considerable girth. He had already made himself comfortable in the deep leather porter's chair by the door and was smoking a pipe. Theresa stared down at him from the stairs, amazed that this buffoonlike figure could pose any threat to Clinton.

The man rose as he saw Theresa and removed his brown bowler. "Forgive the liberty," he said, waving his pipe and coming close enough to Theresa to give her the full benefit of the smoke.

Ignoring his jocular deference, she quietly asked him his business.

"That's with the gentleman himself, madam."

"Lord Ardmore's in Lancaster. Perhaps you could come back another day, Mr. . . . ?"

"Lock, madam." He grinned, revealing a number of broken teeth. "They often remark on it."

"Do they? A better name for a turnkey than a bailiff."

"Sheriff's officer, ma'am," Lock replied with feigned reproach. "I like a joke, though—better for a turnkey. Very good that. Better laugh than cry, that's what I tell them."

"Why not come back in a day or two?"

The bailiff smiled at her sadly. "That's what they often say." He puffed on his pipe. "Never 'Come in and make yourself at home.' "

"You seem to know how to without any help." She fanned away a cloud of pipe smoke with her hand. "If you wish to waste your time, please do so outside or in the smoking room."

Lock bowed stiffly and replaced his hat. "Breath of air, I think."

As he was leaving, Theresa heard scuffling coming from the servants' corridor. A moment later Harris was dragged in by two constables. One of his eyes was closed by a livid bruise.

"Let him go," muttered Lock, jerking his head meaningfully in Theresa's direction. While one of the constables sank down on a small upright chair and gingerly rubbed his ribs, his colleague maintained a firm hold on Harris's pinioned arm.

"Best 'ang on to 'im, Mr. Lock. He were sneakin' out by t'

back. Wouldn't say where and slings a haymaker as Tom tries to stop 'im."

Lock turned gravely to Theresa. "I like loyalty, ma'am. But obstructing a law officer in the exercise of his duty comes under a different head." He sighed and turned to the seated constable. "What about the others?"

"Shut in the servants' hall."

"You've no right to terrify Lord Ardmore's servants," cried Theresa, still shocked by what had been done to Harris.

"For their own good, ma'am. Don't want to have 'em charged with preventing execution of a writ. Not easy these large houses—a sight too many doors."

No longer in any doubt about the bailiff's determination, his good humor now seemed obscene to her. "I told you Lord Ardmore's in Lancaster."

"Happen he'll come back sooner than expected."

When Lock had told the uninjured constable to put Harris in the servants' hall and keep an eye on the back of the house, he sent his still complaining companion to the stables to join another man already waiting there.

"A nobleman isn't likely to run into the woods like a common thief."

"I've known 'em quite elusive, madam," replied Lock, sucking hard at his teeth, as though to dislodge a recalcitrant scrap of meat. "I wonder if I have the honor of conversing with Lady Ardmore?"

"Find somebody fit to introduce you before asking who I am."

A badly suppressed smirk spoiled Lock's pretense of cowed humility. "A very proper answer, I'm sure. My interest was, uh, humanitarian rather than social. As the gentleman's wife I could stretch a point—agree to your accompanying his lordship in my chaise." He relit his pipe and drew on it thoughtfully. "I'm afraid the governor's against all visitors 'cept family."

Theresa turned away with smarting eyes. She badly wanted to ask who had brought suit against Clinton and for how much, but could not face the rebuff which her earlier hostility now made likely. Every minute her suspicion was strengthening

325

that Clinton had expected to be arrested and, knowing he could not prevent it, had kept it from her. On the point of leaving the hall, she froze. The bailiff also heard the sound of hoofs on the carriage sweep and smiled to himself.

Clinton did not at first see the sheriff's officer but, tossing aside his whip, came towards Theresa. "Not waiting for me, love?" His cheeks were glowing after his ride, and he looked happy and relaxed. She drew back; fears that he had misled her were overwhelmed by a desire to reduce the impact of what lay ahead. She wished that he could have come in bad-tempered or indifferent—anything but happy. As Lock coughed discreetly to draw attention to himself, Clinton saw him and started.

Before he could speak, Theresa took his arm. "He's a bailiff. There are other men."

For a moment she wondered whether he had heard her, so sudden was the transformation of his expression; not knowing what to expect, she sighed with relief as she saw his compressed lips relax into a smile.

"So those were your men loafing about my stables?"

"Doing their duty, I hope, sir."

"In the nursery that means another thing." He moved closer and folded his arms. "So what's yours?" The man looked at him blankly. "Your duty?"

"Ah yes, sir," murmured Lock, putting down his pipe and pulling a folded document from his pocket. He cleared his throat. "Are you Lord Ardmore, sir?"

"I am."

"Then I'm sorry to inform your lordship I have a writ against you which I am charged to execute. I must request immediate payment of three hundred pounds at the suit of Messrs Mendoza and Nathan, or the pleasure of your company elsewhere."

"Do many people carry such sums about with them? I'll give you a note for it."

"I'm sorry, sir, but that won't answer."

"Don't be absurd. By the time we get to Lancaster it'll be too late to telegraph instructions to my bank. The creditor can't be as vindictive as you're making out."

"Says he's been used shamefully, sir."

"That old phrase. Have you ever *not* heard it trotted out when harsh measures are taken without warning?"

"Mr. Mendoza's not one who wastes his time. He bought your lordship's acceptance from Mr. Norton in good faith. Your bank wouldn't pay when it fell due."

"Norton's clerk told me the purchaser would renew."

"I can't help that, my lord. Pay the money and there's an end. Otherwise I must arrest you."

"I want to speak to the lady in private. Lock the door if you must."

"Against sheriff's orders."

"Upstairs? You don't think I'd try jumping forty feet?"

"Several gentlemen have made away with themselves like that."

"For three hundred pounds?" exploded Clinton.

"Less, as I recall." Lock phlegmatically knocked out his pipe against the plinth of a classical bust. He caught Theresa's eye. "Perhaps if you'd introduce me to the lady, I could oblige you. The name's Lock, my lord."

"Don't," whispered Theresa vehemently. "If he wants to spy on us, let him."

"To hell with that," said Clinton, picking up his whip and advancing on the bailiff. "Will you take my word that I'll come with you in an hour?"

The sheriff's officer glanced warily at the whip and then at Clinton's face. "Half an hour."

"Very well. Now get out."

Alone, they embraced in silence, tightly clasped, imprinting the memory of warmth and touch.

"How long?" she murmured at last, moving from him.

"Only days. They can't hold me on mesne process after disclosure of my assets in court. Harris will telegraph my solicitor."

"Why not me, Clinton?"

"It'd only hurt you to come to Lancaster. He knows what has to be done. His last officer was in and out of Cursitor Street and the Queen's Bench for all of two years."

"*Two years?* How can you make a joke of it?"

"Because it won't happen."

"If your uncle turns you down, Clinton?" Doing her utmost to remain calm, Theresa could not stop trembling.

"I'd rather think about that when I'm out of Lancaster Castle."

"*You* know the possibilities. Don't *I* have a right to know them too? Must I sit here when you've gone just as ignorant as I was before that man came?" Her voice had become loud and hectoring, but she felt so passionately that he had kept things from her, that she could not hold back. "You must be honest with me . . . you must."

"I'll assign this place; sell what I can. We may have to leave the country." He spoke rapidly as if these things scarcely affected him, then flicked his fingers noiselessly. "Esmond did for me with the trust; that's the truth of it."

"I can't accept that," she whispered fiercely. "I can influence him; I know I can."

He turned away wearily. "What do you think he'd claim as his reward?"

"He'd do what I ask. Let me try." She pressed his hands urgently, but he pulled away at once.

"Swear you won't see him."

"Why?" she asked, shaken by his anger.

"It wouldn't be enough for him to have us in his debt. He wants to drive us apart."

"How could he?"

"Lies, threats. Things are grim enough without that."

"What kind of lies?" she insisted.

"This is not the time," he said quietly, stressing each word, his hostility piercing her.

"If you won't let me do anything," she murmured, "tell me this. Did you foresee today?"

"I promise you, no. I thought the bill would be renewed—was sure of it." He broke off and said with sudden tenderness, "You must listen to me. When I've disclosed my assets in court, they'll let me go and I'll be given time to pay. The real fight comes later. We'll have time to plan."

"I'll get an engagement. I could get work within days, my love."

He looked down at his riding boots and let out his breath in a long sigh. "Shall we leave that till I've got out of prison and seen my uncle?"

She had spoken eagerly, and his dismissive tone hurt her with the force of a rebuke.

He kissed her gently on the cheek. "I must get some things together."

When he had gone, Theresa's mind felt paralyzed as she recalled the weary sadness of his answers. What had been gained by forcing him over ground he must already have explored a hundred times? Of course he would do what he could. When she ought to have expressed unwavering faith in him, her questions had merely underlined his helplessness. In a few hours he would be in a cell as if he were a criminal, and had she even expressed sympathy?

When she opened his dressing-room door, Clinton was leafing through papers in his writing box and did not see her. On the other side of the room Harris was packing clothes. Theresa stepped back, leaving the door ajar. Even when the two men were out of view she could hear them.

"Better put in some candles. They may give us mutton dips, for all I know." As Harris picked up his razor, Clinton laughed dryly. "Think I'll be allowed to keep that? Isn't Lancaster said to be the worst debtors' prison in the country?"

"Quite comfortable after Peking, I'd imagine, sir."

"Or the Black Hole of Calcutta." After a silence, Clinton said, "What happens if the judge is a tartar?"

"You can apply for habeas corpus to bring you up to the Queen's Bench. Wherever you are, bail application takes six days."

"And I'll get it on disclosure?"

"Captain Haswell always did."

"They gave him a room of his own?"

"Most times. Surprised if you don't dine with the governor. Great ones for peers, my captain used to say."

Theresa heard them talk about what food to take and how much china and linen. Then the valet went out into the bedroom. Listening to them, Theresa could not help comparing the man's reassuring matter-of-fact manner and efficient attention to detail with her own fruitless anxiety. Together, master and servant had sounded as unruffled as if planning a stay in a badly equipped hotel or a posting to a new barracks.

Feeling an intruder as she entered, Theresa dreaded that her presence would only drag out the pain of parting. A waiting emptiness seemed to hang about the room. Deep lines across his forehead made Clinton look stern and inaccessible, as if, she thought, only by deliberately denying memory could he endure the future. She walked past the table where he was sitting, aware of the creaking of the wardrobe door. She saw herself briefly in the cheval glass, protective hands clutching her elbows tightly, like a coatless woman in a wind. Glancing at him, her momentary awareness of his personality was so sharp that her own seemed to fade. She stared at the rosewood clock on the mantelpiece: nearly noon. She would not have been surprised to have found it hours later.

Under his silent scrutiny, she let her arms drop, trying to seem more composed, but could not help clutching her hands together, nails driven against knuckles; her whole body ached with tension. On the dressing table was a vase of roses; without thinking she brushed a scattering of petals to the floor.

"Please," he murmured, "stop looking as if we're going to be fed to the lions. Bailiffs are serving writs all over the place. It's really very ordinary." The window was open and the wind bellied in the green curtains with a sudden rattling of rings. Torn rags of blue had opened between the heavy clouds. He stood up, resting his hands on the back of his chair. "Such a wind. At Markenfield the stables' weather vane was a ship; I used to shoot at it when I was bored. God, how it used to spin."

"You needn't say anything. I only wanted to be with you."

"It's like being in a train," he said, "nothing to be done till the next station. Perhaps life shouldn't have gaps, but it always seems to." He smiled. "Like intervals in a play. We used to laugh a lot about melodrama. The hero saved in the nick of time. Imagine—at this moment, a solicitor's clerk spurring up the drive, leaping breathless from the saddle: 'Your uncle's dead, Lord Ardmore. I have five hundred guineas in this purse.'"

He reached out a hand and touched her hair, but she drew

back, not knowing whether his light tone was intended to comfort or prevent her speaking from the heart.

"Just a gap," she repeated softly, looking at the portmanteau and the trunk by the door, imagining them roped to the bailiff's chaise. In Clinton's mind, she fancied he was already looking out across windswept cornfields while the carriage rattled south. For the first time she had no wish either to hasten or prolong the moment. Grief spread through her like a slow stain. "I don't want to see you go," she whispered, thinking how much easier it was to go than be left behind. She kissed him and walked away.

Two days after his committal to Lancaster Castle, Clinton was visited by his solicitor and the barrister briefed to argue his case for discharge before the judge later that week. A complication, he was informed, had arisen. News of his arrest had reached the ears of several of the tradesmen in the town who had supplied him with goods on credit. In alarm, they had lodged detainers with the sheriff, which would prevent his release even should the judge be satisfied with the measures proposed by counsel for settling the original debt. Since judgment could not be expected on new proceedings in anything under three weeks, Clinton was advised to enter an application for bail. Well aware that any delay would expose him to the risk of items in the local press being picked up by London papers with a nose for aristocratic scandals and misfortunes, Clinton did not need his lawyers to tell him that this could alert his metropolitan creditors, and so lead to service of further writs.

A post-dated mortgage deed secured on the Hathenshaw lease, and affidavits disclosing his assets, would, in his lawyers' opinion, get him bail in spite of the detainers, since the unexpired period of the lease was worth considerably more than all the debts which had so far been brought to the court's notice. But any intimation of heavier liabilities would extend his imprisonment until a general settlement with all his creditors could be contrived—a process which the transfer of stock and the sale of chattels would inevitably make lengthy. Even if bail were granted, another judgment summons could see him back in prison in a worse predicament than before. Yet bail, albeit achieved by the forced sale of his present lease, was now essential. A visit to his uncle could not safely be postponed by as much as a fortnight.

After the departure of his legal advisers, Clinton flung himself down on his bed. He had slept very little the night before; and though his room was in few respects like a cell—having been comfortably furnished a year ago by the extravagant younger son of a marquess—the silk curtain concealing the iron door did not palliate the fact of being locked in. At times Clinton came close to dashing his head against the wall. When waking from brief periods of sleep, he was scarcely aware of having lost consciousness.

Because bail could not be obtained before the middle of the following week, Clinton knew that he would have to offer some explanation for his continuing detention to Theresa. Longing to see her, he also dreaded such a visit. Her pity would emphasize the wretchedness of his predicament and perhaps, worse still, fuel his bitter fears that all his happiness with her had been possible only when shielded from everything that might have challenged it. In the past, happiness for him had been perfect or nothing. His present mood and the strangeness of the prison, especially in the hours of darkness, left him so low that he was soon convinced it would be folly to allow himself to see her through the distorting glass of his present uncertainties. Beyond the possibility of failure with his uncle, loomed the shadow of events that made his imprisonment seem a trivial affliction.

When later he began to write, he betrayed nothing of this. Optimism alone would prevent her coming, and this was the mood he grimly sustained.

My dearest,

If stone walls do not a prison make, nor iron bars a cage, I can only assume the poet had no knowledge of this place. The walls are not only stone but ten feet thick, if my jailer is to be believed. The bars are backed by clouded glass, designed to confine the eye as well as the person. Until I saw the gatehouse here, I thought "frowning portals" as poetically improbable as "pearly gates." The second-class debtors (here status is conferred by the scale of a man's financial failings) can be seen behind a vast grating in John of Gaunt's banqueting hall. I once passed by in the evening and all were in nightshirts and caps, singing choruses to the music of a fiddle. The sight made me think myself in Bedlam a century ago.

The governor is a martinet, but a snob too, thank God. So though there are but twenty rooms for most of the debtors in Lancashire (upwards of four hundred), I have one to myself, and no cupboard in size. The governor comes to see me daily and commiserates with me, saying how damnable my incarceration is and quite unlike any other case he knew. I tell him my ordeal would be intolerable but for his solicitude. That way I have been allowed to dine and lunch alone, though I breakfast with the first-class debtors in their day room, which I think was once the castle armory. Cooking is done at one side at a huge open fireplace. The walls are hung with hats, caps, carpetbags, foils, and boxing gloves. Apart from these recreations, the room is large enough to provide a capital skittle alley. My fellow sufferers include two Church of England clergymen and four army officers. Speaking of clerics, the chaplain courts me assiduously to read the lesson in chapel, perhaps as illustration of man's equality in adversity. Since worshipers are actually locked in their pews, the turnkey officiating as the chaplain's clerk with his keys on the desk by his prayer book, one experience of these Hogarthian proceedings was enough for me. The keys by the by are of a size and weight I would have thought impossible except in historical dramas. Visiting regulations beggar all description. Market people come to the gratings of the day rooms at eight in the morning, but no other visitors are allowed in at that hour unless they masquerade by bringing an egg or potato with them, these commodities serving as tickets of admission at the outer gate. The half-hour set aside for friends to the prisoner is a mockery, visitors being locked into a small stone room with a turnkey listening to every word, and the object of their concern standing behind a set of bars which would do credit to the tiger cage in a menagerie. Since it is easier to bear up on paper than to endure a loved face seen through bars, I beg you to write rather than come here.

Lawyers, I fear, are always "proceeding" without ever coming to an end, and though it pains me to tell you that I shall not be out before the 20th, that much, my legal allies assure me, is certain. The preparation of affidavits, notices, and bail papers seems to demand the clerical pains of a monk's manuscript. As soon as I am free I will go south at once to see my uncle. That way we will have more to celebrate than our reunion. Write boldly all you think and feel. I am not repining.

Addio, cara Theresa mia, Clinton

The positive tone of Theresa's reply was a considerable relief to him, and slowly his spirits began to improve. His conditional discharge took place as his lawyers had predicted on August twentieth—a date which in other years had been significant to him as the first day of the open season for black grouse.

CHAPTER THIRTY

 On a hot and windless afternoon, several days before Lord Ardmore was expected back in Lancashire, an elderly man stepped down from a dilapidated fly just within the lodge gates of Hathenshaw. After the ovenlike heat inside the hackney, Major Simmonds was thankful to breathe the cooler air in the shade of the elm avenue leading to the house. The glaring light had made his head throb, and his mouth felt parched with the dust thrown up from the cracked and crumbling roads. He stooped slightly as he walked, and his thin tailcoated figure, crowned by a tall hat and encased in tight-fitting white trousers, seemed a ghostly reminder of an age before the Norfolk jacket and Tweedside suit.

He was considerably taken aback to be admitted to the house by a servant wearing cavalry overalls and smoking a cigar.

"I want to see your mistress," he said stiffly, reddening when the man looked at him with what he took for an ill-concealed smirk.

"What name, sir?"

"I'm her father, so don't go sticking your hand out for a card."

"Please come this way, sir."

335

Overcoming her surprise, Theresa embraced her father. "Why on earth didn't you write and tell me you were coming?" He made no reply, but put down his hat and the gingham umbrella which served as a sunshade in summer. Theresa squeezed his hand affectionately. "You're here, which is the main thing. I hope you're going to stay?"

"The inn at Browsholme suits me nicely." He stared awkwardly at the fender and did not see her smile.

"My dear father, if you're worried about meeting Clinton, he's staying with his uncle."

"Worried?" he muttered gruffly. "Can't see why the deuce *I* should be worried."

"Don't pretend you've forgotten what you've said about him."

"I'm not pretending anything. I don't want to stay under his roof." He sat down and said sharply, "Does he let his servants smoke in front of you?"

"Of course not."

"What about the one who showed me up here?"

"He obviously wasn't expecting anybody. Perhaps he thought you'd be a tradesman."

"At the *hall* door?"

"Isn't it really rather a little thing?" she asked softly.

"Damned if I think it is. An insult to you. That's my view."

"I'll have a word with him. What about tea? The maids don't smoke."

"I'd like a glass of water."

Though used to her father's habit of exaggerating his often genuine irritation over trifles, she had not been slow to recognize that his present testiness concealed a more serious grievance. Since they regularly wrote to each other, his unannounced visit could hardly be explained by a desire to exchange routine news.

When the maid had answered the bell and returned with the water, Theresa sat next to her father. "Did you think if you'd written asking to see me, I'd have tried to fob you off?"

He put down his glass and sighed. "Wouldn't have surprised me. Louise wrote that you were ill enough to need the doctor a dozen times or more." He turned his monocle on her. "Not a word to me. If I did that to you, what'd you think?"

"That you didn't want to worry me."

He let his eyeglass drop down on its black ribbon. "Do you think I'm not worried now? What was wrong with you?"

"What did Louise tell you?"

"Nothing. Said she wasn't told."

"I'm sorry," she whispered, looking away. He made no reply, but when she finally turned, his bowed head and unhappy eyes cut through her previous resolution to say nothing. "I lost a child."

He got up and paced over to the window, his movements jerky with agitation. "The blackguard, dirty blackguard. Small wonder the servants show no respect. If I was younger—"

"If he married me, his uncle would disinherit him. He's virtually penniless."

"That so? And this is the poor house?" He gestured around him, the sweep of his hands taking in the porcelain, portraits, and gilded chairs. "A man's penniless who keeps his coppers separate from the silver in his purse. You tell his lordship that."

"Father, he needs no telling. Please believe me."

The major stood motionless, his chin sunk in the folds of his cravat. "Nothing can excuse degrading you."

"You never accused Esmond of that."

"He wanted to marry you—and no threat of a child to force his hand. A different story with his brother. What did he offer you instead of marriage, when he knew you were with child? Restitution for a blighted career? A covenant for the child's upkeep if you parted? Or did he plead poverty?"

"If I was some sweet young innocent, I'd understand—"

"Better if you were," he cried. "A few years wasted then wouldn't have harmed you. Past thirty, it pays a woman to be thrifty with her time. Think on ten years. I've next to nothing to leave you. Very well, let him squeeze you like an orange, but make sure there's some juice left when he throws away the rind."

"He'll never throw me away."

"Will you never learn?" he asked, in a voice choked with emotion.

With the passing of his bitterness, her father seemed changed: an old man unable to pass on the lessons life had taught him, not understanding how she could fail to see what was so obvious to him. She was tempted as never before to tell him about her marriage. The stiff way her father sat because of the vanity of stays, his tight high collar cutting into his wrinkled neck, the clear definition of the bones in his hands, all moved her intolerably.

He drew back his head like a man about to make a speech in public and for a moment she expected a further onslaught, but when he spoke, his voice was faltering. "Not every girl's a martyr who's seduced. Only fools say that. Takes two to play that game and to share the fun. The rub comes later, and when it does, sharing's a thing of the past." He leaned forward with pathetic eagerness. "Leave him, dear. Leave while you can still help yourself. I beg you to."

"I can't."

"You must tell me why."

"The reasons aren't material."

Fearing his collapse, Theresa was astounded by the quite different effect of her words.

During a long silence, he looked at her with intent reproachful eyes. "I'd much rather you'd confided in me." He paused and stared ahead of him, before facing her with a sudden turn of the neck. "Louise heard a maid say you'd married Ardmore in Ireland."

"How would servants entertain themselves without silly suspicions?"

"Louise claims the girl mentioned the name of a priest and a place."

"I wonder what I wore? Perhaps she mentioned that?"

He twisted his monocle on its ribbon and shook his head. "Only a place, a priest, and a date, when I happen to know you were away."

"Louise knew it too. You realize she doesn't like him?"

"Can't say I'm surprised."

"Well it explains a deliberate piece of mischief. We'd better talk to her. Or perhaps start with the maid? I wonder if Louise named her as well as the priest?"

The major slowly shook his head. "There's a better way. I intend to make inquiries over there."

338

"Suppose there was a secret marriage, can you imagine the priest telling the first person to come asking about it? I daresay if you fail with him, a few pounds in a country place would secure whatever information—"

"I'm sending a lawyer to take sworn proofs. People don't perjure themselves when they can be prosecuted for it."

A scream seemed to struggle up through her silence; her lungs ached withholding it, but she made no sound. The effort of control she had needed to reach even this far with conviction had drained her; only dull anger at his mistrust enabled her to go on.

She got up, the same skeptical smile on her lips. "Suppose you buy these *proofs*, what will you do with them?"

"That'll depend on Ardmore."

"Don't you see what harm you'll do me?"

"Worse than the harm he's already done you? What frightens you if he's honorable?"

"People make promises," she blurted out, losing the sense of his words, immediately horrified by her admission.

"What sort of a man forces a woman to keep a promise that dishonors her? God in heaven, you were with child."

She raised her hands to her temples, dragging back her hair savagely, wanting to punish herself, aware of the stage inanity of the gesture as she sank to her knees. He touched her shoulder lightly but she rocked back on her haunches. "You have no right," she moaned, in a voice not like her own, high-pitched and hysterical. Then, jumping to her feet, she shouted, "My life, mine, mine."

She expected the relief of tears; but though her eyes were congested and her lips quivered, no sound came. At last she rose slowly to her feet.

"Get your proofs if you must," she murmured. "If you do anything without seeing me first . . ." She stopped, suddenly remembering a play—the father of the heroine bemoaning his daughter's sins, and later the pathetic girl destitute at his door. So much of her own life seemed parodied in the melodramas she had acted in.

Before she knew it, she was laughing, more in panic than amusement. "How did we get through them? How, Father?

339

The Maid of Milan, Crazy Jane, Love's Frailties—three in a month sometimes. No wonder we're half mad. Simple morality suits a play; life blurs the lines. If villainy's not punished in life as it should be, so much the worse for life. . . . Isn't that what you think?" She gazed at his unsmiling face, knowing she was right.

"Would you have the good go unrewarded?" he asked.

"Fate isn't in my gift or yours."

He took her hand emotionally. "Don't mock what we did together. What's wrong with letting people hope that life can be better? That's what we did."

"Then give *me* hope. Wait and let him prove you wrong."

He paused, sucking in his cheeks, as though drawing on an invisible cigar. "Two months," he said abruptly. "And I'll find out something in the meantime."

"Is that necessary?"

"I believe so."

He picked up his hat and was reaching for his umbrella when she snatched it from him. "You've no need to send a man asking questions."

"I have every need. What if someone else gets there first? You were right to say money begets lies."

She looked at him beseechingly. "The priest promised secrecy. He might write warning Clinton that questions were being asked. In his place, who would you suspect of breaking faith? Don't destroy Clinton's trust in me."

"Then tell me this," he said with the same stubbornness. "Why should *I* trust any man who makes his wife swear to deceive her father? If I'd been rich or titled, he'd not have dared insult me so. If you were an earl's daughter, could you see him shutting you away miles from anywhere? A different story with my daughter. Let her be laughed at by servants, let the country quack think her a whore. Too bad if she gives birth and half the county thinks her child a bastard." He paused, wiping sweat from his brow with a cambric handkerchief, dropping his hat in the process. "And if his wife has the humanity to tell her father the truth, he'll never trust her again. But *I'm* to trust *him*. I can't do it—can't for the life of me. I'll wait before seeing him, but I'll have proofs of this marriage."

Theresa left the room and returned a few minutes later with the certificate, knowing that otherwise he would see the priest, and possibly return to confront Clinton in person. She waited till he had finished reading. "Do you want to have a copy witnessed by your solicitor?"

"I can't see the need." He seemed dazed.

"Perhaps you trust him now?" She had spoken bitterly, but if she had screamed, her father would not have been troubled by it.

He raised her hand to his lips. "My dear Lady Ardmore," he murmured. "My dear, dear Lady Ardmore."

CHAPTER THIRTY-ONE

On opposite sides of a great shining mahogany table covered with grapes, pineapples, and various kinds of cake, the Honorable Richard Danvers and his nephew sat reading—Clinton cursorily leafing through a leatherbound volume of *Punch* for the year 1860, while his uncle devoted his attention to a book of eighteenth-century architectural drawings. No stranger to his uncle's habit of reading during meals, Clinton was not insulted by it.

Like many wealthy men living alone and completely insulated from any kind of criticism, Richard Danvers saw nothing untoward in subjecting his infrequent house guests to his normal routines, his sole concession being to make himself available for conversation three times a day: during his regular morning walk, while taking the short carriage ride which always followed his afternoon nap, and finally for half an hour in the smoking room after dinner. The bulk of his time was given to his model farm and to omnivorous reading. Few scholars could have claimed to occupy their time with greater exertion than this gentleman of leisure.

By the end of his second day in his uncle's house, Clinton had still not broached the crucial subject that had brought him there. There were still moments when he found it scarcely credible that his elderly host could wield such power over his future. And all because Richard Danvers had married a rich woman, who had not survived her first pregnancy.

Clinton's father had not got on with Richard, and Clinton himself still shared this difficulty. The man's frequent smiles and aphoristic way of talking gave an impression of joviality that was frequently belied by the gravity of his eyes. Usually mild-mannered, he possessed a quick temper. Invariably their conversations had an edge of combat about them. Danvers, who made a point of never talking about himself, would select a subject and invite Clinton's views, which he would then dismiss. Before his marriage, he had been a barrister. He seemed neither to want nor to expect more from people than could be gained in a game of chess or cards. His rare contacts with other people resembled little sips of spa water, taken for his health, like medicine, only when he chose. The idea of seeing his uncle swayed by his emotions seemed as improbable to Clinton as watching him jump fully dressed into a river. To date he had contented himself with assessing the scale of his task, but that evening, while they were drinking madeira in the smoking room, his uncle offered the kind of oblique lead which Clinton knew had to be followed.

Clinton had mentioned his reasons for leaving the army on the first day of his stay, but the subject had met with an emphatic lack of response. So he was considerably surprised when suddenly asked what sum he would need to buy back and how he had ever got into such a scrape in the first place. His uncle's apparent sympathy aroused definite hopes. But, just when Clinton believed an offer was imminent, he was met with a sudden change of tack.

"You know what I'll never forgive your father?" Clinton shook his head, masking his annoyance. "He wasted himself."

"By marrying my mother?"

"He made other mistakes, but that was his worst."

"What else could he have done? He'd compromised her and had to pay the price."

"So did his family—you in particular. *Delicta maiorum immeritus lues.*"

343

"I'm sure it's well known," murmured Clinton, "but I still don't know it."

His uncle smiled and brought his fingertips together below his chin. "Though guiltless, you must expiate the sins of your fathers." He reached for the decanter and filled both their glasses. "Don't know about you," he went on, "but I've never been able to see any possible reason for plumping for a poor woman when rich ones are so plentiful." He stared at Clinton from beneath thick white eyebrows. "I gather you're letting Markenfield go?"

"Not by choice."

Richard Danvers looked at him impassively, a slight nod the only sign of his derision. "You've your father's looks . . . a sound head. Marriage always helps a man's career and never stops him taking mistresses."

Seeing his opportunity, Clinton took it. "But mistresses can sometimes make it hard to take a wife."

"You mean threats of scandal?"

Clinton nodded gravely. "I don't think it'd ever get that far. A woman-to-woman talk at an early stage usually proves more than most young ladies can stomach. The lady in question is an actress with a very caustic turn of phrase."

"Does this creature . . . ?"

"Want me to marry her?"

"Well?"

"No. But she wants to make sure that if I marry anybody else she isn't the loser by it."

"How much is she after?"

"A great deal more than I can raise. At least two thousand."

"You can't believe she wouldn't settle for less?"

"I *know* she wouldn't."

His uncle closed his eyes, and a heavy sigh stirred the ends of his wispy mustache. "A devil of a lot of money." He paused to fortify himself with a sip of wine. "I'll not help you now, I tell you that. You find the right girl, tell me when you're ready to propose, and I'll state my terms."

"That's very generous, but I can't put the question after one or two meetings; and frankly I'd be sure to be found out. Best settle old scores before trying new ventures."

Danvers leaned forward impatiently. "Can't part with money like that. What if she came back for more? What could you do?"

"She's honest."

"Honest? God alive, do you call blackmail honest?"

"I'm afraid the boot's not on my foot."

"Because you're as big a fool as your father. Send her to my lawyer and he'll draw up something—an agreement to pay her something when you get married, and not a day before. And on condition she behaves herself. Try her with five hundred to start with."

Clinton shook his head. "She won't sign anything."

"Of course she will."

"She'd think I might try to use it against her later—supposing she had plans to marry."

"Then send her here and I'll din some sense into her. Thinks she'll get two thousand pounds at the drop of a hat, without conditions? Let her think again." He got up abruptly, and stood tugging at the points of his waistcoat.

"If she won't see you?" asked Clinton mildly.

"I've had enough of her for one day. You'll know my decision before you leave." He picked up his glass and drained it; then, without another glance at Clinton, he left the room and went to bed.

Dejected to have come within measurable distance of success, only to to see his goal recede still further, Clinton had the added anxiety next morning of not being summoned by his uncle's manservant to accompany his master on his usual walk. He now had no idea whether the deception he had committed himself to had been a miscalculation.

His first sight of his uncle that day was at lunch, which as always passed largely in silence. Danvers was reading Lucretius. Behind gold-rimmed spectacles, his uncle's eyes remained inscrutable. After dessert, Danvers put a marker in his place and flicked back a few pages, searching for a particular passage. A moment later he smiled at Clinton.

"*Suave mari magno* . . . I shan't trouble you with the original. 'Sweet it is, when the winds lash the sea with high waves, to gaze from the land at another's troubles.'" He snapped the book shut and tweaked off his glasses, which he slipped into his breast pocket.

"Not a sentiment that would appeal to mariners," remarked Clinton, "Is that how my situation strikes you?"

"Hubris, dear fellow. You're such a positive man that I can't help finding a little humor in it. The biter bit—that sort of thing." He folded his napkin and secured it in a silver ring. "I hope you'll come with me this afternoon. I'm going collecting. Something more rewarding than bugs and beetles." He pushed back his chair. "I've a few things to get ready first."

Though suspecting a joke at his expense, Clinton did not see how, with the limited time left to him, he could refuse the invitation. Already his anger at his uncle's ironic amusement had given way to the familiar and draining fear of failure that had oppressed him from the hour of his arrival. In a moment of optimism, he wondered whether the afternoon's proceedings might turn out to be some sort of test which, if passed, might yield him everything he wanted.

Getting into the open landau, Clinton was puzzled to see the dogcart also drawn up in readiness, but aware that his uncle was enjoying bemusing him, he expressed as little interest in the expedition as he could contrive without rudeness. Whatever the object of their journey, it was evidently important enough to supplant his uncle's normal afternoon sleep.

Their carriage ride lasted just over an hour and ended rather lamely in front of a nondescript village church. Pausing under the porch, Richard Danvers listened anxiously for a few seconds, but smiled to himself as soon as he heard the sound of hammering coming from within. With a finger raised to his lips, he opened the door. The cause of the noise was immediately apparent: a carpenter was at work replacing the pulpit steps. Looking around, Clinton saw nothing of interest. Moving very quietly, his uncle edged his way closer to where the workman was crouching. Within ten feet or so, he sat down to watch. Clinton soon joined him in the same pew and gazed at the royal coat of arms above the chancel arch. He was considerably surprised when Danvers tugged at his sleeve to gain his attention, and then, with another admonishment to silence, pointed to the man's rule and the way he was using it. Instead of bearing figures, the rule was marked out with pins: a different number for every inch. At that moment the carpenter looked up and Clinton saw that his eyes were completely white and partially concealed by deformed upper lids.

He got up in disgust. "He's blind."

Richard Danvers smiled. "Truly remarkable. The only blind joiner in the county. I've noticed he holds his chisel very near the end and marks his wood with it instead of with a pencil. Otherwise, apart from that rule of his, who could tell?"

Outside in the sunshine among the graves, Clinton saw the servants who had come in the dogcart screwing a cumbersome square camera onto a massive tripod. Their answers to a few questions made it plain that his uncle's "collection" consisted not merely of people remarkable for their resourcefulness but of every imaginable human oddity that came to his notice either by word of mouth or through a wide range of local papers. Last month had seen the addition of three fine examples: a man who had not left his bed during the eight years since his wife had deserted him, a woman famous for predicting the dates when people were going to die, and a watchmaker who had cut off all his toes for no reason anyone could discover. Clinton sat down on a box tomb and started to laugh, though deep down he felt something the reverse of amusement.

On their way home, Richard Danvers was in an excellent mood. The carpenter had more than lived up to expectation, counting among his accomplishments making fishing nets and playing the violin in public houses.

"An example to us all, wouldn't you say?" asked Danvers. "Best instance of self-reliance I've ever come across."

Clinton smiled imperturbably, aware of the invidious comparison being invited. "You may do better—a limbless sailor who puts ships in bottles with his teeth?"

"Nothing's too strange to happen."

The landau rolled along on well-oiled springs, through a beech wood where the first yellow leaves were apparent, and out again across open downland dotted with sheep. After a silence, broken only by the horses' breathing and the thud of hoofs, Danvers said reflectively, "I've a curious disposition, so perhaps I'll get some pleasure out of it?"

"Out of what?"

"Helping you." As Clinton's heart raced, his uncle looked at him closely. "You'll have to give a good account of your wooing—the failures too. And I want to meet the front runners in the marriage stakes when you've narrowed the field." He smiled to himself. "The actress must come here to argue her case. I'll know what she's worth."

"If she won't come?"

"No money."

An unmistakable glint of mockery in his uncle's eyes made Clinton freeze. Suspicion turned to certainty. "You didn't believe anything I said."

Danvers raised apologetic hands. "People who want money aren't always particular how they come by it. It was a clever idea, I grant you."

The ground had opened beneath him, and in Clinton's stomach was a ghastly sensation of falling—the breathlessness, the fear. Outside the carriage, drowsy high summer, sunlit clouds, soft green hills. And still he fell.

His uncle said quietly, "If you love someone you can't marry, I'm sorry, but I'll not abet you in your father's mistake. Forget about sending your mistress here. Propose to a suitable woman and I'll pay your debts without condition." He paused and looked at Clinton with sudden concern. "Think of your father. Was there a thing he couldn't have done? But how did it end?" His voice had become very low. "You'll not start on that path while I can stop you. If you won't help yourself by marrying well, I'll cut you off."

Sweat had broken out coldly on Clinton's forehead; in an effort to calm himself, he took out his watch but hardly saw it. His whole personality was crumbling. He thought, This is how it feels to lose all hope, to struggle almost to the shore only to be dragged out again by the tide.

CHAPTER THIRTY-TWO

In London, Clinton soon suffered another reverse. At his bank, where he had hoped to draw out several hundred pounds by pledging the plate and jewelry held for him in the vaults, he was told by the chief partner that since this property was the bank's only security for his overdraft, it could neither be sold, nor used as collateral for a further loan. Since he would have to pay three hundred into court in Lancaster by the end of the week to comply with the conditions of his discharge, Clinton had no illusions about his position.

Apart from meeting this legal obligation, Clinton's other objective was simple—to survive without service of more writs, until he could sell the lease on Hathenshaw, raise what he could on his disposable chattels, and leave the country with Theresa. By failing to meet the court's requirement, or suffering a second arrest on mesne process—no unlikely event while his bank continued to dishonor his checks—he would find himself in the hands of the Commissioners in Bankruptcy.

At all costs, he had to make a large enough payment to his bank to restore his credit for a few more weeks. Though depressed as never before, Clinton found a crumb of comfort in having reached the point where no remedy offering relief could be discarded, however dangerous. His initial steps seemed harmless enough. Three weeks earlier, he had sent Esmond's letters to his solicitor for his opinion. Now he retrieved them and, after making some purchases at a stationer's, set out for Jabez Norton's premises.

Again he was received by the moneylender's clerk and not by the great man himself. Clinton had expected hypocritical sympathy and he got it in full measure. Never for a moment had Mr. Norton expected Mendoza to act with such precipitate ferocity; in fact he had pleaded with the man to be allowed to buy back the bill.

Clinton suffered these lies patiently. "Perhaps he neglected to offer what he got for it," he remarked affably.

The clerk, who had obviously expected furious indignation, looked at him doubtfully. "I wouldn't know the precise sum, but he was very upset about it. We both were, my lord."

"So of course you want to make amends. You offered a loan if my brother underwrote it. I'm glad to say he's agreed to."

The clerk went over to the ledger table and picked up a pen. "How much might he guarantee?"

"Two thousand."

Clinton watched him dip his pen in the ink and write this down as though indifferent to the magnitude of the sum. The wen on his eyelid made it impossible to judge what he was thinking.

"For how long, my lord?"

"A year."

Again the quill pen scratched loudly across the paper. "Over six months Mr. Norton always requires interest in advance."

"I want the two thousand in hand."

"Then you must accept extra bills to cover it. I can't do better than twenty per cent. Mr. Danvers must endorse all your acceptances, including those for the interest."

Clinton frowned. "Can't you draw one bill for the whole sum?"

The clerk opened a drawer and took out a bundle of dock-eted bills, which he untied and started to glance through. "In this instance I feel Mr. Norton would prefer you to take up debts of his own dated a year hence. Mr. Danvers's endorsement will be very soothing to several of our creditors."

"You can't mean there are people who doubt the soundness of your master's acceptances?"

"A sad reflection on the times we live in. There are gentlemen who expect the best rates to be had in London, and still complain about trifling delays. I needn't tell your lordship how it can take a week or two to recover from a client in difficulties." He had now taken out what looked to Clinton like a dozen bills from the larger pile and placed them on top of a closed ledger. He smiled obsequiously. "But, need I say, any bill endorsed by a broker with Mr. Danvers's reputation feels as good as money in the hand to the most skeptical depositor."

"I won't take a great wad of those things. Three or four at the most."

The clerk nodded reluctantly. "Perhaps we can't really expect him to endorse anything under five hundred." He jotted down some figures and then made a final choice of bills. "We'll make it four then. The total's a pound or two over what you want, but that's a fault in the right direction." He put them in an envelope and gave it to Clinton. "Bring them back tomorrow, and you'll have the money by Tuesday."

"Why the delay?" Clinton asked sharply.

"Mr. Norton has to get the money. No help for it—unless you'd care to take it in tea. We've a lot on our hands at the moment. Best quality orange-scented Pekoe—"

"I'm not a tea merchant."

"A joke, my lord. We levied execution on a tea importer last week. Should raise a fair price at auction, but you wouldn't want to have anything to do with trade."

"Borrowing's more my line," replied Clinton, ignoring what had looked very like a sneer; but with a man afflicted by a perpetual wink, it was hard to tell. Clinton left the premises to the accompaniment of effusive expressions of how pleased Mr. Norton would be to be able to render his services.

An hour later in a hotel bedroom Clinton dragged the dressing table across to the window and drew aside the net curtains to improve the light. Then he took out Esmond's letters and the purchases he had made at the stationer's shop before going to

Norton's. He was disappointed by the way matters had gone at the moneylender's, but still intended to go through with his plan. His worst anxiety was that Norton might write to Esmond about the endorsements during the two-day interval between delivery of the bills and production of the money. But on consideration, he thought the likeliest explanation of the delay was that Norton would need to use the endorsed bills to raise the money for the loan. Nor was the moneylender likely to consider the forgery of negotiable instruments a credible occupation for a nobleman, given the severity of the penalties.

He had hoped only to have to produce a single signature, thereby giving Norton no opportunity for comparison. But four autographs would make the smallest discrepancies perfectly apparent. From the outset, Clinton faced another formidable difficulty: when writing to him, Esmond had signed with his Christian name alone. And while Clinton was certain that his brother never adorned his full signature with any loops or flourishes, he was far from happy to have to construct "Danvers" piecemeal, taking a "D" from the opening "Dear," "an" from "and," and "vers" from a sentence containing the expression "chapter and verse." These elements he assembled on tracing paper, joining them as best he could, after a careful study of the way in which similar combinations of letters were linked in other words.

His first efforts at making a freehand copy of his tracing in pen and ink brought him very close to giving up; but thoughts of the consequences of failure demanded perseverance. Nor could he bear to think of returning to Theresa in utter hopelessness.

If he could keep his nerve, he might yet survive. The everyday normality of his surroundings made him momentarily lightheaded—the commonplace furniture, the noise of passing carriages in the street, the sunlight on the drab brickwork of the houses opposite, and the innocent sheets of paper on the table. How could this be the setting for a serious crime? With a steadier hand, he set to work again. Esmond owed him reparation.

Though the shopkeeper had assured him that the pen he had bought was much favored by cartographers because it spread the ink evenly, however carefully he moved the nib, Clinton found that he could not entirely prevent irregular edges to the letters wherever he paused in his laborious imitation. Looking at his work under a magnifying glass, his dissatisfaction grew. Clearly it was hopeless to try to produce a signature stroke by stroke. The tiny blobs and occasional fluctuations in the ink flow suggested the writing of a drunk who, though concentrating for all he was worth, still needed to break off for numerous rests. Success would only be achieved by practicing the signature again and again until he could produce it spontaneously without hesitation. He therefore devoted the next half-hour to tracing over his original construction of the signature several hundred times, interspersing this activity with freehand attempts.

Only when he could produce a run of half a dozen copies with his eyes shut, of a quality little worse than those made with them open, did he feel sufficiently confident to take out the bills. But once again his heart started to thump and he could no longer maintain the relaxation essential for fluency. His hands were sweating and the pen felt slippery. Afraid to get up and walk about, in case he lost the automatic, almost hypnotic response induced by so many tracings, he was equally scared to touch the bills. And if the willpower required for a single signature was all but beyond him, how could he hope to go on and execute another three? He breathed deeply and wiped his palms on his trousers, ashamed of his weakness but unable to remedy it. An error on one bill could be concealed by a blot, but there could be no second chances granted with any of the others. Yet the thought that he had this single reprieve calmed him. The first bill would not be the all-important one; and if he succeeded with that one, nor would the second.

He dashed off three more signatures on rough paper and, having satisfied himself that they compared well, swept all the papers from the table except for the four bills of exchange; these he placed close enough to each other to be able to pass from bill to bill with the least possible delay. At a ground-floor window across the street, a maid was beating a carpet; hundreds of them in London were doing the same. Every possible human activity was happening somewhere at that moment:

murders, thefts, kisses, marriages . . . acts of forgery . . . one or two men sitting undecided in the afternoon heat somewhere.

He picked up the pen, dipped it in the ink, drained off a little with a scrap of blotting paper, and signed the bills. Two hours before, he would have thought the speed and accuracy of his achievement impossible. Since even in authentic signatures, no two were mechanically identical, he was inclined to consider that two slight lapses added veracity rather than detracted from it. When he had turned the bills over and written his own signature under the word "accepted" on their faces, he threw himself on the bed.

He felt happiness but also a peculiar detachment, as though next day he might wake to find that quite different events had happened. One of the net curtains had fallen back across the window and cast a shadow on the ceiling. A slight wind lifted the edges of the bills. A moment later it came to Clinton that the moment of crime lay not in signing but in handing them to Norton. The worst test of all would not come until he returned for the money. That trial would have to wait its turn, but the other Clinton met at once by posting the bills with a brief covering letter.

The candelabra, console tables, and matching buhl cabinets in the anteroom where Clinton had been asked to await Norton's appearance had never disquieted him before; but he was so tense that these spoils from past foreclosures deepened his foreboding. Their sometime owners would have sat in this very room—many of them more confident than he of ultimate salvation. The clerk had been more welcoming than on any previous occasion, but in his agitation Clinton was inclined to see this as sinister. He folded his arms, forcing himself to be still, trying not to start when he heard footsteps outside. Within minutes he would have in his hands two thousand pounds or a warrant for his arrest.

When Norton at last came in, Clinton stood up and moved forward; his legs felt soft and strangely elastic, and he could not keep his eyes on anything. The man's gray mustache, cavernous nostrils, and mottled cheeks stood out in isolation and would not cohere into a whole face. Other vague details were an embroidered waistcoat, velvet lapels, a ringed hand.

"I've some money for you, Lord Ardmore." Dazed with relief, Clinton merely nodded, fixing his eyes on the dragons worked in silver thread on Norton's waistcoat. "Didn't think I was going to be able to do it. My clerk had no right to agree to take interest on an additional acceptance, even at a higher rate." Clinton guessed from the man's tone that he was expected to ask how the matter had been settled, but he could not think of any words. He wanted to take the money and go. Norton said briskly, "I'd have liked to deduct it from the loan and set aside the covering bill, but then I heard that you'd been promised the full sum. Of course it was unthinkable after that dreadful business to have you come here expecting one thing, only to be told another."

"So you stuck to the original arrangement?"

Norton chuckled, a strange noise, closer to a phlegmy cough than a laugh. "Out of the question, I'd be ruined if I waived interest beyond a quarter on large sums. Time's money, don't you see?"

"Of course."

"It's all ready, never fear. Got to tell you how I got round it. You left no address except your club, and nobody there knew where you were staying. Quite a problem. I admit I was most reluctant to ask Mr. Danvers to help, but in the circumstances —not wishing to disappoint, you understand—I threw myself on his mercy."

A feeling of faintness entered him from all sides like an invisible fog. Afraid that his legs would not support him, Clinton grasped the back of a chair; the suddenness of the movement jerked the room back into focus. Norton's face seemed larger; the hairs in his nostrils moved as he breathed.

"What did he say?" Clinton asked.

"I sent a man with a letter. His reply couldn't have been more helpful. Without any prompting from me, he offered to let me have a draft for the interest, said he'd bring it round when I paid over the money."

No longer caring what Norton thought, Clinton sat down heavily. Frozen laughter died in his throat. "Is he here now?"

"Indeed he is, and most eager to see your lordship. He said

to me—purely in fun of course—that he'd not part with the draft till he saw the loan in your hands."

Sharp blades of fear reached Clinton through the insulating numbness of shock. "I know this is awkward for you." He tried to smile at Norton, but his lips felt too stiff. "As it happens, I've a personal and rather pressing reason for not wanting to see him today—something I promised, which I haven't had time to do."

"Mr. Danvers has come here in person."

"Tell him you tried to stop me going."

Norton seemed embarrassed. "I really don't like to, Lord Ardmore." He cleared his throat uneasily. "The fact is, though I'm sure he meant it in fun, he still hasn't given me that draft."

"I'll sign a receipt for you to give him." Trying to be authoritative, Clinton was horrified by the brittleness of his voice.

Norton compressed his lips. "I'd like to please you, but I'm placed in a most—"

"How was I placed with Mendoza?"

"If I'd had any idea that you intended not to—"

"Good God, man, I told your clerk I couldn't meet it."

Norton hesitated a moment but then moved abruptly to the nearest bellpull. When a clerk came in answer, he was told to show in Mr. Danvers. Without raising his eyes, Norton murmured an apology.

One look at Esmond's pale, tight-drawn features convinced Clinton that he would betray him, and had only delayed in order to deliver the coup de grâce in person. Never could he have expected such a perfect opportunity. Certain he could now do nothing to save himself, Clinton faced his executioner. Esmond nodded to him as if acknowledging a routine courtesy and turned to Norton. Clinton braced himself, but Esmond only asked Norton to excuse them for a few minutes.

When the moneylender had left, Esmond said quietly, "You're going to tell me some things now, Clinton."

"You'll repudiate those bills whatever I say."

"Not if you're honest with me."

"Go to hell."

Esmond smiled derisively and nodded to himself as though

the response had been exactly what he had expected. "I don't believe you're stupid enough to prefer ten years in jail to a little loss of face with me." Esmond picked up a pair of silver-handled glove stretchers from a table and examined them. "Somebody came to see me on Sunday evening and told me something rather surprising. Guess what it was." Clinton turned his back. Esmond stood snapping the stretchers open and shut. "All right, I'll come back to that when I've got your interest." He paused. "Quite unintentionally this person re-minded me of something else—something I hadn't thought about for months. Perhaps you remember Mother's story about the Protestant lady and her footman? The marriage that wasn't a marriage?" When Clinton did not react in any way, Esmond said sharply, "If you want my help over those signatures, you'd better answer me."

Clinton shrugged his shoulders. "I remember it. Sounded like something she'd made up to amuse us."

"But she didn't make it up, did she?" Esmond folded his arms and smiled easily. "You must know that, Clinton. You see my visitor was sure you married in Ireland."

"Make your point," murmured Clinton, turning. Apart from the whiteness of his face, he showed no emotion.

Esmond put down the glove stretchers. "Have you told Theresa the implications?"

"Of marrying her in Ireland?" asked Clinton. His brother nodded. "There aren't any."

Esmond clapped his hands together as though delighted by Clinton's reply. "I wonder if she'll agree when you tell her Mother's story. I have to admit it, Clinton, I underestimated you. Not many men would do what you did in cold blood."

"What would you say that was?" asked Clinton, stiffening, his pent-up fury obvious now.

"Deceived her for your own convenience. Don't look so shocked. Why else would you have married her in Ireland? Unless you thought you might need to get out of it later?"

"I was stationed there," Clinton shouted. "If I'd delayed marrying her, I'd have lost her."

"You could have come to England. Steamers leave Dublin

with tolerable regularity." He looked at Clinton with mocking sadness. "All you said about treating her honorably—just a bellyful of cant."

"Did I abandon her when you robbed me of my income?"

Esmond backed away as Clinton came at him. "You still haven't told her the truth, have you? And till you do, you'll go on betraying her every day."

Clinton stood motionless, staring at the floor. "How could I tell her straight after the marriage? Then she was pregnant. Should I have told her the moment she gave me that news? Or when she lost the child and nearly died? After that I had plenty to attend to." He met Esmond's eyes. "I looked on it as marriage. Why should I think I betrayed her?"

Esmond looked at him disdainfully. "Because you knew the law. Must have known it. Any priest would have told you."

To Esmond's surprise, Clinton no longer seemed interested in justifying himself. After a silence, he said with anxiety rather than hostility, "Who told you I married her there?"

"Did you swear her to keep it quiet? Of course you did."

"Just tell me, Esmond."

"Later." Esmond rang the bell and said quietly, "I never intended to give you away over those bills. There'd have been a kind of dignity in going to prison for forging them. Love's last resort." He smiled to himself. "But I won't make you a present of the money either; so don't try running off with it."

Esmond treated Norton to a roguish grin as he came in. "Just a family conference about ways and means."

"A happy resolution, I trust?"

"Entirely." Esmond took an envelope from his frock coat and handed it to Norton with a slight bow. "The draft I promised."

The moneylender held out a bulky packet to Clinton. "Your money, my lord. Shall I count it?"

Clinton tossed the packet to Esmond. "My brother looks after my affairs."

"I hope he's well paid for it," returned Norton with elaborate gravity.

"Pure philanthropy," returned Esmond, already on his way to the door.

358

"Who told you?" urged Clinton wildly as they emerged in the street.

Esmond glanced in the direction of his waiting carriage. A footman had already jumped down from behind and was lowering the step. "Perhaps I can drive you somewhere?"

"Anywhere you're going."

Ignoring Clinton's exasperation, Esmond gave instructions to the coachman and climbed in after his brother.

"Who?" whispered Clinton.

"Her father. I don't suppose you've met him?"

"Damn you. Just tell me what he said."

"He turned up a couple of evenings ago. Tried to get me to tell him if you were as poor as Theresa thought."

"What did you say?"

"Told him the truth—more or less. He wanted me to talk about you and Theresa, but I refused. Anyway, when he'd drunk a fair bit of sillery, he asked me point-blank whether I thought you'd married her. I said he was out of his mind. Where was his evidence? He wouldn't say till I poured such scorn on the idea that he lost his temper. He'd seen a marriage certificate. Where? No answer. Who showed it to him? Nothing. Could he remember the wording? He told me a place with an Irish name. Priest called Maguire. I forget what else." Esmond glanced sideways at his brother's frozen face. "It may be worthless legally, but why the hell didn't you destroy it?"

Clinton stared out in silence at the trees in Golden Square with an expression so distant that Esmond wondered whether he had listened to anything he had said. At last Clinton murmured thickly, "Did he say how he got hold of it—anything at all?"

"Not really. I suppose he must have wormed it out of Theresa. He's as persistent as they come."

When he looked at Clinton again, Esmond saw tears on his cheeks. Seconds later, as the carriage slowed down at a corner, Clinton flung open the door and jumped out. Esmond called after him and started in pursuit, but with twenty yards still between them, Clinton hailed a hansom, which set off at once.

CHAPTER THIRTY-THREE

Though the day had been hot, the elderberries in the dusty hedgerows foretold autumn. On the fells, heather was in flower, and the glory of broom and furze was past. Few birds sang in the still countryside. It was early evening before Clinton dismounted at Hathenshaw after traveling all day. The beech trees cast long shadows on the lawn. Past borders mellow with the russet and ocher of early chrysanthemums, he walked towards the garden door. His first sight of the house moved him not at all, but crossing the soft moss where the lawn ended, the air seemed distended with grief. A feeling that often came to him for no reason he could understand—a warm evening, the smell of leaf smoke, a fox barking at night.

Entering the hall, he felt like a ghost returning to a place last seen not weeks but decades ago. A moment later Harris came in behind him, having seen him crossing from the stables to the house. When the servant told him that the bailiff had been back again with another writ, Clinton's heart seemed to stop. The same tightness in the chest, the same sensation of falling he had known when he realized he had lost all hope with his uncle. For a while every notion of what he had been about to do fell away from him.

Harris had moved closer. "You mustn't stay long, my lord."

Clinton touched the man's arm, moved by his obvious sorrow. Minutes earlier he had imagined going to Theresa's dressing room, searching for the certificate, and handing it to her in silence. Now he merely rang for a maid, asked the girl where her mistress was, and went there at once.

Mother and daughter were making plum and damson jam in the kitchen; their hands and lips were stained by the fruit, now simmering in preserving pans on the range. For several seconds Clinton watched Theresa from the corridor. Her hair was charmingly pinned up with a tortoiseshell comb, and she wore a maid's apron over a pale yellow dress. He stood very still, angry, sorrowful, yet wanting to embrace her, held back by the barrier of their time apart and the sapping consciousness of betrayal—his own and hers.

As he went in, Theresa cried out and ran to him with outstretched arms, hesitating as she saw the coldness of his expression. She asked Louise to leave them and said faintly, "He wouldn't help you?"

"No, he turned me down." He moved closer, and though his eyes were fixed on her face, they seemed to be looking beyond her. "Your father knows."

His calm impersonal voice was death to her, worse than any anger, as if she had already been condemned and this opportunity to speak was offered only as formal justice.

"I didn't tell him," she whispered, trying to contain a rising wave of hysteria.

"But he knows."

"You'd gone to London . . . the first time. You sent that telegram. I'd never felt so alone, Clinton. I was frightened." Ashamed of her pleading tone, she could not help it. She could see that he was relentlessly killing the emotion in himself.

"I repeatedly asked you to come with me."

"I was afraid to be possessive. Then the telegram and Hopkinson. You lied about seeing your trustees. I remembered others. In York, when I saw the letter from your bank, you said it was nothing. You refused to admit anything until things had gone too far to remedy. I needed reassurance."

"So you asked your father for it?"

"No, no," she cried. "I wrote to Maguire. I needed a certificate for the baby's baptism."

"A little early."

"I was stupid, I know."

"You didn't trust me. Perhaps that wasn't so stupid." A dart of unhappy fire sprang from the depths of his gold-flecked eyes; his face looked bruised and crumpled. She wanted to throw herself against his shoulder and weep.

"I didn't tell him, Clinton. How can you believe that? I don't know how Louise found out. I think either she or a maid opened Maguire's reply. Louise wrote to father. He came here. . . . I know he won't tell anyone."

"I'm afraid he's already told Esmond—said you were kind enough to show him the certificate."

"I had no choice. He was threatening to make inquiries in Ireland unless I confirmed what Louise had said. For pity's sake, what could I do?"

"Never have broken your promise by writing to the priest in the first place."

"How was that breaking faith? He knew we were married and understood the need for secrecy." Her eyes were unflinching now. "Are you accusing me of putting Louise up to telling her grandfather?"

"So he'd force me to acknowledge you?" Clinton smiled with half-closed eyes. "I never thought that for a moment, though perhaps it's his intention." He turned away and walked out into the yard.

"What will you do?" she asked, following him.

"Do?" he murmured abstractedly, aiming a kick at a bucket. "It makes no difference. Couldn't matter less." He laughed harshly. "To be honest, I rather hoped you had told him; it might have evened the score a bit. You look at me as if you've done something wrong—*you*. The irony, my God, the irony." She was looking at him with heartbreaking tenderness. He tried to concentrate his mind on what was to come: a few words, and no yielding to the insidious desire to justify or seek forgiveness. He thought, If only it were enough simply to tell her what was done in Ireland. But there was more to say, and though he longed to be done, his thoughts felt like slow-footed groping things. She touched his hand, but he pulled it away as if burned.

He said rapidly, "Nothing's as it seems. I fancy it's either . . . no. We say that man's true as steel, that one a coward. We change so much in and out of love that who can tell what we were and what we'll become?" He broke off as a maid came out of the creamery. Clinton took Theresa's arm and walked with her into the kitchen garden, but there too they were not alone. Two gardeners were at work planting spring cabbages. They went through the narrow gate into the orchard. Under one of the largest trees was a seat hemmed about by forked stakes supporting the more heavily laden branches.

As they sat down, she asked in a low voice, "Why did he refuse you? Why?"

"I couldn't meet his terms. It's over."

"Is that all you'll say?"

"We can't change his mind." A pigeon flapped overhead towards the house, and he gazed after it with restless preoccupied eyes. "You recognized me when we met—the young officer with his heart on his sleeve."

"I always thought better of you than that. From the day you came to the theater—from that first day."

"I'd rather forget." He fell silent, head bowed. At last he said, "It all used to be so simple. No regrets, no fears—life a race to be run, and damn the hazards. Just keep on headlong, leaving caution to the cowards—to anyone ready to sell liberty to buy wealth and safety." The scathing bitterness of his voice shocked him. He drew in breath and said more gently, "And I was quite different. Even my beliefs weren't like any other man's. I took every kind of risk, lived from day to day, did enough for a dozen men, spent more than money. Perhaps I spent myself. And nothing, nothing on earth, could ever bring me down. Such an old story." He dug his nails into a patch of lichen on the arm of the bench. She was about to speak, but he turned away. "I thought the past powerless to touch me, until one fine day it overtook me and blocked the path ahead."

He dropped his hands and faced her despairingly. "I've no faith in the future any more. Even the present's an outpost I can't hold. If things had happened sooner—the writs, imprisonment, the loss of hope after hope—I might have had the strength to go on believing in a new life. Now it's no good. I can't even pay what I promised to the court. I forged bills in London, might have been imprisoned for years. Perhaps I still will be. In any case I'll be up before the commissioners before I can raise enough to save myself." His voice broke and he covered his face. "And all this faith in happiness—nothing but a last throw. An end, not a beginning." He dashed the moisture from his cheeks with the back of his hand. "Listen to me asking for pity already. Imagine six weeks, six months, and God knows how much of it in custody. I went through it before. I know what I can bear. I'd rather die than see you come to despise me. . . . It's over, Theresa. Over."

She was very still and he thought she was crying, but when he looked up he sensed behind her stricken eyes the concentration of cold anger.

"How would it help us to part?" she asked.

He laid a firm hand on her arm, afraid that when he spoke she would tear herself away before he could finish. "The priest had no right to marry us. The law is—"

"The law?" A scream came up into her throat but went no further. "We exchanged vows. Does any law change that? Do you take this woman? Do you take this man? We gave our consent—nothing can wipe that out." She broke from his grasp and struck his chest with clenched fists. "You said that vows spoken anywhere were binding."

"In Ireland the law doesn't allow a Catholic priest to marry a Protestant and—"

She uttered a hysterical little laugh. "The law doesn't allow murder. Does that bring a corpse to life? A man's murdered—a man's married. Facts," she cried, "facts."

Paralyzed with shame, he saw her face as if it were still not too late—all imagined. A fine summer evening like any other, an apron over a yellow dress, warm sunlight on the tower, wasps buzzing around windfalls. He knew that only the smallest searching for emotion would make him weep. He longed to say that all he had said had merely been leading to the sugges-

364

tion of a second marriage in England. A month ago, he would have said just this and meant it, but now the odds had changed, and all his past efforts to deny the inevitable seemed to owe as much to vanity as to honor—a desperate desire to preserve her ideal picture of him, regardless of the ultimate cost to both of them.

In the dappled shade, under the overhanging boughs, her eyes seemed feverishly bright. A thin shaft of sunlight fell on her shoulder and the soft curve of her breasts. The thought of losing her started a pulse of pain under his skin throbbing like a bird's heart, and in all his body was a striving for her, against all matters of time and circumstance. And was he her betrayer? Perhaps only a day or two till the bailiff returned. And then?

"Can't you see how it would be?" he asked, tenderness breaking the rough edge of his voice. "Every penny you earned swallowed by my debts. While I did what? Drank, sold matches in the street? If all my creditors foreclose at once, you know the end of that. How long could we survive that sort of life? In and out of debtors' jails . . . resentment killing every other impulse. Would you have me drag you down into that pit with me?"

Her long silence wrung him as her first outburst had not. She sighed and moved slightly, more puzzled than blackly despairing. "How can I choose? For better for worse, for richer for poorer . . . I knew what the words meant. Desert me, but I'll still be your wife."

"If the priest denied it to your face . . . ?"

"I'd believe what I know." Her voice was hoarse but absolutely level. Her certainty made everything he had said seem unreal to him. She had rejected the basic premise from which everything should have sprung, leaving him as helpless as a man under a net. She said intently, "If I'd made marriage a condition for being with you, I could understand better; but I said it was impossible and in the same breath offered to be your mistress. Everything you did you chose to do. And now you claim I'll be to blame for what follows unless I agree to something that isn't in my power. How can you claim it? How?"

"It doesn't matter whether you agree," he said flatly.

365

"Look at me and tell me you'd go if I begged you to stay." A silence; he shook his head. "You can't?"

"No"—he sighed—"ask it and I'll stay."

"Then you are asking me to agree." She twisted her lips in a parody of a smile and moved closer, turning his face with her hand. "Tell me," she said in a whisper that shook his nerves by its strange tension, its mixture of ruthlessness and suffering. "Will the bridesmaids carry bouquets of snowdrops? How did you describe it?" She paused, her eyes searching in his without mercy. "I'm right, aren't I? You'll go to that girl." She paused, waiting for confirmation or denial. He said nothing. She got up with a light shrug. "Did I ever tell you she offered me money in Dublin? I can't remember what you said to her."

She shuddered as if suddenly cold, and then started towards the house. And the brief time he held her in view seemed to stretch endlessly, like a spasm of impossible pain. Everything that had been most important and luminous in his life was falling away into the widening gap: love, sorrow, and every other desire, until he felt stripped to the bone. He got up and stood hunched and motionless. Without knowing why, he seized a bough of the tree and shook it with all his strength, sending apples raining down around him, unripe and green.

"Over, over," he repeated dully, and the word kept rustling and echoing in the sound of his footsteps through the grass.

In front of the house he hesitated. There was nothing he could say, nothing else. He wanted to leave and never return. The gardens, the redstone walls and mullioned windows, the views of the fells across the meadows, flooded him with sadness. He walked away briskly in the direction of the stables. Inside, the familiar sweet ammoniac odor in his nostrils soothed him at first. He stood in the shadowy darkness, tears forming slowly. Later he laid his cheek against his favorite stallion's neck, murmuring the horse's name, blindly seeking comfort. When his feelings broke, he leaned against the rough wall and wept with harsh gasping sobs, until it seemed to him that he had shed all the tears of the rest of his life.

By the time Clinton returned to the house, the first misty stars were visible in the pale sky. He walked slowly, as though any jarring step might hurt him. But already a curious aching hollowness had absorbed his earlier pain. There could only be one moment of admission, one first discovery of betrayal, and after it the fact could never wound with the same violence—or so he told himself as he climbed the stairs.

She was in her dressing room, sitting writing at the small table by the window, her face pale amber in the candlelight. As he entered, her features seemed to tighten, the mouth narrowing, eyes thrown into wider relief. When he sat down, she left the table and walked round him, attentively but seeming at the same time to be contemplating something remote, the way a sculptor might look at a piece of his work done long ago. Had it not been for the baffled simplicity of her gaze, he would have suspected mockery.

Passing behind him, she lightly touched his hair, letting her hand slip down the line of his cheek and come to rest on his shoulder. "I wish . . . wish you didn't look the same. You aren't, but you still look it." A reminiscent tenderness furred her voice, making him long to call to witness every mitigating circumstance, to say that he still loved her, but he averted his face and said nothing.

She sat down next to him on the chesterfield. "I never trusted anyone as I trusted you. I knew that you lied about money to be kind to me. Perhaps it made you feel stronger to be facing things alone. I could understand that. But the other—" She broke off and looked down at the signet ring on her finger. "Love's very inconvenient—stopping for no reason when everything seems perfect for happiness, or going on when there's no possible reason. Perhaps I ought to hate you; perhaps I will. But now . . . I don't see why I should make anything easier for you. I could very easily stop you marrying that girl."

"And would we have a moment's happiness if you did? Dodging the bailiffs from lodging house to lodging house. Wouldn't the day come when you wished you'd—"

"That I'd agreed to share you with a rich woman?"

"Anything would be better than losing you entirely."

"Better for who?" she whispered, brushing his cheek with her fingers, drawing him to her and then kissing his lips. With her head resting on his shoulder, she slipped a hand under his shirt. "She's young, isn't she, Clinton? How she'll tremble in your arms. First joys . . . How do you think we'll compare? Youth against experience. For a year or two we might be fairly matched." She moved away from him and held up a candle to her face. "Look at the corners of my eyes—my neck. There, I lift my chin a little, smile, and who'd ever know, this year, next year? Standing straight, a slight elevation of the arms when naked, my breasts won't offend you—till you compare. Will you use the same endearments? Never on purpose, I'm sure, but you will in time. She'll have your children—a son and heir. Perhaps she'll buy back Markenfield for you. Esmond said you lacked imagination." She rose abruptly and went back to the table. "You'd better go before I decide I ought to keep you. I love you, but I haven't the will to fight. I couldn't endure your resentment for every misfortune. If you didn't reproach me, it would be as bad. You speak of breaking vows . . . kept what you did from me. How can I hold you to an oath you broke even when you made it?" She lifted her pen but paused after writing a few words. "Don't look so sad. The theater's an excellent school for making last speeches. My real husband died beautifully. Put everything in order calmly, saw old friends, and only wept when they'd gone. So cruel we can't buy things with love—long life, toys for a child, truth."

He made no answer, but watched woodenly as she went on writing.

At last she looked up. "You must send me a written denial of our marriage, signed by the priest, with his reasons. If Miss Lucas is shown a copy, you may depend on my silence." She blotted the paper in front of her and stiffly held it out to him. "So there can be no mistake, I've written this down, also an address." Though her voice was firm and her courage unshaken, he sensed her overwhelming need to finish quickly. Knowing he should go at once, he could think of no parting words. She stood up, and as she passed him he felt her hand against his coat. He wanted to tell her that he could not imagine surviving the waste of days to come. But what use were words now?

After she had gone, searching in his pocket for a handkerchief, his fingers closed on the ring he had given her. He took it out, and, looking at first as if he would dash the little oval bloodstone against the wall, he paused and with a heavy sigh placed this dismal badge of defeat on his own hand.

PART FOUR

CHAPTER THIRTY-FOUR

On a wet and stormy October morning when gusts of wind sent people scudding along the streets like paper figures, and turned umbrellas inside out with spiteful unconcern, Theresa made her way to Deacon's Place for the first time in several weeks. She was admitted by her father's wizened maid of all work, who for thirty years had mended costumes in the wardrobe at the Adelphi. In days of greater prosperity, the major had also employed out of kindness the arthritic old property man as his valet. The maid went up to knock on her master's bedroom door, leaving Theresa among the debris of the previous night's supper party: fragments of lobster shell, empty wine bottles, dirty plates. After a brief interval the old woman returned to tell Theresa her father would see her in his room.

Dressed in a crumpled frock coat put on over his nightgown, the major was shaving by the window; his bowl of steaming water increasing the fetid dampness of the room, beading the windowpanes with heavy drops of condensation. The bedclothes were flung back, revealing a sagging mattress. His white locks hitched behind his ears, her father ran his razor carefully down his cheek, following the line of his whiskers. In the gray light his skin looked pinched and sallow.

"A good party?" she asked quietly.

"Just the baron and Anderson."

For as long as Theresa could remember, Baron von Merck, a penniless German émigré from the troubles of 1848, had been her father's favorite butt and toady; while, for as many years, Ben Anderson, the once famous comedian, had loyally helped the major relive past triumphs.

She caught his eye in the shaving mirror and recognized the mixture of baffled anger and sorrow she had grown so used to during the month she had spent with him after leaving Hathenshaw. There was nothing abstract about his bitterness. It was as thick and indigestible as slabs of Christmas cake; and though he clearly felt pity for her, his every mention of her abandonment was loaded with reproach that she should ever have let it happen.

When he had finished shaving, Theresa began telling him about the progress of rehearsals for the play she was soon to open in.

With an angry gesture he tossed his razor into the bowl and interrupted her. "Did you bring the letter?"

Without replying, she reached under her cape and produced the document her father had been demanding ever since learning that Clinton had promised a letter of explanation from the priest. He took the envelope and went down to the sitting room with it. The page shook in his hand as he read.

Dear Lord Ardmore,

You ask me to state the precise nature of the ceremony performed by me between yourself and the lady you represented as joined to you by a previous contract. I understood that Lady Ardmore's religious conscience was not satisfied by the earlier ceremony and wanted a Church blessing on it. Though I was doubtful about your own religious persuasion, I saw no reason for refusing to oblige you both, since the ceremony I was to perform was only to be the renewal of a consent already given. You will know that for this reason I dispensed with the reading of banns, inquiries about impediments, and so forth. I confess I did not imagine the awkwardness of my position in the event of a baptism. I was therefore obliged to make it clear to her ladyship that the certificate I sent should not be used for any other purpose whatever. I trust if you think I have not been clear enough in any particular, you will not be hesitating to write.

Sincerely, yours in Jesus Christ,
Bernard Maguire

When the major had finished, he put the letter in his bureau and stood staring out of the smudgy little window at the sad-looking sky; across it, dark clouds ran into one another like inkstains on wet paper. "I wonder how much he had to pay the man to write that."

"I'm sure it's the simple truth." She moved towards the desk, but he stood in her way. "I'd like it back."

"Not till my lawyer sees it."

"If you're hoping to get money out of him, you'll have to wait your turn with the rest."

"I want justice, not money," he shouted. The noise of water drumming in a metal basin came from the kitchen. The major crossed the room and slammed the door.

Theresa sat down by the smoldering fire and said gently, "Even if you managed to prove a marriage, it still wouldn't comply with the Irish Marriage Act. You admitted your lawyer told you that."

"He said," replied her father, stabbing at the fire with the poker, "that it wouldn't be binding *if* Ardmore can show he was a professing Protestant at the time."

"You know it's a formality." Theresa sighed, saddened and exasperated by the old man's doggedness. "We both read your man's opinion. Why not get it?" When he made no move, she said patiently, "All right, stop me if I misquote: 'Any baptized Anglican is considered a professing Protestant, within the meaning of the act, unless he proves himself something else by contrary religious observance'—and the example given was regular attendance at Catholic Mass. It's hardly ambiguous, is it?"

The major was laboring with the bellows to make the damp coal ignite. "I don't care if we lose. He dishonored you and ought to pay for it."

"At law the loser does the paying."

"It'd finish him though. He'd be hounded out of the country.

Yes," he gasped, still pumping at the fire, "thousands would be up in arms against an archaic law that permitted such a thing —even if it only happens in Ireland." He straightened up, wincing a little as though his back hurt, and then looked at her beseechingly. "If you'd only bring an action for restoration of conjugal rights, he wouldn't dare contest it."

"But I agreed to let him go. How many more times must I—"

"Why?" he groaned. "Why?"

"Because, whatever the law says, whatever he intended, his lies made it a sham. How could there be any happiness for us after that?"

"Happiness?" he burst out. "What about justice?"

"Do you think he isn't punished?" she cried, beginning to lose her temper.

"I expect he's laughing at his success. By God, I'd go to court without you if I could." He coughed harshly as an eddy of wind from the chimney blew smoke into the room. Abandoning belligerence, he eyed her sadly. "Try to explain it to me. I want to understand. You went to church, exchanged vows, the priest went through the marriage service, you signed your name afterwards as Lady Ardmore. He said you'd become his wife." He raised his monocle. "Surely you believed you'd married him?"

"I'd never been more certain of anything in my life."

"Then why," he burst out, throwing up his arms, "don't you still believe it? Because of that damn fool law?"

"No, not by itself." Theresa paused a moment. "There were three of us at the altar. Take the priest first. He believed he was salving my conscience, conferring a blessing. He spoke the words because Clinton had told him we were already married. He thought I wasn't happy with a civil ceremony, so he read the service in church for my peace of mind. That's what his letter says. He didn't intend to marry us."

"But he spoke the words, and so did your husband."

"Clinton spoke them," murmured Theresa, "knowing there was a law that made them void. He didn't believe he was marrying me. He knew the priest only intended a blessing. How can I think myself married now I know he never meant to give his consent? He lied to the priest and lied to me. He never told me about the law, never said a word about what he'd told the priest. He knew his vows were worthless." Her voice had risen and she was close to tears. "I was the only one who believed in it. It was a fraud, not a marriage."

Her father raised a conciliating hand. "He may have meant every word he said at the time. Suppose he learned about the law later? He could have dreamt up all the lies to get you to release him."

"There's the priest's letter," Theresa replied wearily. "And I don't believe any priest would accept money to deny what he thought was a perfectly good marriage, so don't suggest that again."

"He sent you a marriage certificate."

"Because he thought we were already married. Of course he didn't want to deny the child a proper baptism. He said in his letter I shouldn't use the certificate for any other purpose." She looked up reproachfully. "I have given it all a lot of thought."

"So have I," the old man replied quietly, "and I think he's your husband."

"There's no point in arguing about it."

"None."

Theresa had very much hoped that Maguire's letter would finally persuade her father to abandon his persistent efforts to get her to reconsider her position. Seeing she had failed to change his mind, she nonetheless decided to make one more effort to settle another matter. "I've brought the money to repay what you lent me."

"I've told you I won't take it. A husband's responsible for his wife's debts. Get *him* to pay me or forget about it."

"The loan was to me. I have a right to repay it."

Simmonds shook his head and smiled. "A married woman can't make an independent contract. If she borrows money, the legal debtor is her husband and not herself. You pledged your husband's credit, not your own."

Theresa got up and walked to the door; beside it the broken barometer still pointed to "fine and dry" as it had done for a decade. Without turning, she said, "You took some papers of mine when I was here. I want them back."

377

"I don't deny it. I was surprised he had the decency to return the letters you wrote him. Do you want to burn them?"

"They're mine."

When she faced him, he did not look away. "They're evidence."

"Which you can't possibly use."

"Unless you change your mind about going to court. It's my duty to see the choice isn't thrown away in case you ever want to take it." He followed her into the dark little hall and stopped her. "I'll give them to you when they've been copied."

She turned on him furiously. "Can't you understand what I said? I've finished with it all. Finished."

Before he could answer her, she was walking down the court towards the mews, the wind catching her bonnet ribbons and puffing out her skirt. He stood watching her from the doorway until she turned the corner and was gone.

CHAPTER THIRTY-FIVE

Around him, décolleté busts and jeweled dresses contrasting with black evening coats, a hubbub of conversation punctuated by the discreet popping of champagne corks, footmen and waiters moving silently behind the chairs as course followed course in stately progression; and all the time Esmond could not help admiring the Lucases' spirited hypocrisy. Clinton had treated their daughter abominably, yet here they were, laughing and smiling, marking the day of Sophie's betrothal to her former tormentor with a magnificent celebratory dinner, and appearing for all the world to be as proud and pleased as if the girl had been accepted by a royal duke.

From the moment he had received his invitation, Esmond had looked forward to this December evening in London with keen anticipation. The wedding itself would not take place until the spring, but for all the chances of escape now open to him, Clinton might just as well have undergone ten marriages. Yet somehow this event, which Esmond had so often lived through in imagination, in reality brought only a fraction of the happiness he had expected. Ever since losing Theresa, he had made the present endurable by looking to the future, and the habit had become so ingrained that even Clinton's downfall could not prevent him running on towards the days to come when he would make his bid to win Theresa back.

Looking down the long table between the branched candelabra and flower-filled epergnes, Esmond caught occasional glimpses of Clinton's face. And though he could feel no sympathy for him, at moments when Clinton's mask of brittle gaiety slipped, Esmond sensed an emptiness of feeling so ghastly that he could not look at him without shuddering. After dessert, before the ladies withdrew, Mr. Lucas rose, his face very red above his white ruffled shirt. As the sounds of conversation subsided, faint chords of music came from the ballroom beneath, where the orchestra was getting ready for the dancing. Through all the clichés of his future father-in-law's speech, Clinton's smile did not falter.

"I have the good fortune to have known Lord Ardmore since boyhood, and if, as the poet says, the child is father to the man, any defects of character would long since have been apparent to me." He paused briefly to mop his forehead with a napkin while the ripples of polite laughter died away. "Until Cromwell fought the King, Ammering and Markenfield were part of one estate. The Lucases were Roundheads, the Danverses Cavaliers. Well, you know who won that battle. The third viscount lost half his land and was lucky not to lose his head. We Lucases got the land on that occasion and kept it. We're all royalists now, so I'm not complaining that the time of restitution is at hand. When Sophie weds Clinton, Ammering comes home to Markenfield, ladies and gentlemen. If not at once, it will when I join the majority. I make bold enough to say that I predicted this years ago when his lordship first entertained Miss Sophie in his nursery. . . ."

As the speech ground to a close, Esmond looked up and met Clinton's gaze. The glance was brief, but Esmond read the ironic complicity, as though his brother were once again saying those well-remembered words: "I, mortgaged acres, take thee, money in the funds, to have and to hold . . ." A moment later, Clinton got up to reply and did so with a perfectly judged blend of banter and seriousness ideal for such occasions.

If Ammering coming to Markenfield sounded a bit too much like High Birnam Wood coming to Dunsinane for his taste, it was not spears and branches that had brought him to his knees, but two far more formidable weapons—the character and beauty of an English lady. And for Esmond, almost every word his brother spoke rang with irony. Afterwards amid prolonged applause, Clinton solemnly lifted his glass to Sophie, who rose by his side like Aphrodite from a foaming sea of tulle and muslin. The sight of the betrothed couple raising their glasses to each other was one that would haunt Esmond for many weeks to come.

Shortly after midnight, a footman attracted Clinton's attention as he was dancing with Sophie. Minutes later, having murmured his apologies, Clinton left Sophie dancing with a cousin and hurried from the ballroom to the hall. Already dressed in hat and cape, Esmond was waiting for his coachman to drive round from the mews.

"I'm sure you won't refuse me a favor on this night of nights," murmured Clinton, placing a hand on his brother's shoulder. "I'd like to leave with you."

Under the portico of the Lucases' town house, Clinton moved away from his brother and looked up at the overhanging balconies and tall lighted windows. "Do you think," he said, "that Judas would have killed himself if it'd been thirty thousand pieces of silver?"

Esmond stared in silence at the bare black branches in the square; beyond them, on the other side, carriage lamps and gaslights showed indistinctly through the fog.

Clinton laughed as they got into the carriage. "Poor Esmond, you never had much humor." As the coachman spread rugs over their knees, Clinton chuckled. "You know something, Esmond? There's not much to separate one woman from another when all's said and done. I mean take Sophie and Theresa . . ." He paused as the landau swung forward and began to gather pace. "Sophie hasn't quite managed the queenly dignity, but she's good at pretending to be languishing and sentimental; they're as tough as each other in different ways. There aren't many who'd have shrugged off the humiliations I dished out to Sophie over the years. Between the two of us, I even told her about Ireland. Of course she was upset. But I think it's going to help her in the long run. She can despise me, which should take the edge off her worries about buying me. . . . She's also vain enough to believe that I'll come to love her for herself. Actually I'm already giving her definite signs that—"

"I can't listen to this," cried Esmond.

"Because you're to blame? Don't be so sensitive. I'm going to be an excellent husband. I admire her—the way she stood out for what she wanted against every kind of opposition. I don't love her, but that isn't my fault. Anyway I'll give a very creditable performance—the best sort of distraction."

As they passed the gates of Apsley House and clattered into Piccadilly, Esmond glanced at him. "What did you want to say to me?"

Clinton looked at him intently as they passed a streetlamp, but said nothing until the carriage drew up outside his hotel in Half Moon Street. His face no longer bore traces of ironic insouciance. "She's in a new play."

The tight harshness of his voice did not escape Esmond. "You don't mean you've been to see it?"

"Certainly. Can't say I cared for her kissing that actor, but I stayed in my seat. What about you?"

"I haven't seen it."

"Good," he breathed with chilling quietness.

"What do you mean by that?" asked Esmond, affecting not to feel the powerful pressure of his brother's hand on his arm.

Clinton released him and flicked aside the rug on his knee. "Only that if you try to wheedle your way back into her favor by acting the faithful friend, I'll put a bullet through you."

A moment later he was walking briskly to the door of his hotel.

CHAPTER THIRTY-SIX

 There is no gaiety as gay as the gaiety of grief, and the majority of those who met Clinton during the weeks after his engagement found him excellent company. As the future husband of an heiress, his social value was far greater than it had ever been when he had merely been an impoverished nobleman. His uncle had paid his debts, and now he had money to spend. In the Cavalry Club he was envied and became the recipient of numerous invitations to dinners and house parties. On various excuses, he refused all of them, but he still paid visits to the club.

In private he was a different man. He was unable to come to terms with what had happened, and his moods shifted with dizzying speed from sullen anger to icy detachment. The pain he suffered was unlike anything he had ever known, as if a vital part of him had been sliced away. By any normal laws of anatomy, he ought not to have survived the amputation; yet somehow a little of him lived on. Even when behaving quite naturally, he often felt that a stranger was speaking and acting for him. His life was alien to him and seemed to continue its most real existence in other people's minds. For the benefit of the Lucases he gave a spirited imitation of himself, fleshing out the part with little details rather as an artist might add tints and shadows to a face. Such pretenses formed the most effective distractions he could discover. Alone, when he was sober, his yearning for Theresa was savage, humiliating, and not beginning to be tamed.

He had told Esmond that he had been to see Theresa act not because he really had but because it had helped him make the point he had been determined to force home. But the temptation had been constantly with him ever since he had seen notices of the play in the papers. One evening he gave in. He hardly thought it possible that his unhappiness could be increased. On his way to the theater he tried to persuade himself that the sight of her might bring some alleviation—a theory he knew to be as false as a habitual drunkard's plea that one more glass will end his craving.

She was on stage when the curtain rose, standing still for what seemed an age to him, but might only have been seconds. He felt stifled and faint, unable at first to follow her words. Her voice was as natural as he had ever heard it, the words seeming to flow as if they had never been spoken before. As the play progressed, the tightness in his throat eased, and he found mixed with his pain a bewildering pleasure in simply watching her. Through an opera glass, her face seemed close enough to touch; isolated from the rest of her body and the other actors, it floated before him, lips forming words he did not hear, eyes wide and expressive. Suddenly he fancied himself at Hathenshaw alone with her. He found he could no longer hold the glass steady. Longing to rush backstage, he knew that every other man in the theater had a better right than he. Twenty yards away, she remained for him as remote as the farthest planets. With violent abruptness he rose from his seat and hurried from the theater. A row of hansoms saved him from indecision; like a man wading through water, he tore his eyes from the lighted sign above the stage door and crossed the street.

Later he lay on his hotel bed like a wounded animal and wondered how he would endure the night ahead and the day after it. Though he did not *feel* it, reason told him that if he stayed away from her his memories would slowly fade. Just as unconsciousness saved men from unendurable physical pain, grief too had its limits. Either the sufferer bore it or went mad —survived or broke.

During the next few weeks, Clinton began to feel less apathetic and detached. His attitude to Sophie and her parents gave him his first inkling of this. Their trust in the person they took him for bound him to sustain the role of honorable man. Though he had told Sophie everything about Theresa, she still firmly believed that he had been ensnared by an older and cleverer woman. Her determination to see only good in him ran much deeper than flattery, and often Clinton could not help being touched. Sometimes he was so bitterly aggravated by her happiness that he deliberately said hurtful things. Though she never wept, her misery was so obvious that he invariably felt ashamed afterwards.

She tried her best to please him, was modest and reticent. She was rarely guilty of pretending to a maturity she did not possess, and her reliance on his opinion over quite trivial things —the choice of a dress or present—produced feelings not far short of affection. The way her face changed when he entered a room restored him. To be valued so highly when feeling himself worthless was both strange and affecting. She was proud to be seen with him and, in spite of everything he had done to discourage her, adored him without reservation. Though nervous with him, she could still be amusing and spirited. The growing solicitude and responsibility Clinton felt for her might have been more appropriate to a father than a husband-to-be, but they were sincere emotions. When he had first proposed to her and been accepted, his debts and the fear of a breach of promise action had been the ropes binding him to a future marriage. Now, respect for her feelings was his only concern. In loyalty to this young girl he saw a measure of redemption.

He did not return to the theater, but sent a check for the precise sum raised on the Hathenshaw lease, with a letter begging Theresa to accept it for his sake rather than hers. It was never presented at his bank. When the play was taken off, Clinton made no attempts to discover where she had gone.

CHAPTER THIRTY-SEVEN

During the two months after his brother's betrothal, Esmond weathered the worst financial crisis of his life, and did it by pure audacity: splitting his shipping company and creating the Southern Steamship Line, with the sole intention of paying the Greek & Oriental's shareholders their dividends out of the new company's subscriptions. He also formed two other "paper" companies to raise the short-term capital needed to consolidate early successes in the trans-atlantic grain trade. Esmond overcame his fearsome liquidity problems by blandly transferring nominal assets from company to company as the need arose—one company "selling" to another and advancing the money at a high rate of interest. The interest was then entered in the books as increased value, and when a premium had been paid, this was described as earned profit. Though checks passed round the companies, never a penny of actual money changed hands. So long as the public continued to subscribe, he knew his depredations could continue undetected, giving him the time he needed to recoup his previous losses.

The constant risks he had needed to take almost daily to survive had not been without effect on Esmond. He was far more confident than before, and Clinton's threats did not prevent his considering when the time would be ripe to renew relations wtih Theresa. If he had lost her by seeming weak, he would not make the same mistake again. This time nothing would deter him. When Clinton was safely married, Esmond intended to begin his campaign in earnest.

In the third week of February, just over six weeks before the day fixed for Clinton's wedding, Esmond's hopes were shattered in so unexpected a manner that for some time afterwards he could hardly believe that the blow had been fatal. On the day in question, Major Simmonds came to his house and told him that he intended to bring an action against Clinton in the courts unless he received conclusive assurances. Since Esmond had already given considerable thought to the major's possible recourse to law, and had confidently concluded that he was completely powerless without Theresa's active cooperation, Esmond was not unduly alarmed. In fact to begin with, he adopted a manner of polite skepticism, in keeping with a growing belief that the threat was a thinly disguised attempt to extort money.

"This action," Esmond asked agreeably, "would it be for restoration of conjugal rights?"

"How could it be?" demanded the major brusquely.

"Very easily, I'd imagine—if Theresa brings it."

"Well she won't."

Esmond smiled sympathetically. "I can't quite see what you can do without her testimony."

"That's what the first two lawyers I saw told me. Luckily the third had more sense."

The man's obvious confidence had started to worry Esmond, but he said lightly, "I suppose lawyers can afford to be philosophical about starting proceedings. Win or lose, their fees are paid."

A curious expression crossed the major's face; it became smooth and arrogant. "The man's prepared to act for me for nothing."

Esmond glanced at him with raised eyebrows. "Nothing? What about the public notice that scandals usually attract?" His heart was beating fast, but he managed to maintain a front of contemptuous amusement. "I think the best person to talk to is my brother. Perhaps you'd like his address?"

The major pulled at the loose skin above his tight stand-up collar as if seriously considering the suggestion, then shook his head. "I think you'd be better at persuading him. He'd only lose his temper with me. I want to give him a proper chance."

Looking at the old man's stubborn forehead and pale curiously opaque eyes, Esmond no longer supposed that money was his objective. He said harshly, "You'd best tell me what I'm supposed to say."

"Nothing easier, dear fellow." A flicker of irony moved across the wrinkled face like a shadow over ruffled water. Like a card player with a good hand, he seemed in no hurry to finish the game. "You see, I lent Theresa some money a couple of months back. Nothing very much, in fact a trifling sum. I'm told I'm perfectly entitled to get it back from your brother—husbands being liable for their wives' debts." His tongue flickered over his upper lip as he watched Esmond attentively. "The action will only be for the recovery of a few pounds, but the real issue being tried will be your brother's marriage. If he's her husband, I get the money; if he isn't, I don't."

"I did make the connection," Esmond replied dryly. He moved away to the window and turned sharply. "Suppose I settle the debt for my brother?"

"I won't let you."

"Has Theresa tried to pay you?"

"Indeed she has. Of course I wouldn't take anything." He smiled at Esmond. "By law, a wife can't contract debts of her own."

"In practice, wives frequently incur personal debts and honor them."

The major nodded affably. "But when a wife defaults, her creditors can't enforce payment against her personally. They can only sue her husband for recovery."

"How can that be relevant if she's perfectly ready to settle?"

Simmonds frowned as if perplexed by his obtuseness. He said reasonably, "Ask yourself why her debt isn't enforceable against her. I'll tell you. It's because she's pledged her husband's credit. She can't make a valid contract of her own. The

388

real contract's between her husband and the creditor. That's why her husband is the one who has to be sued if she defaults."

The major's assurance made Esmond shudder. Longing to argue, he could think of no way to refute his argument.

"What I'm saying," Simmonds went on pleasantly, "is that when I lent Theresa money, the real contract was between your brother and myself; so I'm entitled to get my payment from him. No creditor has to accept settlement of a debt from anyone except the person legally answerable for it. If Theresa gives him the money and he passes it to me, that's a different matter. I'd settle at once."

"Has it crossed your mind," Esmond burst out, "that if Theresa denies everything under oath, the case will be thrown out in minutes? If you can't prove a marriage, Clinton's going to sue you for defamation."

"Theresa won't perjure herself."

"You mean you'll subpoena her to give evidence against her will?"

"If I have to. In any case she won't be the only witness. My solicitor's in Ireland taking proofs of evidence."

The old man had spoken with a lightness that was almost jovial. Esmond felt sick. His own relationship with Theresa would come out in court. Public prejudice against the theater being what it was, she would be represented as little better than a courtesan; Clinton would be socially ostracized for life, and Sophie made virtually unmarriageable. And yet the man was smiling with the self-righteous air of a moral fanatic.

"Will Theresa thank you for doing this?"

The major sighed, his breath coming thinly, like a thread of air blowing through a crack. The sudden change of mood astounded Esmond. "She's said she'll never speak to me again."

"Then why?" cried Esmond in amazement.

Standing by a lamp, one side of the old man's face was in shadow, the other eye socket sunk in deep relief. He raised his thin hands in a gesture of simple regret. "She's no longer capable of rational thought."

"You mean she won't ruin three lives?"

The major turned on him with flashing indignation. "You'd

rather it came out later? These things do. Louise knows already. How do you know who she's told? Who saw them at the church? The priest may be a drunkard, for all I know. And what if the truth was ever printed? A libel action, imputations of bigamy . . . And the girl he's going to marry—would you have her disgraced, her children made bastards?"

After a long silence, Esmond managed to rally. "The marriage can't be proved," he murmured dully.

"I think it can."

Esmond shrugged his shoulders. "Just tell me your terms for dropping the action."

"Lord Ardmore must break off his engagement."

"And acknowledge Theresa?"

The major puckered his lips and was silent for a moment. "I won't insist on that. He can sign a confession."

"To stop him marrying anyone else?"

Major Simmonds nodded and picked up his hat. As he moved to the door, Esmond walked after him. He felt as if he were suffocating. Clinton would believe this was his final act of vengeance; nothing on earth would persuade him otherwise. How could anybody who did not know this old man, with his moth-eaten old fur coat and battered stovepipe hat, ever credit that on his own, ignoring his daughter's pleas, he would embark on such a course? Every external frailty denied the strength of his inner will.

"See him yourself," Esmond groaned. "Get your solicitor to write. I can't do it." He rang the bell violently and leaned against the wall. When the footman came, he said faintly, "This gentleman is leaving. Never admit him again."

Alone, Esmond gazed around the room as though he had never seen it before. With hallucinating clearness he saw Clinton holding out a scrap of lace from a child's cuff—the precise expression of nonchalant inquiry—and suddenly Esmond was weeping, not just for his brother but for himself, Theresa, and for everything that had happened since the day when Clinton had come back on his first leave from Ireland.

CHAPTER THIRTY-EIGHT

When Clinton first learned that Major Simmonds intended to sue him, he immediately suspected that Esmond was involved. But a single conversation with his brother was enough to change his mind. Far from showing alarm when he suggested that they both go to question Simmonds, Esmond obviously welcomed this chance to clear himself. He was also so clearly alarmed by the possible effects of a family scandal on his business interests that Clinton soon knew he had misjudged him. Throughout their meeting, Esmond's distress impressed Clinton as forcibly as any of the arguments he advanced in his defense.

Not trusting his temper enough to risk going to see Simmonds, and in any case knowing that his lawyers would deplore anything done without advice, Clinton went on from his brother's offices to the Cavalry Club. He did not particularly want to go there, but he wanted to be alone even less. Lunch was being served as he came in, and during it he witnessed a scene that increased his depression. A young officer ordered a bottle of burgundy, which the wine waiter refused to bring. The servant tried to do this tactfully, but the officer flew into a rage and began shouting abuse so that the whole room could hear. After an interval the steward was fetched, and the officer, and all those at his table, learned that the treasurer's instructions were that he should have nothing else on credit until he had paid what he owed. Without a word the young man jumped up and ran from the room.

Later Clinton went out and found him white-faced and trembling on the stairs. "Can't I pay for your wine?" he asked softly. "I'll have a word with your waiter, who'll say a mistake was made."

The officer shook his head vehemently and covered his face. "The disgrace," he muttered. "How can I ever go in there again?"

Clinton did not reply and after a few seconds went back into the dining room. Almost every week of the year, one member or another would feel that he had been disgraced by some trivial injury to his pride: inability to pay a gambling debt, failure to raise his stakes with the rest during a game, a feeling that some disagreeable remark, ignored at the time, had really been an insult requiring an apology. And what was any of this nonsense in comparison with real disgrace?

That afternoon Clinton's lawyers were to meet Major Simmonds and his advisers to see if any compromise could be achieved. The results of failure were very clear to Clinton. He would still be able to avoid fighting Simmonds in the courts by breaking off his engagement with Sophie—in effect choosing to be sued for breach of contract by Sophie's father as the lesser of two evils. Even though he would be unable to meet the costs and damages of the case, the public disgrace in store for him would be mild in comparison with the hysterical execration he could expect if he tried to disprove the Irish marriage in court. Actions for breach of promise were numerous enough to be forgotten within a year or two, not so a case that would inevitably become an instant cause célèbre.

Yet almost from the beginning Clinton knew he would rather suffer anything than renege on his engagement. Pride and honor had little to do with it; nor was he worried by the thought of people supposing he had shirked a challenge. He had never admired the obstinate pride that still led to occasional duels. There were many forms of cowardice, and one was the terror of being called a coward. More important to Clinton was a purely intuitive sense of what seemed just. If he were to be punished, then let it be for his real fault and for no other reason. Deeper still, he was blindly angry. Although Esmond had warned him about Simmonds's obstinacy, Clinton could not believe that any man alive could stand firm against Theresa's most passionate persuasion. It seemed impossible that she had done her utmost to dissuade him. Esmond had said that the major was one of the only men he had ever met who might for the sake of a principle have his daughter subpoenaed to give evidence against her will; but this had not entirely convinced Clinton.

He could not bring himself to believe that when he had parted from Theresa she had entertained thoughts of one day going back on her assurances. And yet resentment had been known to change the firmest resolutions. She had met Sophie. Perhaps only when seeing the engagement in the papers had she found herself unable to endure the thought of his marriage to her. If so, Theresa probably thought that the threat of court proceedings would be enough to make him abandon Sophie. Of course Simmonds alone might be responsible, but either way, both of them would feel sure that he would not dare let the case proceed. Theresa would hardly be touched by the notoriety of a public trial. What would ruin him beyond all hope of recovery would merely increase the size of her audiences. Though shocked with himself for thinking her capable of such betrayal, he had to know.

"My thoughts and general state of mind are probably of little concern to you," he wrote, "but in case you are in any way counting on my nerve breaking before we renew our acquaintance in court, I solemnly swear that I will defend a dozen actions rather than accept your terms."

Above the blazing fire in the club library, a handsome gilded clock, once the property of Napoleon, ticked portentously. Another day and he would know whether Major Simmonds was going to make concessions. At that moment, Clinton thought it as likely as the assassination of the entire Royal Family or a mutiny in the Brigade of Guards. After finishing his letter to Theresa, he wanted to weep.

The following morning Clinton went to Lincoln's Inn for his first conference in the chambers of Mr. Serjeant Alderson, a

Queen's Counsel with a formidable reputation in matrimonial disputes. Mr. Yeatman, Clinton's solicitor, also attended with his managing clerk. Clinton was not surprised to learn that a compromise with the other side had been brought no closer by the previous day's meeting.

Alderson was a slight, dapper man, who reminded Clinton of his boyhood dancing master. A wave of dyed black hair swept across his forehead like a frizzy breaker. But there was nothing amusing about the lawyer's manner. He smiled with his lips but not his eyes, and his carefully framed sentences often ended in a peculiar nasal sneer. His occasional pauses suggested the calculated naturalness of a skillful actor rather than genuine hesitance.

Already acquainted with the facts by Yeatman, who had taken a lengthy deposition from Clinton, Alderson did not question him, but instead studied him in silence with a gaze that was both searching and detached.

"If this action is brought," Alderson began silkily, "we have broadly two lines of defense. If I can persuade the jury that Mrs. Barr went to church knowing the ceremony would be no more than a device to ease her conscience, then we needn't bother with our second resort—I mean that deplorable Irish Marriage Act." He paused and moved some papers on his desk. "Frankly, my lord, if you gain the verdict by invoking that statute, the damage to your reputation will cancel out any advantages in winning."

Clinton bowed his head. "I can't possibly claim that she thought the marriage was a sham. I know she believed in it."

Alderson's expression softened. "Nobody can ever be sure of knowing what someone else believes."

"In this instance I have no doubts."

"My lord," said Alderson sharply, "to suspect something, however strongly, is not the same as to know it."

"All I meant," murmured Clinton, "is that if you ask me on oath what I thought she believed, I could only repeat what I've just told you."

"Very well," the serjeant replied briskly. "Consider what I have to say carefully, Lord Ardmore." He folded his arms and leaned back in his chair. "A Catholic woman—call her Mrs. Barr—falls in love with a man who for various excellent reasons would be most unwise to marry her. She understands these reasons so well that she actually writes to him admitting that marriage is out of the question. That's what you told Mr. Yeatman, Lord Ardmore. Anyway, barely ten days later, this same lady goes through a ceremony with her lover in an isolated church. Were all the man's difficulties magically removed? What could have happened to explain so sudden a volte-face? Who better to tell us than the officiating priest? And some months later he does just this when he describes the ceremony not as a marriage but as a blessing." Alderson brought his hands together noiselessly. "So how does the impartial juryman suppose the ceremony came about? 'Ah,' says he, 'because the man and woman knew a proper marriage would have disastrous consequences, they put their heads together and worked out a way of giving their liaison an aura of matrimony without the legal reality.' "

Sensing that Clinton was about to speak, the lawyer raised a hand. "Unfortunately a dispute arises at a later date, and it comes to court. The lady swears she is a lawfully wedded bride, the gentleman that nothing more than a blessing had been intended. A simple matter of her word against his.

Somehow the jury must decide who to believe: the lady with a coronet to be won by perjuring herself, or the gentleman who by facing his blackmailing mistress in open court loses his good name whatever the verdict." Alderson broke off and looked at Clinton agreeably. "I'm not a gambler, my lord, but my money's on the gentleman."

Clinton's eyes moved from a discolored print of a late Lord Chancellor to the narrow window overlooking Lincoln's Inn Fields. "And where would your money be," he asked quietly, "if no heads had been put together?"

"In my pocket, save several shillings on the other horse."

"No help for it," said Clinton curtly. "It's not a point I intend to lie about."

"All right"—Alderson sighed—"let's suppose we don't argue when the lady tells the jury she thought her marriage was good. Well, what can I tell the court?" He glanced up at the ceiling with half-closed eyes and then leaned forward. "Gentlemen of the jury, my client does not deny that he deceived the lady and lied to an ordained minister of God, nevertheless he claims immunity from the consequences of his behavior by virtue of an enactment of the reign of George II. Gentlemen, that statute, I agree, was framed solely to restrict the spread of Catholicism in a more bigoted era than our own, but odious and archaic though many of you may think it, I must remind you that it remains the law of the land. If I can prove that my client was a Protestant at the time of the ceremony, his marriage can have no validity, and so he is entitled to your verdict." He shrugged, and turned down the corners of his mouth. "I daresay I could dress it up more decorously, but opposing counsel would soon reduce it to its naked form."

Clinton swallowed hard; he could feel his cheeks burning. Only now was he beginning to see precisely how it would turn out. The man's tone of voice, the mixture of sarcasm and virtuous indignation he could expect from the other side. He said rapidly, "Can't you conceive of a jury believing that a man might intend to honor vows which he knew weren't legally binding? I meant to go through a civil marriage afterwards. You know the problems that prevented me. Only fools wouldn't understand why I retracted—as much for her sake as my own."

Alderson let out his breath and looked steadily at Clinton. "Lord Ardmore, if you claim in court that you meant to honor your vows, mutual consent is proved, and the law will strongly presume that the legal requisites for a valid marriage were complied with. Even if we rely on the Irish Act, you still weaken your case by claiming you meant to do anything other than deceive the lady." He had spoken with quiet sympathy and added gently, "Perhaps you now appreciate why it would be wiser to adopt the first approach I mentioned to you."

"Can't you understand me?" Clinton groaned. "I'm finished whatever happens. I don't care if I win or lose. All I want is to explain how it came about."

"I wish," murmured the serjeant, "I could believe your opponents will have such honorable intentions." He sat thinking for over a minute and then said slowly, "I ought to ask Mr.

Yeatman to find another man for his brief, but I'm not going to. You see, the lady's trust in you isn't a fact to me."

"It will be the moment she opens her mouth in court." Alderson surprised Clinton by grinning broadly. "I'll be opening my mouth too. Let me tell you the order of things. Opposing counsel will open. Then Mrs. Barr will give her evidence. After that I cross-examine her." The serjeant smiled apologetically. "Forgive my arrogance, but I think by the time I've finished with her you may change your mind about your own evidence. It's providential that you won't be called till the second or third day." For the first time Alderson's eyes entirely lost their coldness. "Don't let 'em destroy you, man. She agreed to release you. Even put it in writing. Would a conscientious Catholic have done that if she'd thought herself truly married?"

"She'll explain it perfectly."

"We'll see about that, my lord." He thrust out a hand to Clinton, who found himself smiling as he took it. Serjeant Alderson accompanied them to the oak door of his chambers.

Going down the uncarpeted stairs, Clinton's solicitor, who had listened in gloomy silence to everything that had been said, turned diffidently to his client. "I'm surprised he's agreed to act for us. Outspoken, but believe me a very—"

"His qualities are obvious, Mr. Yeatman."

"I presume you want me to retain him?"

"Please do."

Outside, Yeatman looked at the sky apprehensively. "Looks like snow, my lord."

"Better than blood, I suppose," replied Clinton, putting on his hat.

Yeatman chuckled halfheartedly as they came out into Lincoln's Inn Fields. As they parted, a few soft flakes of snow began to fall.

A few days later Clinton received Theresa's reply to his letter.

Clinton—

Are you mad or am I? In the name of everything we did and said, how can you think me guilty? I will testify only under threat of contempt of court. I have done everything in my power to stop my father, even refusing to see his lawyers. If the worst happens, I will say what I can for you, helping you in every way short of perjury. Since no memories seem to weigh with you, I beg you to ask your lawyer one question. Why, if I am really the prime mover, am I not suing for restoration of conjugal rights? Should my father win his action, the court will only compel you to pay what is claimed. It cannot force you to maintain me. I am also told that the verdict cannot be evidence in any other proceedings. In a successful suit for conjugal rights I could claim thousands from you, and the jury's decision would not be reversible on appeal. Ask yourself why I have refused to do something so obviously to my advantage, and never, never accuse me so unjustly again. Though you disbelieve it, I remain, as always the woman you once loved.

Theresa

Pained by the letter, but thankful to be able to exonerate her, Clinton showed it to Serjeant Alderson at their next interview. The lawyer's skeptical response surprised him. Certainly restoration of conjugal rights would be of greater value to the lady. But she could still sue him for them afterwards. And if she did, though the first trial could not be referred to, it would be most unlikely that a later jury could be entirely ignorant of the earlier proceedings. The lady would also know that by appearing in an action brought by her father she could seem reluctant to testify, and this would win her the immediate sympathy of the jury.

He was unimpressed by these remarks, but another of Alderson's suggestions did disconcert Clinton, since it arose from questions that had already troubled him. Why had Theresa never spoken to him before writing to the priest for the wedding certificate? And how had it then been allowed to fall into Louise's hands? Alderson's inevitable explanation was that Theresa had always doubted the validity of the marriage and had therefore set about strengthening it. As soon as her father and daughter were persuaded that a genuine marriage had taken place, the later chances for retraction would be greatly reduced. Clinton rejected this at once, but still could not satisfactorily explain why she had at first kept the certificate a secret from him. But remembering how fears of her reaction had originally discouraged him from quickly disclosing the true basis of their marriage, he did not feel inclined to leap to definite conclusions.

Nothing said by Alderson against the other side made Clinton as bitter as the humiliating interviews he had with Sophie and her father later that week. The wedding invitations had not been sent out, but Sophie had already discussed her dress with her dressmaker, and the bridesmaids and pages had been chosen. Worse for Clinton than Sophie's grief had been her unshakable belief that the court would vindicate him. He did his best to warn her what to expect, but her powers of self-deception seemed invincible. He tried to persuade her that they ought not to be seen together until the case ended, but she hotly disagreed. He had told her about Theresa before proposing, and she had not rejected him then. Should she do so now because he was being threatened by the woman? The girl's unswerving faith in him hurt Clinton more than any indignation could have done.

Sophie had listened in stricken silence while he had explained matters. Her normally phlegmatic father wept, and later became uncontrollably angry. He told Clinton that if Sophie refused to break off her engagement, it was his duty to break it for her. Clinton refused, offering to retract only if it were put in writing that he did so solely to avoid involving Sophie in his public difficulties and had stated his willingness to honor his contract with her. Clinton suspected that Lucas wanted to sue him for misrepresentation, but since this would be impossible to prove until judgment in Simmonds's case, there was nothing further the outraged father could do except to forbid all further meetings with his daughter till the conclusion of the case.

Two days later, *The Times* carried a terse statement on the court page to the effect that the marriage between the Viscount Ardmore and Miss Sophie Lucas, previously announced for April, had been postponed. From the country, Sophie sent

Clinton a miniature of herself, but in spite of the note enclosed with it, promising never to give him up, Clinton was sure that her father would cut her off rather than let her keep her pledge. If she did not realize this now, newspaper accounts of the proceedings would soon persuade her.

CHAPTER THIRTY-NINE

 In late June, Theresa was served with a subpoena to give evidence in the forthcoming trial of Simmonds v. Ardmore. A month earlier she had warned her father that if he went ahead, she would reveal in court that she had been Clinton's mistress before her supposed marriage, and had also stood in the same relation to his brother. But the old man had remained unmoved—his composure evidently founded on his absolute certainty that Clinton was bluffing and would back down before the trial opened. Convinced by his lawyers that Ardmore had no chance of winning, the major thought it was out of the question that he would risk adding a galling public defeat to his other humiliations.

With the trial still a month away, Theresa accepted a part in a burlesque at the Marylebone Theatre; anything seemed better to her than sitting thinking about what lay ahead. During the first private dress rehearsal, just as she was leaving the stage at the end of the second act, she was astonished to see her father arguing with the prompter and several stagehands. She led him away from the scene flats to the back of the wings. Above them shaded gaslights burned blankly against bare brickwork. The property man and a carpenter pushed past, dragging a large table towards the stage.

Her father said dully, "He's going to go through with it."

"It's what I've always told you. What's finally changed your mind?"

"His counsel's made an application for a change of venue. He wants the case tried in Ireland."

Theresa's eyes conveyed faint derision. "I thought your lawyers told you he'd never dare invoke the Irish Marriage Act."

"It won't help him," he replied sharply, his confidence belied by the nervous movements of his hands. "He'll outrage every Catholic in court, and lose any chance of a fair trial."

Theresa said mildly, "Possibly his counsel has other ideas?"

"Just shows the funk they're in. They can't deny a marriage took place, so they're reduced to that despicable Act of Parliament as a last resort."

A crowd of loud-voiced perspiring girls in short fancy petticoats clattered past them in the direction of the dressing rooms. A callboy came up and told Theresa that her dresser was looking for her.

She turned to her father, whose face seemed gray in the dim light. He looked haggard and very frail. "You'd better say what you want," she said gently.

He did not answer at once, but looked at a group of men clustered around the limelights changing the glass filters to red. Smoke braziers were being put in place. The last act started with the hero's escaping from a fire.

"Father, please," she whispered.

He nodded and raised his hands. "I know, I know. The fact is—though there's still plenty of time for him to throw in the towel—he may not."

"He won't. He thinks I've betrayed him."

The major flapped the loose sleeves of his cape like some enormous bat. "*You* did? That's good, very good." The smoke had started to swirl about and made him cough. He moved closer to her and took her hand tenderly. "You've got to see my counsel. They'll try to blacken your character. He's got to take you through the sort of questions you'll face in cross-examination."

"I won't deny what happened in church."

"They'll try to make out you knew it was a fraud."

"Then I'll disagree."

"Just one interview with the man—just one," he implored. She hesitated a moment before shaking her head.

He said flatly, "I'm done for if we lose."

"Then stop it now," she cried. "You can't owe counsel much yet."

"I can't stop. Do you think I haven't been tempted to? Haven't seen myself as a fool for my pains? I'm not just fighting him, but you too. And that damned Act gives him a chance of a verdict. Listen, if you let yourself down in the witness box—" He broke off and hung his head.

"Give it up then," she said coaxingly. "None of us gain by it. Why should we be estranged from one another—you and I?" Somewhere above them a bell clanged noisily.

"But you *married* him," he burst out at last. "You still believe it. I'm not blind. I know that." His voice had sunk very low. "You might have had his child, and he deserted you. . . . Did *that*, and you still want to protect him." He shook his head helplessly, and she saw tears glistening in his eyes. He turned away abruptly and said in a shaking voice, "He'll not dishonor you. Not while I've strength left to prevent it. How can I let you cheat yourself? See another woman's child get everything yours should have had?" As she moved away, he came after her. "If you prove yourself his wife, you won't have to live with him. There'll be a judicial separation."

"I want to forget," she shouted, suddenly distraught.

He leaned against the wall, apparently drained; but as she hurried away he still pursued her. "Would you rather see him tried for bigamy in a few years' time?" Again the smoke caught in his throat and he doubled up coughing. "It'll come out in the end," he gasped as his parting shot, but she was already too far away to hear.

One of the men near the limelight clapped him on the back. "Don't you worry about bigamy, old man. Just you keep asking." He broke into a spluttering laugh. "Ain't it bloody marvelous, at his age—and with that one too."

All around him people were laughing. The major looked at them in disbelief.

CHAPTER FORTY

Clinton's counsel's application to the High Court to have the trial conducted in the Irish courts—on the grounds that they alone had jurisdiction in cases involving points of law arising from specifically Irish statutes—was contested by the other side. Because of the complex judicial and constitutional relationship of the two countries bequeathed by the Act of Union, three months were to pass before the legal argument was finally resolved in Clinton's favor.

Before embarking on this preliminary litigation, Mr. Serjeant Alderson had been at pains to give his client vivid examples to show the weight of public prejudice that would be arrayed against him if he claimed immunity under the Irish Marriage Act. He would probably need protection during the trial, and it would be unsafe for him to stay in a hotel or visit any public resort. To the serjeant's surprise, Lord Ardmore had seemed entirely undismayed by the prospect of events which the barrister himself viewed with such apprehension. Nevertheless, after careful consideration of Father Maguire's proof of evidence, the serjeant had felt that opposing counsel's chance of establishing the *fact* of a marriage was too good to justify pinning the defense too tightly to that issue. If the judge seemed likely to rule that a marriage had taken place, then its legal validity could only be challenged under Irish legislation. Alderson prided himself on having won cases for a number of exceptionally unpopular defendants.

Having started by believing Lord Ardmore a scoundrel, the serjeant had soon revised this opinion. Placed in a similar predicament, he had no doubt at all that he, and most other men he knew, would have attempted to make almost any compromise to avoid defending such an action in court—hoping that as time passed and tempers cooled, a day would come when the other side would agree to settle for money. This course should have been particularly tempting to a man with expectations from an elderly relative. But when the serjeant-at-law had tactfully tried to suggest that there could be ways to smother the scandal, Lord Ardmore had hardly listened. Failure to defend himself, he had argued, would not only be seen as an admission that he had proposed to a girl, knowing he had no right to do so, but also as proof that he had all along considered himself married to somebody else—and worse still, to a woman whose loyalty and forbearance he had exploited in order to desert and betray. Alderson had pointed out that, if matters were carefully handled, very few people would ever have the opportunity to entertain such partisan suspicions. These few people, Ardmore had replied, were the only ones who concerned him. Society at large could think what it pleased.

In spite of a habitual mistrust for anything that smacked of self-righteousness or chivalrous fidelity to a lost cause, Serjeant Alderson had been unusually impressed. When, shortly afterwards, Clinton had shown a wonderfully astringent sense of humor, the barrister had been entirely won over. A week or so after the first appearance of speculative press comments linking Lord Ardmore's name with an impending scandal, the secretary of the Cavalry Club had asked for his resignation in front of several witnesses. While Clinton had been able to forgive journalists for being curious when a nobleman decided to defend an action for the recovery of a small debt in the Irish courts, he had been less charitable to the club secretary and had served him with a writ for slander. Afraid that they had made a mistake, and not wanting to pay for it, the committee had not supported the secretary, who had been obliged to make an unreserved apology. A few days later Clinton had resigned, telling the secretary in front of a roomful of members that he did not care to belong to a club where an official could remain in office after admitting he had slandered a fellow member.

In due course all the witnesses required by both sides had been traced and interviewed, material documents secured, and the original pleadings amended. In September a trial date was fixed for the third of November.

There was a good deal about the case that interested Serjeant Alderson professionally and personally; but he had a number of worries, and the worst by far was his uncertainty about what Lord Ardmore would say in the witness box. Alderson's strong impression was that his client had decided to reserve his position until he heard what coloring his former mistress chose to give her evidence. The barrister therefore reluctantly made up his mind not to press any more emphatically until the trial was under way. On balance he believed he would be able to shake Ardmore's faith in her sufficiently during the opening stages to make him reconsider his evidence.

The serjeant-at-law was keenly aware that the first two days would win or lose him the case. Success would largely depend on his cross-examination of the actress. That she would be accomplished and beautiful, he had no doubt. Lord Ardmore was not a fool, and yet, because of this woman, he had done a remarkably foolish thing. The other side's solicitors had disclosed three letters written by her to the defendant, and these very clearly showed that she was quick-witted and intelligent. The impetuous tone of various passages encouraged Alderson to believe that he would do best to make her lose her temper. Even a clever actress would find it hard to maintain a pose of pathetic innocence while trying to hide burning indignation. The serjeant counted on learning a lot during her examination by opposing counsel, which would precede his own.

When he left Holyhead for Dublin two days before the trial was due to begin, Mr. Serjeant Alderson was not despondent. As always before a case, he thought victory possible, but he could not remember any other action in which, at this stage in the proceedings, he had been quite so incapable of forming a realistic estimate of his chances. The case would largely swing on the behavior of the two protagonists in the witness box, and any predictions on this score could only be guesswork. Whether the judge would direct the jury fairly was also an open question. Public pressure on him to do otherwise would inevitably be very great.

The serjeant had many attributes envied by his colleagues, and one was his ability to snatch moments of sleep in almost any circumstances. Though the sea crossing to Dublin was unpleasantly rough that week, while most of the other passengers were being sick, Lord Ardmore's advocate slept soundly.

CHAPTER FORTY-ONE

Although well warned what to expect when the trial started, Clinton was depressed to discover on his arrival in Ireland that the local press had already given the case considerable attention. The eminence of the counsel involved and the fact that the Lord Chief Justice of Ireland would preside had been clear enough indications to newspaper editors that something more than the recovery of eighty-nine pounds was at stake. How they had discovered what this something was seemed plain to Clinton. The interviews conducted by Major Simmonds's solicitor with possible witnesses, in and around Rathnagar, would have alerted the more quick-witted inhabitants to the kind of sums to be obtained by selling information to Dublin journalists.

But not even the anticipatory build-up, and the malicious interest aroused by all cases involving erring aristocrats, had prepared Clinton for the enormous crowds around the Four Courts on the morning of the first day of the trial. These stretched in both directions along Inns Quay from the classical portico, and blocked Richmond and Whitworth bridges to all traffic crossing the Liffey at this point. Most matrimonial actions were popular, but no case for over a decade, with the exception of political trials, had started in this fashion. The prospect of seeing a titled army officer who had recently fought the Fenians do battle with an actress over a disputed marriage would have been involving enough in itself, but when to this was added a widespread rumor that the trial would witness the first airing of the notorious Irish Marriage Act for almost twenty years, fiercer emotions were engaged.

High above the brown waters of the Liffey and the thronged bridges, an orange winter sun touched the great copper dome of the Four Courts and palely lit the grimy figures of Justice and Mercy perched on the pediment. From the time Clinton and his solicitor left their carriage, it took them the best part of a quarter-hour to force their way through the crowd into the building. What struck Clinton most was the surprisingly high proportion of well-dressed people hoping to gain admittance. Looking at the sea of faces, he was stunned by the thought that they were there on his account. As yet he was unrecognized, and for all the notice taken of him might have been a casual spectator. But when he took his seat in court beside his solicitor, all that would change. Next to the journalists on the press bench were artists commissioned to sketch the litigants for the papers.

The Court of Common Pleas was filled to capacity by the time he entered, and the usher was already swearing in the jury. He felt nervous, and yet part of his mind remained curiously detached as he glanced about him. At the far end of the room was the judge's dais under a canopy of faded red moreen, surmounted by the royal arms. Immediately in front of the dais was the clerk of the court's table, piled with books and papers. To the left of this table and facing across the court was the jury box, which slightly reminded Clinton of a Smithfield sheep pen. On the opposite side, directly facing the jury, was the witness box, looking to Clinton not unlike a Punch and Judy stall. There was something inexpressibly dreary about the place, an air of forlorn neglect compounded by many details: the tarnished gilding of the lion and unicorn supporters of the royal arms, the ink-stained desks, the jurors' nondescript hats and coats hanging on pegs behind them, the grayness of the walls.

Set back slightly, so not to obstruct the jury's view of the witness, were the rows of benches for counsel and solicitors. These extended across the floor of the court and faced the judge's bench and the clerk's table. Split down the center, the right side of these benches was for the plaintiff's lawyers, the left for the defendant's; the front row was reserved for leading counsel, the second for junior counsel, and the third for solicitors and their clients. Behind these were the public benches and, high up at the back of the court, the public gallery.

Serjeant Alderson was conferring with Mr. Fernley, the other Q.C. acting for Clinton, and with Mr. Owen, the junior on their side, when his solicitor, Yeatman, came up to introduce Clinton to the two barristers he had not yet met. Out of the corner of his eye, Clinton saw the people in the gallery craning forward to try to see his face. Alderson smiled and remarked wryly that he hoped they would be able to live up to such high expectations. In his wig and gown, everything that Clinton had found ludicrous in his appearance had disappeared. He seemed almost inhumanly composed. Bending close to Clinton, he murmured, "If Mrs. Barr pretends to be overcome when she sees you, I don't want you walking out. If counsel tries to get the judge to ask you to withdraw, I'll contest it."

A moment later, the usher intoned solemnly, "Be upstanding in court."

The Lord Chief Justice entered in scarlet robes. As soon as the Right Honorable Sir James Monahan had taken his seat on the bench, the clerk of the court called out, "Simmonds against Ardmore." ·

Suddenly Clinton found everything like a dream—the breathless silence after the babble of talk, the stolid-faced jurymen picking up pencils to make notes, the large number of ladies in court, and above all the extraordinary atmosphere that was so like the tense stillness in a theater just after the curtain rises. Clinton's heart was beating fast, and yet for some reason he wanted to laugh. One of the jurors blushed as he caught his eye. A few yards away the artists were already at work.

"May it please your lordship, gentlemen of the jury," began Serjeant Mason, leading counsel for the other side, "I appear in this case for the plaintiff, Major Arthur Simmonds. The defendant is the Viscount Ardmore. The plaintiff's claim against the defendant is for eighty-nine pounds advanced by him to the defendant's wife. The defendant denies that the recipient of this sum is his wife. This is the only issue raised by the pleadings."

Serjeant Mason paused and adjusted his pince-nez, a gesture which Clinton was soon to realize had nothing to do with a defect in their design, but was used by the barrister as a device for punctuating his remarks and presenting them to the jury in easily digestible morsels. Mason was a tall emaciated-looking man with a surprisingly deep voice. "This action," he continued, "rests on the well-settled principle of law that if a husband turns his wife out of doors without cause, he sends her into the world as his accredited agent, and is responsible for her reasonable support. The plaintiff in short seeks to make Lord Ardmore responsible for this duty. An ordinary action of this kind is quickly disposed of, since the relationship of husband and wife is invariably acknowledged; but this case, gentlemen of the jury, is not an ordinary one."

The serjeant's expression grew somber and he drew himself up very straight. "The defendant brazenly denies any legal relationship with the plaintiff's daughter. I am prepared to prove first that Theresa Barr became his lordship's wife, and that he then treacherously abandoned her and drove her penniless into the world. If these facts are proved, my client will be entitled not only to the unreserved respect due to any parent who champions an ill-used daughter, but to this court's verdict. Gentlemen of the jury, I am confident that when you have heard this case you will rejoice to find for my client, and thus assert the cause of virtue against deceit and immorality." After the serjeant delivered these words in a stern commanding voice, his face softened as he tugged reflectively at the sleeves of his silk gown. "Gentlemen of the jury, it is absolutely necessary for me to confide to you some details of Theresa Ardmore's unhappy history. . . ."

For the next ten minutes Clinton listened to a highly colored account of Major Simmonds's financial difficulties and his daughter's loyalty. A moving sketch of her marriage and early widowhood followed, and Mason lost no opportunity to stress the courage Theresa had displayed in continuing her career rather than allowing herself or her child to become a burden to her father. For eight years—and Mason made this period sound like eight centuries—she had struggled to win professional recognition, only to be denied fame by failing health and exhaustion. Threatened with destitution, what was she to do?

Clinton had wondered how counsel would lead up to Theresa's time with Esmond in order to make her relationship seem less discreditable. It had never occurred to him that she would be prepared to lie on oath about being his mistress, but soon he felt less confident. Yeatman had interviewed a number of Esmond's servants, who to a man had denied the existence of any impropriety. Esmond would have paid a great deal to stop their giving accurate testimony. When Esmond's offer of marriage was used by counsel to suggest that Theresa's virtue was irreproachable, since gentlemen did not propose to immoral women, Clinton's misgivings began to grow.

"Gentlemen of the jury," asked Serjeant Mason emotionally, "how many women in the lady's plight would have hesitated for a moment to accept such an offer from a financier of Mr. Danvers's standing? From a man who was honorable and loved her as sincerely as ever man has loved woman? But Theresa Barr did more than hesitate. She asked for several months in which to consider whether she could give herself with the love and devotion she believed to be a wife's sacred due to her husband. For her, the respect and admiration she felt for Mr. Danvers were not enough. She would suffer hardship rather than marry for material advantage."

While the serjeant once more paused to adjust his pince-nez, the Lord Chief Justice intervened: "Serjeant Mason, I think it would be of more assistance to the jury if you dealt with the facts you intend to prove rather than with the lady's character. I would have thought your closing address a more appropriate place for a tribute of this sort."

"If your lordship pleases," said Mason, "but in view of the publicity attached to this case and the wholly unjustifiable moral prejudice voiced by some papers against female members of a hard-working and exacting profession, I thought it desirable to say these few words at the outset."

"Very well," replied the judge, "you have said them. Perhaps you will now confine yourself to the facts you have undertaken to prove."

Mason passed on to Clinton's first two meetings with Theresa, which he said little about. He then looked sorrowfully at the jurors.

"In October 1866, Lord Ardmore stayed with his mother at Kilkreen Castle, County Mayo, at a time when his brother and Theresa Barr were also house guests. Gentlemen of the jury, counsel for the defendant may suggest that Mrs. Barr had by this time refused Mr. Danvers. If he does, I trust you will ask yourselves whether it is conceivable that Lady Ardmore would have received her as a guest in those circumstances? The idea is ludicrous. Gentlemen, you may find this hard to credit, but I must ask you to. In his mother's house, and knowing his brother's feelings, Lord Ardmore professed himself passionately in love with Mrs. Barr."

A loud murmur of hostility came from the gallery. The serjeant shook his head grimly. "This avowal was so distressing to the lady that she left the house several days before she had planned to go. Horrified to have been the innocent cause of such ill-feeling between the two brothers, she took a theatrical engagement in the city of York. At this time she intimated to Mr. Danvers her final and painful decision not to marry him. In December, Lord Ardmore made inquiries about her whereabouts and followed her to York, where he renewed his attentions. If the defendant claims that he took carnal possession of her there, he will do so to persuade you that he had no need to marry since he had already gained his objective. Do not listen to such falsehood. In his secret thoughts he had already resolved to make the lady his wife. Is it possible that any nobleman would seduce and degrade his future wife before bringing her to the altar? Why then should he wish to assert it?" The serjeant stared hard at the jury. "Because, gentlemen, only by swearing that his intentions were dishonorable from the beginning will he be able to give a shred of credence to his miserable claim that a solemn and binding marriage was a deliberate act of imposture."

Serjeant Mason folded his arms and rocked back on his heels. "No matter, I will show him a better man than that. I will prove that from the day he left York, he *intended* nothing except marriage. I will do so by putting in the witness box a man who I believe will swear that two days after leaving York, Lord Ardmore confessed that marriage was his one and only intention. This witness will also tell you that he saw Theresa Ardmore before she went to Dublin and that he repeated to her what he had heard Lord Ardmore say about his intention to make her his wife. When you have heard this, you will know what to think of any claim by defending counsel that the lady went to Ireland knowing that Lord Ardmore's intentions were dishonorable. The truth is the exact opposite."

When the barrister went on to relate how Theresa went to Dublin in early January, Clinton was no longer listening. Obviously the unnamed witness was Esmond. There was no other possibility. But the profound shock Clinton felt owed nothing to thoughts of whether Esmond would try to damage him with his evidence. What made Clinton's stomach turn was fear of what Esmond had told Theresa in York. Of course he would have warned her to expect a proposal of marriage and would have advanced every possible argument against acceptance. It was the next logical step that horrified Clinton. Wanting above all else to stop Theresa's marrying in haste, wouldn't Esmond have been sure to warn her against an Irish marriage? Esmond had not forgotten their mother's anecdote about mixed marriages two years after he had first heard it, so it would certainly have been even clearer in his mind when he saw Theresa in York. Clinton's suspicion hardened. When Theresa went to the altar at Rathnagar, she *could* have known as much as he did about the possible defects of the ceremony. Esmond would have had every reason to tell her.

The mass of misrepresentations in Mason's speech had hurt Clinton far more than he had anticipated, making him wonder how he had ever been naïve enough to suppose that the facts would somehow mitigate what he had done. But now, with all his attention focused on what Esmond might have told her, he began to take the insults more calmly. The trial at last had a purpose for him.

Counsel had now moved on and was telling the jury that Theresa had agreed to secrecy concerning the marriage, not because of any doubts about its soundness but solely to protect the financial expectations of the man she loved. The characteristics of Mason's manner were becoming clearer to Clinton: the tenderness of his tone whenever he mentioned Theresa by name, his contempt whenever he spoke of "the defendant." His gestures too had elements of theatrical caricature: feigned reluctance to make a damning accusation expressed by lowered eyes, incredulity conveyed by upward glances and exaggerated smiles. He was pausing again, touching those wretched pince-nez, leaning forward slightly as he always did when wishing to speak to the jury with particular intimacy.

"So now"—he sighed—"we have come to that fateful day—to the time of the celebration of the marriage. On January the sixth, 1867, shortly before High Mass, they went together to the chapel at Rathnagar. Theresa Ardmore will tell you under oath what occurred, and I do not believe that Father Maguire's testimony will differ in any material way. Suffice it for me to say that Lord Ardmore and his future wife found the priest robed in his vestments. They knelt down before him at the altar, and he pronounced the marriage benediction over them after they had pledged their troth. Gentlemen of the jury, when the defendant comes to give his evidence, I cannot believe that he will deny the words which were spoken on that occasion. I venture to say that when you have heard him, you will find it incredible that a man who had plighted his troth before an ordained minister of God, in God's house, could within a year find it in his heart to repudiate his bride."

The serjeant drew in a long breath and shook his head. "I fear, gentlemen, the answer the defendant will give you is that there was no marriage on that occasion, that he took her in there merely to ease her conscience and to legitimize her relationship to him as his more confiding mistress." As Mason paused, Serjeant Alderson looked round at Clinton and pretended to wipe away a tear. Clinton smiled back and felt real tears in his own eyes. His new-found composure began to crumble as he sensed that Mason was only warming to his task. The thought that this man would try to break him in cross-examination had been apparent to him from the beginning, but never with such clarity.

"What will you say to such a man?" Mason cried to the jury. "What *can* be said to any man prepared to stand in that box and say that he went to the chapel with a ring in his hand, intending to profane the altar and deceive the woman who loved him? Could any man be so lost to all honor? I think not, gentlemen of the jury. He will wish you to think that he withheld the consent which is the essence of a valid marriage. The priest may support him, and call what he did a blessing." A few people laughed in the gallery. Serjeant Mason turned and looked up. "In this country I am delighted to think that the words of the Catholic solemnization of matrimony are tolerably well known. If not, I am prepared to jolt a memory or two. Possibly the priest has been threatened with prosecution for marrying a Protestant. If that is so, I can understand his desire to call the ceremony something else." Again there was a ripple of muted laughter.

The Lord Chief Justice said with sudden impatience, "Serjeant Mason, I am always most reluctant to interrupt counsel, but I must ask you to wait till after the examination of witnesses before making any more remarks of this sort. I have been very lenient, but this cannot continue."

Mason bowed deferentially. "If your lordship pleases." He hugged the sleeves of his gown around him and smiled. "Gentlemen of the jury, I will submit in evidence a marriage certificate under the priest's hand, which may help you to reach a decision on the matter. If you decide when you have heard the evidence, that a marriage was performed, this trial ought to be at an end. I may not tell you what the defendant will say, but I will tell you this: There is an Irish statute, enacted in days when Catholics were treated as criminals. The wording of this Act will speak for itself, will explain how it has remained in force only through the neglect and oversights of our legislators in Parliament. Listen to this: 'Nineteenth George Second, chapter thirteen, section one. Whereas the laws now in being to prevent popish priests from celebrating marriage between Protestants and Papists have been found ineffectual; for remedy therefore, it is enacted—by the King's most excellent majesty, with the consent of the lords spiritual and temporal,

416

and by the authority of the Commons in this Parliament—that every marriage celebrated after the first day of May in the year of our Lord 1746 between a Papist and any person who had professed the Protestant faith at any time within twelve months before such celebration, shall be and is hereby proclaimed absolutely null and void to all intents and purposes, without any process, judgment or sentence of law whatever.' The same Act, gentlemen, provides that the officiating priest should be guilty of felony." He paused and then looked gravely at the jury. "Gentlemen, I am confident that I can prove that Lord Ardmore was not a professing Protestant at the time of his marriage, and that he had been nothing of the sort at any time during the twelve preceding months. If I also convince you that a marriage was performed, then it will be your duty, and I believe your pleasure, to hold the defendant to what he swore at the altar. Your verdict for the plaintiff will dash aside a dishonorable plea and defend the marriage service from being made the trick of libertines to gain possession of innocent women. Such a verdict will rightly merit the praise and gratitude of every honest man and woman in the land." He sat down abruptly to tumultuous applause.

The judge rapped sharply with his gavel. "At any other time I would have the court cleared. But since this is a convenient time to adjourn for luncheon, I shall be indulgent. Do not expect the same forbearance again." His lordship glared down at the public benches and then rose.

Leaving the court, Clinton was spat at several times. Affecting not to notice, Serjeant Alderson took his arm. "Could have been worse, my lord. In fact I've a feeling he's worried about his witnesses."

In the deserted corridor outside the robing room, Alderson eyed Clinton closely. "You didn't expect them to call your brother?"

"No."

"I was watching you. Why are you so worried?"

"I think it's possible he told her about the status of Irish marriages."

"Before she went to Dublin?" gasped the serjeant. Clinton

nodded. Alderson stared at him in amazement and burst out, "My dear man, it's a gift from God if you're right. Don't you see? If she knew the thing was false—"

"Of course I see," snapped Clinton.

"Then what's the matter with you? You ought to be thanking your—" He broke off as he saw Clinton cover his face.

"I loved her," he whispered, "loved her. Don't you understand?"

After a long silence, Alderson took out his watch and murmured gently, "My lord, it's crucial that you put me in the picture. Believe me, every minute counts."

Soon Clinton was blindly following him across the central hall towards the rooms allotted to them for the duration of the trial.

When Theresa entered the witness box and took the oath, the noise of people moving forward in their seats to get a better view made her almost inaudible. Clinton was sickened to see women raising lorgnettes and even opera glasses. She was dressed in black and wore a short veil, but as she turned he caught a fleeting glimpse of her face, which was haggard and very pale. For several moments he was in danger of breaking down, so powerfully did he feel for her. Only when he heard her firm voice and saw how steadily she faced counsel did his instinctive trust begin to weaken. Looking at her frail old father sitting with his solicitor, Clinton once more found it hard to believe that Simmonds could have had the will to bring the case to trial against her wishes.

His head was throbbing and he was aware of a parched dryness in his throat. And all the time Clinton knew that his nervousness had nothing to do with whether Theresa's evidence turned the case against him. All he prayed for was that her replies to counsel's questions would give him back his faith in her. If she denied being his mistress before the ceremony or needlessly damaged him, their love and sufferings would lose all meaning.

To begin with, Serjeant Mason asked her straightforward questions aimed at verifying all the meetings mentioned in his opening. These inquiries did not go into the nature of the relationship or require her to answer in detail. Though she seemed reluctant to testify, Clinton could not help remembering Alderson predicting this. Just after Theresa stated with her usual brevity that she had accepted him on the evening before her marriage, Clinton knew from the intentness of Serjeant Mason's gaze that an important point had been reached.

The barrister said quietly, "On the evening you accepted the defendant, did he say anything that in any way alarmed you? Did he for example—"

Serjeant Alderson jumped up and faced the judge. "I trust my learned friend isn't about to lead the witness."

"Certainly not," snorted Mason.

The Lord Chief Justice inclined his head. "You may put the question again, Serjeant Mason."

"On the evening of January fifth, did Lord Ardmore say anything to alarm you?"

"About the marriage?" asked Theresa, apparently confused.

Mr. Serjeant Mason smiled encouragingly. "You must have talked about it. What did he say?"

The long silence which followed the question clearly disconcerted Mason. Clinton felt the rapt attention of the court like a physical presence enclosing him.

Theresa said softly, "I asked whether he minded being married by a Catholic priest and he said that we—" She stopped, as if suddenly bewildered.

"Well?" murmured Serjeant Mason. Theresa merely shook her head and stared blindly at the clerk's table.

The Lord Chief Justice said in a firm but kindly voice, "Madam, please will you answer learned counsel's questions. He wishes to assist you but may not put words in your mouth."

Theresa paused a moment more and then said, "He told me he disliked Catholic ceremonial."

Her reply brought an emotional tightness to Clinton's throat, since it was so plainly not the answer Mason had expected.

The barrister said firmly, "He disliked Catholic ceremonial. Was that so very alarming? After all, he'd been quite happy to arrange matters with the priest. I suppose he knew he was a Catholic minister?"

Serjeant Alderson intervened. "This is no way to conduct the examination. The witness plainly stated that the defendant on the eve of his supposed marriage expressed a serious reservation about the form of the Catholic marriage service. I object to my learned friend trying to persuade her to deny the obvious implication of this remark."

The judge made a note and said to the jury, "You heard what the witness said. You should discount the personal opinion expressed by Serjeant Mason about the importance of that reply."

Serjeant Mason appeared quite unmoved. He folded his arms. "Madam," he went on almost cheerfully, "are you a Roman Catholic?"

"Yes."

"Were you one at the time of your marriage?"

"I was. I hadn't been a good one for several years."

"But you were a Roman Catholic and believed in the doctrines of that church at this time?"

"Yes."

"Before you went to the altar with the defendant, what did you do?"

"I made my confession."

"And after your marriage, what did you do then?"

"I received communion."

Mason looked at her with a guileless smile. "Confession and communion are sacred acts, are they not?"

"Yes."

"It is blasphemy to perform them insincerely, is it not?"

"Yes."

"I ask you then by virtue of your oath and as a Roman Catholic, would you have made your confession or received the host if you had understood that what was also done that morning was no marriage but a sham to ease your conscience?"

Theresa lowered her eyes as if reluctant to speak. At last she whispered, "I thought the marriage a true one."

"Thank you, madam," murmured Mason with a slight bow in the direction of the jury.

"May I explain something?" asked Theresa looking up at the judge.

"You may."

"These questions have been hard for me because I felt very

420

emotional at the time, and Lord Ardmore may have tried to tell me something which I did not understand."

Serjeant Mason pursed his lips. "I'm sure your sense of fairness does you great credit, madam, but would you not say that an actress is better able than most people to judge the effect and meaning of spoken words?"

"In general, I would agree."

"Do the words 'blessing' and 'marriage' carry quite different meanings for you?"

"They do."

"The words do not sound similar to you?"

"No."

"Do you think marriage has one or many meanings? I should perhaps have said the ceremony of marriage."

"It has one meaning to me."

Mason leaned forward on the raised rail in front of him and breathed out heavily, as though completing a task that had not been easy. His apparent struggle to obtain what he wanted had at first almost restored Clinton's faith in Theresa; but then he realized that her hesitance had not defeated Mason, and in the end had lent her evidence greater impact. The jury would now believe whatever she said. Mason continued: "I suggest to you that no woman with a clear view of marriage could fail to recognize even a mild statement at variance with her opinion on the matter. That she should fail to notice, if such a statement were made by the man she intended to marry, passes my comprehension."

"My lord," said Serjeant Alderson, "I strongly object to counsel for the plaintiff making speeches to the jury under the guise of examining a witness. If he wants to ask her whether she thinks that Lord Ardmore tried to explain his actual position and intentions before the ceremony, then let him ask her that directly."

"I've finished with the subject," Mason replied blandly.

"You may depend upon it that I have not," remarked Serjeant Alderson.

"Now, madam, will you tell us what was done at the altar with the defendant kneeling by your side?"

Serjeant Alderson, who had only just resumed his seat, rose

again. "I have no desire to keep interrupting my learned friend, but this is quite improper. The witness has said nothing about the altar or the defendant doing anything by her side. He may have been by the font and she in the vestry, for all I know."

The judge turned to Theresa. "State all that occurred in reference to the ceremony from the time you entered the church."

When Theresa had finished an account which almost exactly coincided with Clinton's recollections, Mason put questions to establish that cohabitation had followed the ceremony and that for six months Theresa had thought herself the defendant's wife.

"And during these months, you never thought of yourself as his mistress?"

"No."

"Bearing this in mind, let me read you this memorandum which you gave the defendant in September 1867. It begins: 'I abhor what you did—' Did you give him that letter at the date stated?"

"Yes. Shortly before we parted."

"In it you wrote, among other things, 'I will release you and remain silent only if you send me a denial of our marriage in Father Maguire's hand.' You also insisted that he should prove to you, if he wished to marry another woman, that this lady was shown this letter before he made any proposal to her. Why did you write this to the defendant?"

"Because I believed him when he said there was an Act of Parliament that made our marriage legally void."

"Otherwise you would have felt that you had no right to release him?"

"That's true."

"I have no other questions."

When Serjeant Alderson rose to cross-examine, the nerves seemed to tighten around Clinton's heart. Though he knew that Alderson had decided to reserve for his examination of Esmond all questions about what Theresa had learned in York, there were other issues of great importance to Clinton which he hoped would be made clear—not least whether she would support her counsel's claim that she had remained chaste until after the ceremony. Longing for an end to his uncertainty,

Clinton nevertheless dreaded seeing her humiliated by his advocate, especially since he believed nothing conclusive would be proved until Esmond was called.

He had supposed that Serjeant Alderson would attack from the beginning, but instead his tone was gentle, even friendly, as though all he wanted to do was clear up a misunderstanding that might have nothing to do with her.

"Madam, I think you told my learned friend that you have a clear idea of what constitutes a marriage?"

"I did."

"Would you agree that you pledged yourself before God to honor certain vows?"

"Yes."

Alderson looked confused. "I admit this puzzles me. You see, a moment ago you said that because of an ancient Act of Parliament you considered your marriage void. I heard you correctly?"

"You did."

"You also told the jury that you believe in God." Alderson frowned. "And you swore that you thought your marriage was a true one in God's eyes—*and yet* you took it upon yourself to release the defendant." The slight smile on Alderson's lips faded and was replaced by his familiar sneer. "Madam, are you asking the jury to believe that a sincere God-fearing Catholic would risk damnation by knowingly overturning what Serjeant Mason insists is a holy union because of a man-made statute?"

A second or two passed, and Clinton felt his heart begin to race. Then with an unhurried graceful movement, she lifted her veil, as if to show counsel she was not afraid of his eyes. "I did what I did," she said, "because when Lord Ardmore told me about the statute, I was forced to believe that he had never meant to give his consent. I thought that my own consent had no effect without his."

The judge said, "I must remind the jury that they must take the law from me. Later I will tell you what amounts to a lawful marriage and you will have to decide, on the evidence before you, whether a lawful marriage took place. The witness's opinion about the validity of the ceremony *after* its performance can have no bearing whatever on its legal effect or lack of it."

423

"Mrs. Barr," asked Alderson sharply, "do you expect me to believe that you accepted what the defendant said without question, although his saying it was proof that he had lied to you before?"

"I believed him."

"You had just heard from the defendant that he had deceived you at the altar, and you believed everything else he told you?"

"The main point . . . yes."

"On the word of a man who had done something so abominably dishonest, you decided to dash aside a union which only moments before you had thought binding in the eyes of almighty God?" Alderson's derision was blatant.

"I told you my reason."

"I heard it, madam. I have attempted to show why I find it inadequate." He paused. "I put it to you that it is inconceivable that you would have agreed to desecrate and deny your marriage so readily, unless you had known it was an imposture from the start."

"I never thought it an imposture before Lord Ardmore left me."

"We will see, madam. In December 1866, you wrote a letter to the defendant. Members of the jury will find it on page four of the printed documents." The serjeant paused a moment while the original was handed to Theresa.

"Did you write that letter within a week of going to Ireland?"

"Yes."

"Attend to this. You wrote, 'I think it is a great shame one cannot go on trial with marriage as with other things. It is a formidable affair for life. Enough of it. For us it will never raise a problem, being impossible.' So, eleven days before the ceremony in the chapel at Rathnagar you wrote saying that marriage was impossible. Listen to how you continued: 'Since I am no lover of convention, I like getting off the beaten track and am proud rather than ashamed that we cannot do what others can or follow rules to the letter. What cannot be got straight has to be enjoyed crookedly.' I put it to you that because you already knew that marriage was impossible, you were hinting at another way—a way in which the strict rules could be disregarded and the advantages of marriage enjoyed, in your own words, 'crookedly.' By virtue of your oath, madam, were you not referring in this letter to a church ceremony that would be less than a marriage?"

Up to this moment, Theresa had seemed at ease, but now the letter trembled in her hand. Her cheeks were flushed. "The meaning's perfectly clear to anyone who wants to see it. I was telling Lord Ardmore that I was ready to be his mistress, and that he need not fear that I'd end our relationship if he didn't marry me. I was scared that his uncle would disinherit him if he married me. I was scared on his account."

Alderson smiled condescendingly. "But the marriage was secret, was it not?"

"He only told me it would be secret when he proposed to me. Otherwise I would have refused him."

"You are an actress, madam. I believe secret marriages are common enough in modern plays."

"I can think of two plays like that."

"If you weren't ashamed to offer to be his mistress, why were you so modest about suggesting such an obvious way out of your difficulties as a secret marriage?"

"It was for him to make suggestions about marriage."

Alderson nodded solemnly. "And for you to make other sorts of suggestions. . . . I appreciate these niceties of etiquette. But, madam, you wrote that marriage was impossible. Are you now telling me that what you actually meant was *perfectly possible?*"

"I explained what I meant," she replied in a shaking voice.

"Can you swear that only your sense of etiquette prevented you making a suggestion which could win you a coronet?"

"Etiquette was your word, sir. I said that in our situation it was for him to make that sort of suggestion."

"I suggest to you, Mrs. Barr, that the real reason why you didn't make that obvious suggestion was the knowledge that Lord Ardmore had no intention of making you his lawful wife. Wasn't that why you conceded that it was *impossible?*"

The judge said quietly, "The witness has given her answer. You may not be satisfied by it, Serjeant Alderson, but you can't go on rephrasing the same question."

"If your lordship pleases." Serjeant Alderson drank some water and said harshly, "Did you or did you not become the defendant's mistress in York? I warn you that I can call witnesses to—"

Serjeant Mason shouted, "This is outrageous. The jury are being tempted to believe that any answer the witness gives now is given because of that threat. We will see what these witnesses are worth when they're called."

"Gentleman of the bar," said the judge, I am endeavoring to discharge a difficult and unpleasant duty, and I must beg of you not to turn my court into a bear garden. The witness may answer now."

"I first became his mistress at Kilkreen Castle in October. I was his mistress in York too. I never intended to deny it."

A strange murmur rose from the gallery—a sound which seemed to Clinton like a drawn-out sigh of disappointment. In this at least, she had not betrayed him. The pity he had felt when Alderson had quoted from her letter wrung him more fiercely now.

"As a Catholic, madam, did you feel guilt?"

"I wasn't practicing my religion at this time."

"Because you believed you were living sinfully?"

"Yes."

"Your conscience troubled you?" Theresa made no reply; she seemed drained, stricken. "I won't press the question. Let me put another. Were you not in a position where any ceremony that might quiet your conscience would have been a great help to you?"

"How could a fraudulent ceremony have eased my conscience?" she cried.

"With respect, madam, if the priest intended the ceremony as a blessing, and you and the other party shared that view of it, how could it be fraudulent?"

"It would have been futile self-deception. I pledged myself sincerely. Can't you understand that I'll never say anything else?"

"That may be so, madam, but it remains my duty to ask you questions. When Lord Ardmore came to York, he left a letter for you at the theater, or his valet left it for you. The jury will see it as item one." The clerk of the court's assistant gave the letter to Theresa. "Lord Ardmore accused you of dragging him across the Irish Sea like a monkey on a chain, he described theatrical offices as greasy and theater agents as posturing men. If you refused to see him, he offered to break the heads of more actors and theater staff than there were seats in the theater. Madam, would a gentleman write in those terms to any woman he considered might one day be his wife?"

Theresa looked wearily at the advocate. "The letter demands a sense of humor, sir."

"Was it humorous to insult your profession?"

"Possibly the joke is a little labored."

"I put it to you that under a veneer of humor the tone is hectoring and rude. The way a nobleman might address his mistress, but not his future wife. What do you think?"

"I don't know enough noblemen to make a reliable guess."

"This trial is not an amusing matter for the defendant, madam."

"I meant my answer seriously. You mistook my tone."

"I shall endeavor to do better. I would like to ask you some more questions about that letter on page four of the printed documents." Clinton's letter was taken from her and she was once again handed the letter Serjeant Alderson had already quoted from. "Eleven days before the ceremony, you wrote to the defendant that you would like to be a vivandière. Of course this was meant humorously, but how would you describe the life led by these women in the French army?"

"My lord," said Theresa, "I find this intolerable. The question's absurd and insulting."

"Serjeant Alderson," asked the judge, "how can it be material what the witness thinks about cooks and camp followers in the French army? They have a reputation for immorality, but many were killed in front of their regiments in the Russian war, leading them as our pipers do in the Highland regiments. It may be strange that the witness should in any way compare herself with these women, but she could hardly wish to be one. The witness need not answer."

"If your lordship pleases. A little earlier in the same letter you wrote, 'You know where I am in London, so all you will need do is whistle and I'll come to you, my lad. You know the rest of that verse I'm sure.' Well, Lord Ardmore may have known it, but can you recite it for me?"

"The author is Robert Burns. It's well known."

"That is not an answer, madam."

"I can't remember the precise words."

"Are they not to this general effect? The girl narrator says that she will come to her lover if he whistles for her. Though her father and mother may go mad, she tells him that she'll leave her back gate open, and asks him to be careful and come as if he were not coming to see her. 'Come as ye were na comin' to me.' Is that a fair rendering?"

"The girl ends up asking him to be faithful to her."

"Would you say the poem is a moral one?"

"It starts worse than it ends."

"Is it moral?"

"No."

"But you forced it on the defendant, days before the ceremony. Again, madam, is that the way a woman would write to the man she might soon marry? Doesn't it suggest that you envisaged a very different relationship?"

"I didn't expect to marry him when I wrote the letter."

"Of course. You were too shy to suggest secrecy. 'Come as ye were na comin' to me.' I've finished, madam." Theresa stood very still as if she had not heard him. Alderson said, "You may leave the stand now." She remained a moment longer and then followed the usher from the courtroom. Clinton shut his eyes.

There was a delay of several minutes before counsel for the plaintiff called his next witness, and Serjeant Alderson took advantage of it to encourage his client. Sitting down beside him, the serjeant murmured to Clinton, "I assure you I was kindness itself in comparison with what Mason's going to try to do to you."

"It was hateful reading those letters." He looked away. "Do you know something? I wish to God she'd lied."

"But she did," said Alderson, wiping his forehead just below the line of his wig. "Not about being your mistress—how could she? Must have known we could call half a dozen maids from York and Dublin to swear that only one bed was slept in. They wouldn't all have been disbelieved. Her counsel knew that." Alderson glanced at his downcast face. "She lied, I'm telling you. You said your brother didn't want her to marry you. He *must* have warned her against marrying in Ireland."

"But if he *did*, "whispered Clinton urgently, "why did she ever agree to go through the ceremony?"

"She decided to take a risk. She wanted to be Lady Ardmore, and any kind of marriage seemed better than none. She obviously thought she could hold you to it. Remember the certificate." Clinton said nothing. "Look, man, if she'd turned down your proposal in Ireland, she'd have had to admit she didn't trust you. And then you would have resented that and maybe got cold feet later. That was the last thing she cared to risk."

"I don't know what I think any more. When you read that letter . . . You told me I ought to have settled out of court. I wish to hell I had."

"I'm thankful you didn't. I think you'll win."

"Did she really lie, Serjeant? I know what you said, but I saw the way she gave evidence." Clinton looked imploringly at his advocate.

"My lord, I haven't the least doubt of it. It always hurts to find one's been made a fool of, but that's no reason to pretend it didn't happen." He paused slightly. "Least of all in a place like this."

The next witness called by Mason was not Esmond but Father Maguire. While the priest was being sworn and asked the necessary formal questions, Clinton remembered the man's sparsely furnished room and the scaffolding around the church. If only he had refused me thought Clinton. But there would have been another priest needing money just as badly, and in the end he would have found him. Maguire, who had seemed so stolid to Clinton, now looked distraught and painfully nervous. Serjeant Mason treated him severely from the beginning.

As soon as the priest had said who he was, he turned to the Lord Chief Justice. "I beg leave, your worship, before I give evidence in this case—"

"I won't allow this, my lord," said Mason. "The reverend gentleman is trying to make a speech."

"I wasn't going to."

The judge gazed at him reproachfully. "You are sworn now as a witness, and your duty is to answer such questions as you may be asked. Later, if you think you should, you may give explanations. In here you must address me as my lord."

Mason leaned forward. "Did Lord Ardmore and Theresa Barr, as she then was, enter your church together on Sunday January sixth, 1867?"

"Yes."

"And were you at the altar when they came in?"

"I was inside the altar rails—My lord," asked the priest in desperation, "may I be allowed to—"

"Not yet, sir. Did they kneel down before you?"

"Yes."

"Did you ask the man whether he would take the woman to be his wife, and did you ask the woman would she take the man to be her husband?"

"Yes, but I must—"

"Answer this, sir. Was a ring produced?"

"I have no knowledge of seeing a ring; except when I gave a short exhortation after the ceremony, he had his hand on her hand."

"Putting the ring on her finger—come now?"

"Holding the ring."

"What did he do with it?"

"I saw him turning it."

"Did you ever see a wedding ring put on a finger before?"

"I did often enough. I don't think he put it on."

"Perhaps it was too small?" asked Mason with heavy sarcasm.

"Possibly, sir."

"Did Lord Ardmore say these words, repeating them after you: 'I take thee, Theresa Barr, to be my wedded wife, to have and to hold from this day forward'?"

"He did."

"And did he continue right through the form of words after you?"

"They both gave their verbal consent in that way, but the marriage ceremony was not complete."

430

"That isn't for you to decide."

"I did not end with the normal form of benediction."

"That was out of turn, sir."

Maguire blurted out, "The words of the service when the parties plight their troth, include the expression 'if holy church will permit.' In my opinion—"

"You must behave yourself," put in the judge, "and only answer learned counsel's questions; otherwise I will send you to prison for contempt of court. Do you understand?"

"Yes, my lord."

"Now, sir, did both parties pledge themselves distinctly?"

"Yes."

"And she kneeling by his side at the altar?"

"Yes."

"And you married them?"

"I renewed a consent which I understood—"

"I object to that answer. I object to anyone, be he the Pope or the Archbishop of Canterbury, telling us what marriage is. If he went through the form, it is for your lordship to decide what it is."

"Did you go through the form?" asked the judge.

"Yes, but without the customary form of benediction."

"How can that change the fact of their consent?" demanded Serjeant Mason.

"I will rule on that later," replied the Lord Chief Justice.

"When the defendant came to see you alone, before he came with the lady, did he say he was a Catholic? Surely you would have had nothing to do with him otherwise?"

"He said he was of no religion."

"He attended Mass after his marriage. Do you swear he said he had no religion?"

"Yes."

"What was your fee?"

"For attending at the ceremony?"

"I call it marriage. But tell me your fee?"

"Twenty pounds."

"What is the usual fee for a marriage?"

"Two pounds."

"The defendant could have been ten times married for his fee, could he not?"

"He wasn't though, sir."

Serjeant Mason asked for the marriage certificate to be shown to the witness.

"You sent that certificate now produced?"

"Yes."

"You wrote it?"

"My curate did."

"By your authority?"

"Yes."

"And with your knowledge and assent."

"Yes."

"I have no further questions."

Serjeant Alderson in the opening questions of his cross-examination got Father Maguire to admit that if he had thought he was marrying the couple, he would have made more diligent inquiries about Lord Ardmore's religion. He had not done so, he said, because he had never intended to do more than renew a consent given at an earlier marriage. Thus at the outset Alderson managed to inform the jury that Maguire had probably been mistaken about Clinton's lack of religion. To Clinton this seemed very little to set against Serjeant Mason's efforts.

"In your church," continued Alderson, "I believe there is a particular dress to be worn by clergymen celebrating marriages?"

"I object to that," snarled Serjeant Mason. "If he'd had a sack on his head, it wouldn't make any difference."

The Lord Chief Justice said that Serjeant Alderson could put his question.

"What way were you dressed then? In those special vestments?"

"No, sir. I wore a soutane."

"No other clerical dress at all?"

"No."

"Before the ceremony, were the banns registered?"

"They were not."

"Were two witnesses present in accordance with the law?"

432

"No."

"Did the parties swear to the lack of any impediment?"

"They did not."

"Did they sign the register of marriages?"

"They signed in another book. They knew it was not the church register."

"You told them that?"

"Yes."

"What did their refusal to sign the proper register make you think?"

"That the lady knew the ceremony was a blessing. I had never been in much doubt, but this convinced me."

"Did you have any other reason? What had first made you think the lady knew?"

"I had an instinct."

"Had it to do with confession?"

"I will not answer anything about confession."

"I certainly won't press you to. I have no more to ask."

"My lord," said Serjeant Mason, rising to re-examine, "the last exchanges were outrageous. An insinuation was made that cannot be challenged because of the seal of confession."

"The jury should discount the insinuation," replied the judge.

Mason looked at the priest with derision. "In the certificate you sent the lady, you described what you did as marriage. You also stated that this marriage had been recorded in the register. Do you deny that?"

"No. May I explain, my lord?"

"Answer this one question first," said Mason. "Since the lady knew the marriage was to be kept secret, was there anything strange in her agreement to sign a private register?"

"I thought so then."

"Why, sir?"

"An impression. I can't be more precise."

"You were precise enough with your certificate."

"When may I explain about it?" moaned the priest.

"You may do so now," said the judge.

"The lady told me she was expecting. I didn't want the child to be denied baptism. If I'd ever suspected the purpose the certificate was to be used for, I'd have cut off my hand before I gave it."

"You explain this in your letter to Lord Ardmore. It is on page twelve of the jury's printed documents." Maguire was handed his letter. "Did you write this to the defendant?"

"Yes."

"Why did you not produce his letter which prompted it?"

"I destroyed it."

"Why?"

"I foolishly thought I could forget the whole business. I wished I'd never seen the man."

"Didn't you destroy it because Lord Ardmore in his letter to you gave you warning that you could face prosecution for marrying a Protestant unless you wrote what he asked you to?"

"That was not my reason. I swore an affidavit on this. I swore the truth."

"We have under your hand as evidence two documents. They contradict each other, do they not?"

"For the reasons I gave."

"But one of them is still a falsehood." Serjeant Mason paused. "Before you go back to Rathnagar, answer me this question: Generally speaking, which do you consider the more important of these two—a letter or a certificate of marriage?"

"In general, the certificate."

"Tell me one more thing, and I am done. Is it usual for Catholic priests to issue false certificates of marriage?"

"It is not."

"That is all, sir."

The day ended on a note of bathos. Serjeant Mason decided not to call Esmond till the following day. Instead he put in the box a jeweler who claimed to have sold a wedding ring to Clinton—and actually had done—but who sounded unconvincing when cross-examined. Next came a maid and a waiter from the hotel where Clinton and Theresa had spent the night after their marriage. Both swore that Clinton had spoken of Theresa as his wife. Serjeant Alderson was not impressed, and destroyed them by asking whether in their experience many hotel guests who were unmarried cared to advertise the fact. And

434

last came the old man who had first driven Clinton to Rathnagar. His evidence favored the idea that Clinton had intended to marry somebody, but was almost entirely discredited by his admission that he had suggested Father Maguire because he would not be as scrupulous about regulations as most other priests in the district.

That evening, after the court had adjourned, Clinton, with Yeatman's clerk acting as intermediary, paid out over thirty pounds in a vain attempt to discover where Esmond was staying. But Esmond had clearly foreseen this, and had chosen not to stay in any of Dublin's principal hotels. In Clinton's opinion, Esmond not only held the key to who would win the case, but his words, and his alone, seemed destined to answer the question which tormented him above all others. Had Theresa practiced on him deception that made his own fault insignificant? That night he slept very little. It was bitterly cold, and from a clear sky the stars shone as brilliantly as on the evening he had set out with Theresa on the journey that was to take them to Rathnagar. He wondered whether in some other room in the sleeping city she too was looking at the stars—remembering.

CHAPTER FORTY-TWO

 During their short carriage ride from their hotel in Merrion Square to the Four Courts at the start of the second day, Major Simmonds handed Theresa a copy of the *Morning Register* folded open at the leader page.

We have no notion of making a martyr of such a person as Mrs. Barr. She is an adventuress, launched into the world nobody knows how, with a previous history that has never fully been told. Her father claims to have been an officer, but in what regiment or country we are not informed. He has been a speculator in many melodramas, and doubtless hopes that this new undertaking will bring him and his daughter richer rewards than their previous endeavours. The lady, if such she can be called, is made up of passion and prudence; of hard intellectual vigour and sensuous thoughts and feelings. She writes as no modest woman would write, and schemes as no modest woman would scheme. She has religious scruples, but they do not restrain her from living sinfully. The best that can be hoped for is that she will abandon that elevated world on which she has aspired to force herself. After this unseemly trial, we confide that society will do her the infinite kindness of consigning her once more to those theatrical regions where her talents will find more appreciative auditors.

Though the piece wounded Theresa, she was not surprised by it. The press had prematurely represented her as an innocent Catholic heroine and were going to punish her for their mistake. Like Romans at a gladiatorial combat, people would now only be interested to see which side inflicted the ugliest wounds. She handed back the paper in silence.

Her father looked as if about to weep, but instead he blurted out, "The adventuress . . . The whore. Isn't that what you'll be next?"

"They can't make me anything."

"Can't they?"

She looked out the window and said nothing. Dazed by her own misery, she felt neither anger nor pity for her father. At times she saw the trial as something so extraordinary and alien that it seemed impossible that it could have anything to do with her; then suddenly it's reality would dwarf and crush her own existence. She had felt, when Clinton's counsel had read out and derided her letters, that her memories no longer belonged to her; they had been wrenched and smeared now, beyond recognition. The people being talked about were not her or Clinton but strangers existing in another world. Yet there in the distance were the crowded bridges in front of the courts; the carriage was jolting across cobbles; in a few hours Clinton would be called to give evidence. Her perceptions could do nothing to diminish the reality of what was happening.

Her father said, "I suppose you know what people will think, because you were mad enough to say you *wanted* to be his mistress whether he meant to marry you or not? They'll say you only let him go so you could share that rich girl's money with him. I heard that said at the hotel."

After a silence, Theresa turned to him. "Have you thought what'll happen to him if you win?"

"He'll have to make amends for what he did to you."

"Could any man face the divorce courts or an appeal after this trial? That girl's family will sue him for breach of contract. And if they do, what will happen to him? He's as proud as you are."

As if unaware of her suffering, Simmonds said bitterly, "I don't think you need trouble your conscience. You did your best to ruin yourself yesterday." He picked up the newspaper on the seat between them and threw it to the floor.

Approaching the courts, they were recognized through the carriage windows. Men and boys started running alongside them, jumping up to get an unobstructed view. Blurred and senseless faces, bobbing in and out of sight like grotesque puppets or jumping jacks. Theresa shuddered as the coachman whipped up the horses to avoid being forced to a halt; and as the faces fell away, she could not help remembering Clinton laughing as he drove full-tilt at the angry crowd barring their way out of a small market square in the west.

Neither side wished to call her again, so Theresa was allowed to watch the proceedings in court. Her father was the first witness to be examined that day, and since he was only to be asked to confirm that he had lent her the sum which was now claimed from Clinton, Theresa did not expect his stay in the witness box to be long or eventful. But when Serjeant Alderson began to cross-examine with the same supercilious smile he had worn so often the day before, she saw her father grow rigid with anger. Alderson started by trying to get her father to say what he thought her theatrical earnings had been in the six months after she parted with the defendant.

When Alderson failed to establish a figure, his smile faded. "I put it to you, Major Simmonds, if loans were to be made during this period, Mrs. Barr was better able to make them than yourself?"

"Not when I advanced the sum in question."

"Well, we know she earned more than that soon afterwards. I suggest that she asked you to lend her money so that Lord Ardmore could be threatened with proceedings like these. So he would be forced to acknowledge her as his wife?"

"She begged me not to bring this action."

"That may be so, Major. But did she beg you not to *threaten* to bring it?"

"She wanted nothing to do with it in any shape."

"Come now, Major. Wasn't it only when she saw that Lord Ardmore wasn't going to be cowed by threats that she begged you not to bring the issue to an actual trial?"

438

"That's not true, sir."

"Well, whether she wanted him threatened or not, I can understand why she begged you not to let it come to court. She begged you not to, didn't she?"

"She did, sir."

Alderson nodded, his smile once more seeming as fixed and permanent as an engraving. "I put it to you that she begged you not to because she was not Lord Ardmore's lawful wife and knew it. Isn't that what she told you?"

Then her father began to shout, and though the judge warned him, Theresa could see that nothing would stop him. "She still loves him, sir. That's your reason why she begged me. Didn't want him harmed. So she lied on oath—brought shame on herself to protect him." Again the judge intervened and was ignored. "She was never his mistress, only his wife. I know her, sir." Even when her father was escorted from the box, he was still shouting. "She was going to have his child . . . nearly died. She wouldn't see my counsel . . . wouldn't even do that. She hopes he'll get off . . ." The doors of the court swung shut behind him, snuffing out his voice with eerie suddenness.

Theresa looked at the shocked faces of the jury as she heard Mason apologizing for his client's behavior. But what her father had said meant nothing to her. What made her want to scream was the dawning fear that Clinton might believe his counsel's arguments. And now there was nothing she could do to let him know that she was guiltless. Even if she could speak to him alone, she wondered whether he would believe that she had played no part in his ruin.

When Esmond took the stand, it took Serjeant Mason few questions to elicit from him that he had told the lady that Lord Ardmore wanted to marry her. He stared straight ahead of him, and spoke in a quiet dead voice.

"When did you tell her this?"

"About two weeks before she left for Dublin."

"Did you suggest anything to her which might have made her think Lord Ardmore contemplated any other form of relations with her?"

"You mean other than marriage?"

"Well?"

"Marriage was the only word I used."

When Mason had finished, even though Theresa realized that if Esmond's evidence convinced the jury it would effectively clear her of having knowingly participated in a fraudulent ceremony, she felt despair rather than relief. She had sworn that she had thought the marriage true only because she had been unable to bring herself to lie about it. Esmond too had sworn truthfully, and between them they had brought Clinton almost to destruction.

Serjeant Alderson's manner was as unruffled as at any time in the trial when he rose to cross-examine. "Mr. Danvers," he began softly, "did Lord Ardmore make Mrs. Barr his mistress at Kilkreen Castle?"

"I believe so," murmured Esmond, coloring deeply.

"He gave you good reason to dislike him, did he not?"

Suppressed laughter came from the gallery.

"He did."

"Very well, sir. When you saw Mrs. Barr in York, what was your purpose?"

"To persuade her not to marry Lord Ardmore."

Alderson pulled a handkerchief from his pocket and blew his nose as though suddenly bored. Then he rapped out, "By virtue of your oath, sir, was there ever any occasion, before you saw Mrs. Barr in York, when you heard the Irish Marriage Act spoken of in Lord Ardmore's hearing?"

After a long silence, Esmond nodded. "My mother once mentioned reading about a court case involving it. There was no particular reason why. The subject arose by chance."

"When did this conversation take place?"

"The autumn before last—1866."

"Do you recall anything Lord Ardmore said during this conversation?"

"As far as I remember, he showed no interest."

"I see," said the serjeant suavely. "Now, sir, your brother had told you he was thinking of marrying Mrs. Barr. Did you subsequently give any thought to where this marriage might take place?"

"Not beyond the fact that it would be in an out-of-the-way place."

"The need for secrecy would have made Ireland very suitable?"

"No more than many other places."

Serjeant Alderson leaned forward. "I put it to you that because Lord Ardmore was stationed in Ireland it must have occurred to you that he would consider marrying her in this country."

"It may have crossed my mind. I can't remember."

"Sir," snapped Alderson, "since Lord Ardmore had shown *no interest* in the possible legal pitfalls, didn't you think it advisable to warn Mrs. Barr about the consequences of marrying your brother in the country where he was stationed?"

For the first time since taking the stand, Esmond appeared shaken. He said vehemently, "If I'd mentioned it, she would have thought I was trying to damage him in her eyes. She wouldn't have listened."

"You didn't consider it worth telling her in case she did listen?"

"It could have made her doubt the other reasons I put forward to persuade her not to marry."

Serjeant Alderson shook his head sadly. "Mr. Danvers, did you not say you wished to dissuade her from accepting your brother?"

"I did."

"Well then, sir, it must surely have been clear to you that if you told Mrs. Barr what your mother had said in Lord Ardmore's hearing, and he had then suggested an Irish marriage, her confidence in him would have been considerably reduced?"

"I said nothing to her about it. I explained why." Esmond broke off and then burst out bitterly: "You imply that I came here to harm my brother by protecting the lady. It's not true. I never wished this on him—never. I'm here because I was subpoenaed by the plaintiff's lawyers."

Alderson looked at him with raised brows. "*I* made no accusation of that sort, sir. You may go down now. I have no further questions."

At that moment Theresa glanced at Clinton, and the misery and tension in his face overwhelmed her. Though Esmond had indeed said no word to her about Irish marriages, Alderson had undermined him so skillfully that perhaps the majority in the courtroom would now believe that he had warned her. Nothing Theresa had suffered during her cross-examination approached the pain she felt as it dawned upon her that Clinton would think this too. And if he did, her evidence would seem perjured to him, and every claim she had ever made about belief in her marriage a pack of lies. Because Alderson had undoubtedly helped the defense by discrediting Esmond, Clinton's dejection could only be explained by loss of faith in her and in everything they had once shared. In a daze, Theresa heard Serjeant Alderson begin his opening speech for the defense.

"May it please your lordship, gentlemen of the jury, it is now my solemn duty to lay before you the case for the defendant. Before drawing your attention to the evidence, I must first warn you against the absurd error of looking upon this case as one between Major Simmonds and Lord Ardmore. In this action, the major is a mere stalking-horse for his daughter."

Alderson went on to remind the jury of various answers Theresa had given in cross-examination, and quoted again passages from letters—especially the comments she had made on the impossibility of marriage in her letter to Clinton sent shortly before the ceremony.

"In the same letter," he continued blandly, "she quoted a dissolute French monarch's complaint about marriage with relish: '*Perdrix, toujours perdrix.*' I confess I rather enjoy partridge, but really, gentlemen, was that a fit way to speak of the life of mutual dedication which she wishes us to suppose she had in mind when she went to Rathnagar? Gentlemen of the jury, I have no intention of doing the lady the injustice of trying to give you a better picture of her than the one she herself presented in her letters and in the witness box. Who can gainsay that she can be witty and clever? In her own words, she is 'no lover of convention.' I have no doubt that she knows Latin as well as she knows French. I am sure, if asked, she could instruct us all in the wiles of the sirens who lured men to disaster.

"Actresses, gentlemen, must be women of the world. Without resourcefulness and cunning they would hardly make their livings in so ruthless a profession. I leave it to you to judge which of the two would be most likely to lead the other—the experienced actress or the young army officer whose upbringing had been so very different from the lady's? Counsel for the plaintiff will have us believe that the lady was seduced and led astray by my client. The poor actress scarcely knew what she was about when she gave herself to Lord Ardmore at Kilkreen Castle and again in York. I flatter myself that you will laugh at such an absurd proposition. She captivated Lord Ardmore and, having done so, ran away to York. I ask you to consider what could have been more enticing than this sudden virtuous flight after she had given him a single taste of pleasure? Could any action have been better calculated to excite a hot-blooded man's passion? I don't deny that Lord Ardmore behaved foolishly in taking the hook that she had so temptingly baited. Doubtless he should be censured morally. But, gentlemen, if any man in this court is tempted to throw stones, let him think of his own youth, and ask whether his conscience is clear before he judges too harshly."

Serjeant Alderson bowed his head and sighed. "Gentlemen, I do not intend to challenge the testimony of Mr. Danvers. I rely too much on your good sense. You must decide whether it is likely that a man who wished to stop a marriage would not have used the one piece of information most likely to prevent it. Well, he swore that he never breathed a word about Irish marriages to the lady, and we can only wonder at it. No matter; he told the lady that lawful marriage to her would ruin Lord Ardmore, and I think you will agree that Mrs. Barr is no witless innocent, unaware that a wife falls with her husband. You must draw your own conclusions.

"Gentlemen she asked you to believe that secrecy banished every difficulty. I won't remind you of my questions to her on that subject and her prevaricating replies. Her testimony is that she entered the church perfectly confident that an impeccable marriage was to be celebrated. She saw nothing strange that the priest was wearing the garb he rides about his parish in and hitches up when he digs his garden. I mean no disrespect, but such was the case. No banns had been registered, the church was locked and no witnesses allowed in. They never signed the public register, the priest did not make the routine inquiries whether they were free to marry. And this travesty Mrs. Barr chooses to see as a perfect marriage and not the imposture it obviously was. Well, gentlemen, when she released Lord Ardmore, she proved what she really thought was done at the altar. Certainly she made her confession first, but would she be the very first Roman Catholic who ever received absolution and then committed a sin an hour or two later? Gentlemen, one thing you may be sure, we are not talking about a saint.

"It is up to you whether you believe that she indeed thought herself his wife; but if she did, what possible use could she have had for a marriage certificate? And more pertinent still, why did she keep her correspondence with the priest a secret from Lord Ardmore? I confidently assure you that he will swear that she did. Is it not certain that she needed that piece of paper because she hoped to force my client to make that mock marriage into a binding union? Can there be any other explanation? Gentlemen, that certificate was obtained by a miserable subterfuge. She told the priest it was only to be used for a baptism. You heard the use Serjeant Mason made of that document, so you can judge how well the lady kept her promise to the man who had tried to help her. Why then did she not use it?

"Lord Ardmore will tell you that she agreed to free him shortly after he had been imprisoned for debt, and within days of his failure to gain financial assistance from his uncle. As proof of this intention, she gave him the written undertaking which you have already seen. No, gentlemen, I do not ask you to believe that any practicing Catholic would have agreed to free a husband whom she believed she had wedded before God. If he had owed millions, I would not believe that of Mrs. Barr."

He paused to drink some water. At times as she listened, Theresa had been numbed far beyond resentment or despair; the man's words came at her, wave after wave, too fast for her to recover from the impact of one falsehood before the next broke around her, and all surging by with a plausibility and force that made her fragmentary recollections seem light and useless. For brief intervals she heard and saw everything with perfect lucidity, and then individual words struck her like darts of pain: *travesty, imposture, subterfuge.* And all she could remember was her happiness on that day, and her certainty that in no place in any country could she have been more truly married. Never, she thought, never would they be able to unravel this web of lies; what was being done would never be mended.

"What induced the lady to go back on her word is not a subject on which I intend to speculate," continued the barrister. "Jealousy, vindictiveness—I cannot tell. But one thing is beyond question—she decided to bring the defendant to this court, and by doing so has brought about his utter ruin. Gentlemen, do not misunderstand me; I do not condone what my client did in the church at Rathnagar. Though the priest abetted him, the marriage service was used for a purpose for which it was never intended; and that was a great fault. But that is no reason why you should decide he is married. The more you condemn him, the more you will see that he meant no marriage. Is that not his real fault, gentlemen?

"A few more words and I will be done, so bear with me. Regardless of any words spoken at the altar, and even if at the end of this hearing you believe what I do not—namely that a marriage took place—then I must remind you of that Act of Parliament which my learned friend so much detests. Gentlemen, if I prove that Lord Ardmore was a professing Protestant at any time in the twelve months before the ceremony, then you cannot find for the plaintiff. You must perform your duty according to the truth and in your hands I now leave the case."

When Clinton was called to the witness box a few minutes later to be examined by his counsel, Theresa could not bear to look at him; she felt that if he repeated the lies she had just heard, she would lose her reason. As he began to speak the words of the oath, she left the courtroom. Yet outside in the circular hall she was no better off; her heart was still beating wildly. Like a fog that could penetrate closed doors, the atmosphere of the court still enveloped her; she was hemmed in, imprisoned by it and would never breathe pure air again until she had lived through what was to come. She imagined herself walking away along the quays, watching carriages pass, the brown river flowing on, everything continuing—everything except her. Minutes were passing, and indecision held her: a feeling of deep destroying panic. She had to go in again. Behind those doors her life was being lived for her against her will; no attitude of hers or physical absence could change that fact. And still she did not move. Her past was a lost continent, the future quite unknown; her only way to reach it was to return and hear him speak. That alone would free her.

She had been away longer than she thought, because Clinton's counsel only asked a single question before sitting down. Apart from Mrs. Barr's written undertaking to let him go, had there been anything else done at their parting to make him suppose the lady thought her marriage void? Clinton said that the ring she had worn since the ceremony was returned to him.

Then Serjeant Mason rose and asked in the indifferent tone he might have used to inquire about some trivial detail, "Lord Ardmore, did you ever love Theresa Barr?"

"I did."

"Did you ever love her purely and honorably?"

"Yes."

"You're not ashamed to make that answer?"

"No."

"Then answer this: Is seduction of a gentlewoman pure or honorable?"

"I think I'd use other words."

"Do you deny that you seduced her?"

"In the sense that you mean it, yes."

"Words can mean what you like, can they? Then try another one. Is she a gentlewoman?"

"A woman of gentle blood?"

"Is blood all that makes a lady, sir? Has education nothing to say to it, think you? Belief in religion? Accomplishments? Manners?"

"I respected her sincerely."

"You thought her a lady fit to marry any man, whatever his rank?"

"Yes."

His quiet firm voice and counsel's hectoring self-righteous tone froze Theresa.

She heard Mason's grating voice: "Was it not shameful to seduce such a woman?"

"There are seductions and seductions."

"Don't fence with me, sir. Do you mean to tell me that the seduction of a gentlewoman can sometimes be laudable?"

"When a woman's eagerness is equal to the man's, and her marriage, or hope of marriage, isn't endangered, then a liaison can't be so harmful to her."

"So that's your morality, is it? A deed is only blameworthy if it's found out."

"I said nothing about blame. A man who has a liaison with a woman who isn't dependent on her family or a husband obviously knows he can't ruin her. I don't say it excuses him, but I think it's an important consideration."

"Then you think it's perfectly acceptable to seduce a woman who is clever enough to earn her own living? Is there no blame in interrupting the career of a widow obliged to support herself and her child?"

"I gave up my own career so I could support her while hers was interrupted. I believe when my own resources failed, she resumed it with tolerable ease."

"And was there no moral harm? Has a man the right to defile a woman simply because his action won't make her a beggar?"

"You'd do better to ask a clergyman."

"Because you have no morals of your own? Perhaps you can answer me this, sir: Did you first determine to make the lady your mistress when she was a guest in your mother's house?"

"I determined nothing."

"Events surprised you, did they?"

"Yes."

"I intend to discover how surprising that seduction was. How did the first indecent familiarities come about? Where were you at the time?"

"My lord," objected Serjeant Alderson, "how can such details be material? This is a court of law and not of morals."

"Since you dispute what occurred in church, I believe such details are material," replied the judge. "I cannot see how counsel for the plaintiff can be expected to throw light on what actually occurred without trying to establish the previous circumstances and attitudes of the parties. For this reason I allowed you to examine Mrs. Barr about her letters. It would be wholly inconsistent if I now refused to let Serjeant Mason ask the defendant about his intentions and behavior toward the lady prior to the ceremony." The judge looked up at the gallery and said loudly, "I am not going to order the ladies in court to leave while this cross-examination continues, but I give you due warning that counsel's questions may be indelicate, and in my view you will avoid exposing yourself to an unpleasant scene if you go out now."

Theresa felt sick as she watched almost every woman in the crowded courtroom rise and leave. Earlier she had observed not a few looking at Clinton with silly smiles that they could not conceal. Clinton appeared completely indifferent to the departure of the women; evidently resigned to the worst, he seemed inhumanly detached. Yet when Mason addressed him again, Theresa saw his hands tighten on the rail of the witness box.

"Well, sir, when and in what manner did familiarities first take place betweeen you?"

"Do you mean, when did I first touch her?"

"Quite so."

"I kissed her in the saddle room of the stables at Kilkreen Castle. Incidentally, I should be obliged if you would stop calling it my mother's house. I own it, and she has a life interest."

Mason bowed. "I stand reproved." The barrister folded his arms in the sleeves of his gown. "Isn't it somewhat singular, Lord Ardmore, that you asked Mrs. Barr to join you in a deserted room in the stables, when according to your word you had no intentions of any sort concerning her?"

"I found her attractive. I said to you that I never had a conscious design to make her my mistress."

"Was it chance that brought you both into the saddle room at the same moment?"

"She had been watching the horses. I suppose I suggested she looked at the rest of the stables."

"That won't do, sir. We must be more particular. In his speech my learned friend suggested that Mrs. Barr is such a calculating siren that an innocent young gentlemen like yourself would hardly have known what he was doing when he was in her company. Just let loose from your mother's apron strings, you had no chance against the wiles of this temptress bent on dragging you to the altar. That was what my learned friend implied. Well, sir, did the siren lure you into that room against your will?"

"I told you I made the suggestion."

"With what object, sir?"

"I wanted to be alone with her."

"And she, thinking you a gentleman, did not suspect your motive?"

"I don't know what she thought."

"Did you make the first move, Lord Ardmore, or did the enchantress surprise you before you could resist?"

"We took that fence together, sir."

"Just like that? Without premeditation?"

"Would you have had us discuss it first?"

"I ask the questions, sir. Is it normal in your experience for titled army officers who have distinguished themselves on active service to be surprised into kissing women with no previous idea that they might do so?"

"I doubt it."

"Of course you do. You took her in there determined to dishonor her, did you not?"

"I did not."

"What were your next dealings with the lady?"

"I tried to tell her that we ought not to see each other again."

"Tried to? Was it so hard? Perhaps the siren frightened you."

"It was hard because I loved her. I was alarmed for a number of reasons—money, my brother's feelings, the impossibility of offering her much. I considered marriage out of the

449

question. Anyway she cut the ground from under me by imitating the sort of speech men make on such occasions."

"And that changed everything?" asked Mason with scathing mockery.

"I loved her more for it. That was all. I couldn't face making a decision there and then. I suggested we go away from the house to discuss what we ought to do. I wanted time. We drove in an open carriage. It rained and we took shelter in a barn. Yes, it was my suggestion."

Mason tugged at his wig, as if bemused. "I understood that you wished to prevent an entanglement with the lady. Was that why you took her out alone with you in a carriage and then, for the sake of a shower of rain, invited her into a barn?"

"It was more than a shower."

"Come, sir. If the sun had been shining, would you not have gone in there?"

"No."

"Did you attempt her virtue in that building?"

"I won't answer the question phrased in that way."

"Find your own words, sir. I offer you the whole vocabulary."

"She became my mistress."

"Again without premeditation on your part? Were you too innocent a young gentleman?"

"I made the first move and she responded."

"Because you seduced her. Because you drove her to that place and then invited her to go in with you. Is that not so?"

"I volunteered that information myself."

"When she went in with you out of the rain, had she not the right to suppose herself safe with an officer and a gentleman?"

"If she had found what I did unwelcome, I wouldn't have been left in ignorance for long."

"When she removed to York, did she encourage you to follow her?"

"No."

"And was it your proposition that she should stay with you in Dublin?"

"It was."

"Did she think you loved her honorably?"

"I believe so."

"Did she trust you?"

"I thought so at the time."

Theresa heard his qualification with a painful contraction of the heart. Apart from flickers of impatience, his answers often sounded coldly retrospective, as though the events described had long since ceased to concern him deeply. But she knew he would be determined not to allow counsel or the gloating audience the satisfaction of seeing his wounds. Theresa had dreaded hearing him lie; and yet as long as he answered truthfully, he stood before her as victim and scapegoat. While this continued, regardless of betrayal, their past still strained and tightened about her heart.

Mason said, "You told us your love was honorable. Now, sir, by virtue of your oath, did you take her into God's house intending to deceive her?"

"I did."

Relief and savage disillusion warred within her, their impact softened by succeeding waves of shock. She was trembling.

The barrister leaned forward. "Were your vows at the altar nothing but mockery?"

"I meant to sustain and protect her for the rest of my days. I believed that the ceremony was not good in law, but I felt bound in conscience."

"In conscience bound as her husband?" Counsel's excitement communicated itself to every corner of the court.

"I believed that until we married in England, we would not be man and wife."

"So you intended to marry her?" cried Mason triumphantly.

"By another ceremony. I was afraid to let her leave Ireland without thinking herself bound to me. I was afraid I would lose her if I did. That was the construction I put on her letter when she said marriage was impossible. The priest warned me the ceremony would have no effect. I believed him, but decided to go through with it."

"What prevented you going through a second ceremony?"

"My debts. The certainty of imprisonment. I should have been truthful with her about the ceremony far sooner. But I thought it'd be easier for her after a few months. Then she became pregnant; later she was ill. And all the time I delayed my position grew worse."

His only emotion as he spoke seemed one of flat regret, as though he were recounting something inevitable and final that freed him from all need to speak with grief or defiance. Facts were facts regardless. Theresa looked at him in astonishment. In the space of seconds he had overturned the seemingly impregnable castle his counsel had built for him and left it a mound of useless rubble. But for all the concern he showed, he might have said nothing of any importance. Even Serjeant Mason was speechless. At last he recovered and began to question Clinton about his church attendance. How many times had he been to church parade? Had he been to any other Protestant places of worship? Was it true that he had been to Mass with Mrs. Barr after the marriage ceremony? Had he ever attended the Anglican church at Browsholme when living at Hathenshaw? At this last question, Theresa was surprised to see Clinton smile, as if this inconsequence suited the trial better than solemnity or indignation.

After several more questions, Serjeant Mason said, "So the year before the ceremony, you attended military church parade five times and never once took the sacrament?"

"True, sir."

Mason looked at him almost with pity. "Lord Ardmore, how can that make you a professing Protestant?"

"I was listed as a Protestant in the regiment's quarterly returns."

"And *that* is proof of religious belief?"

"In the army it is."

"Your duty obliged you to march your men to church once every two months and *that* made you a Protestant?"

"I wouldn't have been required to do it if I'd been a Catholic."

"Isn't church parade referred to in the army as prayer drill?"

"In the cavalry any sort of drill is taken seriously."

"Come, Lord Ardmore, didn't most of your men sleep or play cards under the pews? Isn't that the level of devotion displayed on these occasions?"

"It never was in my regiment."

452

"Because you put them on charges if they did?"

"Certainly."

"They behaved themselves under threat of loss of pay or being confined to barracks?"

"Some of them. Others may have been afraid of hell. I never acted as their confessor, so I can't vouch for them."

"Then vouch for yourself. What solemn act of religious observance can you claim to have performed beyond the bare performance of a routine military duty?"

"I once read the prayers when the chaplain was ill. I believe that was a profession of Protestantism."

"You mean you spoke the words of certain prayers?"

"Spoke them aloud in front of five hundred witnesses in a Protestant church."

"Lord Ardmore, as regimental adjutant wouldn't such a duty inevitably have fallen to you in the chaplain's absence?"

"The colonel or second-in-command might just as well have discharged it."

"Perhaps they were ill too. I have no other questions, sir."

Throughout his evidence, Theresa had never once seen Clinton look at her. But just before he left the box, he gazed at her steadily for several seconds. Long afterwards she could still see his face with piercing clarity—calm at first, almost amused, as though willing her to share an ironic joke, then clouding opaquely like a dead eye. So, although she never looked away, she felt later that her answering gaze had made no more impression than a pebble skittering across thick ice. Her throat felt tight and weary as if with weeping.

Through tears she saw the blurred courtroom: unknown faces against dirty walls, the judge's canopy, black legal gowns. Beyond the tall windows was the city they had walked through in hope—the Castle, the barracks, their hotel—and every detail clear to her. She thought, Nothing dies completely until forgotten. An hour ago their whole past had seemed soiled and outraged beyond recognition. But suddenly she knew it was not so. At last she thought she saw why Clinton had not tried to save himself with lies. Had it not oeen to salvage something of their past and what they had been to each other? *And does he think I betrayed him?* She looked round fearfully, hoping to learn something from his face, but he had not returned to his usual place.

When it ends, she told herself, I shall explain everything to him. And though she did not know how, or even whether he would agree to see her, the thought soothed her. For a moment it seemed to her that sanity and forgiveness had stolen unnoticed into the hushed and hostile room.

CHAPTER FORTY-THREE

Theresa did not go to the Four Courts on the third day of the trial to hear the closing speeches of opposing counsel. Like the courtroom itself, the whole city had become for her a stifling closed-in world, a place she had to escape from, if only for a few hours. She engaged an inside car and told the driver to take her westward in the direction of Lucan. Passing the Phoenix Park, she heard through the windows the music of a band and saw a thin crowd pressing against the park railings. The sky was a muddy sepia, and swathes of mist lay under the dripping trees. The music grew louder, a gay confident march. Through gaps in the mist she saw ghostly formations of foot soldiers and cavalry moving in front of the viceregal lodge; the brightness of uniforms and the gleam of metal were soft and muted in the morning light. Her driver slowed down and told her that they were rehearsing for the Lord Lieutenant's birthday review. He seemed surprised that she did not ask him to stop. There was a pause in the music and she heard words of command and a bugle call.

In memory she was crossing a barrack square with Clinton, absorbed by his pride in everything he showed her. A lost world now, a thousand times less substantial than the dimly moving figures in the mist. She felt anger as well as sadness.

455

Pride in position, pride in esteem, even pride in love—pride that could not admit the fault, which, if admitted in time, could have saved them.

The band again, its music fainter now but still as sprightly and full of purpose. She could not bear to hear it.

The judge began his summing up at the start of the fourth day by thanking the jury for their attention with polite formality, and then outlining the form and substance of the action.

"Gentlemen," he continued, "the plaintiff, Major Simmonds, rests his case on establishing that the ceremony which took place on January sixth, 1867, in the chapel at Rathnagar was a lawful marriage. In law, marriage is a contract which can be proved like any other by a clear intent expressed by the parties. Counsel for the defendant wished us to believe that there had been no such intent and that Mrs. Barr had known beforehand that the ceremony would be a blessing rather than a marriage. Now if the defendant himself had supported his own counsel's argument, your task would not be a very hard one. However Lord Ardmore did something else entirely. He said that his intent was to marry, and he only considered he had not done so because a certain law made the ceremony void.

"Gentlemen, I will return to that law later, but now let me tell you plainly that if a man plights his troth before a minister, his unspoken reservations make no difference to the validity of his spoken vows. It is laid down in numerous judgments that all acts done by a person competent to contract are presumed to intend what they appear to, unless there is overwhelming evidence of fraud. Lord Ardmore's testimony shows that there is no such evidence in this case. There is no conflict of testimony about the words spoken at the altar, and regardless of any omissions in ceremonial, I have no hesitation in telling you that what occurred on that occasion amounts to a marriage in fact."

The Lord Chief Justice paused a moment to allow the murmuring in the gallery to subside. He then went on to explain that the marriage could only be lawful if it complied with the Irish Marriage Act, and went on to quote the relevant words. If the defendant had been a professing Protestant at the time of the ceremony, or during the twelve preceding months, the marriage could not be legally binding. The judge then repeated the evidence advanced to prove the defendant's religious allegiance.

"Gentlemen, it is my duty to tell you the law as clearly as I can, and then it will be yours to form your own opinion on the merits of the evidence placed before you. Profession of a particular faith is proved where an individual can establish that he has regularly performed religious acts which no member of any other church would have done. You must decide whether reading the prayers at church parade is such an act. Whether you think so may depend upon the weight you give to Lord Ardmore's presence at Mass at Rathnagar and the absence of all other religious acts unconnected with military duty. I must however remind you of Lord Campbell's recent ruling: Unless a man clearly breaks with the religion he was brought up to profess, and does so by positive acts and not simply by omission, then it should be assumed that his original religion remains. Well, Lord Ardmore's upbringing was Protestant. So, did he sever that childhood allegiance by positive acts? The Reverend Mr. Maguire swore that Lord Ardmore claimed to have no religion. If you discount the reverend gentleman's testimony, you should ask yourself whether Lord Ardmore's presence at Mass after his marriage in a Catholic church can be deemed an act sufficient to nullify the presumption of Protestantism arising from his upbringing."

When the Lord Chief Justice went on to cite more cases, Theresa's mind became blurred. What could these trials of years ago have to do with what she and Clinton had done so recently? That his reluctant decision to attend Mass should be elevated to an act of awesome solemnity dumfounded her. Everything she was hearing seemed to have the absurd logic of a nightmare, absurd but unchallengeable. The names of judges and litigants of the past echoed in her head with no more meaning than nursery doggerel. When she saw the jurors taking notes, she wanted to shout at them to stop being such fools. With an effort she listened to what the judge was saying.

"I do not think it improper to assist you with this final observation: Where a marriage has been solemnized, the law strongly presumes in favor of its validity. Therefore the onus of proof that he had professed himself a Protestant is squarely on the defendant. The plaintiff is under no equivalent obligation in this respect to disprove what the defendant avers. Gentlemen, your decision on this matter will determine for you whether the marriage complies with the laws of this country. If you conclude that it does, then you will find for the plaintiff. Otherwise the defendant is entitled to your verdict. It is now for you to consider these questions and in due course to inform me of your conclusion."

When the jury had retired, fear swept away Theresa's incredulity. What would be done if they decided she was Clinton's wife? She looked around but could not see him anywhere in court. Twenty minutes passed before the jury returned and the Lord Chief Justice once more took his seat on the bench. Silence fell spontaneously without the usher's intervention.

"How say you, gentlemen?" asked the judge. "Was there a lawful marriage?"

"Yes, my lord," replied the foreman.

"Then you find the defendant was not a professing Protestant in the twelve months preceding his marriage?"

"We believe he was not, my lord."

Before the foreman had finished speaking, a ragged cheer rose from the back of the gallery where the less well-to-do had congregated—a sound not so much of moral satisfaction as of sporting delight that an actress had got the better of a nobleman and won herself a coronet. The proud had been humbled, and the meek exalted, which was rare enough in life. Whether her ladyship deserved her good fortune was beside the point; like the winner of a lottery, her luck itself was worth applauding. The Catholics had beaten the Protestants, and that was something else to celebrate. A lot more money had been staked on the woman than the man. Only the respectable preserved an enigmatic silence. Aristocratic scandals were undeniably entertaining, but they tended to make ordinary people insolent.

That evening Corporal Harris brought a note from his master to Theresa's hotel. In it, Clinton told her that he intended to go to Kilkreen for a few days and suggested that she come there to discuss their future before their lawyers met to decide a settlement. Harris had personally placed the letter in Theresa's hand, and waited outside the room while she read it.

After several minutes he knocked. "Is there any answer, my lady?" The man spoke softly but his eyes were cold and hostile.

"Tell him I'll come." As the servant was walking away, she called after him, "And, Harris, never call me 'my lady' again."

CHAPTER FORTY-FOUR

A week after the trial ended, Theresa was at Kilkreen. Finding on her arrival that Clinton was out with the land agent, she decided to go in search of him rather than wait for his return. Her anxiety to get their first confrontation behind her and the memories the house evoked combined to make any course preferable to passive idleness. She sent a maid to the stables to summon the coachman, but the girl returned with the news that the old man had refused to get out the barouche for anyone except his mistress, and had claimed to have no idea where his lordship might be. The maid suggested that Lord Ardmore's valet might be more helpful. Though she did not want to call on Harris for assistance, the sight of the circling rooks through the leaded windows, and her constant fear of hearing the dowager's cane on the stairs, persuaded Theresa to accept the man's services.

Half an hour later she was seated beside him in the same trap that Clinton had driven on the day that had changed their lives. Around her the same brown hills and sparse fields, the same small reedy tarns and limestone rocks. A woman in a blue petticoat who had been digging in a patch of bog near a cabin threw down her spade and ran inside as soon as she caught sight of the trap. Then a man came out and blew several sharp blasts on a horn. Without moving his eyes from the road ahead, Harris explained to her that because Clinton had given notice of eviction to over a dozen families near Clonmore, the tenants for miles around were nervous about the sudden appearance of bailiffs, and had taken precautions to warn each other.

"Says he should have done it years back." Harris grinned. "He's clearing two hundred acres of best arable land. Can't leave it just for grazing with such arrears owed on it."

Theresa nodded abstractedly while Harris talked about plans to drain other areas and to resettle the graziers on hill farms. She found it incredible that Clinton could be concerning himself with such things so soon after the trial. Some snipe rose above a lake away to their right, and Harris raised an imaginary gun. He was dressed in the strange combination of civilian and military clothes she remembered from Hathenshaw.

They did not find Clinton in the village, and returned in the direction of Kilkreen along the coast road. The tide was out, and on the sands local people were gathering the reddish colored seaweed in cartloads. On a promontory near a makeshift jetty were some fishing boats, and back from the shore a few stone houses. Just past this hamlet, Harris raised his cap and shouted. A hundred yards away across the sand, two mounted men were talking to some more weed gatherers. Another shout, and Clinton turned his horse and trotted towards them, followed by his agent. As his master dismounted, Harris got down from the trap and took his horse. When the valet and agent had gone on ahead, Clinton clambered up next to Theresa.

After a long silence broken only by the wind and waves, Theresa turned to him. "Why didn't you try to help yourself?"

He smiled and looked down at the reins. "Nothing dies harder than the desire to think well of oneself."

One of the laden carts was leaving the beach, men pushing from behind to help the donkey drag it across the soft sand.

"Manure for the spring sowing," he explained with deliberate bathos. He lifted the reins and clicked his tongue. A little later he said, "The damage was done when we went to court. Losing made no odds at all."

"No odds when it made me your wife?"

"You won't find it hard to get an annulment."

461

His tone was calmly factual, and not bitter. But its remoteness still cut her to the heart. Every sentimental illusion she had brought with her, every hope that something might be retrieved, was fading now. He pulled at the nearside rein to avoid a mound of shingle thrown up from the beach, and said quite gently, "I could only have won by calling you a liar."

"Why didn't you?" she whispered.

"I believed Esmond's evidence. Don't look so grateful. I'd have lied like the devil if I'd thought you'd pushed your father into it. But when I saw his exhibition in court, I had to change my mind." He looked out to sea and sighed. "After that, I said what I had to—my own opinion mattering more to me than the court's."

Suddenly she was breathless with excitement. "But don't you see, Clinton, that changes everything? You trust me." His silence scared her. "Say something to me."

"What's happened stays the same."

"No," she said vehemently, "our view of things changes them."

He looked mystified. "My view of things? Will it help me when I'm sued for breach of promise? When I have to pay your father's costs? Will it wipe away what was said in court?" He glanced at her and took her hand. "Of course I'm glad they didn't make us hate each other. Don't think I'm not. But I'm still done for."

"Only if you believe you are."

He smiled at her and shook his head. "It's kind of you to say so. But I'm afraid belief doesn't come into it. It's very uplifting to think one can adapt to anything. I only wish it was true."

They drove on in silence towards the house.

Before Theresa had come to Kilkreen, Clinton's mother had told him that she would not leave her room while "that woman" was in the house. For this reason Clinton and Theresa dined alone. The meal was well advanced when he began to talk about the trial, but very soon, in spite of his ironic manner, Theresa understood what hurt him most—the idea that counsel's jibes and mockery had made their suffering absurd.

Though he did not mention the worst questions, she recalled them all. Did you defile her in there? Would you not have gone in if the sun had been shining? Everything reduced to grotesque indignity. Tragedy made farcical.

"Did it make what we did together seem futile to you?"

He put down his knife and thought for a moment. "If I could find words for it, it might not seem so bad."

His calmness and resignation suddenly made her angry. "Why did you ask me here, Clinton? Why? Why?"

"To ask what you want."

"You've already decided—annulment. I didn't dream what you said."

"Tell me then," he murmured.

"We're married. We ought to try again. Are you too proud to accept a second chance simply because you didn't choose it?"

His eyes were fixed on the tureen between them. He did not raise them. "I was accepted by another woman after deserting you."

"But the reasons!" she cried.

"Oh yes, reasons." He met her eyes at last. "Do you think it's a good foundation to build on?"

"How do I know? Don't we have to try first?"

He rested his chin in his hands. "I don't know. I can't say what I feel. Perhaps in a month or two." He paused. "No, I admit I thought you'd want an annulment. I wanted to tell you what sort of settlement I could manage . . . before the lawyers made an even greater mess of it. I thought you ought to know I'm not going to appeal. I came here to put the estate in order. Not just money. I needed something to do."

"And what were your plans after leaving here?"

"To go abroad."

"It wouldn't have occurred to you to try to change my mind about an annulment?"

"I doubt it."

"Even if you still cared for me?"

"Even if I still cared for you."

"Why?" she whispered fiercely.

"I betrayed you."

"And if I don't care?" Her voice had risen and she was trembling. She saw him looking at her closely, a glint of anger in his eyes.

"When I left you, remember what you said—I'd killed your desire to try to stop me going. Was that not caring about what I'd done?" He drained his glass and looked at her blankly. "Perhaps I don't understand anything any more; perhaps it's perfectly possible. You know the way quite little things can make people give up. . . . What I did wasn't a little thing." He brushed her cheek gently with the tips of his fingers. "So give me a few weeks. Will you?"

She nodded, sure he had already made his decision. She said, "I can't believe everything we went through can have been for nothing."

He looked at her with great gentleness but did not reply. When she thought of the man who had sat in the same chair on the day he had gone out to break the rent strike, the change in him struck cold horror to her heart. And over again she thought, Did I do this? The stuffed birds in their cases along the wall, the dense black glass of the windows, and the white candlelight became blurred as her tears rose. But then he started to talk about buying tenant rights, and how a new Scotch manager would din into ignorant heads the advantages of clover and turnips. And after a while she asked questions, which he answered, and the evening went on somehow, until eventually they went to bed in their separate rooms, treading gently as they passed the dowager Lady Ardmore's door.

Next morning when Theresa came down, Clinton had evidently been up for several hours. When he came into the dining room, where she was having breakfast, his clothes were splashed with mud and his cheeks were glowing from the cold morning air. He pulled a chair over to the fire and called for Harris to help him out of his riding boots. And though nothing was said while this went on, Theresa could sense that something was different. His face seemed relaxed and carefree, as though some inner conflict had finally been resolved. He smiled at her, reflections of firelight kindling in his eyes. When Harris went out, Clinton rose, poured himself some coffee, and paced over to the window, his cup chinking in its saucer as he walked. When he stopped and looked at her, he seemed excited and yet slightly bemused.

"I think I know," he said hesitantly. "It really is clear to me at last. Isolation—I've been alone too much these last few months. That's what's been wrong. Not just that, obviously." He smiled at her. "Don't look so doubtful. I can't cope with myself single-handed—that's what it amounts to. When I was always doing things, I was all right. Now I can't survive on my own without that sort of active life. Self-sufficiency's just affectation for someone of my temperament."

"So what will you do?" she asked, puzzled and alarmed not to know what he meant.

He spilled some coffee and put down his cup. "Surely you see?" he said urgently. "I need you—that's what I meant. I've been a fool." He kissed her with cold lips and placed his hands on her shoulders. Behind him the sun shone palely from a pastel sky. When she did not speak, he went on rapidly, as if to persuade her: "You know how it feels when you don't sleep for several days? Everything's strange—not quite solid; faces, rooms, streets are all different—not quite there. Like things in a mirror. You know the way noises seem louder than they are when you've heard nothing for hours? I'm trying to explain about solitude, being cut off. That's how it was yesterday. I couldn't reach you." He touched her hair and turned her face towards him. "Can't you understand?"

She nodded dumbly and pressed his hand against her cheek. Her eyes were glittering. "Why don't we go away, Clinton? Go now, go anywhere you like. But away from everything that's hurt us."

"We will, we will, my love."

"Why not now, Clinton? For God's sake, why not today?" Her arms were round him pulling his face to hers.

He disentangled himself gently, kissing her as he did so. "In a few days, when I've finished here."

"But if it happens again? Like yesterday . . ." Her voice trailed off. With an effort she calmed herself.

"How can it?" he said softly. "I tried to root out the past. I found it was the ground under my feet. I know better now."

465

"Then come today," she implored him one more time; but again he refused, and talked to her very calmly and rationally about his reasons for wanting to finish what he had set in hand. The costs of the trial would mean . . . But she did not listen; she accepted it. They would need money; he would have to stay a little. There must be no cause for future reproach. She knew that now.

Later, in the drawing room, she went up to the mantelpiece. She had been about to talk about what they had said in this room before they drove out together for the first time—the way she had taunted him—but her eye was caught by the embroidery to the right of the carved chimney piece. She saw the knife held to the stem of a vine and under it Clinton's motto, "*Virescit vulnere virtus*," and remembered the first time Lady Ardmore had drawn her attention to it. "Courage grows stronger through a wound," she repeated to herself wonderingly.

And at that moment, thinking back over everything that had happened to them, she saw that nothing had been gratuitous. In ten days he would follow her to London—ten days. In her heart she no longer felt any fear; the pattern of their lives was unbroken. Because she had lived there, Clinton spoke of going to France. Louise's education would be easier there than in many other countries. His words enfolded her like gentle hands. Later that day she would leave, but the thought did not trouble her any more. At that moment, a spirit of intercession and tenderness seemed to be watching over them. The same events that had brought on them the disaster of the trial had now carried them beyond it.

CHAPTER FORTY-FIVE

After Theresa had left Kilkreen, Clinton was puzzled that he had ever supposed matters could have turned out differently. And yet before her coming he had clung to a frail thread of hope. If even a little of what they had once been had survived the trial, a miracle might still be possible. What appeared broken past all mending might magically be made whole again. But for Clinton that was all dead and buried now.

Theresa's optimism and passionate faith in the future had only caused him dismay and disbelief—as if he had blundered into a room where two strangers were talking and somehow, without rhyme or reason, found himself not just the object of what was being said but also one of the speakers; or so it had seemed until another illusion had taken hold of him. It was as though they were walking together but could not manage to keep the same pace. Either he kept falling behind, or she was forever moving ahead; one way or the other, their words had constantly fallen into empty air.

Then during dinner he had suddenly *seen* her again—really seen her as he had always done in the past before they parted. Not just the shadows of her hair, or the softness of lips, but the warmth in her, the life. She was moving forward because she still felt with her whole being that there was more ahead of them than a rickety imitation of past happiness. And looking at her, hearing her, his own hopelessness had overwhelmed him. He had thought, This is what it's like to be over, to have ended, to be a ghost watching someone who is still alive. Everything she was saying was as real as the room was real, as the minutes they were living through were real. And yet he could not believe in it. Even their past suffering seemed remote, almost nothing to do with them. She had worn a white dress in York, they had swum together in a mill pond on summer days, and like other lovers had seen significance in trifling things. He had not forgotten even the most unremarkable facts of their relationship; but without the emotion that had given them meaning, they dropped through his mind like beads from a broken necklace.

From the moment on the beach when he had first realized that she wanted to revive their marriage, Clinton had known himself lost. To feel as he did, yet not find it in him to end her hopes, was madness. But her refusal to admit defeat had touched a deep nerve of sympathy. Ashamed of himself for doubting her during the trial, he had not had the heart to reject her a second time. Before her arrival he had known he would only escape the ruinous damages of a breach of promise action by fleeing the country. He had reconciled himself to the prospect of a lifetime abroad—but *on his own*, without anyone there to pity him or make comparisons with what he had been.

That night he had imagined precisely how it would be, living with her in a succession of foreign towns. Whatever their privations, she would rarely admit to being downhearted. He would never hear her blame him for what his betrayal had done to them. However isolated they might become, she would still say that being together mattered more. Out of honor and compassion he would agree, feigning an optimism he did not feel, pretending to be still the man he had been before he left her for Sophie. For a time he would convince her; but when she read his despair—as sooner or later she would—and knew the humiliation he felt for everything he had lost, even her courage would waver. No love could survive for long if forced to bear the weight hers would be called upon to bear. Her disillusion, when it came, would be more terrible after so much hope.

As the night had worn on and the sky had grown lighter, a strange sense of ease had washed through him—a feeling of peace which sometimes follows the crisis of a serious illness. She asked him to honor their marriage. Very well, he would agree to do so rather than endure the guilt of a new betrayal. By pledging himself to live out a life that was impossible, he would seal his fate. There could only be a single way to avoid failing her. He felt no sadness. The same feeling after he had been·taken prisoner in China: relief to be beyond the reach of false hopes.

In the past, the doors of choice had been slammed against him from outside; this last remaining door he would close himself; close it against his future. As soon as this course was clear to him, everything that had happened, which he had thought perverse or nonsensical, now fitted precisely. This was the point he had been traveling towards all the time; and as if he had been there before, he recognized it perfectly.

So he had dressed himself and shaved and gone out for his usual morning ride before returning to persuade Theresa that he had changed his mind. And when he had convinced her that he was sincere, he had talked realistically about that future which would never happen. He had felt calm, and as near contentment as he had been for many months. And all the words he had spoken had seemed right and inevitable, as though all the time they had been waiting to be used.

After she went away, not much had remained to be done, though what there was had to be done well.

Absolute normality was the first rule. For two days Clinton went on with his tasks on the estate, trying to persuade the tenants he had asked to quit to do so peacefully and accept other holdings. He visited the resident magistrate at Westport and arranged for notices to be served a week hence on the hardest characters. Wherever he was seen, he showed no signs of any change. The land agent and the servants saw nothing to remark upon. His apparent indifference to his humiliation in Dublin evinced grudging respect in the neighborhood, though those likely to be dispossessed in the clearances inevitably saw it as added evidence of inhumanity. He had two bitter arguments with his mother about the impending evictions and on both occasions left her in tears. He had already made it clear that he would not discuss anything to do with Theresa or any legal steps he might be contemplating. His relations with her were neither better nor worse than they had been at any time during the past few years. He wrote an affectionate letter to Theresa, reaffirming what he had promised and giving her a definite date on which to expect him in London.

Late on the evening of the fourth day after Theresa's departure, Clinton went to Harris's room and stayed talking to him for almost an hour. A maid passed through the stableyard under the lighted window and heard shouting, but did not stop to listen. She had been meeting a married man near Clonmore and did not want to be seen. After leaving his valet, Clinton paused in the harness room and leaned heavily against the wall. What had seemed so natural and so firmly fixed to him had been violently attacked by the servant whose obedience he had taken for granted. The man had said that he was mad, that the woman was not worth his little finger, that the judge ought to be hanged; and not a word Clinton had said could get across the reasons which were so obvious to him. When he had finally told the man that he would do what he proposed either with or without help, Harris had broken down and agreed to do what was asked of him. From the harness room, Clinton heard the sounds of harsh sobbing.

Over by the window, an oil lamp was burning dimly. Clinton stared at it with deep preoccupation. Behind it the black window. Before birth, darkness—after death, the same darkness. A lamp was no worse off when it was put out than it had been before it was lit. Dozens of times since reaching his decision Clinton had found new proofs of the logic of his proceedings in a wide variety of trifling events. Almost anything could become a sign or omen. Already he felt absolved from all personal responsibility. Earlier the same day he had seen a dead hedgehog, and even that had served him with further reinforcement of his purpose. The animal with its bloody snout and dirty spines had been living too, just as flies and lice lived. There could be nothing very remarkable about this spark of life that was shared with such humble creatures.

He walked out across the stableyard under the stars and felt the cold air on his face, saw squares of yellow light in the black silhouette of the house. Life was this act of seeing and feeling; that was all it could be: squares of light, shadows, the noise his shoes made on the ground. A beating in the chest. Only these things. Wine tastes a certain way, love feels like this or that, fear and pain were known to him, pride and courage. What else could there be? Some unexpected sensation or pleasure? More likely boredom and the pretense of still liking what was stale. And what then? Complain about life, like those wearisome people disparaging what they had forgotten how to enjoy? To hell with that. Anyone dissatisfied with the terms should submit with a good grace or get out. The length of a play never mattered, only how good the acting was while it did.

Clinton locked the door of his room and took off his coat; then with great care he cut several small rents in it and ripped the fabric so that the tears concealed the cuts. He also tore his shirt at the collar. He would have liked to have drunk a lot, but that might have looked wrong afterwards. Instead he lit a cigar. Attending to these details, he knew none of the nervousness he had felt when forging Esmond's signature or waiting for Norton. The despair and wild hopes he had lived through that summer seemed improbable now—touching, but a little theatrical. But then the consequences had been unknown, the odds of success imponderable. This time the end was not in doubt. He was all-powerful now.

The fact that nobody except Harris would ever know the truth pleased him. Courage so carefully disguised as something else possessed a special poignancy. Irony made perfect. It occurred to him with peculiar inner laughter that those who spoke with such hatred about death were even bigger fools than men who bleated about the horrors of war without having tasted them. Nothing should be condemned without fair trial.

Again he began thinking about the details. There would be no second chance; it had to be right the first time. He picked some coins from the top of the dressing table. Enough money to scatter on the ground. He looked at his watch. No, he would leave breaking it till later. If there was any broken glass, the bits should be there to be found. He caught sight of himself in the mirror and looked away; he suddenly realized that he did not want to see his face. It had looked ordinary and unchanged. A young man smoking a cigar, picking up money, considering when to break a watch. A man of almost thirty who might live till old age. For a moment he felt diminished and pitiable. But the feeling passed; reality—his special reality —returned. It had nothing to do with the young man in the mirror but was somewhere else, hidden deep within him. He covered the mirror and sat down. His world closed in again and he was safe. He slipped the watch into his waistcoat pocket. Time wasn't in those cogs and wheels any more, or in the arithmetical progression of years and seasons; time was the beating of his heart. Time began and ended there.

A little later he wrote two brief letters, both for Harris's use. One was to be sent to Dick Lambert; in it Clinton told his friend that because he intended to live with Theresa he would not be able to keep Harris in his employment, since she disliked the man. Clinton asked whether Dick could give him a position. The second letter was a simple statement that he intended to kill himself, and was only to be used in the unlikely event of an arrest being made; otherwise it should be burnt.

Two hours before dawn, Clinton loaded a revolver in the gun room and went out into the garden; behind some bushes, he rubbed his torn coat on the muddy grass and then put it on. He also smeared mud on his knees. Harris was leading out his horse as Clinton arrived. The mare's hoofs were muffled with sacking. The valet's face was the color of candle wax and his lips were drawn tight. Clinton handed him the letters; he had already explained what would be in them. Neither of them spoke. Out of sight of the house, Clinton bent down and removed the sacking before mounting.

A gray blear of light was growing in the east when Harris reached the point which Clinton had described to him barely eight hours earlier in his room—a place where a rough track skirted the beech woods near the domain park wall. From a distance Harris saw the mare standing alone tethered to a tree. He had drunk half a bottle of brandy but still felt stone sober. Another two hundred yards and he found his master's body. He knelt down on the black slippery leaves and choked back a mouthful of regurgitated brandy. There was blood all down Clinton's coat sleeve as well as trickling from his head. He had shot himself in the arm first. Some money was on the ground a few feet away and his watch was hanging from his pocket on its chain; the glass was cracked and the hands pointed to a few minutes after nine o'clock—still three hours in the future. Choking back retching sobs of shock, he took the revolver from Clinton's hand and pocketed it. Then he swung the blackthorn he had brought with him hard down on the dead staring face. He rained other blows on the chest and legs.

Then he turned and ran. Gasping in deep gulps of the splintering air, he stumbled to where the horse was tethered. The mare whinnied at his approach. This too was agony to him. He freed her and then hit her hard across the quarters with the stick. When she still stood confused, he shouted and then struck out wildly until the animal stampeded into the woods, snorting with pain and fear. Afterwards Harris dragged his way homewards. The blackthorn he threw down in a weed-choked ditch, and the revolver he flung far out into the heronry pond. The mud gripped at his boots as he walked on. No birds called to break the labor of his breath as he blundered on towards the back of the house. Above him in the misty sky the moon was a milky disc. Twigs cracked under his feet like brittle bones; his flesh shuddered. The dark stain on his hand where he had held the gun was blood.

Shortly after half past ten the mare came limping home. Harris told the coachman that Lord Ardmore had gone out for his morning ride at about seven o'clock as usual. Alarm spread rapidly. The search began.

CHAPTER FORTY-SIX

First there was the despairing ever-present craving to see and touch him—a longing sharper than the most exacting physical pain—and behind it the knowledge that nowhere, never again, would he enter a room, smile at her, or speak. And every other living face, every door that opened to a hand not his, every alien voice, was a violation to her, shouting out, Not him, not his. Theresa's world was filled by his absence. Her loss closed in around her like a dense cloud.

Weeks later, a floating emptiness as if she too did not exist. After that, thoughts, and one which it seemed would never leave her in peace: He had gone out hopefully, thinking of the years to come, and had been brutally cut down. And because fate had held out this second chance, only to dash it aside, everything that had gone before became a savage joke to her.

This too had passed. To die hoping was surely better than to die in despair. Yet this crumb of comfort also proved ephemeral. Already she knew that one day she would have to find out everything she could about the last days of his life. She never doubted the truth of the coroner's verdict of murder by persons unknown; her fears were all concerned with the state of mind that had caused Clinton to stay behind and take the risks that had killed him. Time and again she was haunted by memories of his strange volte-face during her last hours with him. Without his voice and presence to persuade her, she no longer knew whether she had let her own hopes deceive her. What else could he have intended by setting in hand clearances than a deliberate tempting of fate? Why, if he had ever believed in their future, had he ridden alone each morning, unarmed, and knowing how much he was hated?

Apart from Kilkreen itself, Dublin was the last place on earth Theresa would have wished to return to; but when she learned that Harris had re-enlisted with the 15th Hussars at Richmond Barracks, she had had no choice in the matter.

A fresh spring day when even the gray Georgian streets looked vivid. A day for open windows, walks, and the first airing of summer clothes. Voices and street sounds carried clearly; in squares and crescents, buds on the trees were swelling, and here and there splashes of new green.

The man was summoned for her from the riding school, and from the moment she could see his face distinctly, she sensed the hatred his civility concealed. Standing stiffly in his blue uniform, answering each question with cutting brevity, his manner said more eloquently than words, You ruined him; how dare you come to me for consolation. He told her next to nothing. It had never been his habit, he said, to try to guess Lord Ardmore's thoughts. Couldn't he at least tell her the things Lord Ardmore had said? Had he seemed to be aware of the dangers involved in the evictions?

Harris smiled to himself and kicked at the gravel with a glistening boot. "He said they hadn't the guts to shoot crows. That's how worried he was."

Reassured, she murmured, "Did it surprise you that he stayed in Ireland after the trial?"

"Surprise me?" The man's derision was blatant. "Did you think he'd run off and hide himself?"

"He wanted to show people that he didn't care? Is that why he went to Kilkreen?"

The eagerness in her voice seemed to confuse him. He said harshly, "What's the use? Talking won't bring him back."

"But what do you think?" she insisted.

He had become very pale, and was looking at her as if seeing something else. His lips moved but no sound came.

"That day," she murmured, "why did he go out without a gun?"

"Perhaps in case he got ideas," Harris blurted out, suddenly beside himself. "Wasn't the coroner's verdict enough for you? What more do you want?"

"Why are you so angry?" she asked, appalled by his sudden fury.

"Didn't I find him?" he muttered. "You think I want reminding?"

"Won't it help us both if you tell me everything?"

As he moved away, the sun caught the tiny brass buttons on his coat, dazzling her.

"Go away," he said weakly. Then, drawing in a deep breath: "He didn't go round begging people to have a shot at him—he knew better than that. He wasn't any different from any other time—just himself, that's all." His voice had risen again, and his fists were so tightly clenched that the knuckles shone white. "Another thing . . . he gave me notice two days before—told me he was going abroad with you, so I'd have to shift for myself. Said you couldn't abide me. That good enough for your ladyship?"

Some sparrows that had been chirping and fluttering in the dust at the edge of the parade ground rose suddenly at the sound of his voice. Small white clouds passed overhead. Some officers were laughing on the steps of the mess.

"I'm sorry," she managed to say at last. "You cared for him . . . found him dead . . . I'm sorry."

"You've no cause."

"I'd like you to have something of his." Because she had never seen his dead body, the things that had been with him at the time of his death were especially precious to her. She reached inside her mantle and held out Clinton's watch. Harris froze and then turned away with violent abruptness. Seeing his shoulders shaking, Theresa thought her offer had moved him to tears.

"Please take it," she said softly.

476

He faced her again, moving very slowly. His cheeks were wet, but his lips were drawn back in a grimace of agonized resentment.

She drew back in dismay, not understanding what she had done. "Tell me," she faltered as he began to walk away. She moved after him quickly.

"Leave me alone," he shouted, but she still followed.

"What have I done?" she implored.

He stopped, and gazed at her in stupefaction as she drew level. "*What have you done?*" A breathless moan left his lips. He moved a step closer, his face darkened by the blood rising in it. "Killed him—killed him, d'you hear?" He broke off, seized by the most frightful bewilderment. His face crumpled. "God forgive me."

Theresa felt herself swaying. Panic was tightening in her chest, squeezing out her breath. "He was murdered," she stammered. "You said so."

"Yes, I said so," he repeated with frenzied eagerness.

Shock hit her like a falling wall, hurtling down on her. Either she or the whole world was disintegrating. Beyond any doubt, she knew that he had killed himself. She wanted to scream, to run away and get out of herself, but she was rooted, held in suspension. She had no idea how long she stood there. At last she heard a voice coming from somewhere else; a thin wild voice; hers: "Don't lie any more. I have to know."

As if returning to herself, she took in the barrack square and the man standing in silence. Rage caught her by the throat. She grasped his arm with all her strength. "Tell me. *You've got to tell me.*"

As he pulled away, the watch was knocked from her other hand. He stared a moment, then bent down and closed his fingers round it. "Why?" he moaned, "why did you show me that thing?" His torment of remorse reached her through the cloud of her own distress.

"It can't matter to him what you tell me. Nothing can hurt him now." He gave her back the watch but still said nothing. She said gently, "Don't be afraid."

Slowly he raised his eyes. "He broke it before he killed himself . . . to make it look as though he'd struggled for his life. I found money scattered on the ground. His clothes were torn." Tears spilled over his lashes and his breath came harshly. "But the worst . . . was . . . He fired into his arm first, so they'd never doubt murder." He looked at her in anguish. "Think of going on after that—the pain, and then . . ." Harris raised a hand to his head, held it there a second before letting it fall. "He went through all that to spare your feelings. And *I* told you." He crashed a clenched fist to his forehead. "*I told you.*"

A dream; she was inside it and yet watching, seeing clearly: white clouds, men leaving the riding school, her shadow moving as she began to walk. The shock of his death, the moment of it, his last deliberate acts, pressed in on her, filled the barrack square. She heard the first shot, saw him raise the gun again. In agony she thought, I could have stayed with him, could have saved him. His happiness on her last day at Kilkreen seared her now that she knew the reason for it. Even then he had already decided. Already chosen death. Her skin was cold and she was shivering. So little could have spared him: their child's birth, his uncle's help, her father's pity. And how it was that none of these things had happened, she could not tell. Nor why they had ever met, and loved each other, and suffered. What purpose had there been? What purpose? Each word, each kiss, each day together, had served one end—to lead him on to death.

She had reached the gateway, and saw the sentry in the street stamp past, spurs ringing on the stones. Clinton had come towards that arch, had welcomed her a dozen feet away, the guard had saluted. A man respected, honored, confident, and free. She saw Harris watching her, heard him say, "You mustn't go. Please don't go." She looked at him in bewilderment. "You should be with someone."

"Don't be afraid of that," she said quietly.

They stood in silence as the sentry tramped back again, the sun flashing on his scabbard. She wondered, If I had known how it would finish, would I ever have loved him? And even as the question formed, she knew the answer. He had risked death too often to fear it as others would. She had known his pride— had known.

She felt the broken watch heavy in her hand. She turned. "You say he did those things to spare me?"

"Yes, my lady."

She thought of the dawn. The silent house. Her man leaving it to die, still with thought of her as he rode to the place. Those acts before the end had been his last gifts to her, so she could think only chance robbed them, could still dream and hope when all his own had gone. She knew another day might usher back despair, but as that moment, in the sunshine, beside a barrack square, new faith lived in her. With love, the purpose could transcend the fate it led to. The end be changed utterly in its fulfillment.

Harris was still looking at her anxiously.

She touched his sleeve. "Don't worry. I'll survive." The ghost of a smile moved her lips. She stood still a moment longer, remembering, then launched herself, like a swimmer leaving the shore.